WINTER'S

Ceri Houlbrook is a lecturer at the University of Hertfordshire, and has published academic books and articles on contemporary folklore and domestic rituals. *Winter's Wishfall* is her first novel and combines her academic interests with her love of magical realism and creative writing.

She lives in Manchester with co-adventurer Mark and their little pirate Captain Jojo.

WINTER'S WISHFALL

Ceri Houlbrook

BLACK & WHITE PUBLISHING

First published in the UK in 2023 by Black & White Publishing
An imprint of Black & White Publishing Group
A Bonnier Books UK company
4th Floor, Victoria House, Bloomsbury Square, London, WC1B 4DA
Owned by Bonnier Books, Sveavägen 56, Stockholm, Sweden

Paperback ISBN: 978-1-7853-0551-1
eBook ISBN: 978-1-7853-0550-4

A CIP catalogue record for this book is available from the British Library.
Typeset by IDSUK (Data Connection) Ltd
Printed and bound in Great Britain by Clays Ltd, Elcograf S.p.A

1 3 5 7 9 10 8 6 4 2

Black & White Publishing is an imprint of Bonnier Books UK
www.bonnierbooks.co.uk

Chapter One

Oh, the weather outside is frightful . . .

Frank Sinatra's words reached my ears from a nearby shop just as my umbrella flipped inside-out for the final time. Wind and rain buffeted me from all directions as I desperately pulled on the spokes and yanked at the runner, but it had well and truly given up the fight. I'd never felt so betrayed by an inanimate object. It was made to serve one single purpose and couldn't even do that.

Fortunately, I had a waterproof hood.

Unfortunately, as I discovered two minutes later, 'waterproof' – contrary to popular belief – doesn't actually mean impervious to water. The rain seemed to soak through it like a sponge and by the time I'd jogged to the end of Market Street, I was thoroughly sodden. I turned a corner and could see the coffee shop in the distance, but I was wavering.

Maybe I shouldn't go. The Universe seemed to be telling me it wasn't a good idea. Nothing had gone right all day. I'd woken up with a cold sore the size of a Christmas tree. I'd spilt orange juice all over my only smart shirt. My plan to cycle into town had been thwarted by the ominous clouds. The bus had been even later than usual

1

and my hopes of sitting in peace to enjoy my cinnamon roll had been dashed by the sardine-squish of passengers. I'd stumbled off with relief, choking down my thoroughly squashed breakfast, when the heavens decided to open.

They were all First World problems, as my brother would say, but I couldn't help thinking they were also all signs.

I need this job, I told myself, forcing my legs into gear as thunder rumbled overhead. I covered the last few yards to the coffee shop in a run, splashing through puddles on my way. Of course, my shoes proved not to be waterproof either. I checked my watch as I pushed open the door. At least I was still early and would have time to wring my rain-frizzed hair out in the toilets before—

'Ms Lancaster?'

Seriously? Forcing a smile, I turned round. Sitting at a corner table were a man and a woman. They both looked to be in their thirties, but that was where the similarities ended. Even sitting, I could tell the man was at least a head taller. He had dark, almost black hair, cut smartly, with a neat beard, dark brown eyes and a mouth set in an unimpressed line. He wouldn't have looked out of place on the front cover of the *Wall Street Journal* in a crisp suit and teal tie. The woman, on the other hand, had a round face with bright blue eyes, a button nose and a wide smile. Her lips were painted the same hot pink shade as her bobbed hair. She was wearing a knitted white jumper, the chest adorned with a pair of suggestively positioned Christmas puddings. I had a vague sense of recognition but couldn't think where I'd know her from.

2

As well as two mugs, the table in front of them held a stack of files and a clipboard.

'Ms Lancaster?' the man repeated.

'Yes, that's me,' I said, suddenly feeling nervous. They rose politely and I peeled a saturated glove off to shake their hands. 'Please call me Ellie.'

'I'm Clementine Jones,' the woman smiled, 'and this is—'

'Mr Jones,' the man interrupted in a clipped tone. 'Thank you for coming.'

Their accents were Scottish, but I didn't know the country well enough to place them more specifically.

'Thank *you* for inviting me,' I countered sincerely, trying to remove my 'waterproof' without shaking water everywhere. 'I'm sorry if I look a state, it's—'

'Raining, yes,' Mr Jones said, sitting back down. Based on his abruptness, I assumed he'd already found me wanting, but the woman – Clementine – was still smiling.

Clementine . . . Clementine . . . Where did I know her from? Suddenly it clicked: one of my brother's recipe books sported her photo on the front, standing in a bright kitchen, wearing an apron with the words *Life's Short, Eat Cake* across the chest, a delectable pastry in each hand, her hair electric blue.

I gasped. 'You're Clementine of *Clementine's Calorifica*?'

She grinned at me. 'You know my book?'

'I *love* your book. I bought it for my brother last Christmas. We made my niece your Mile-High Marshmallow Pie for her birthday.'

'Ooh, good choice.' She nodded approvingly. 'I can't believe you bought my book.'

'Only me and ten million others,' I pointed out. '*Clementine's Calorifica* was in all the book charts. Didn't it make it to Christmas number one?'

She waved a dismissive hand but was clearly pleased. 'Well, now that we've established your excellent taste in cake, can I get you a drink?'

'Oh, that's very kind of you, but I'll get—'

'I insist.' She'd said it cheerfully enough, but her tone brooked no argument. She lifted her clipboard and waited expectantly.

'Erm, thanks. A hot chocolate would be great.'

Her smile widening, she noted something on her clipboard. Perhaps she was worried she'd forget my order, simple as it was, though I sensed there was more to her scribbling. 'Cream? Marshmallows? Syrup?'

I glanced at Mr Jones but his expression gave nothing away.

'A shot of gingerbread syrup if they have any?' I hazarded, wondering ridiculously if there was a right answer to this.

Clementine gave an eager nod and jotted something else down. 'Uh-huh, uh-huh. And anything to eat? Cake? Mince pie? Candy cane?'

'Clementine,' Mr Jones growled.

'I actually wolfed down a cinnamon roll on my way here,' I admitted. 'Just a drink would be great.'

'A cinnamon roll, huh?' More scribbling. 'Righty-o, I'll be back in a second with your *gingerbread* hot chocolate.'

She leant towards Mr Jones with a grin, emphasising the word, as if making a point, and then veritably skipped over to the counter.

I turned to Mr Jones with an expectant smile, wondering if there would be any small talk before the interview or if he'd launch straight in. But in the absence of Clementine, he seemed to have forgotten me entirely. He pulled out a binder from his briefcase and began flipping through pages. The minutes ticked by in awkward silence. I noticed a stray pastry crumb on my shirt and dusted it away. He turned a page and made a couple of notes. I glanced at my watch. He turned another page. I looked out of the window at the Christmas shoppers battling the wind and rain. He turned another page.

'Awful news I'm afraid!' I jumped at Clementine's voice. 'They're out of gingerbread syrup. Really, they should lose their hot chocolate licence for that.' She seemed genuinely put out as she placed the brimming mug in front of me. 'I asked for cinnamon instead. I figured if you'd had a cinnamon roll then you must like cinnamon.'

'Your powers of deduction are staggering, Clementine. As ever,' Mr Jones said dryly as she sat back down.

'Now,' she said, retrieving her clipboard. 'To business. What – and this is a serious question – is your favourite Christmas film?'

I laughed, guessing she was trying to put me at ease. 'That's a tough one,' I admitted, cupping my hands around the hot mug. 'But the old ones are the best. *White Christmas* maybe – I love musicals. How about you?'

5

'Clementine isn't the one being interviewed here,' Mr Jones cut in coolly.

'Oh, I—'

'I love musicals too,' Clementine beamed. More scribbling. 'The cheesier the better, right? *Mr Jones* here loves them too, though he'd never admit it. You don't suffer from vertigo, do you?'

The transition of topic was so quick I nearly missed it. 'Vertigo? Erm, no, I never have before. Why?'

No response other than more scribbling. 'And now, if I could just ask you to show me your socks . . .'

I'd just taken a nervous sip of hot chocolate, which was a mistake. I sputtered mid-swallow, spraying flecks across the table – and, of course, over Mr Jones's crisp white shirt.

'Oh God, I'm so sorry!' I gasped, searching for a napkin. But he'd already reached for one and, without a flicker of emotion, was dabbing at the specks.

'It looks more interesting that way. Pollockesque,' Clementine waved a hand dismissively. 'Anyway. Socks?'

'I, er . . .' *I need this job.* Maybe it was some kind of weird take on psychometric testing. Self-consciously, I pulled up the hem of my trouser leg to reveal an orange sock designed to look like a carrot, damp from my leaky shoe. I could feel my cheeks reddening. 'I would have worn something more interview appropriate if I'd, er, known . . . And I walked through a puddle.'

Clementine was studying my sock in earnest, but Mr Jones's eyes were focused on my chin. He was frowning. I squirmed self-consciously. 'Do I have something on my face?'

6

'Yes,' he replied mildly. 'Hot chocolate.'

Mortified, I wiped my chin with my hand.

'I'm so sorry about that,' I said. 'Perhaps we should cut straight to the interview now.'

Clementine, nibbling on the leg of a gingerbread man, looked confused. 'But you've already done it.'

I glanced at Mr Jones, perplexed. His expression told me he didn't necessarily agree with Clementine's statement, but wasn't going to argue.

'But you've not asked me anything.'

'We've asked you enough,' Clementine assured me firmly. 'We've seen your CV. You've worked in archiving for five years. Do you enjoy it?'

I didn't have to fake any enthusiasm. 'I love it.'

'What do you love about it?' Mr Jones asked. It suddenly began to feel like an actual job interview. My stomach knots, which had gradually loosened, abruptly tightened again, but at least I could answer honestly.

'I've always been intrigued by how people lived. Historical documents can give us the answers. Well, some at least. If they're doorways into the past, archives are corridors full of those doorways. Sometimes they take us to court rooms, or council offices, or hospital wards. Sometimes they take us into people's homes and show us how people lived their everyday lives. If we're really lucky, they can even show us what people thought, what they felt. Just the other week a local woman donated her great-grandmother's collection of family letters. They were amazing, not just full of historical details, but of character. I feel like I know her, even though she died seventy years ago. It was . . .' I stopped, taking in Clementine's look of amusement and Mr Jones's raised eyebrows. Blood flooded my cheeks. 'I'm sorry. I'm rambling. I'll stop now.'

'There's absolutely no need to apologise,' Clementine assured me. 'So, you love working in archives. And you speak six different languages. Impressive.'

'Well, five and a half,' I qualified sheepishly. Mr Jones made a questioning noise. 'My Mandarin's only passable.'

'Have you moved around a lot?' Clementine asked.

'No, I've only ever lived here.'

'Travelled a lot?'

'Not really,' I admitted. I then remembered that this was a job interview. 'But I've always had a knack for learning languages.'

'Well, that's precisely what we're looking for,' Clementine nodded enthusiastically, her pink hair bobbing around her face. 'And we've got your references here,' she added, briefly tipping her clipboard to show the tops of two envelopes.

'But I haven't given you my reference details yet—'

She cut across me. 'And we'd be very happy to offer you the job.'

I sat in stunned silence, unsure of whether to laugh or run away from the clearly crazy people.

Mr Jones cleared his throat. 'Would you give us a moment, please?'

'Of course.' As I left them to it, taking a seat at another table, I caught the word 'unsuitable' from Mr Jones.

Clementine responded loudly. 'It's my decision.'

'This is a joint decision.'

'Nuh-uh. You've already had your choice with Mr Grey-Socks-Black-Coffee. It's my turn to choose.'

There was a – long – silence then Clementine called me back.

Mr Jones slid a wad of paper across the table towards me. He didn't look happy. 'If you could sign the contract, please.'

'Contract? But I don't even . . . I haven't . . . You haven't told me anything about the job,' I finished lamely.

'You're a multi-linguist archivist. We're seeking to employ a multi-linguist archivist.' Clementine shrugged cheerfully. 'What's there to tell?'

'Well,' I laughed nervously, 'where the archives are, for one.'

The pair exchanged looks. 'Ah, well, that's a little complicated.'

'This job,' Mr Jones explained carefully, 'is . . . location sensitive.'

I looked from one to the other expecting clarification, but none came. 'Is it in Manchester?'

It was Clementine's turn to sputter. 'Oh, sweetie.' She reached over and patted my hand.

'So . . . it's not in Manchester,' I concluded. 'Is it at least in the UK?'

'It's not *not* in the UK,' Clementine replied cryptically. 'And you don't need a passport to get there.'

'We cannot disclose any further information until the contract is signed.' Mr Jones passed me a heavy fountain pen. 'Read it thoroughly.'

I looked at the pile of papers, at least ten sheets thick, dense with impossibly small print. 'Can I take it away with me?'

'No.' Mr Jones reached to another table for a newspaper. 'We can wait.'

'Don't worry, it's all above board,' Clementine smiled encouragingly. 'He's a lawyer.'

Probably best not to admit that made me trust him even less. 'Well, can I at least have a magnifying glass?' I joked, picking up the first page and squinting.

Clementine chuckled but neither of them said anything, so I began scanning the pages.

I consider myself a fairly intelligent person, but I didn't understand most of the words in the first sentence. Or in the second, or third, or fourth. One paragraph further down the first page struck me: 'Given the highly confidential nature of the work you will undertake, you will not at any time during your employment or afterwards, disclose to any person any information as to the affairs, business, dealings, practice, know-how, details of clients, transaction details or geographic location of the employer. All information held about the employer or in connection with the employer and the entailing work you are employed to undertake, is to be regarded as confidential.'

Other phrases like 'breach of contract', 'gross misconduct', 'grounds for dismissal', and 'legal action' littered the rest of the pages. My hands were sweating by the time I'd finished reading. I leant closer and lowered my voice, unable to stop myself from asking, 'Is this some kind of Secret Intelligence Service thing?'

Clementine's lips twitched. 'You could call it something like that.'

But Mr Jones blinked at me from over his newspaper. 'No.' Both his tone and expression clearly communicated that he'd never heard a more ridiculous question.

I felt myself blush, but was determined to maintain an air of competence. 'OK. Not MI6 then. But some kind of . . .' I grasped for a term that didn't sound silly, and failed, '. . . secret archive? And this contract basically says that if I disclose any information about it to anyone then I'll be sacked?'

'As well as held subject to criminal charges,' Mr Jones appended.

I gulped.

Clementine punched Mr Jones in the arm. 'Stop scaring the poor girl!'

'Ms Lancaster needs to grasp the severity of the consequences if she breaches the confidentiality clause.'

'Oh, I'm definitely grasping it,' I assured him. I put the contract on the table and went to push it back towards them, unsigned. This was ridiculous. How could they expect me to sign a contract for a job I didn't know anything about? Who would be reckless or naive enough to agree to that?

And if the job wasn't in Manchester, I'd have to move. That wasn't something I could consider, not with everything I had here.

My brother and niece.

11

My mum. Who'd recently retired, sold the family home and jetted off for the sun, promising she'd be back for Christmas dinner. Maybe.

My job. Well, ex-job.

My boyfriend. Well, ex-boyfriend. Who'd claimed my now ex-apartment.

The weather. Ha!

OK, so the list is short, I admitted to myself. But starting again, somewhere new? The idea terrified me. And every Universe-sent sign today had been yelling at me to run in the opposite direction, back home. Well, back to my brother's couch, where I'd been sleeping for the last month. Back to exciting Saturday nights watching *Peppa Pig* with my niece (actually, I loved that part). Back to my self-storage unit, where everything I owned was in boxes. Back to uploading my CV onto job sites and signing on at the job centre and failing to even get short-listed and waiting for things to get better.

I grabbed the pen and signed.

Chapter Two

Although I know now that the stars began aligning years before, it felt like everything started one evening a few weeks before the interview, when I'd arrived at my brother's house with nothing but my bike, a small backpack and a sodden tissue tucked up each sleeve. I'd rung the doorbell, which I noticed dully had been re-tuned to play 'Jingle Bells'. Toby answered with a roll of wrapping paper under one arm and a row of cut sellotape striped across the other. One look at me and his smile dropped.

'What did he do?'

Without giving me a chance to answer, my brother pulled me inside and into a bear hug. He then shepherded me into the living room, where he and his daughter Izzy had clearly been wrapping Christmas presents for the myriad people in my niece's friendship group. For a six-year-old, she had a far superior social life than I did.

'That one's for Ms Khan,' Izzy announced, pointing to a box of Quality Street. 'That's for Mrs Newton, the dinner lady. This one's for Dan the lollipop man.' She paused, studying the various boxes of chocolates arrayed before her. 'Or maybe I should give him the Quality Street – the chewy ones are his favourites. But

Ms Khan likes the purple ones. And what about Trevor the postman? There aren't enough chocolates.'

'There are *never* enough chocolates,' I agreed mournfully, rummaging in an open box to find that all the green triangles had gone. I glowered at my brother, the obvious culprit, but he was focused on his daughter who looked close to tears.

'Remember when we talked about First World problems, sweetie.'

'Why don't you give Dan the postman the Roses?' I suggested. 'There are chewy ones in there too. Ms Khan can have the Quality Street. And then you could make a Christmas card for Trevor. I bet he'd love that.'

Izzy chewed this over gravely for a moment before nodding.

'Excellent,' my brother enthused quickly. 'We'll get the crafts out tomorrow. For now, why don't you write your letter to Santa? Me and Auntie Ellie have some grown-up talking to do.'

Once my niece was happily stationed at the table with paper and a set of felt-tip pens, Toby placed a steaming cup of peppermint tea in my hand and ordered me to tell him everything. Within minutes, he was grinding his teeth.

'He called you *boring*?' he repeated, incredulous. 'Gary, the guy who couldn't come to Izzy's birthday party last year because he was attending the launch of a new handkerchief, called *you* boring?'

'He said all I do is work, read and sleep. Which is true,' I added, pre-empting Toby. 'But it still hurt. Apparently he wants somebody who'll go out with him on a Saturday night . . .'

'To handkerchief conventions?'

I smiled despite myself. 'He wants someone with, I quote, "more spark".'

'You've got truckloads of spark,' Toby bristled. 'What a ba—' He glanced at my niece. 'Banana-head.'

'Banana-head indeed,' I nodded, taking a sip of tea.

'Where's the list?' my brother demanded.

'What list?'

He gave me a level look. 'It's you. There's always a list.'

Grudgingly I reached into my pocket and handed it over.

Smirking, he unfolded it. 'Item one: "Exact revenge." Ticked off. How exactly did you exact revenge then?'

I glanced down at my feet. 'I'm not proud of it.'

'What did you do?'

I reached for my backpack, unzipped it, and pushed it towards him. Nestled amidst my clothes were ten lightbulbs of various shapes and sizes.

Toby raised an eyebrow. 'You exacted revenge by robbing a light bulb shop?'

'Of course not. They're *my* light bulbs. All the ones I bought for the apartment.'

His lips quirked. 'You stole Gary's light bulbs?'

'I paid for them,' I replied, indignant. 'Why should he keep them?'

'Let me get this straight. You took out your anger, hatred, and burning need for vengeance by going around

15

the apartment, turning off light switches, and unscrewing bulbs? Wow, that's truly *spiteful*. Supervillains of the world beware: Ellie Lancaster is going to out-evil you all.'

'That's not all I did,' I muttered, re-zipping the bag.

'What other monstrous acts did you commit?'

'I de-alphabetised his DVDs, snuck a red sock into his white laundry pile, squeezed washing up liquid into his running shoes . . .'

Toby was laughing. 'Oh, the horror.'

'. . . and changed the password for all his social media accounts.'

'OK, now I'm impressed.' Toby snorted. 'What did you change it to?'

I looked over at my niece. 'A variant of banana-head.'

He held up my list again. 'I'll allow you your tick then. Revenge duly enacted. So, item number two: "Be unboring."'

'I'm still working on that,' I admitted. 'I was thinking of taking up lion-taming.'

'You're allergic to cats.'

'Volcano-surfing then.'

'Perfect. You can borrow Izzy's kneepads.'

'Thanks. I'll get started tomorrow.'

'Excellent. OK, item number three: "Find a job."' It took Toby a second to compute. 'But you have a job.'

'No. I don't.' I didn't want to admit this was hurting me far more than the break-up, but couldn't stop the tears.

With a groan he grabbed a tissue and stuffed it into my hand. 'What happened?'

'Restructuring,' I said through shuddering breaths. 'They told us on Friday. Council cuts hit the library and archives hard. Half of us have to go.'

'Oh fu—fudge.' He passed me the entire box of tissues. 'So in the space of one week you've lost your job and your banana-head of a boyfriend.' My brother always did tell it like it was.

'And my apartment,' I pitched in, feeling thoroughly sorry for myself. 'Banana-head is saying that he paid the deposit, so . . .' I gestured to my backpack. 'Your sofa pulls out into a bed, right?'

'You're not letting him keep the apartment,' Toby growled.

'I can't afford it on my own. Especially not without a job.' The waterworks started again, and I buried my face in a new tissue.

'Of course you can stay here, for however long you want. Izzy and Mike will love having you around.'

'I'll pay rent . . .'

'Don't be ridiculous. I'm not charging you a penny for sleeping on my lumpy sofa-bed.'

'I warn you, I won't be leaving that lumpy sofa-bed anytime soon. I'm going to cocoon myself in a duvet and hibernate until spring.'

'You'll do no such thing,' he sniffed, rifling through the box of chocolates and muttering about no more green triangles. Settling for an orange crisp, he turned back to me. 'You've had a crappy week but that's all it is. Next week will be better.'

17

I raised a cynical eyebrow at him, but he went on. 'Do you know why? Because you have *the* best brother in the world, who also happens to be the Merlin of recruitment. I'm going to work my magic. I'll write you the don of all CVs and then I'm going to find you the perfect job.'

Two weeks later, an email arrived in my inbox from 'Jones Associates' and the rest, as they say, is history: come January, I would be embarking on what I'd decided was going to be a grand adventure.

* * *

Stage one of my grand adventure involved a lot of boredom, soggy sandwiches and doubting whether I really wanted a grand adventure after all. I was in yet another nondescript waiting room, twelve hours into a journey that had thus far involved a car, a train, an airplane, a ferry and a bus. I was tired, smelly, grumpy and over five hundred miles from home.

'Why on earth would archives in the Shetlands recruit from Manchester?' I'd demanded, a week after my interview when I received a formal job offer conspicuously giving no details whatsoever about the job itself, other than to specify the wage (surprisingly generous) and to say that food and accommodation would be provided for the duration of my employment (generous and suspicious in equal measure). It was signed *Mr Jones and Ms Jones*. There was also a detailed travel itinerary accompanied by a series of tickets. The final, perplexing destination was apparently a fishing pier in Baltasound on Unst, a place I'd never heard of. (A quick search online revealed Unst to be the northernmost island of Britain.)

Did they really expect me to travel all the way to the Shetlands, a set of islands almost closer to Norway than to the British mainland, on so little information? This was feeling more and more like an elaborate prank.

Of course, I'd tried researching 'Jones Associates'. And of course, the online search engine had proffered one hundred and twenty-five million results, ranging from letting agents and surveyors to an arboricultural planning consultancy. Filtering the results to include the name Clementine narrowed them down to baking websites and news articles. My computer screen filled with images of mouth-watering cakes interspersed with images of Clementine, whose hair colour seemed to change with every photograph. (*Clementine's Calorifica* had been even more successful than I'd realised, winning several culinary awards, and there were thousands of gushing online reviews.) Clementine even had her own Wikipedia page, but other than a photograph – hair poppy red – and information about her book, there were few other details. Under 'Early life and family' was a single sentence: 'Her favourite childhood toy was a baking spatula called Elspeth.'

Not a single result mentioned archives.

Toby, self-proclaimed Merlin of recruitment, took it upon himself to dig up some details on the company, but his search was fruitless as well. Most people in his network had heard of a Jones Associates, but none with archives and a Clementine.

'How did you get me a job interview with them then?'

'I didn't,' he'd replied, moodily. 'They must have found your CV on the job site.'

I'd hoped that when the offer letter arrived, I'd get some answers. But there was nothing in that envelope except more questions.

'This is way too fishy,' I decided, shoving everything back into the envelope.

Toby, who was busy putting the finishing touches on Izzy's Christmas play costume – she was starring as Ebony Scrooge in her school's 'gender blind' version of Dickens's classic – rolled his eyes. 'Coward.'

'Cowardly is just a synonym for sensible,' I'd retorted firmly.

'No, it really isn't. And even if it was, is that what you want your tombstone to read: "Here lieth Eleanor Lancaster, she lived and died sensibly"?'

'The sensible live longer and die later,' I'd grumbled.

'Or they don't live at all.'

I stuck my tongue out at him.

Toby finished pinning the paper hat to Izzy's curly hair and turned to me, his expression earnest. 'Look, it's up to you how you live your life, but may I remind you of those two currently unticked items on your "make life better" list?'

Be unboring. Get a job.

'It's all a little weird,' he allowed, 'but maybe that's just what you need.'

I ignored him and admired my niece in her make-shift Victorian top hat and tails. 'You look amazing, sweetie.'

As I sat in the audience later that evening, beaming with pride at Izzy, Toby's words were playing on repeat in my mind: *It's all a little weird, but maybe that's just what you need.*

The following day, instead of my usual morning routine of scouring the internet for a job, I'd cycled to the nearest bookshop and bought a travel guide for Scotland's Highlands and Islands.

When Toby, Mike – my brother-in-law – and Izzy had seen me off at Manchester Piccadilly train station two weeks after Christmas, I'd been 50 per cent nerves and 50 per cent excitement. I'd felt bold and optimistic; an intrepid explorer, backpack shouldered as I stepped out into the big wide world – accompanied of course by my trusty travel guide.

The ratio had shifted the further away from home I travelled.

Boarding the plane to Sumburgh Airport in the Shetlands in the early hours, nerves had increased to seventy per cent. Stepping off the ferry at Ulsta, on the isle of Yell, they'd risen to eighty. Disembarking the next ferry, at Belmont on Unst, they were pushing ninety.

Just one more bus journey and I'd be at the final destination: Baltasound, a mere seven miles north of Belmont. I suddenly felt very sick, and it had nothing to do with the short but choppy crossing.

I paused when descending the gangplank, getting my bearings. A small queue of cars was waiting to replace the ones filing off, for the trip back. On the other side of them I could see a small, sheltered bus stop. It took more willpower than I care to admit to step off the ferry and make my way towards it.

The timetable printed at the bus stop agreed with my travel itinerary that the next bus was at 10.20 a.m., only ten minutes away. I took the opportunity to pull out my phone and message Toby. The signal bar shimmied back and forth between low and non-existent, so I typed out a quick message.

Still alive. Journey nearly over. Weak signal so don't worry if I don't text for a bit. Hug Izzy for me x

My phone deliberated for a long moment before sending. I wiped away a tear, annoyed at myself for missing them so much already. I'd never lived more than a few miles away from my brother and was used to seeing Izzy and Mike at least weekly – a lot more since moving in with them. Right then, I felt very, very far away from my family.

Just then a bus trundled up. I asked the driver if he was going to Baltasound. He seemed amused by the question. I gave him the last of my tickets and settled on a seat, halfway between a pair of elderly ladies and a teenage boy fully immersed in a paperback. It was only a twenty-minute journey but by the time the bus pulled into Baltasound, the clouds had parted and the sun was

22

shining. I stepped off and grinned widely. In front of me was the most bizarre and wonderful bus stop I'd ever seen – not that I'm in the habit of ranking bus stops.

I'd read about the bus stops of Unst as an attraction in the travel guides and had been a little cynical about the term 'attraction', but I understood now. Structurally it was your average bus shelter, but kitted out to look like a cosy living room, complete with floral window valances. A comfortable chair had been placed next to a beautifully painted set of drawers topped with a telephone, teapot and vase of flowers, and a coffee table held a pile of books, some crafting material and a football. Perched outside was a statuette of a vigilant-looking puffin who, judging by the writing across his chest, was named Bobby. A couple of woolly-hatted tourists were taking a selfie in front of him. It was a relief to see them – to know I wasn't the only person on this part of the island.

'Do you mind?' the woman asked in an American accent, holding out her phone.

'Of course not,' I smiled, snapping a few photos of them flanking Bobby. I handed the phone back and looked up and down the road. They were the only people in sight. 'I don't suppose you know where the pier is?'

'Sure.' The man pointed to where I could make out a row of neat, slate-roofed houses – the only buildings I could see, bar the bus stop. 'About a mile that way.'

I left them admiring the bus stop and headed in the direction the man had pointed. It was a long straight road, with flat green fields stretching to my left and grey-blue water to my right. Whether it was the walking or the improving weather, I felt my mood lighten with every step. Suddenly the descriptions in the travel guides (I'd read three) of beautiful glens and ancient rugged coastlines didn't seem so exaggerated. This was the *perfect* place for a holiday – given the right clothing. The sun may have begun to shine but the wind was relentlessly icy, biting at my nose and cheeks.

In the distance there were the bobbing masts of some fishing boats and a cluster of low buildings, one of which I assumed would be my new place of work. Maybe even my home for the foreseeable future. I nervously revisited some of the theories Toby, Mike and I had proposed over the last few weeks, ranging from the reasonable to the ridiculous. A fishery perhaps – but why all the secrecy? A reclusive billionaire's private library, maybe? The archives of some secret society? My favourite suggestion was an archive of cake recipes. It would make Clementine's interest at the interview in my choice of syrup and breakfast pastry *slightly* more understandable. But sadly, the likeliest theory was that this was a hoax. I was fully expecting a TV crew to jump out at me from behind one of the drystone walls. I even moderated my expression for the camera, aiming for a bold and intrepid smile – but probably only achieving an anxious grimace.

But nobody appeared as I neared the pier. And, as I scanned the handful of buildings, my heart sank. There were no archives here, just a couple of domestic bungalows with the curtains drawn and what looked like a storage facility or depot with a vacant JCB digger outside.

Suddenly feeling very sick, I dug in my pocket for a folded piece of paper. On it were the instructions I'd been sent, the final line reading, 'Once alighting the bus at Baltasound, make your way to the pier.'

'Right,' I said aloud to myself, trying to sound decisive. 'Right. OK.'

I weighed my options.

One: knock on the bungalows and hope somebody answers.

Two: sit on the pier and wait.

Three: turn round and go home, adventure over.

I still don't know which one I would have chosen. I like to think the first or second, but knowing myself, it probably would have been three. Fortunately, I didn't have to make the decision, because a movement caught my eye. Two men were standing on one of the smaller fishing boats – the hand-painted name on the bow read *Valkyrie* – waving at me.

I made my way towards them.

'Miss Lancaster?' one of the men asked as I approached, in a strong accent that was part Scottish and part something else. He was the older of the two, but his age was difficult to determine. Grey stubble and lined, sun-damaged skin put him in his sixties, but his broad build made him seem younger.

The second man was probably in his late twenties. Trendily shaggy, sandy hair framed a boyishly handsome face, set with bright blue eyes. He was wearing jeans, a striped shirt and a leather jacket – and looked absolutely freezing, his cheeks flushed and his hands thrust deep into his pockets – but he gave me such a warm smile that I forgot how inappropriate his outfit was for the North Sea in January.

'That's me,' I said, smiling expectantly from one to the other. 'I'm in the right place then?'

'Almost,' the older man replied, gesturing to the gangway.

'Oh,' was all I could think of to say. 'I'm, erm, looking for Jones Associates . . .?'

He gave a curt nod, pointed to the gangway again and disappeared into the wheelhouse.

'I wasn't expecting the boat either,' the younger man admitted with a sheepish grin. His accent was a softer Scottish. 'But apparently we've got one more step of the journey to go.'

I baulked at this. It was one thing to travel by plane, ferry and bus, but it was quite another to board a fishing boat with two strangers and set off into the open sea.

'You're a new recruit too?' I asked hesitantly.

'Yep. With no idea of where we're going or what I've been hired to do.'

Although I would have liked answers, his ignorance was strangely comforting. It meant I wasn't alone.

I lowered my voice. 'And you trust him?' My eyes flicked to the man in the wheelhouse.

'He knew my name,' he shrugged. 'Which is Aiden Haw, by the way.'

'I'm Ellie Lancaster.'

'Nice to meet you, Ellie.'

'And you think we should go with him?'

'Sure. We've come this far. Granted, it's not a normal first day at work but, let's face it, what part of this has been normal? Mysterious email. Interview in a coffee shop. Thousand-page confidentiality agreement.'

'So I am in the right place then,' I concluded, eyeing the gangway warily.

'If I am then you are. And if he turns out to be a crazy serial killer who's lured us here under false pretences, then at least there are two of us and only one of him.' His cheeks dimpled as his grin widened.

Whether it was Aiden's logic or his dimples that decided it for me I still can't say, but despite my better judgement I climbed onboard. *I could certainly check* be unboring *off my list now*, I thought, countering it with *if I survive long enough to see my list again*.

Seeing that I'd boarded, the older man came out from behind the wheel and handed us each a bright orange life jacket. They looked brand new.

'Written in my contract,' he muttered, almost embarrassed. 'You've got to wear them, or I don't get paid.'

This was a good sign, I decided, pulling the bulky jacket over my head. If he planned on murdering us then he wouldn't be giving us life jackets, surely.

'Orange isn't really my colour,' Aiden joked. 'Have you got anything in blue?'

The man – from books I'd read, I was fairly sure you'd call him the skipper – gave him an unamused look and returned to the wheelhouse without comment.

Within seconds we were away from the pier and cutting through the waves, the shoreline to our left. I'd had the romantic notion that I'd stand out on the deck, the wind tousling my hair and the salt air filling my lungs. But, as with most things, the reality was very different, and after thirty seconds of being whipped by icy blasts and salt spray, both Aiden and I retreated ruefully to the wheelhouse. I squeezed into a corner trying not to get in the skipper's way, while Aiden stood beside the wheel, chatting easily.

After some time, a lighthouse came into view, perched atop a small rocky island a little out to sea. There was no sign of life there, other than the seagulls wheeling overhead.

'Is that Muckle Flugga?' I pointed.

The skipper nodded.

'Muckle . . . what?' Aiden asked, nonplussed.

I recited what I remembered from the travel guides. 'It was Britain's northernmost inhabited island until the lighthouse became automated in the 1990s. The name comes from Old Norse. There's some folklore about it.'

'I'm not surprised,' Aiden said, eyeing the island.

'There were two giants,' I went on, 'and they both fell in love with a mermaid. They fought over her by throwing rocks at each other, and one of those rocks became Muckle Flugga.'

'I hope she was worth the trouble.'

'She killed them both,' I replied with a grin. 'She promised to marry whichever of them could follow her to the North Pole. They both followed and – as neither of them could swim – they both drowned.'

Chuckling, Aiden shook his head. 'Well, isn't that a lovely story?'

I wondered excitedly if Muckle Flugga was our destination. The lighthouse could, I supposed, contain a small archive. *What a wonderful place that would be to work*, I thought, picturing myself waking up in a lighthouse every morning. But we skirted round the island and, to my surprise, veered north, away from the coastline.

According to the travel guides, there was nothing north of here. Norway would be to our west, and the Faroe Islands and Iceland to the north-east, but straight up was nothing but the Norwegian Sea. Anxiety mounting, I reached for the guide I'd strategically placed at the top of my backpack and flicked through the pages.

'Erm, excuse me,' I said to the skipper. 'Where are we going?'

He replied with a single, unfamiliar word. 'Osk.'

Aiden and I exchanged perplexed glances. 'And what's that?'

'Osk,' he repeated. 'An island.'

I held up my travel guide. 'According to this, there aren't any islands north of Muckle Flugga.'

The skipper merely shrugged.

Now I was getting really worried. How stupid and irresponsible I'd been to just climb aboard a stranger's boat and let him take me out to sea. What was his plan? To take us far from land, far from help, before murdering us? Almost more than fear, I felt anger. Anger at myself for giving up my safe, ordered life to *be unboring*. Well, being bloody *unboring* meant very little when you were dead.

Okay, I told myself firmly. *So you made a mistake. But there's still time to fix it. You're not murdered yet.* I considered my options. I needed a weapon. I glanced furtively around the wheelhouse, but the few objects scattered around were either useless or firmly secured. My eyes rested on a large flask for hot drinks or soup. It looked hard and heavy enough to knock somebody out if it hit the right spot with enough force. But did I know the right spot, and did I have enough force?

I was too busy formulating a plan to notice what was up ahead.

'Look,' Aiden said suddenly, pointing.

I followed his finger and found a grey cluster of clouds, too thick and formed for mist, lying low on the water. We seemed to be heading straight for it.

'Well, that isn't ominous at all,' Aiden muttered, and I could tell he was finally worried too. About time.

'Is it safe to be driving into that?' I asked the skipper.

He shrugged. His staple gesture it seemed. 'Sure.' He didn't even slow the boat as we plunged into the cloud, our visibility instantly cut off.

For long minutes the world around us was an impenetrable silvery grey; it would have been beautiful if it hadn't been so unsettling. And then the cloud began to thin and suddenly we were out the other side.

I let out the breath I hadn't realised I'd been holding – and gasped. Directly ahead of us was an island.

It wasn't just some rocky outcrop, but an actual island. I couldn't gauge the size, but it was significantly larger than Muckle Flugga. What looked like grass and heather covered most of it and – most surprisingly – there was a building at its centre, smoke spiralling out from its chimney. Relief came first and then confusion.

'But there aren't any inhabited islands north of Unst . . .' I flicked to the map of the Scottish islands in my guidebook. Nothing but sea.

'Clearly there are,' Aiden said. He seemed curious, but frustratingly untroubled.

I turned to the skipper. 'Is this Osk?' I tried to imitate his pronunciation. It sounded more Scandinavian than Gaelic, and probably had roots in Old Norse, but I wasn't an expert.

He nodded.

'Is it still part of Scotland?'

I thought it was a simple enough question, but the skipper seemed amused by it. He considered for a moment and then gave a wry smile. 'Sure.'

Chapter Three

If Clementine hadn't been easily recognisable with her bright pink hair, I never would have disembarked. But there she stood, at the end of a small wooden pier, waving her arms enthusiastically at us. She looked incongruously real against the ethereal background of a dark heather-covered island that shouldn't exist.

'Land ahoy!' she shouted in greeting.

I was so relieved to see her – and equally relieved *not* to see dour Mr Jones with his long silences and disdain – I could have hugged her.

'You made it,' Clementine exclaimed, beaming at us both. 'I'm so glad you did. And not only because it means I've won a wager. Willum!' She turned her broad smile to the skipper, who'd shut off the engine. 'Thanks for getting them here safely.'

'No problem, Miss Clementine,' he replied, tipping his woolly hat at her in a comfortingly old-fashioned gesture.

'How's Mary? Has she shifted that cough yet?'

'Oh, she's right as rain now. She appreciated that cake you sent back last time. Mind you, so did I,' he added with a wink. 'There's a letter from her somewhere in that lot,' he nodded towards two small crates on the deck.

'You're a lifesaver Willum, thank you.' Beside her was a trolley, which she wheeled over as the skipper – Willum – unloaded his cargo. Aiden and I followed, clambering out onto the pier.

'Did you manage to get it?' Clementine asked, clearly excited by whatever was in the crates.

'Mary tracked it down.'

'Oh wonderful,' she preened, caressing the top of one of the crates. I studied them, wondering what they contained, but they bore no telltale words or logos. 'Tell that miracle of a wife of yours that I owe her another cake. Join us at the house for a cuppa?'

Willum shook his head. 'Thank you but I'd best be getting back.'

'I thought you'd say that.' She proffered a flask and handed it to him, along with an envelope. 'Another list of supplies. Can you make it back in a fortnight?'

He nodded, pocketing the envelope and smiling gratefully as he took the flask. 'You take care now.' He glanced at me and Aiden, a glint of amusement in his eye. 'And mind you be keeping this city pair out of trouble.'

'But trouble's the best place to be,' Clementine grinned as Willum reboarded the *Valkyrie*. She turned to me and Aiden as the boat's engine started. 'Last chance to return to civilisation.'

Realising with a prick of panic how true that was, I very nearly leapt back onboard. But politeness and curiosity won their battle with self-preservation, and I stayed, watching as the boat slipped away.

'Wellies.' Clementine gestured to where the pier met the land and I saw two pairs of boots propped up against a birch tree. 'It's about a mile up to the house and, well . . .' She looked pointedly at my sensible suede boots and Aiden's trendy sneakers.

She loaded the crates onto her trolley while Aiden and I pulled on the wellingtons – mine slightly too large and Aiden's slightly too small. 'Can I take the crates for you?' Aiden asked.

'Thanks but no,' she smiled. 'I wouldn't trust this precious cargo in anybody else's hands. 'Tis a treacherous path.' I thought she was joking, but within one minute of setting off from the pier, I'd slipped in the mud, tripped over a rock, got one foot caught under a tree root and sunk my other foot in a puddle so deep that water had poured traitorously over the top of my boot. The track was less of a track and more a set of boot prints in the soggy earth.

'What is this island?' I asked, trying for a breezily curious tone.

'We call it Osk.'

'It isn't on any of the maps I've seen.' No response. Clementine suddenly seemed very focused on manoeuvring her trolley around a cluster of rocks. Once she'd safely skirted them, I went on. 'I didn't think there were any inhabited Scottish islands north of Unst.'

Clementine smiled over her shoulder at me. 'You like geography?'

'Of course,' I replied. Who doesn't?

'Well, there are lots of things I can tell you about the island,' she mused – the implication being that there were also lots of things she couldn't tell me. 'It's roughly six miles around. Mostly heather and mud, as you can tell, with some nice beaches on the east side and cliffs on the west. We get puffins on the cliffs – so cute! – and sometimes seals on the beaches. We get a *lot* of weather too, which is great, but does mean you need to prepare for anything. I never venture from the house without raincoat and wellies, even if it's sunny. The island likes to lull you into a false sense of security, so be warned.'

'Do you live here?' Aiden asked, his tone sympathetic.

'Most of the time. It's the best place for me to work, plus I grew up here.'

'You grew up here?' I asked, stunned. Having spent my entire childhood in Manchester, I couldn't imagine growing up somewhere so isolated and wild. 'You must have had some great adventures,' was all I could think of to say, not sure whether I envied or pitied her.

'Me and my brother Cole – oh, sorry, *Mr Jones* – got into a fair number of scrapes,' she grinned roguishly.

'Mr Jones is your brother?' I asked, incredulous. I couldn't picture the two as distant cousins, let alone siblings. Although, I reminded myself, Toby and I were as different as chalk and cheese.

'What, did you think he was my husband?' Clementine snorted. 'Trust me, I have better taste than that. Anyway, we both hit our teens and couldn't wait to get away from the island and each other. In case you hadn't guessed, ours is the only house here, and I was desperate for some other company. Not to mention clothes shopping, cinema, restaurants, boys . . . But once I'd escaped to uni, I couldn't wait to come back. It's not perfect – where is? – but it is home. Speaking of which . . .'

We'd reached the top of a particularly steep section of muddy track, and there stood the house. Originally, it would have been a small two-storey building of dark grey stone, with four square windows, a chimney either side of the slate-tiled roof and a slightly crooked wooden front door. But over the years, various extensions had been added. They were all in the same stone, but I could tell by the shade of grey and the neatness of the bricks that the section added to the left had come first and the section on the right more recently. Despite the asymmetrical sprawl of windows and side doors, the house still managed to look cosy.

'I need to get these treasures into my part of the house,' Clementine patted the crates and gestured to the most recent wing. She opened a bright red side door and kicked off her wellies in the doorway. We followed suit, both smiling as the warmth hit us. Clementine ushered us through, wheeling in the crates and closing the door behind us.

My senses registered various things at once. First was the heat, so glorious after hours of finger-numbing cold. Second was the smell: tantalising scents, both sweet and savoury, enveloped me and made me realise how hungry I was. Thirdly, music was playing, just loud enough for me to recognise a 1990s power ballad. And fourthly, my eyes took in the most cheerful looking kitchen I'd ever seen. There was no hint of grey stone; the walls were painted sunflower yellow, and every surface was covered in patterned tablecloths – gingham, stripes, polka dots and flowers – and brightly coloured appliances. The microwave was turquoise, the stand mixer orange and the toaster the same tone of pink as Clementine's hair. Wooden beams crossed the ceiling and a vast, ancient-looking Aga cooker stood in one corner, emanating heat and those mouth-watering smells. Stretching across the middle of the space was a large table surrounded by mismatched chairs painted every shade of the rainbow. Clementine gestured for us to sit.

'First things first: something hot to drink.' She filled a copper kettle with water – I was relieved to see a running tap – and lit the hob of the Aga. 'If I remember rightly, you're black coffee,' she pointed to Aiden, who nodded gratefully. 'And you're a hot chocolate with syrup kind of girl.' She opened a cupboard, revealing an entire shelf of bottled syrups. 'Pick your poison.'

'I think I'm in heaven,' I whispered, scanning the labels. 'Toasted marshmallow syrup?'

'I'd recommend,' Clementine said, filling a pan with milk and placing it on another hob. Humming along to a second power ballad, which seemed to be coming from a retro cassette player on the windowsill, she rummaged in a wicker basket next to the door and pulled out two pairs of slippers in the shape of snowmen. 'Second things second: your feet. I didn't know if you'd brought your own giant fluffy slippers . . .'

'I don't think I've ever even owned giant fluffy slippers,' Aiden admitted, taking a pair gingerly from her.

'Nobody's perfect,' she reassured him, handing me the other pair.

I gave a sheepish smile. 'I did bring my own, but these look much cosier.' I peeled off my damp socks – I couldn't remember the last time my feet had stayed dry all day – and sighed happily pushing my feet into the warm woolly snowmen.

'And third things third: food.' Clementine donned a pair of polka dot oven gloves, opened the Aga, and pulled out a loaf of plaited bread and a dozen scones. The smell was heavenly. She set them in the middle of the table, along with a couple of plates, a breadknife, butter and a congregation of condiments. 'Tuck in!'

I didn't need telling twice. As Clementine prepared the drinks, I merrily burnt my fingers cutting into the still-hot bread and slathering it with butter and raspberry jam. 'This is amazing,' I said, knowing even before my first bite that it would be. 'Thank you so much.'

Aiden cut himself a smaller slice and dolloped a little chutney onto it. 'Yes, thanks. I've had nothing but airport salad for what feels like days.'

Once Clementine had prepared the drinks and set them in front of us in mugs – 'Hot drinks always taste better in mugs rather than cups, don't you think?' – she turned to the crates. 'Now if you guys don't mind, I'm just going to do some unpacking.'

'Can we help?' Aiden asked, making me feel guilty for just sitting there, hugging my mug of gloriously thick hot chocolate.

'No, no, you just enjoy your drinks. I know where everything goes.' She opened the first crate and peered in, grinning with delight.

I craned forward, wondering what this 'precious cargo' contained. Hoping it might provide some clue as to why we, still none the wiser, were there. But nothing became clearer as Clementine pulled out her first 'treasure' and my eyes took in a little plastic jar bearing the words 'Gum Tragacanth'. She held it aloft like a trophy. 'Oh, it's like Christmas morning all over again!'

Aiden and I exchanged bemused glances. He was braver than I was. 'That's great and everything but . . . what is it?'

Clementine looked aghast. 'It's gum tragacanth!'

'I repeat,' Aiden said, his lips quirking, 'that's great and everything, but what is it?'

'Oh, you philistines,' she declared with an exasperated shake of her head. 'It's a baking ingredient, for firming up fondant. I ran out weeks ago but it's so hard to find on Unst . . .' She gave the jar a little affectionate caress and placed it in a cupboard.

'There's nothing worse than saggy fondant,' Aiden said, throwing me a wink.

'Absolutely,' Clementine enthused, beaming as she heaved out an industrial-sized sack of flour, followed by muscovado sugar, almonds, about twenty bars of plain chocolate and a punnet of strawberries. She stored them all in various cupboards and fridges before diving back in again.

'Are you planning on doing some baking?' Aiden asked, as she revealed a colossal bag of icing sugar and three cartons of eggs.

'Only every day for the rest of my life,' she laughed, laying the eggs down into a bowl. 'It's what I do.'

'As your job?'

'I make people fat and happy for a living.'

'Her cake recipes are amazing,' I told Aiden, who was looking perplexed, then turned back to Clementine. 'I did wonder whether you'd hired us for a baking archive . . .?' I left it hanging, a hopeful question.

'A baking archive?' Clementine repeated before bursting into laughter. *I guess not then*, I thought, sipping self-consciously at my hot chocolate.

'I know, it was a silly idea,' I murmur.

'Oh no, not silly at all. I wish it were the case. Wouldn't it be wonderful?' Her expression turned dreamy. 'Aisles and aisles of catalogued recipes.'

'So,' Aiden cut in, 'if we're not here for a "baking archive", then . . .?' He let his question trail off, peering over at Clementine expectantly.

'Oh yes, sorry!' she cried, closing a cupboard and turning back to us. 'I totally forgot why you were here. You must have so many questions.'

'Just a few,' Aiden admitted with a disarming smile. 'But you finish unpacking. We can wait.'

I gritted my teeth. *He* might be able to wait, but I was bursting with curiosity. Fortunately, Clementine seemed to sense this.

'No, no, you've both been waiting long enough. I wanted to tell you as soon as you got the jobs, but Cole insisted that we wait until you were here. Well, now you're here, so let's begin.' She stood looking at us for a moment, and her smile began to waver. 'Hmm. This is harder than I thought it'd be. Cole was meant to be here to do this, but he's been delayed with work, so I guess it's up to me . . . I knew I should have written a speech or something.' She drummed her fingers on the table in deliberation and then, after a moment, gave it a decisive slap. 'You'll just have to see for yourselves. Come. I'll show you the archives.'

Chapter Four

The door was much like the other doors we'd passed through to reach the oldest section of the house: wooden, old-fashioned, otherwise nondescript. But instead of opening onto a hallway or a cosy sitting room, it opened onto a set of stone stairs, leading down. Clementine, who was carrying a cling-filmed plate of buttered bread, scones and – inexplicably – two small, seemingly uncooked eggs, led the way.

I followed Clementine, and Aiden took up the rear, the staircase too narrow to walk side-by-side.

The wall on my left was lined with thick cables and industrial lights, the latter bright enough to see that the walls were stone as well as the steps and were – I realised with surprise – natural rather than brick.

'Where do you get your electricity from?' Aiden's voice echoed down from behind me. 'You can't be on the grid here.'

'We used to just have a diesel generator but recently my brother installed solar and wind power on the island. Don't ask me how it works. He's the expert.'

She must have more than one brother, I decided, unable to picture Mr Jones the lawyer, in shirt and tie, setting up wind turbines and solar panels.

Clementine was blocking my view ahead so I couldn't tell how far down the steps went, but we walked for what felt like minutes. The steps grew more uneven and the air colder the further we descended. And then abruptly Clementine stopped, stepped to one side, and I gasped.

It was truly the most breathtaking thing I'd ever seen. We stood on a narrow platform overlooking a cavern, far larger than any cathedral, and far more beautiful. Twisting down into the cavern was a path hewn into the rock face – actually, several paths, crossing and merging and diverging. They wound down and down and out of sight like a colossal spiral staircase, illuminated by warm amber electric lights, which shone from wall fixtures every few feet. Running beside each path, as far as I could see, were niches pockmarking the rock, from the floor to head height. Judging by the regularity of their shapes – long, horizontal rectangles – they had been deliberately carved, and acted, I realised, as shelves. The 'shelves' on our level were empty, but this wasn't the case further down the spiral. Below, they were packed tightly with what appeared to be scrolls, stacked atop each other, their ends facing out so that nearly every inch of the rock face was obscured behind tight circles of rolled-up parchment. It looked like a giant honeycomb.

'What is this place?' I breathed.

'The archive,' Clementine replied simply. And with a tip of her head, she gestured for us to follow her down one of the paths.

It descended gradually, but the flooring was rough, in some places slippery and so narrow that we had to remain in single file. I was glad that whoever built this magnificent place had thought to run a simple metal railing along the edge of the path, separating me from the precipitous drop. It probably still wouldn't pass health and safety regulations though, I noted, eyeing sections so heavily rusted that a tap with a finger would see it crumbling to dust. I thought back to my interview and Clementine asking if I suffered from vertigo. It made sense now.

After the first spiral of the cavern (which took us about a minute, such was its size), we reached the first set of filled shelves. Clementine didn't slow and Aiden was directly behind me, so I couldn't stop to examine them, but I managed to make out a few details. Each niche seemed to contain at least a hundred scrolls, probably more. As far as I could tell, they seemed to be the same size and colour. Most shockingly for an archive, there didn't appear to be any identification markers or shelf numbers. *How on earth can anyone find anything?* I wondered, anxious at the thought of trying to locate a single item amidst the thousands – probably millions – stored here. The only numbering system I noticed was a *1997* carved into the rock above the first set of populated shelves. The year?

Here the path forked. One continued its gradual descent clockwise and the other veered sharply anticlockwise. Both were flanked by the scroll-filled niches; I caught a glimpse of *1987* over the first set on the stairs, but Clementine was leading us in the other direction. After two spirals of the cavern, I noticed a *2002*. Half a spiral later and the path forked again; a moment later, another opening as well as a *2001* and a *1986*.

Every now and then we passed a bright red fire extinguisher, incongruous in such an obscure setting – but no doubt wise.

I'd lost track of time, but the bottom of the cavern was still nowhere in sight and we had yet to see another living soul. Suddenly, the industrial lights that had accompanied us this far down transitioned to incandescent light bulbs, which gave off a weaker glow. The air was icy cold; I kept my hands firmly in my pockets and made a mental note to wear multiple layers tomorrow.

I was beginning to wonder if we'd become trapped in a Penrose staircase, spiralling down and up simultaneously, never reaching the end, when Clementine disappeared into one of the passageways leading off from the cavern. The winding spiral had become so hypnotic that I almost didn't notice, and Aiden had to tap me on the shoulder.

This passageway was just like the others: flanked on both sides by scroll-upon-scroll-upon-scroll. It was wider than the walkway in the cavern, but more claustrophobic, and I began to think about how much hard, heavy, merciless rock was above us.

Clementine's humming – I recognised another 1990s power ballad – was a little reassuring, but I was still relieved when the passage opened up into a high-ceilinged cave-cum-room. Here the shelving went much higher, and there was a set of rolling library ladders pushed up against one wall. There was also a hodge-podge of old furniture scattered about – a faded armchair, a couple of tables and chairs, a bureau topped by a vintage gramophone – making the space feel almost cosy. They weren't the first things I noticed though. The first was the warmth, provided by a small but clearly effective portable gas heater. The second was a pair of stuffed ravens, bafflingly positioned on top of the gramophone. And the third thing I noticed was the man.

His age was difficult to determine, but I guessed at somewhere between sixty and seventy. He was a small man, in both height and build, with wiry grey hair. His skin was paper-white and as lined as a page in a book, but his eyes were bright. He wore cord trousers, braces, a crisp white shirt and a bow tie; the only things missing, I decided, were a flat cap and a cardigan with elbow patches. Then I saw the cardigan draped over a chair and smiled.

He hadn't noticed us as he stood over a large mahogany desk and cross-referenced a document with a German-to-English dictionary, his pencil scratching as he made notes. Behind him was a wooden bookcase, filled with more dictionaries. I considered myself old school, but even I rarely used foreign-language dictionaries and they were not, I noted, alphabetised or even ordered by continent. My fingers itched to rectify the oversight.

'Uncle Joe,' Clementine sang, and the man looked up with a smile. His eyes fell on Clementine first but the moment he saw me and Aiden, his smile faltered. He dropped his pencil and straightened, as if standing to attention.

'These are the people I was telling you about,' Clementine said, placing the plate of food on the desk in front of him. 'Ellie and Aiden. They're here to help you.'

Although he gave us both nods of welcome, an emotion I couldn't quite place flitted across the man's face. Regret?

She kissed him on the cheek and peeled back the cling film on the plate. 'You didn't come up for lunch, so you're going to eat all of this. Well, not these.' She picked up the eggs and threw them in the direction of the gramophone. To my surprise, the stuffed ravens leapt up with a caw and caught the eggs in their hooked black beaks. *Not* stuffed then.

'Are those . . . pets?' Aiden asked incredulously.

Clementine looked towards them affectionately. 'They've been with the family for . . . a long time. But they do whatever they please, including taking chunks out of the hand that feeds them.' She held up a plastered finger. 'So be warned: they bite.'

I'd never been in such a surreal situation. Hundreds of feet below ground, in a labyrinthine archive of mysterious, seemingly identical scrolls, being warned not to stroke the ravens. I focused on the man and his translation task, something familiar I could hold on to.

'I can read German quite well if you need help with that,' I offered.

He nodded but said nothing, turning back to his work. Clementine gave me a reassuring smile and gestured for us to return the way we'd come. 'Don't forget to eat,' she called to him as we headed down the passageway.

'Who else works here?' I asked, glancing back over my shoulder at 'Uncle Joe', hunched over his translation.

'My parents dip in and out but they're away at the moment. It's a family business but Cole and I, well . . .

47

We had other ideas, so it's fallen to Uncle Joe.' Her expression touched on doleful for the briefest moment before she gave a grin and gestured to me and Aiden. 'And that's why we're extending the family.'

I was desperate to hear more about the archives, about what those scrolls contained. But Clementine was either being deliberately coy or deemed it irrelevant, because she said nothing more as we wound our way back up to the house. (I timed the journey and it took us twenty-three minutes from cavern to door.)

'So, you should have tomorrow to settle in, unpack, explore the island and then start work the day after. How does that sound?' she asked as we luxuriated in the warmth of the kitchen.

A whole other day before I got some answers on what those archives contained? No, thank you. 'I'm more than happy to start tomorrow,' I said, hoping she'd pick up on just *how* happy I'd be.

'Me too,' Aiden chipped in.

'I like your enthusiasm.'

'What time do we start?'

'Oh, erm . . .' Clementine shrugged. 'Whenever you want really. I'll be making breakfast around ten, so come eat and then get started.'

Ten? I was used to having been in work for two hours by that time.

'Now,' Clementine went on. 'Do you guys want anything else to eat or would you rather hit the sack? I know it's been a long day for you both.'

Glancing at my watch I saw that it was only half past three, but it felt much later. Partly because I'd been travelling for what felt like a thousand years, and partly because, looking through the closest window, I could see it was already dark outside. I'd known the sun sets early this far north but hadn't realised quite how early.

'Honestly? I'd kill for a shower and a bed,' Aiden admitted, and I had to agree. Although I didn't think I'd sleep, I was eager – and a little apprehensive – to see where I'd be staying. Today had been so full of surprises, I didn't want that to continue into my sleeping arrangements.

We headed to the kitchen to grab our luggage, and then Clementine led us back through the old part of the house and over into the other extension. Through a door, down a corridor, through another door, up a flight of stairs, right turn by the window. Compared to the subterranean labyrinth of walkways and passages we'd just navigated, the house was easy, but I still knew I'd get lost finding breakfast in the morning.

'The rooms aren't en suite I'm afraid, but you're the only two who'll be using the bathroom. I'm over on the other side of the house and Uncle Joe's rooms are in the old section, although he usually sleeps down in the archives anyway.' Clementine stopped on a hallway on the first floor and pointed to three different doors. 'Bathroom. Aiden's room. Ellie's room. You should have everything you need but just tell me if anything's missing.'

'I'm missing one thing,' Aiden said, holding up his phone. 'Signal.'

Clementine barked a laugh. 'Didn't I warn you? Signal isn't weak here – it's non-existent. We don't have TV or internet either.'

'What?' Aiden asked, clearly taken aback. 'Nothing?'

'Nothing at all. No signal can find us, not even using satellite phone. The island doesn't really . . .' Clementine cast her hands out for the right words, '. . . like or allow it.' It was peculiar phrasing, I thought, as if the island had both an opinion and the right to impose it. And how could we be beyond the range of a satellite? My knowledge of technology was limited, but even I found it odd that a satellite phone wouldn't work here.

'Totally cut off from all that noise. Great, isn't it?' Clementine smiled.

'Erm, not really,' Aiden replied. 'For one, how do I contact home?' I'd been worrying about that too, although Toby had warned me I might not have signal, so hopefully wouldn't be too concerned when he didn't hear from me straightaway.

'Snail mail,' Clementine informed Aiden. 'Willum will be back in a fortnight – pass on any letters you have to him. Your friends and families can send their replies to him. He's used to acting as postman when he comes over every couple of weeks.'

'Every couple of weeks?' Aiden repeated, bemused. 'But that means it could be a month before I hear from anyone.'

'More if the weather's particularly bad,' Clementine replied cheerfully. 'Now, I've put some clean towels on your beds and—'

'No signal whatsoever?' Aiden pressed, fiddling with his phone. 'Have you tried a booster?'

'It wouldn't make a difference. We don't get anything here. We consider ourselves lucky to have plumbing and electricity! But don't worry, there are plenty of other ways to pass the time. We have a whole cupboard full of board games and we do have a video player.'

'Video player . . .' Aiden closed his eyes, took a deep breath. 'That's great. Board games and a video player. What more could we need?'

'Precisely! Now I'll leave you both to your beds. I hope you sleep well, and I'll see you for breakfast.' Clementine gave a salute and headed back down the hallway.

I turned to Aiden and found him studying his phone again, as if sheer willpower would make a signal appear. I muttered a 'goodnight' and headed into my new room.

It was small but, without a doubt, cosy. One wall was exposed grey brick and the others were painted a warm russet, which matched the sheets on the single bed. A small square window looked out onto darkness, but candles were clustered on the windowsill and mantel-piece. Embers still glowed in the fireplace, explaining the warmth in the room, and kindling, a coal bucket and a box of matches lay ready to one side. I'd have to ask Clementine to teach me how to get a fire going.

Smiling contentedly at my new, if temporary, home, I began to unpack. I'd brought only what I could carry, so it didn't take long. Clothes in the wardrobe. Books – mainly travel guides – on the desk. I plugged in my phone charger only because I'd need the alarm, and draped my flannel pyjamas over the bed. Then, grabbing my toiletries, I headed to the bathroom – only to find the door locked and the sound of a shower running within.

My shower, when I finally had it, was significantly shorter than Aiden's. It appeared he had used up all the hot water, and the bathroom was a lot colder than the bedroom. I rinsed the conditioner out of my hair in the sink, brushed my chattering teeth and padded back to my room, throwing daggers at Aiden's closed door.

I'd expected to lie awake for a long time. Not only because it was still technically afternoon, but because anxiety had been causing insomnia for the last few weeks and, today of all days, I'd predicted many hours of staring up at the ceiling, running over the journey in my head and puzzling over the mysterious archives. But I was asleep faster than you can say 'gum tragacanth'.

* * *

I woke before the sun did, the sky just blushing pink. For a moment I was disoriented, wondering why Toby's sofa-bed was suddenly so comfortable. My head quickly cleared when I pulled off the myriad blankets and felt the frigid air. Slipping my feet into the snowman slippers and wrapping one of the blankets around my shoulders, I moved to the window. Beyond the ice-cloaked glass I could make out the path leading up to the house and the frosted heather sloping down into the sea, which looked almost purple in the early morning light. Two birds danced in the sky but otherwise the world was still.

I guessed it was about half past seven and was surprised I'd slept for so long, even after the mammoth journey. So when my alarm suddenly started blaring, signalling 8.30 a.m., I jumped. How had I slept for sixteen hours? I'd obviously benefited from it, though. I hadn't felt this fresh and eager to start the day in a long time.

I rushed through my ablutions in the bathroom, dragged my frizzy, straw-coloured hair into a bobble, pulled on multiple jumpers and set off in search of a door leading outside. The house was dark and quiet; I suspected that both Clementine and Aiden were still in their beds. Not wanting to disturb them – and feeling like an intruder in somebody else's home – I moved quietly and resisted the temptation to peer into the rooms I passed. There would be time for that later.

Somehow, I managed to find my way to the kitchen, dark but far warmer than the rest of the house because of the Aga. I pulled on the wellies I'd left by the door, popped on my woolly hat and stepped out into the fresh morning air.

My breath came out in clouds as I crunched over the ice-dried mud, hands stuffed deep in my pockets. A few different paths led away from the house, but I stuck with the one we'd climbed up the day before. The red-bricked streets of suburban Manchester had been my home all my life, and this was another world entirely. The way the sea mirrored the sky as it danced from crimson to amber to teal. The way the frost-coated heather glistened as the sun, winter-weak, began its slow ascent. The way the waves embraced the rocks below, surging and crashing.

Both Clementine and Aiden were in the kitchen when I arrived back. Clementine, in a fluffy purple dressing gown, was standing at the stove, cooking something in a frying pan, while Aiden was sitting at the table, hunched over a cup of coffee. He looked dishevelled and half-asleep, and all the more boyishly handsome for it. I checked the clock, worried I was late, but it was eight minutes to ten.

'You were out early,' Clementine observed as I yanked off the wellies. 'Hope you weren't out there looking for a Starbucks.'

'I just went for a walk. It's such a lovely morning. Can I help with anything?'

Clementine, waving me to the table, gave a suspicious frown. 'You're not a . . . *morning person*' – she whispered the words as if they were dirty – 'are you?'

I laughed. 'Afraid so, sorry.'

'Crazy person,' she shook her head. 'I'm not functional before nine thirty. And this one here doesn't look like he'll be functional until midday.' She nodded to Aiden who simply grunted into his coffee cup. 'Care for some pancakes?'

'Always,' I said eagerly, just as my stomach grumbled.

'That's what I like to hear. This one' – Clementine nodded again to Aiden – '"doesn't do breakfast".' She gave a tsk of disapproval and emptied three American-style pancakes onto a plate in front of me. 'Syrup in the jug, orange juice in the fridge, coffee in the pot. Help yourself.'

'You're spoiling us,' I said, drenching my pancakes in syrup.

'I've not had people to cook for since . . . well, since my parents went away – Uncle Joe doesn't really count – so you're doing me a favour. And these,' she proffered three brown paper bags, 'are your lunches. Please try to get Uncle Joe to eat something.' And with a wave, she was gone.

I was impatient to head down – partly because I hated the thought of being late on my first day, and partly because of those tantalising scrolls. I'd finally find out what the archives were housing. But Aiden was taking his sweet time, pouring himself a second cup of coffee and, when he finally looked conscious, getting his phone out and peering morosely at the screen.

'Do *you* have any signal?' he asked me.

'Sorry, no. Do you think we should be going now?'

He took another slurp, dragged his fingers through his hair, and finally pulled himself up. 'I suppose that is why we're here.'

I grabbed our packed lunches and turned eagerly for the door. Aiden followed, less eagerly. But at some point between the top of the stone staircase and the bottom, he perked up. Clearly the caffeine had kicked in, and when we reached the first set of scrolls, beneath the *1997* etched into the rock, he elbowed me playfully.

'Go on, I dare you.'

'Dare me to do what?' I asked, innocent.

He rolled his eyes and tapped the edge of a scroll. 'I saw how you were looking at these yesterday. You were like a kid in a sweet-shop.'

'Don't you want to know what they are?'

55

'Of course, but you're the one practically drooling. Go on, open one.'

I glanced around furtively. 'But what if . . .'

'I don't really think you need to worry about CCTV,' he said dryly, gesturing at the bare stone walls and ancient lighting. 'And I won't tell anyone, cross my heart.' He made the sign of a cross on his chest and inched a random scroll out teasingly.

He was right of course; nobody was watching us. But for some reason it felt wrong. It must have been the setting: the vast cavern, the dim lights, the secrecy that had surrounded our journey there. There was also the memory of that colossal contract I'd signed, and Mr Jones's stern gaze.

'I can wait a little longer,' I said firmly, keeping my hands by my sides. 'I like the suspense.' That was an outright lie and Aiden knew it.

'Coward.'

I smiled, reminded of Toby. 'Do you think Uncle Joe will be in the same place as yesterday?'

'I bloody well hope so, otherwise we'll still be looking for him by the time our contracts end.' And with that he took the lead. To my relief he had a good sense of direction, and only hesitated a couple of times as we reached forks in the walkway.

As we walked, Aiden slightly ahead, he explained it was digital archiving he was interested in.

'Does this place have digital archives?' I asked doubtfully as we continued to wind our way down.

Aiden snorted. 'No, and that's why they hired me. But I'm curious as to how they think I can digitise *all* of this,' he gestured into the vast cavern, 'with only a year on my contract.'

'They want *everything* digitised?'

Aiden shrugged. 'They didn't tell me much. They didn't tell me *anything*, actually. But it was my digital archiving skills they were mainly interested in at the interview, so I'm guessing.' He glanced over his shoulder at me. 'Did you get any more information out of them?'

'Not at all.'

We'd reached the entrance to the passageway and suddenly my first-day-in-the-job nerves overtook my curiosity. What if I wasn't good enough? What if they'd made a mistake when they hired me, and I didn't have the skills they'd been expecting?

It was with this fear churning in my stomach – and making me regret that stack of pancakes – that I followed Aiden down the passageway and into the room Uncle Joe had occupied the day before. It was empty of both archivist and ravens.

Another passageway led off the room, lit by the same incandescent lightbulbs, but there was no indication anybody was down there. Aiden and I glanced at each other, unsure of what to do.

'I guess we just . . . wait?' I asked.

'Guess so.' Aiden was circling the room, clearly looking for something. I tentatively approached the desk, where the German dictionary had been replaced by a Portuguese one, and where the cling-filmed scone and buttered bread sat untouched beside a tightly rolled scroll.

'There aren't even any power outlets in here,' Aiden announced, dismayed. 'Where are we going to plug in the equipment?'

'Equipment?'

'Well, I can't digitise with pen and paper. I'm good, but I'm not *that* good.'

'Maybe there's another room . . .' I trailed off as a noise reached me from the other passageway. A rhythmic squeaking, distant but growing closer. 'Do you hear that?'

'What? Oh yeah.' Aiden moved to peer down the passageway. 'Sounds like bedsprings.' He raised a suggestive eyebrow at me.

I rolled my eyes and hoped my blush wasn't obvious. 'Or maybe . . . a trolley?'

'I prefer my theory, but . . .' Standing by the entrance to the passageway, he could see more than I could. 'Sadly it looks like you're right.' A few seconds later, Uncle Joe appeared, pushing a trolley piled precariously with scrolls.

'Hi there,' Aiden said cheerfully.

Uncle Joe froze. A scroll fell to the floor and Aiden rushed over.

'Here, let me get that for you.'

Uncle Joe nodded what could have been a thanks, before pushing the trolley to the desk. Then he lowered himself into the chair, pulled over the Portuguese dictionary, unfurled the scroll – anchoring one corner with the plate of untouched food, to my horror – and began working.

Aiden and I stared at each other over Uncle Joe's bent head. For a very long moment, we simply stood listening to him rifle through the pages of the dictionary.

'What now?' Aiden mouthed at me.

I shook my head: no idea.

To my relief, Aiden broke the silence first. 'We've been told to call you Uncle Joe. Is that right?'

The old man paused in his rifling to give a brief nod, and then resumed.

'Well, it's great to meet you, Uncle Joe. I'm Aiden and this is Ellie.' Aiden held out his hand expectantly. Uncle Joe glanced up long enough to acknowledge me with a tip of his head and gingerly shake Aiden's outstretched hand, then went back to work.

'Sorry to disturb you,' Aiden went on after another moment's silence, 'but we were told that you'd be showing us the ropes down here. I don't suppose you know what we're meant to be doing?'

Uncle Joe gave an apologetic smile, not quite meeting our eyes. 'Afraid not.'

'I think I'm meant to be digitising some of this. Do you know anything about that?'

Another apologetic smile before he continued his work. I was flummoxed and Aiden looked equally so. We stood awkwardly listening to the pencil scratchings for what felt like a very long time when I finally stepped forward.

'Can I help with your translations? I don't know Portuguese but if there are other languages in there, I could take a look?'

It took him a moment to answer. 'Only one pencil.'

I hadn't thought to bring anything down with me, expecting everything we needed to already be here. Apparently I'd been wrong.

'Could I maybe . . . look at the scrolls?' I ventured, trying to keep the eagerness from my voice. Despite everything, I still wanted to come across as professional.

A hesitation and then a nod.

I reached gingerly for one of the scrolls on the trolley. Aiden sidled up next to me as I unrolled it. The parchment was white, crisp, contemporary; even so, I took every care not to damage it as I opened it out. There were only a few lines in the centre; a lot of paper for so little writing. It was handwritten and, judging by the large, uneven lettering, had been composed by a child. The ink was silver but didn't look to have been from a pen; there was no indentation where the nib would have met the paper. Perhaps some kind of printer? However it had been produced, the wording was Croatian.

'Do you know Croatian?' I asked Aiden.

He gave a soft snort, not deigning to respond.

It was a language I'd barely studied, and although I could have looked for a Croatian dictionary on the nearby bookcase, I was too impatient. I carefully rolled it back up and tried another. The paper was the same as the first, as was the silver ink, but the handwriting was different, probably that of an older child. And the words were in Italian, which I *could* read.

It began, *Caro Babbo Natale . . .*
Dear Father Christmas.

Chapter Five

Dear Father Christmas,
*   I have been a very good girl this year. I have done my homework and looked after grandmother and washed Whisky when she got muddy. I would like a new pair of ice skates please and a cover for my phone, the one with a puppy on. Thank you very much.*
From Alessia

In the top corner of the letter, in the same handwriting, was the address of an apartment in Trento, Italy.

Not wanting to disturb Uncle Joe's silent working, I whispered the translation to Aiden.

'What the hell?' he muttered.

I carefully re-rolled the scroll and took another from the trolley. This one, in the same silver ink but different – though undoubtably a child's – handwriting, was in English.

Dear Santa,
*   Can I please have Elsa's dress and a pair of blue shoes (I am size 12 and a half) and an Olaf teddy.*

*I will put carrots out for Rudolph and some choco-
late out for you because you will be bored of mince
pies.*
    Love from Lacey xx

This one was addressed Stoke-on-Trent, England.

The third scroll I unrolled was in German, addressed
Wernigerode. The first line, again in silver ink, read,
'*Sehr Geehrte St Nikolaus . . .*'

I looked up at Uncle Joe, head still bent over his work,
and breathed, 'What are these?'

He glanced up, seemingly surprised that we were still
there. He looked from me to the scrolls and said, 'The
tardies. I mean the LRNCs.'

'The LRNCs?'

'Just working my way through them.'

'What are LRNCs?' Aiden asked.

'The ones that didn't get here in time,' Uncle Joe replied,
his voice so quiet I had to turn my ear towards him.

'Oh right,' I said, not understanding even a little bit.

'In time for what?' Aiden's tone was both amused and
exasperated.

'Last year's shortlist,' Uncle Joe murmured.

'Shortlist for what?' Aiden persisted. His tone was
light and friendly, but Uncle Joe seemed uncomfortable.
His hands reached out to briefly touch the objects on the
desk in front of him, the plate, the scroll, the pencil – a
nervous habit?

'They'll go in the running for this year's,' he said, not
really answering the question.

Aiden opened his mouth no doubt to ask another question, but I intervened. We'd already invaded this poor man's personal haven; it was unfair to stand here interrogating him. Even if we had been hired to do a job . . .

'Clementine asked us to bring you some lunch,' I said, placing the brown paper bags on the desk.

He nodded a thanks to me, touched each item in front of him once more, pulled himself creakily to his feet, emptied the top layer of scrolls onto the desk and, without saying a word, began pushing the trolley back down the passageway he'd emerged from.

'Should we follow?' I whispered to Aiden.

But Uncle Joe halted, turned to us, and shook his head. It was the first time he'd made direct eye contact with either of us and was enough to stop us both in our tracks.

'Anywhere else. But not down here,' he said, his voice still quiet but firm.

When the squeak of his trolley had faded away, Aiden and I turned to each other, bewildered.

'Do you think it's a hoax?' I asked.

'Either that or we've fallen through the rabbit hole and my name's Alice. Come on,' he said decisively. 'Let's get this straightened out.'

Twenty-five minutes later we were walking back into the kitchen. Clementine, semi-obscured behind a cloud of icing sugar, exclaimed a greeting. 'Back already? You guys work fast.'

'We haven't worked at all,' I admitted apologetically.

Clementine lowered the sieve she was shimmying and looked from me to Aiden. 'Oh? Couldn't you find Uncle Joe?'

'Oh, we found him,' Aiden replied with a smirk, standing across the table from her. 'And we've figured it out, so the camera crew can come out from wherever they're hiding.'

'Camera crew?' Clementine looked to me for an explanation.

I gave an awkward shrug. 'It's just that . . . none of this makes sense.'

'None of what?'

'The mystery boat ride. The island with zero signal,' Aiden answered, counting off on his fingers. 'The isolated house. The ancient cave full of scrolls. The letters to Santa. The pet ravens. The senile old man—'

'He's not senile,' Clementine cut in, and it was the first time I'd seen her look annoyed.

'But the rest is real?' Aiden countered.

'Well, yes.' She held her hands out in a helpless gesture. 'What do you want me to say? It's real. There's no hoax.'

'Prove it.'

Clementine seemed amused by this, in the way a parent is amused by a child. 'How would you like me to prove it?'

Both Aiden and I were stumped for an answer.

'Look,' Clementine finally said, dusting off her hands on her apron. 'I'm not going to be able to convince you this is real, but I can promise you that after a month's work you'll get paid. The money will be there, sitting in your bank accounts. *That* will be real. So does it matter what *this* is?' she asked, gesturing around the room and to herself.

'We won't know the money's there though,' Aiden pointed out. 'We can't exactly access our account details here, can we?'

She pondered for a moment and then smiled. 'In a month I need to go to Lerwick for work. I'll take you with me. You can check your accounts there, while having a weekend back in civilisation. How does that sound?'

'It sounds good to me,' I said, surprised at the certainty in my voice. It wasn't just the words *be unboring* that were spurring me on. It was the thought of the archives lying beneath my feet. All those scrolls, all those doorways to the past. How could I possibly leave them?

Aiden seemed surprised by my certainty too, raising his eyebrows at me. But, smiling, he gave a shrug. 'If you're game, El, then so am I. Even if it is a hoax, it'll be a good laugh.'

'Great,' Clementine beamed. 'That's settled then!'

'Only . . .' I countered hesitantly.

'Go on.'

'Well, I don't really know what I'm supposed to be doing.'

'Hasn't Uncle Joe told you?'

'Uncle Joe hasn't given us the warmest of welcomes,' Aiden admitted.

'I'm not sure he likes us being there,' I reluctantly added.

'Nonsense!' Clementine cried, waving a dismissive hand. 'Uncle Joe's just used to working with . . .' She seemed to stop herself, re-arranging the words in her mind. 'Working on his own. He'll get used to you.'

'Whether he does or not, I can't do my job without the proper equipment,' Aiden said, sounding frustrated for the first time. 'I take it you hired me to digitise the archive, but there isn't a single thing down there that can help me do that.'

For a second, Clementine looked uncharacteristically flustered. 'That might be my fault. Everything was rushed. This is the first time we've ever recruited, you see. The first time we could afford to, what with Cole's salary and my royalties. And, to be honest, the first time we've felt the need to bring people in, but it was necessary after—' She stopped in her tracks, and there was that sense again she was holding something back. 'It's necessary now. But like I said, it was all rushed. Cole left me in charge of ordering what we'd need for you.'

Aiden and I exchanged uncertain looks. 'I hate to ask this,' Aiden broached, 'but what did you actually order?'

She wafted a hand airily. 'Oh, you know. Extra towels, bedding, food supplies. Giant fluffy slippers.'

'So, we have absolutely no equipment for digitising, but we're good for slippers?'

'I'm glad you're seeing the silver lining,' Clementine grinned, clearly seeming to think all was settled. She returned to sieving. 'I'm sorry I can't be of more help. I did help out a lot when I was younger, and I chip in when it gets to the busy season, but things have changed since – well, since I worked there.' There it was again – the impression that she was stopping herself from saying the wrong thing. But then she added ruefully, 'I paid absolutely no attention to the running of things. My parents and Cole know much more than I do. Cole will hopefully be here soon, and he can give you the "formal induction"' – she drew quotation marks in the air – 'and order whatever equipment you need.'

At the news that Mr Jones would be arriving soon, my heart sank. If anyone could see instantly how incompetent I was at the job, it would be him. And from what I remembered of that strange, uncomfortable interview, he wouldn't be shy about telling me.

'In the meantime,' Clementine went on, expertly cracking an egg into the bowl one handed, 'I guess just . . . translate and document.'

Ten minutes later Aiden and I were back at the archives – with our laptops this time, and I'd brought pencils and a notepad – looking out across the vast cavern of scrolls.

'Come on then, Alice,' I said. 'Back down the rabbit hole.'

Uncle Joe wasn't there when we arrived, but his lunch bag had disappeared and the trolley was freshly laden with scrolls.

'So . . . what do we do and where do we start?' I asked.

'Well, I don't know about you, but I'm pretty curious about where that leads.' He nodded to the passageway Uncle Joe had disappeared into. 'What do you say? Further down the rabbit hole?'

'He seemed pretty adamant we shouldn't follow him.'

'We're not following him. We're exploring.' Aiden ambled towards the entry and peered down.

'I really don't think we should,' I said, trying to sound assertive. It wasn't just that I didn't want to get into trouble; it was a sense that whatever lay down that passageway was not for our eyes and we should respect that. No matter how curious we might be.

I expected Aiden to ignore me, but he shrugged. 'Fine. I can be good too. But I have every intention of exploring the rest of the cavern.'

'Me too,' I admitted. 'But first, do you think we should carry on with these?' I looked at the scrolls piled onto the trolley. 'What did Uncle Joe call them? The LRNCs?'

Aiden shrugged again. 'Sure, but what do we do with them?'

'Translate them. What languages can you read?'

'English.'

'Oh well. That's the joy of computers I suppose,' I said, tapping my laptop. 'Do you have translation software on yours?'

'I have Google translate.'

'Not here you don't,' I pointed out. 'For now, how about I read and translate, you transcribe?'

Aiden flipped open his laptop. 'Sounds like a plan. Tell me what to write, boss.'

I unfurled the first scroll to find it was in English. This one, addressed Cardiff, Wales, was simply a long list of computer games and Marvel merchandise, signed *From Noah*. I placed that to one side on the desk and reached for another. This one was in Finnish, a language I didn't know at all, so I started a second pile of scrolls I'd come to later, armed with my laptop. The third scroll was in English: addressed *To Santa* in a spidery scrawl, it asked for a new baseball bat, a new pair of sneakers, and for 'my big sister to be nicer to me'.

The fourth, to my pleasant surprise, was in Japanese. This was a language I knew and loved.

'Ooh, here we go,' I said, laying it down on the desk. As I tried to read though, both ends of the scroll curled inwards and I sighed with frustration. 'Why didn't I think to bring a set of snake weights?'

'That's precisely what I was thinking,' Aiden said. 'How could I have forgotten my trusty snake weights? I do, of course, have a dozen of them up in my room.'

'Really?' I asked, delighted. 'Could we—' But then I looked up and saw his expression. 'Sorry, apparently I don't have an ear for sarcasm.'

'You will after a few days of working with me. Just put your laptop on one end,' Aiden advised, gesturing to the re-furled scroll.

'I can't do that,' I replied, indignant. 'That's an unforgivable offence in any archive.'

'Any other archive,' Aiden corrected. 'This isn't exactly your run-of-the-mill establishment, is it? But if it offends you so much, here, I'll do it. Now *I'll* go to that special circle of hell reserved solely for the sinning archivist.'

I couldn't help but smile.

It was, like the other scrolls we'd read, a letter to a version of Father Christmas.

Dear Santa-san,

I guess it must be very cold in the North Pole. How are you? I hope you and the reindeer are well. This time of year must be very busy for you. I am sorry this letter is late. I already sent you one for me, but my baby sister was just born. Her name is Yua. She cannot write yet, so I am writing one for her. I hope that is all right. She cannot even talk yet so she cannot say what she wants, but she would like an Anpanman toy. It would make her smile and stop crying. Thank you very much. Please take care of yourself on your journey.

Sincerely, Hinata

'That's very sweet,' I said, smiling as I re-rolled the scroll and placed it at the far end of the desk.

'And polite,' Aiden added. 'My letters to Father Christmas just consisted of pages ripped out of the Argos catalogue with big arrows pointing to the toys I wanted.'

'Subtle,' I laughed, reaching for another scroll.

There were three more in English (one addressed to Father Christmas and two to Santa) and four in languages I wasn't fluent in. I translated one from German asking for a camera and a new pair of shoes. Another from Poland requesting a puppy, informing *Mikolaj* that they had moved house in the last year, and providing their new address. And one from France, which was more of a series of curious questions to *Père Noël* about where he lived and how his reindeer flew, with a plea for the latest book in a series I'd never heard of tagged on at the end.

At this point, Aiden declared it was lunch time.

'I make a pretty sexy secretary, right?' he asked, snapping his laptop closed and running his fingers through his sandy hair. 'But I should warn you: I don't do coffee runs.'

'I want a coffee a lot less than I need the bathroom,' I admitted. I looked around. 'Where do you think Uncle Joe goes?'

Aiden grinned. 'There's a bucket in one corner I haven't been brave enough to look in.'

'I'm not *that* desperate.'

Aiden was tearing open one of the brown bags Clementine had given us and pulling out a sandwich. 'Hummus and veg? I half expected cake with a side of cake topped with cake.'

'I wouldn't have minded that,' I laughed, unwrapping my own sandwich and then pausing. 'We really shouldn't be eating in here.' Food in the archives was another unforgiveable offence.

Aiden snorted dismissively. 'We can't exactly nip to the canteen. Besides, Uncle Joe had food down here.'

Realising that some of my rules were going to have to be bent a little while working here, I gingerly opened the rest of my sandwich, careful not to spill crumbs. 'Okay, but I'm drawing the line at peeing in the bucket.'

As we sat and ate, it was the first time I truly appreciated how quiet the place was. Archives were usually hushed places, but there was always the scratching of pencils, the tapping of keyboards, the squeaking of trolley wheels, whispered conversations. Here there was nothing but the sound of Aiden munching and the muted hum of his laptop and the gas heater.

'I think I know what this place is,' I finally said, finishing off the last of my sandwich.

Aiden fished in the paper bag and pulled out an apple. 'The North Pole?'

'Sort of,' I smiled. 'I've heard of charitable organisations who set up a kind of postal service, so that letters addressed to Father Christmas or to the North Pole get sent there. Then they answer the letters, so the kids think it's come from Santa. It's sweet really.'

Aiden considered this for a moment as he tossed the apple from hand to hand. 'Sounds like a lot of work for something the parents could do instead.'

'Maybe,' I say, not agreeing in the slightest, 'but I think there are quite a few places that do it. The Royal Mail do it in the UK, the NSPCC as well, and I know there's somewhere in Finland and in Germany. They receive letters from all over the world. I read an article about it once. Volunteers dressed as elves write responses.'

Aiden raised an eyebrow. 'No amount of money in the world is going to get me wearing an elf costume. You'd make a cute elf though.'

I rolled my eyes, not naive enough to take the comment seriously. I hadn't known Aiden long, but had quickly identified him as a serial flirter. It was entirely unprofessional – and if we'd been in a normal office environment, he'd probably have received a stern warning – but he was so impishly brazen about it that I was more amused than offended.

While he finished his lunch, I studied the shelves of scrolls and considered my theory, which didn't explain why all the letters were written on the same paper in the same silver ink . . .

'Okay,' Aiden said suddenly as he tossed his apple core into the paper bag. 'It's time to explore.'

I was torn between carrying on with my work – the work I was being paid for – and seeing the rest of the archives. But, I reasoned, I was entitled to an hour's lunch break.

'A quick look,' I relented. 'And then we crack on with the LRNCs.'

'Yes, yes.' Aiden was already heading back up the passageway.

I grabbed my notepad and pencil and followed, catching up with him as he reached the central cavern.

'Further down the rabbit hole?' he asked, indicating the descending path. 'I want to see how far it goes.'

'I don't mean to alarm you, but I think we're being watched,' I whispered, and gestured across the cavern to where the ravens perched on a shelf in the rock wall. They were too far away to make out in detail, but it felt, disconcertingly, as if they were studying us. 'What did you say about this place not having CCTV?'

As previously, the path snaked around the rock walls of the cavern, flanked by scroll-filled shelves on one side and a sheer drop on the other. The fence separating us from a fatal fall was rustier than ever, with whole sections missing, and even Aiden trod those parts carefully. We came to our first fork – sharp right down or straight ahead – and I began to think we should have been leaving breadcrumbs (had that not been in direct violation of the rules of an archive).

'I'll remember the way,' Aiden assured me, ploughing straight ahead.

We passed more and more numbers carved above the shelves: *1982, 1979, 1978, 1980, 1981, 1976* ... I made note of them as we went. Although the numbers were jumbled, they were getting gradually lower.

After we'd descended a few levels, I noticed the ravens again. They sat on the fence opposite us, their beady eyes focused on our movements.

Aiden seemed eager to cover as much ground as possible, but I wanted to inspect some of the scrolls. Were they also letters to Father Christmas? I stopped at a set of shelves marked *1974* and delicately pulled one out, glancing at the ravens as I unrolled it, wondering – ridiculously – if they would object, but they simply sat there, watching. I returned my gaze to the scroll. It was the same paper, though less crisp – a sign of age, I supposed – and the same silvery ink. The writing, slightly neater, was again in a child's hand. It was from a boy living in Vancouver, asking for 'Hot Wheels, Monopoly, and a puppy that stays small. Daddy won't let me have one but ive been asking sinse I was 3.'

Aiden had stopped too and was reading over my shoulder. I replaced the scroll and we continued down.

'How many do you think there are?' I wondered aloud.

'Millions. Probably billions.' Aiden shook his head. 'It would take decades to digitise it all.'

1971, 1970, 1962, 1965 . . . Another fork and we went straight on again. *1959, 1960, 1958, 1951* . . . Another fork. By now, the levels beneath us were obscured; the lights seemed to die away.

I stopped under *1949* and pulled a scroll out at random. It was in a Serbian or Bosnian dialect I couldn't translate, so I returned it and continued down.

Under *1944*, one girl in America asked for nylon stockings, a new pair of saddle shoes and a doll pram for her little sister. She asked Santa how old he was and how many elves worked for him. The one sitting next to it was in German, and it bore only two lines.

'Please can I have a *Glückskind* doll with real hair. And can you please stop the bombs.'

The words brought tears to my eyes.

'You could trace history through these scrolls,' I breathed as we passed through the 1930s interspersed with some 1920s. If the letters were genuine, they were testimonies to the wishes of generations of children. What a precious thing to be hidden away on a non-existent island in the North Sea.

Aiden was already moving on, but he didn't get far. Up ahead the platform was shrouded in darkness, and I could now see why. The electric lighting ended.

There was a sudden caw and flash of black wings as the ravens flew by, a hair's breadth from our faces. We both jumped back with yelps, pressing ourselves against the stone shelves. A second later, the birds had disappeared into the shadows ahead.

'I've got a torch on my phone,' Aiden said, but even he sounded hesitant.

'I think we've used up our lunch hour,' I replied, peering uneasily after the ravens. I'd seen enough horror films to know you don't go wandering blindly around pitch-black subterranean passageways. 'Let's go back up.' Aiden didn't argue.

We returned to the 'office', half expecting Uncle Joe to be there. He wasn't, but the ravens were. One sat on the gramophone and the other perched on a shelf, both watching us with their unnerving gazes.

'Sneaky little devils, aren't they?' Aiden observed, switching his laptop back on.

Eyeing the pair warily, I reached for a scroll and began the afternoon's work.

Aiden's laptop died soon after starting, so we moved onto mine. 'Cute picture,' he commented as he noticed my wallpaper: me and Izzy on last year's Easter egg hunt. Izzy proudly holding up her basket full of eggs while I leant over her, pretending to steal one.

'Thanks. That's my niece.'

'She looks just like you.'

I smiled at that. Lots of people said the same thing.

We got through twenty more translations before my laptop ran out of charge. I suggested continuing with paper and pencil, like Uncle Joe, but Aiden vetoed the idea.

'It's the end of the day anyway.'

Looking at my watch I realised, with surprise, that it was nearly six. Where had the time gone? We'd worked our way through most of the scrolls on the trolley, but there was a large pile of letters in languages I wasn't familiar with. They would take a lot more time to get through. But, as we had no idea what else we were meant to be doing, I supposed that was a good thing.

I wrote 'translated' on a piece of paper and propped it up beside the pile of scrolls we'd finished with, in case Uncle Joe returned. The ravens, who hadn't moved all afternoon, stayed where they were as we packed up our laptops. But as we headed towards the exit, they took to the air and flew into the passage Uncle Joe had disappeared down hours before. The shift was over, they seemed to be saying. I sensed we'd be seeing them again tomorrow.

Chapter Six

'You survived your first day then,' Clementine observed brightly. My nose told me something with cheese and garlic was cooking in the oven; I hoped it was meant for us.

Aiden and I had headed straight for our area of the house after emerging from the archives, to empty bladders, wash up and put our laptops on charge. Aiden clearly wasn't down yet.

'I enjoyed it,' I said, and it was the truth. Provided with a task I could competently achieve, I was happy. I was also looking forward to tackling the languages I didn't know.

'I'm glad to hear it.' Clementine glanced at the clock on the wall. 'Dinner's nearly ready. Hope you're hungry?'

'You never have to ask me that,' I assured her. 'Can I help?'

'You could set the table, thanks.' She gestured to a cupboard.

'How many of us are eating?'

'We'll set the table for four, but I doubt we'll see Uncle Joe.'

I began pulling out plates, all mismatched, brightly coloured and slightly chipped.

'We've not seen him at all this afternoon. Do you think he's okay?'

Clementine waved her polka-dotted, oven-gloved hand dismissively. 'He'll be fine. Sometimes he disappears for days on end, but he always shows up again.'

'But ... where does he go?' I asked, perplexed. I hadn't seen much of the island, but couldn't imagine there were many places to disappear to.

'Oh, you know, here and there.' Clementine said evasively. 'So, what did you get up to today?'

'Translating some of the LRNCs – if that's the right acronym?'

'Beats me.' She pulled out a colossal lasagne, cheese bubbling on top. 'We used to just call them the tardies, but Cole insisted we "standardise the jargon".' She rolled her eyes. 'He throws a tantrum if we don't use the "correct terminology". I *think* it stands for "Late, Rollover for Next Christmas" or something like that. It's a bit corporate, I know.'

'Oh. Okay.'

Either way, it didn't clarify much.

'It's great you're here to help Uncle Joe with the translation work,' she went on. 'He enjoys it, but it takes up so much of his time. Did you come across any for the shortlist?'

'The shortlist?'

Clementine grimaced. 'Sorry, I'm getting ahead of myself. Don't worry, this will all be part of your "formal induction". In the meantime, carry on with the translations.'

At that moment Aiden strolled in. I noted, amused, that he was still carrying his phone, almost like a child's comfort blanket. He shoved the useless device into his pocket morosely, but seemed to perk up when he saw the lasagne.

'I was wondering about the ravens,' I began as Clementine dished up.

'Have they been causing mischief again?'

I didn't want to admit how unnerving I found their gazes, and Aiden, sitting across from me, seemed more interested in the lasagne than the conversation, so I shrugged. 'Not at all. They're just . . . unusual. Do they have names?'

Clementine placed a bowl of salad in the middle of the table. 'They've had lots over the years. When my father and Uncle Joe were young, they were Bill and Ben. My grandparents called them Charlie and Simon.'

Aiden and I shared a glance across the table. I guessed he was thinking the same thing I was. While I didn't know anything about the lifespan of ravens, I was fairly certain they shouldn't outlast three human generations.

'When Cole and I were kids, we came up with new ones. Cole's is Cicero,' Clementine rolled her eyes. 'He always was a geek.'

'And yours?'

'Fluffy.' She said this so earnestly that I choked back my laugh.

'Exactly the name I would have chosen,' Aiden agreed, poker-faced, reaching for the salad bowl. 'We could take them some food tomorrow. Although I've no idea what ravens eat.'

'Making friends by appealing to their stomachs?' Clementine grinned. 'I approve. I'll pack something for them.'

'That would be great, cheers. And you can consider *me* a friend for life after this meal.'

I took my first mouthful of the lasagne and nodded. 'This is so tasty. Thank you.'

'Like I said, I enjoy having people to cook for.' Clementine speared a lettuce leaf with her fork and pointed to Aiden and me with it. 'And on that subject, I was hoping you could both help me with a project I'm working on.'

'Oh?' I asked, intrigued.

'All shall be revealed with dessert,' Clementine assured me mysteriously.

When our plates were empty, Clementine proffered a cake tin. 'Take out one of each but don't eat them yet,' she instructed, passing it to me. Inside were ten tiny chocolate cakes, all beautifully crafted and delicately decorated. As per Clementine's instructions, I plucked out one of every type so I had five lined up in front of me. Aiden took the tin and grimaced apologetically.

'I'm not a fan of chocolate,' he admitted.

Clementine did a double take and my jaw dropped. 'How can you not be a fan of chocolate?' we asked simultaneously, aghast.

'That's like saying you're not a fan of oxygen,' Clementine added. She seemed personally affronted, but then took a loud, dramatic breath. 'But that's okay. We're all entitled to our own opinions. Even if they're wrong,' she added in a mutter. 'But I'm afraid, unless you're allergic, you're going to have to sample them. It's a condition of your room and board here.'

'I don't remember that being in the contract,' Aiden protested, amused.

'It was, just in really small writing. Anyway, I want you to taste each of them, taking a sip of water between each bite – this is a serious cake tasting. Then I want you to rank them in order of preference.'

More than happy to oblige, I tasted each, sipping water in between, and wondered how I could possibly rank them. They were all delicious. When I said as much to Clementine, she simply growled at me to 'do it or pack your bags'.

One, a little darker than the rest, was slightly bitter for my taste, while another had a sweet, alcoholic edge. Feeling sorry for them but thoroughly intimidated by Clementine's glower, I placed them at the bottom of my ranking. A nutty one went in the middle while second place went to one with salted caramel. It was the lightly spicy one, strongly cinnamoned with a hint of something hotter, that I awarded the top spot.

When I looked at Aiden's rankings, I laughed aloud. His were the opposite to mine.

'Interesting,' Clementine observed, and I realised that her clipboard had made a re-appearance. She unclipped two pieces of paper and placed them in front of us, along with pens. 'Now if you could just answer a few questions.'

I'd assumed the questions would be about the cakes, but it was more like a personality quiz. What is your favourite colour? If you could be any animal, what would it be? On a rating scale of one to ten, how assertive are you? The book is always better than the film: agree or disagree?

I glanced up at Aiden, expecting him to be as baffled as I was, but he seemed to be enjoying the quiz far more than the cakes. Then I looked over at Clementine, who gave me an encouraging nod and began scribbling behind her clipboard. I answered the questions as honestly as I could – blue, pygmy owl, two, agree – and flipped the piece of paper over before sliding it across the table, not wanting Aiden to see what I'd written.

'Thank you both very much,' Clementine beamed, snatching up our answers. 'Same again tomorrow.'

Perhaps because we'd spent all day asking questions, or perhaps because we'd accepted it was going to take us some time to begin to comprehend this bizarre place, neither of us pressed Clementine to explain.

We cleared the table. Aiden washed the dishes while I dried and Clementine stayed at the table, lost behind her clipboard. She was still writing feverishly when we bade her goodnight and departed for our rooms. I was hoping to shower before Aiden used up all of the hot water but he managed to get to the bathroom before me again.

Day two on the island followed a similar pattern to day one: a solo frosty morning walk down towards the pier, breakfast with Clementine, the descent to the archives. Uncle Joe was still absent, but the ravens – Cicero and Fluffy – were perched in what I was beginning to think of as their office. They didn't acknowledge

our arrival, but it certainly felt as if they had been waiting for us. Aiden, armed with a handful of nuts gifted by
Clementine, tried befriending them. Braver than I would
have been – ravens were larger than I'd thought and their
beaks a lot sharper – he held out his palm towards them.
They ignored him until he placed the nuts on the gramophone, and then they pecked at them with indifference.

I opened my laptop and resumed work on the LRNCs.
I set aside the remaining scrolls in English, one of which
had come from Nigeria, and translated two in Italian,
one in Japanese and one in Finnish, while Aiden transcribed. Then we moved onto languages I didn't know,
so while Aiden began typing up more English letters on
his laptop, I loaded up my translation software, eager
to begin. My first was in Swedish. I learned that '*öns-
kelista*' meant 'wish list', and that a girl called Ebba,
who lived in Edsbyn, wanted a hamster and a Barbie
for Christmas.

At lunch we both made our way up to the house,
partly for the exercise, partly to re-charge our laptops,
and partly because we needed the toilet (to my relief,
Aiden had been joking about the bucket). We ate our
sandwiches as we walked, and on the way back stopped
at various sections to read random scrolls. Neither of us
suggested returning to the cavern where the lights ended,
although I knew we'd have to eventually – preferably
with two really powerful torches. And maybe a couple
of Clementine's kitchen knives.

The afternoon passed by in a blur of wish lists. Most
were clearly children's but there were a couple written by

adults. One Latvian woman asked *Ziemassvētku vecītis* to help her conceive. *No presents under the tree this year*, I translated. *But please, a baby in my belly*. Reading that, my throat tightened.

I was so absorbed in my translations I didn't notice Aiden readying himself to leave until he waved his hand in front of my face. It was already six o'clock, time to head up. As before, the ravens took their leave before we did, cawing their goodbyes and disappearing down the passageway.

After a dinner of stir-fry, Clementine presented us with a selection of miniature cupcakes. We chose our rankings – again, Aiden's was opposite to mine – and answered random questions about our personalities and favourite things. Then we cleared up and said our goodnights. Again, Aiden got to the bathroom before I did. I'd just have to accept morning showers from now on, I decided, sinking once more beneath my mountain of blankets.

Day three followed the same pattern. That evening we sampled bite-size cheesecakes and answered questions about the types of music we liked.

On day four we came down to the office to find that our large pile of translated scrolls had been removed and the trolley re-stocked. The food we'd left out for Uncle Joe the day before had disappeared as well.

'I guess the old man's still alive then,' Aiden said. 'But how many more of these bloody LRNCs are there?'

I didn't admit that I was glad to see more scrolls. They may not have granted us insights into the past as the older scrolls did, but they still spoke of people's lives. And I was enjoying the excuse to delve into so many languages. When day five saw even more scrolls added to the trolley, Aiden eyed them in silent resignation, while I rubbed my hands together in glee.

That evening, Clementine asked us what we'd be doing with our weekends.

'Is it Friday?' I'd lost all track of days. To be honest, I'd lost track of months. Was it still January?

'In the absence of bars, restaurants, a cinema and a gym, I think I'll spend my weekend sleeping,' Aiden declared. Clementine placed a plate of miniature cookies in front of us and he added, 'Maybe I'll go for a run as well.'

'Good idea,' Clementine enthused. 'There are lots of tracks around the island. How about you, Ellie?'

'I might explore the island a little more.' I didn't want to admit that so far I'd only walked down to the pier and back.

'I might join you, if you don't mind? Even I need a break from baking every now and then. Mind you, it'll have to be in the afternoon. Weekend mornings don't exist for me.'

'Of course,' I laughed. I'd be glad of the company. Without it, I probably would have ended up heading back down to the archives and spending my weekend lost in translations.

'Great. Now earn your keep and eat the cookies.'

That evening, I finally asked Aiden if I could shower first. He seemed happy to oblige but five minutes after he went in after me, I heard him swearing over the sound of running water. I fell asleep smiling.

After a deep sleep, I woke early, my body refusing to lie in. I'd been missing Izzy and Toby all week but felt it most acutely that morning. Even before I'd moved in with them, we'd spent Saturday mornings together. We'd go to our favourite café for breakfast and stay there well into the afternoon working on crosswords together or teaching Izzy chess. I wondered morosely if they were following the same tradition without me or if they were doing something new, and didn't know which would hurt more.

Because it was Saturday, the weather was, of course, terrible. Dense dark clouds sputtered out rain in short sharp bursts and the wind whipped it sideways. But Clementine didn't seem deterred.

'We're on a tiny island in the North Sea,' she reminded me as she pulled on her wellies. 'If you don't go outside in bad weather, then you don't go outside.'

'We follow the same philosophy in Manchester,' I assured her. 'All Mancunians have webbed feet.'

Clementine took the lead as we stepped out into the cold. The rain was holding off for now, but we put our hoods up to combat the wind.

'Where are we heading?' I asked as we circled round the back of the house.

'I'll show you the cliffs. The puffins won't be there this time of year but they're still pretty spectacular.'

As we walked, Clementine talked and I listened. She pointed out features I never would have noticed, each attached to a childhood memory. The gnarled tree she'd seen struck by lightning. The moss-covered boulder she and Cole had commandeered as their pirate ship. The slope perfect for sledging down. The rectangle of heather brittle and brown after years of pitching the tent in the same spot, and the section of heather greener than the rest, regrown after an ill-fated campfire. I was beginning to get a sense of what Clementine's childhood had been like, and it was very different to mine.

I was also beginning to wonder how somebody so sociable and full of conversation could live in such isolation.

'Doesn't it get lonely?' I asked.

'Nah, I've got Uncle Joe. And—' She stopped abruptly, and again there was the sense she was keeping something back. 'And my parents are often here – they'll be back from their holiday soon. And Cole and Alex come to visit a lot.'

'Alex?'

'My nephew. He used to be my favourite person in the world – until he became a teenager.'

I couldn't imagine Mr Jones with a teenage son. Partly because he seemed too young, but mainly because I'd not detected any paternal (or any other type of) softness in him. I wondered if he made Alex sign contracts about tidying his room and doing homework.

'Plus I'm not always on the island,' Clementine went on. 'I travel to Edinburgh a lot to meet with my editor. And in the summer I do the food festival circuit and generally eat myself into a sugar coma. All in the name of research, of course.'

We'd crossed an expanse of heather and were now gradually climbing. Ahead, I could see where the ground seemed to vanish into the steely sky and assumed we were nearing the cliffs. Sure enough, we'd reached the edge of the island and a precipitous drop lay between us and the crashing ocean below.

'When me, Cole, and – when we were kids, our parents wouldn't let us come to the cliffs on our own.' Clementine gave a roguish smile. 'So, of course, we came nearly every day.'

This didn't surprise me, and again highlighted how different our childhoods had been. Even growing up I hadn't a single rebellious bone in my body. I probably would have been the one telling my mum not to play on the cliffs.

'You see that ledge?' Clementine was pointing a few metres down, where a narrow shelf jutted out of the rock face. 'I climbed down there when I was nine and got stuck.'

'What happened?' I gasped, my stomach churning at the prospect. There was a very long – and very fatal – drop between that ledge and the rocky sea below.

'Oh, it was fine. I was only stuck there for two hours before Uncle Joe came to my rescue. He got me up with only a few scratches and bruises. He didn't even tell my parents. But he did tell me that my dad had got stuck on the exact same ledge when *he* was nine.' She cocked her head to one side. 'Thinking about it, maybe that's why he'd warned me away.'

To my relief, Clementine moved back from the edge and steered us inland. The cliffs were beautiful, yes, but I had no desire to take a closer look. I valued being alive.

'So your father and uncle grew up here too?'

'Oh yes. My family's lived on this island for as far back as . . .' She shrugged. 'Well, for as far back as I can trace my family tree.'

'And the archives – they've always been run by your family?'

'Yep. We're hereditary archivists, whether we want to be or not.'

'And they've always been . . .' I waved a vague hand, not knowing how to describe them.

Clementine seemed to know what I meant. She gave a sage smile. 'There's magic there but we don't understand it. We don't even try.'

'Magic?' I tried to keep the cynicism from my voice, but Clementine stopped walking and turned to face me.

'You still don't believe this place is real, do you?' She didn't sound annoyed or offended. If anything, she seemed amused.

'Well, I . . .' I gave a helpless shrug. What could I say? And what was *she* saying? *There's magic there* – what did that mean?

With a laugh, Clementine shook her head. 'When we get back home, I'll show you something.'

An hour later we were standing in the kitchen, Clementine holding a folder bearing my name.

'Read this,' she said, pulling out a sheet of paper. As far as I could tell, it was the same type of paper as the scrolls, and I caught a glimpse of silver writing. 'I haven't had chance to re-shelve it yet.'

'What is it?'

'The reference that got you this job.'
Perplexed, I took it and began to read.

Dear Santa,

I need you to get antie Ellie a pressent. She needs a new home and a new job after banana-head took them from her. She is a really good antie and always seys nice things to me and I don't want to see her cry. She is at my house now so you can send them here.

Thank you.

Love from Izzy Lancaster-Roberts

PS. If there is room left in the slay for anuva pressent then I want a new art set please.

Chapter Seven

Uncle Joe had re-emerged. We found him sitting at the desk on Monday morning, hunched over a translation. Aiden and I both stopped in our tracks at the sight. Other than Cicero and Fluffy, we'd grown used to having the office to ourselves. I suddenly felt nervous. What if he wasn't happy with the work we'd done?

I needn't have worried. When Uncle Joe finally noticed us, standing awkwardly in the entryway, he glanced up, nodded in greeting, and then pointed to the pile of scrolls I'd marked as 'translated'.

'Thank you,' he said in the gruff, quiet voice of someone who hadn't spoken in a while.

It wasn't praise exactly but I was pleased. 'The translations are saved on our laptops,' I explained, tapping the computer under my arm. 'Would you like to read them?'

Uncle Joe hesitated. 'Soon,' he said. 'When we start the shortlisting.'

There were still more scrolls on the trolley and the desk was large enough for the three of us to work at. Aiden pulled over a chair while I sifted through the scrolls for some English ones to tide him over. Then we began our day's work, Aiden keeping up his usual chatter as he typed.

I would have preferred to work in silence, partly for Uncle Joe's sake and partly for mine. I was still mulling over the letter Clementine had showed me. I'd been thinking about it all weekend. I hadn't told Aiden and didn't know why. Perhaps I felt it was my mystery to solve. How had my niece's letter ended up on this island in the middle of the North Sea? Had Toby posted it here?

I'd planned to write Toby a letter, to send c/o Willum, letting him know I was alive and enjoying my new job (keeping the details vague as per Mr Jones's confidentiality contract). I now made a mental note to ask where Toby had sent Izzy's letter to Father Christmas. I was confident I already knew the answer though. Toby and Mike usually posted Izzy's letters to Royal Mail's 'Letters to Santa' service; Royal Mail would then send a response from 'Santa'.

I'd begun to wonder if this was where Royal Mail kept all their letters, but why here? And then there was the matter of the silver ink. I'd been in the room when Izzy had written her letter to Father Christmas, and I was fairly sure she'd used brightly coloured felt-tips. Were the letters scanned somewhere and printed out in silver? And if so, why?

If Clementine had expected the letter to ease my mind, she'd been wrong. I had more questions than ever. But once I began translating a letter to 'Santa Klaus' in Filipino, those questions became quieter, fading to the background. Aiden's voice faded too as I let myself sink into the work.

I resurfaced at lunchtime (no matter how engrossed in work, I never forget to eat). Clementine, as usual, had sent us with an extra packed lunch for Uncle Joe. He took the brown paper bag with a grateful nod and disappeared with it back down into his passageway. It was, I sensed, Aiden's chatter that had driven him away.

'I need to get some exercise in, especially with all the cake Clem's been force-feeding us. What are we supposed to do? Go running in the mud? Don't get me wrong, I like the outdoors as much as the next person, but would it kill them to get a treadmill in here?'

As grateful as I was for Aiden's company, I wished I could have disappeared down that passageway too.

It was only after we'd returned to work that Uncle Joe came back. He padded quietly up to the desk, briefly touched the various items he had set up around him, and leant over his translation. Although he never looked up, I could see his lips tighten every time Aiden sat back from his laptop, gave a dramatic sigh, and launched into yet another description of how life on the island would be easier if . . .

'Are you heading back up with us?' I asked Uncle Joe as we packed up at the end of the day.

He shook his head. 'Thank Clementine for my lunch.'

'We will,' I assured him. 'See you tomorrow?'

He gave a small smile and gestured to the large pile of scrolls marked 'translated'. 'Maybe. Thank you for your work.'

I beamed all the way back up to the house.

The next day I 'forgot' to bring my laptop down to the archives.

'I'm really sorry,' I lied to Aiden. 'Do you mind fetching it from my room, while I dig out some English letters for you?'

'Of course not. It's good exercise.' His affability made me feel a little guilty, but it was worth it for the grateful smile Uncle Joe threw me as Aiden jogged out of the office.

We enjoyed an hour of companionable silence as we worked our way through more translations. I guessed that Aiden had taken a few detours on his way to my room, but I really didn't mind.

That evening, as Clementine distributed miniature brownies, I finally asked about the cake and question-naire exercises.

'Oh, haven't I told you?' She seemed surprised.

I shook my head and sighed in delight at the first bite of gooey chocolatey goodness.

'Well, I'm working on my next book. It's going to be called *The Psychology of Cake* and it's based on the fact that everyone has their one true cake.'

'One true cake?' Aiden asked, amused. 'Like their one true love?'

'Everyone, even if they claim to not like cake . . .' She gave Aiden a meaningful glance '. . . has one cake they can't resist, even if they've not found it yet. And I've been testing the theory that you can determine a person's one true cake by knowing enough about them: their personality, their likes and dislikes, their tastes in other aspects of life.'

'You're trying to create algorithms?' Aiden asked, and he sounded genuinely curious.

'Precisely.'

'Confectionery algorithms,' I supplied, delighted by the idea.

'Confectionery algorithms?' Clementine laughed. 'I like it. That can be the book's subtitle. Don't worry, I'll credit you both. So far, I've been quite successful at it. I figured out that Alex's mum Andy can't resist banoffee pie and that Alex's one true cake is Black Forest. But, other than Willum, not too many other people come to the island – except for Cole, Uncle Joe and my parents. And I already know their true cakes. So,' she declared, passing out her questionnaires, 'you guys have the honour of being my test subjects.'

'Have you worked out our true cakes yet?' I asked, intrigued.

'Not yet, but I'm narrowing it down.'

'I don't know cake,' Aiden declared, leaning forward with more enthusiasm than I'd seen in him since arriving on the island. 'But I *do* know algorithms. This is something I can help with.' He cracked his fingers in a gesture of confidence. 'What system are you using?'

'System?'

'Computer system.'

'Computer system?'

The two looked equally nonplussed. 'You're trying to calculate this . . . by hand?'

'Well, I type up my findings,' Clementine replied, indignant.

With a laugh, Aiden put his head in his hands and muttered something about the Stone Age. Clementine tossed a tea towel at him. 'Mock me at your peril, mister. I'm the one signing your payslips.'

'I'm not mocking you. Well, I am. But I'd love to help you.'

Clementine cocked a suspicious eyebrow. 'Help me how?'

'Give me one week with your findings and I'll see what I can do.' He turned to me. 'I'm not exactly a huge help in the archives at the moment. Without equipment, I can't digitise anything. Put me to good use on your algorithms, and once we get the digitising tech, I'll go back down to the archives. What do you say?'

Clementine looked to me and I gave a shrug. 'I don't mind. Of course, he is a help with the transcribing work – you *are*,' I insisted to him, 'but if he can be more useful to you . . .' I let my words trail off, trying not to sound hopeful.

'Well, I have no idea how useful you'll be because I have no idea what you're offering to do,' Clementine admitted, 'but I'm happy to give it a go. However,' she held up a finger and nodded towards Aiden's unfinished brownies, 'this doesn't get you off tasting duties.'

And that's how Uncle Joe and I got our peace and quiet. For the next three days, we worked alongside each other in near total silence. I was a little worried my typing would bother him, but he was there every morning when I arrived and stayed all day, not even retreating down his passageway when we broke for lunch.

For the first two days we ate without speaking. It didn't feel awkward or uncomfortable – if anything, it was refreshing – but on the third day, I made a gentle attempt at conversation. I was curious about this reticent old man who lived in a labyrinth of letters, alone and seemingly perfectly content.

'How long have you been working here?' I kept my voice quiet, but it still made him jump.

He gazed down at his sandwich and I wondered if he would refuse to answer. But he seemed to be pondering my question. Finally, with a small smile, he said, 'Lost count.'

I smiled back, relieved that he didn't seem annoyed by my query. 'Have you ever worked anywhere else?'

He pulled a face as if to say he couldn't imagine anything worse.

'I don't blame you,' I assured him. 'These archives are . . . wonderful.'

He looked back down at his sandwich and nodded. 'That they are.'

I felt we were on the same page when it came to the archives. Did he see them the same way I did? Each scroll a treasured insight into a person's life and desires, all the more precious for their brevity.

On our fourth day without Aiden, I asked him about Cicero and Fluffy, who still stood vigil on the gramophone. 'I hear you and your brother call them Bill and Ben. Can you tell which one's which?'

Uncle Joe pointed to the one on the left. 'Bill. Longer beak.'

'They made me nervous at first,' I admitted. 'But now, I don't know. I find them reassuring.' Their watchful presence didn't have quite the same effect as a cat curled on your lap, but there was comfort in it.

'Been here forever,' Uncle Joe said, studying them. There was clear affection in his gaze and something else. Respect, perhaps.

'Do they ever go outside?'

'Oh yes.' And he gestured towards the passageway I still hadn't been permitted down. 'There are ways out.' Then, with his slow, deliberate movements, he swept the crumbs from his desk into his lunch bag and returned to work.

Day five felt like a real breakthrough. Uncle Joe wished me a good morning as I entered the office and, halfway through the morning's work, completely unbidden, began a conversation.

'We'll finish the last of the LRNCs today.'

Startled, I looked up from translating a Polish letter from a thirteen-year-old boy, who claimed to not believe in *Święty Mikołaj* but was hedging his bets, just in case. So often, I forgot Uncle Joe was even there. We both looked towards the trolley. There were probably ten or so scrolls left on it.

'Oh.' I felt a flare of panic. I'd been enjoying this work; I was good at it. What if this was where my usefulness expired?

'What do we do once the LRNCs are finished?' I asked, trying to sound casual.

'The shortlisting. Then more arrive and we translate and shortlist again. Won't be long now. They start to come in earlier and earlier every year.' He frowned in concentration. 'Where are we? June?'

'Erm . . . January?' I formed it as a question because I honestly didn't know myself. The days had all bled into one, as they always did when I was enjoying my work.

He shook his head. 'Can't be. Never finished the LRNCs this early.' Then he looked at me contemplatively. 'Guess my niece and nephew were right.'

'About what?'

'Hiring you.'

My cheeks were burning as I ducked my head in embarrassment. 'Thanks. I hope so.'

That evening, for the first time since I'd arrived on the island, Uncle Joe came with me to the house. Our walk up through the archives was slow and quiet, with several breaks along the way, but I didn't mind. The vast catacomb of scrolls still filled me with awe, and I enjoyed being able to take a closer look at the different sections.

'How far down does it go?' I asked, peering cautiously over the railing as we stopped at *1985*.

'All the way,' he replied.

I threw a smile at him over my shoulder. 'That's very cryptic.'

He returned my smile and nodded, setting off again.

Aiden did a double take as we walked into the kitchen, but Clementine greeted her uncle nonchalantly.

'You picked a good night to join us,' she told him, pulling open the oven. 'I've made one of your favourites: meat and potato pie.'

Uncle Joe's eyes brightened as he took a seat at the table, at the place we always set for him. I noticed him glance at an empty spot part-way down the table and hastily look away again. The brightness had been abruptly replaced by something else. Sadness? But it was gone as quickly as it came, and his attention turned to straightening his cutlery.

'Maybe it was the smell that lured you up,' Clementine suggested, dishing him out a generous slice and adding a side of vegetables. 'I want to see all of this eaten, by the way. I'll be thoroughly offended if I see so much as a crumb left on your plate.'

Uncle Joe's lips quirked. 'Yes, ma'am.'

I had thought it would be strange having Uncle Joe with us, but he seemed to fit naturally into our little group. And, I reminded myself, this was his home after all. We were the intruders, but he didn't seem to mind. Like me, he seemed to enjoy listening to the conversation – and, as usual, Clementine and Aiden made sure there was plenty – more than participating.

'No taste-testing tonight,' Clementine declared when the last of the pie was finished. 'I fancied apple crumble and there's no way to improve apple crumble.'

Chapter Eight

My excitement at seeing the *Valkyrie* cutting through the waves was short-lived.

The figure standing on deck was unmistakable, even without the suit and tie. The island I'd so quickly come to view as my home, my sanctuary – was soon to be invaded by a briefcase-wielding lawyer.

I felt a stab of anger at this intrusion, as irrational as it was. This island was far more Mr Jones's home than it was mine, as evinced by Clementine's many childhood stories. And besides, I barely knew the man. I shouldn't judge him too much based on our brief meeting in the coffee shop, no matter how awkward. But panic followed the stab of anger.

All week I'd been braving different routes around the island on my morning strolls. I'd returned to the cliffs one morning; on another, I'd ventured east, finding a small copse of silver birches, slanted by the wind. The following day, I'd stumbled across a tiny pebble beach, which I'd planned to return to at the weekend.

So why, oh why, on that morning had I decided to head to the pier? I could have gone anywhere, but no, there I was, striding *down* the track that Mr Jones would soon be striding *up*. I really did not want to have to walk to the house together in silence – or worse, strained conversation.

Perhaps I could avoid him still. The *Valkyrie* hadn't reached the pier yet and, even though I was close, there was every chance Mr Jones and Willum – busy chatting – hadn't noticed me; I had time to make my escape. I could venture off the track, cross to the left, and loop back round to the house unseen.

After a moment's deliberation, I gave the *Valkyrie* one more furtive glance and stepped off the path. I was pretty sure I'd crested the rise before Willum had time to drop the gangplank, and then I was out of sight.

I was breathing a sigh of relief when I hit the swamp. Both feet were in before I realised how deep the water was and how adhesive the mud. My wellies became submerged almost to the knee and when I tried to take a step forward, there was no shifting them. The mud had me firmly in its grasp.

Grunting, I put more force into the movement and managed to take a step – but realised too late that my right foot had come free of both boot and sock, which remained stuck while my bare foot squelched into the sludge. Panicking, I stumbled forward and lost my left boot. I felt the icy mud between my toes and let out a long string of my choicest swear words. Ten curses in, I heard a polite cough from behind me.

I didn't need to turn round to know who was there. Really, I should have expected it all along.

I glanced over my shoulder to see Mr Jones standing on top of the rise. His bland expression suggested he wasn't particularly surprised to find me in such a state.

'Ms Lancaster,' he said with a nod of greeting.

'Mr Jones,' I replied through gritted teeth. At least I was too cold for my cheeks to burn.

We stood in painful silence for a moment before he observed, 'You appear to have lost your boots.'

If I'd been hoping he would arrive on the island as ill-prepared as I had – and I'm not saying I was hoping that – then I would've been disappointed. He wore seasoned green wellingtons over waterproof trousers, and there wasn't a briefcase in sight.

'I've not lost them,' I said, aiming for haughty but achieving only peevish. 'I know *precisely* where they are.'

The corner of his lip may or may not have twitched. 'Shall I help you retrieve them?'

Logic fought a quick battle with pride, and lost. 'No. Thank you. I'm fine.'

I expected him to argue, to insist on coming to my rescue, and part of me – mainly my numbed feet – hoped he would. But he simply nodded and turned away. 'I'm sure I'll see you up at the house soon.' And then he disappeared back over the rise.

The second he was gone I covered my face with my hands and half-laughed, half-cried into them. 'Of course,' I mumbled to myself. 'It was pretty inevitable really.'

And then I began the long, sludgy process of extricating feet, boots and socks from the swamp, and trudging up to the house, squelching all the way.

By the time I reached the kitchen, Mr Jones had settled himself at the table with a cup of coffee and was talking with Aiden while Clementine sizzled bacon in a frying pan.

'What I really need,' Aiden was saying, 'is the TTI Digiflex 45ei camera with a BetterLight Super 6K-HS, which I can mount on a copystand. That will give us the best quality digitisation. But I'd also need—'

'Write me a list,' Mr Jones cut in, giving me a cursory glance as I entered and began peeling off my boots.

Aiden followed Mr Jones's gaze, took in my feet, and burst out laughing. 'What on earth happened to you?'

'What *have* you been doing?' Clementine gasped, looking over her shoulder.

Mr Jones raised his eyebrows at me, as if he too were curious about my answer.

'Swamp paddling,' I mumbled miserably. Three pairs of eyes blinked at me, bemused. 'Would someone mind getting me a towel? I don't want to traipse mud through the house.'

'Perhaps you should have thought about that before going swamp paddling,' Mr Jones suggested dryly, as a chuckling Aiden went to get me a towel.

'You poor thing,' Clementine sympathised as she shimmied the bacon onto a plate. 'Some breakfast and a pair of warm fluffy slippers will fix you right up. Cole, go get her slippers.'

Cole gave his sister an incredulous look but before he could refuse, I cut in. 'It's fine. I'll need to head upstairs anyway to wash.'

'I'd recommend it,' Cole said, sipping his coffee. I willed him to spill it – not enough to hurt himself, but enough for a thorough humiliation. Of course, he didn't.

Aiden returned, and I hastily towelled off the mud and retreated upstairs. Once clean, I had to fight every urge to climb into bed and hide under the duvet. I didn't know quite what it was about Mr Jones, but he either irritated or intimidated me. At first, I'd thought it was the crisp suit and the interview setting, but there he was in a woollen jumper in Clementine's colourful kitchen, and still he managed to unnerve me.

The second I returned to the kitchen, Mr Jones rose from the table. 'We'll wash up later, Clem. It's time to head downstairs.'

Downstairs? What a painfully prosaic way of describing the vast labyrinth beneath us.

'But Ellie's not had her breakfast yet,' Clementine protested as Aiden gathered the crockery from the table and dumped everything in the sink.

Mr Jones glanced pointedly at the clock.

'I'm fine,' I insisted. 'It *is* time to start work.'

Clementine rolled her eyes. 'You've only just arrived, Cole. Why not chill for a bit?'

'I want to see their progress,' he replied, moving to the door and gesturing for us to follow.

Clementine mouthed 'sorry' to me as we left. I smiled back, hoping I didn't look as nervous as I felt.

At least there was no awkward silence as we made our way down into the archives: Aiden kept up a constant monologue about the various technologies he could employ to get the scrolls digitised and the equipment Jones Associates would need to purchase. Every now and then Mr Jones would interrupt him, repeating the instruction to write up a list. I sensed he was listening as little as I was.

I wondered if Uncle Joe would have sensed the lawyer coming and made himself scarce, but he was in the office waiting for us. I'd expected a formal greeting but to my great surprise, the two men moved easily towards each other and hugged – and was that a smile on Mr Jones's face?

'It's good to see you, Uncle Joe,' Mr Jones said with uncharacteristic warmth, patting the old man on the back. 'Are you keeping well?'

They parted and Uncle Joe gave a little nod. There was a brief flash of sadness again behind the smile. 'Clemmy looks after me. And it's good to see you too. Been too long.'

'I know. Work's been busy.'

'How are Alex and Andy?'

'Both fine. They send their love.'

'Would be nice to see them soon too,' Uncle Joe remarked.

Mr Jones glanced over to Aiden and me as if just remembering we were there and cleared his throat. 'We'll catch up properly later, Uncle Joe. We should get down to business.'

With a chuckle, Uncle Joe reached up and patted his nephew on the cheek. 'As you wish.'

Mr Jones pulled out a smartphone and began tapping in digits. 'Update on the LRNCs?'

'Nearly finished.'

When Mr Jones looked up in surprise, Uncle Joe gestured to the sparsely populated trolley. 'That's the last of them.' Then he nodded towards me with a smile. 'The new girl works fast.'

Mr Jones glanced my way briefly and then tapped in more digits. 'So, ahead of schedule then. Good. You'll be starting the shortlisting soon.'

'Probably tomorrow.'

'Where are the translations?'

Uncle Joe looked to me and I felt suddenly as if I was back in the interview. 'On our laptops,' I croaked.

Mr Jones gave Aiden and me a level gaze. 'The contract clearly stipulated that no material would be stored on personal devices.'

'Well, there was nothing else to use,' I bristled defensively.

'Unless you count paper and pencil,' Aiden chipped in.

'I do count paper and pencil,' Mr Jones replied.

'We needed the translation software on my laptop.' He looked towards the bookcase, but I spoke before he could. 'We'd never get it all done using just dictionaries. I honestly don't know how Uncle Joe managed all this time.'

'He used a computer too,' Uncle Joe said suddenly. 'He said my way took too long.' For a second, I thought he was speaking *about* Mr Jones, but he was looking *at* his nephew. So, who was 'he'? I asked as much, tentatively, but neither of them answered.

Finally, Mr Jones cleared his throat. 'I have some new equipment, including encrypted laptops, down at the pier. I'll transport them to the house today, and tomorrow you can transfer everything. Of course,' he added, 'your personal laptops will need to be wiped.'

'Wiped?' Aiden sputtered.

'Wiped. You may continue using them today though,' he allowed magnanimously. 'Finish the LRNCs and we'll begin the shortlisting tomorrow.' And with that, he turned and left.

That evening brought our first awkward meal on the island. Clementine tried to pull everyone into conversation, but Aiden was sulking about his laptop and I felt uncomfortable speaking with Mr Jones there. I'd probably say the wrong thing and he'd accuse me of violating my contract. The lawyer was equally quiet, responding to his sister's questions with short, perfunctory answers. Eventually Clementine gave up and, like a frustrated parent, announced that there was no dessert and we were all excused.

The next morning, I approached the door to the kitchen with caution. I could hear somebody moving around but no talking, and when I peered in, saw only Clementine.

'The boys have already gone down to the archives,' she said, ushering me into a seat. 'Cole roped Aiden into carrying some equipment down there. Have some breakfast before you join them. I've cooked your favourite to make up for yesterday.'

Once I'd eaten the mammoth stack of pancakes, Clementine fixed me with a firm look. 'I know my brother can be a bit of an arse, but don't let him get to you. Just do what I do: agree with him and then do the opposite.'

'I'll try,' I said with a weak laugh. 'I'll let you know how it goes.'

'No need.' She pulled her apron off and moved towards the door. 'I'm coming with.'

We found the office re-arranged, a desk either side of Uncle Joe's, each bearing a shiny new laptop connected to a printer and what I recognised as a power bank. Aiden was sitting at one of the desks with his personal laptop hooked up to the new computer. Uncle Joe was absent, as were the ravens, but Mr Jones was there, arranging two piles of scrolls on a fold-up table in the centre of the room. As I entered he glanced at his watch, saw that I was on time, and gestured to the vacant desk. He frowned when Clementine walked in behind me.

'I didn't realise you'd be joining us.'

'I'm here for comic relief and moral support,' she replied cheerfully, perching on the edge of my new desk.

'I don't need—' he began.

'Not for you, you eejit. For this poor pair who have to put up with your pernicious pedantry.'

'Nice alliteration,' I whispered.

She grinned.

Sighing, Mr Jones turned to me. 'You've brought your laptop? Good. Transfer the relevant files onto the new machine and then we'll get started on the shortlisting.'

I obeyed, feeling like a schoolchild taking a seat in an exam hall. Aiden threw me a knowing wink as I opened my laptop.

'I've set your password as xRd29Ngy, upper case R and N,' Mr Jones informed me.

'That's a little too easy to guess, don't you think?' Clementine asked. 'Maybe you should choose something less obvious.'

I hid my smile behind the laptop and Aiden managed to convincingly turn his bark of laughter into a cough. Mr Jones said nothing.

'Oh and by the way,' Clementine said chirpily, 'after some discussion, my brother and I have agreed your personal laptops don't need to be wiped. We'll just delete the relevant files.'

Aiden looked to the ceiling and mouthed 'thank you'. Mr Jones glowered at his sister and I wondered how much 'discussion' there had actually been.

Once my translations were stored on the new computer, I was instructed to print them out. Mr Jones gave them a cursory read, made no remark, and then gestured for us to assemble around the two piles of scrolls.

'Once the LRNCs are complete, we move on to the shortlisting,' he explained. 'This year's potentials start arriving soon, and then it's a mixture of intense translating and shortlisting until year's end.' He was making little sense. 'Have Clementine or Joe told you anything about shortlisting?' When Aiden and I shook our heads, he pointed to the smaller pile of scrolls before us. 'These are from 1935s shortlist. The larger pile didn't make the cut. Have a read. Tell me what differentiates them.'

'You missed your calling as a schoolteacher, Cole. Will this be graded?'

Mr Jones ignored Clementine and gazed at Aiden and me expectantly. I glanced at Aiden who motioned for me to go ahead, so I chose a scroll at random and carefully unfurled it. Clementine and Aiden clustered around and we read in silence.

> *Dear Santa Claus,*
> *Is it cold in the North Pole? Don't forget to wrap up warm. How many elfs do you have? I would like to meet an elf. It is Christmas soon so you must be very busy. Please can you bring a present for Mama? Papa has gone away and she cries because he is not home. Please can you bring Papa home?*
> *Your friend, Ellen Walker*

At Mr Jones's bidding, I opened another.

> *Dear Father Christmas,*
> *I haven't been a very good boy this year. I pushed Arthur wen he was anoying me and Mam says I don't help her enuf so don't deserve pressents. Maybe you shud give pressents to the orphans insted. They need Christmas too. I will be better next Christmas and you can bring me pressents then.*
> *David*

Mr Jones passed me a couple from the larger pile and we read.

Dear Father Christmas,

My friends don't believe in you but I do. Mother says you must be real otherwise where do the presents come from? I don't want much this year but would like a foot ball and some books please. If you are real. I will leave some milk out for you.

Sincerely, Freddy

Dear Santa,

Please bring me a Shirley Temple doll and I will look after her really well. I have been a good girl. Thank you very much.

Betty, Age 7

'Well?' Mr Jones asked as I re-rolled.

I said the only thing I could think of. 'The ones in the shortlist ask for things for other people, not just themselves?'

Clementine gave a clap. 'A+++++++++ for Ellie!'

Mr Jones nodded. 'Exactly. The shortlist consists of the selfless requests.'

'Oh yeah,' Aiden said. 'Mama and the orphans. Sweet but a bit weird. I wouldn't have asked for anything like that as a kid.'

'Which is why your letters never made it into the shortlist,' Mr Jones remarked matter-of-factly, and Aiden gave an easy laugh.

'Fair enough.'

'Every year we draw up a shortlist like this,' Mr Jones went on, indicating the smaller pile. 'It's our primary

113

job. The translations are simply a necessary precursor for the real work. So, Mr Haw, while you're waiting on the digitisation equipment, you and Ms Lancaster can work with Uncle Joe on the shortlisting.'

Aiden nodded. 'Righty-o. Sounds easy enough.'

'It is now,' Mr Jones said as he began packing the 1935 scrolls onto the trolley. 'But wait until winter when the letters come flooding in.'

'There just aren't enough hours in the day,' Clementine agreed. 'Which is why we've hired this beautiful and talented lady here.' She beamed at me and I ducked my head, embarrassed.

Mr Jones gave an exasperated sigh. 'Unless you want a sexual harassment charge filed against you, I'd recommend not objectifying our employees.'

Clementine gave an even louder and more exasperated sigh. 'Oh, do shut up.'

'Question,' Aiden said, clearly unfazed by the squabbling. 'What's the point of the shortlist?'

I was glad he'd asked.

Clementine looked about to answer but Mr Jones got there first. 'That's not pertinent.'

'Not pertinent?' Clementine cried. 'It's the whole *purpose* of their jobs.'

'Not at the moment it isn't.' His tone brooked no argument and Clementine relented, muttering under her breath.

'While we're taking these back to their shelves,' Mr Jones went on as he placed the last scroll onto the trolley, 'there's something I want to show the two of you.' He opened a drawer of Uncle Joe's desk and pulled out three wind-up torches.

'You don't need to show them—' Clementine began, but Mr Jones raised his hand pompously.

'They need to know why we've made the decision to digitise.'

'We've made the decision to digitise because this is the twenty-first century,' Clementine replied, as her brother began winding up the torches.

'That was part of it, yes. But only part.'

'You're determined to blame him,' she snapped, suddenly and unfathomably angry. I had no idea what she was talking about and, judging by Aiden's bemused expression, neither did he. But Mr Jones was shaking his head.

'This isn't about . . .' He began, equally angry, but then stopped himself and sighed. 'Mr Haw and Ms Lancaster need to know so that they can . . . guard against it.'

Clementine made a gesture with her right index finger and clenched left hand. I vaguely recognised it as sign language for 'arsehole' and covered my mouth to hide a smile.

Mr Jones surprised me by signing in response, holding his thumb up and shaking his hand back and forth in a gesture I didn't know but could interpret easily enough. With that, he turned and motioned for Aiden and me to follow.

I'd hoped he would take us down the prohibited passageway, but instead he pushed the trolley back towards the main cavern. Feeling like the child of divorced parents being forced to choose, I glanced uneasily at Clementine, who gave me a reassuring smile but stayed put.

We descended the archives, passing through the 1970s, 60s, 50s, 40s and stopping to re-shelve the scrolls from 1935.

'The shortlist goes on the top shelf,' Mr Jones instructed.

'Is there no other identification marker?' I asked, and he shook his head.

'We make a record of the shortlisted requests and addresses but – no.'

'What if they get mixed up?'

'If it concerns you, feel free to implement an alternative system. Just run it by me first.'

I began stacking the scrolls onto their respective shelves. Once the trolley was empty, Mr Jones continued the descent, Aiden and I trailing after him until the lighting stopped. Mr Jones turned his torch on and we followed suit, casting shadows amid pools of pale white light.

We began to slow in the 1920s and it was then that I noticed the smell. Not the mossy, mushroomy smell of a million paper scrolls, but something acrid and charred.

'Is that . . .' Aiden began to ask, sniffing.

'Just wait,' Mr Jones said, and he swung the light of the torch onto a set of shelves ahead of us.

There were no scrolls. Just ash and the odd blackened fragment of what once had probably been paper. The rock was scorched, and we saw that the singed stone stretched across several sets of alcoves, all empty.

'What is this?' Aiden asked quietly.

'1921,' Mr Jones replied stiffly. 'Or what's left of it.'

'The whole year?' I whispered, stepping closer.

'The whole year lost, yes.'

I closed my eyes at the tragedy. 'What happened?'

'A fire,' he said, quite redundantly, and I sensed we'd get no further details. 'I've since installed fire extinguishers. We should have done it years ago; it's easy to say that now but we need to ensure it doesn't happen again.'

Aiden reached out to pick up a seared fragment and I winced as it crumbled between his fingers.

'So, candles and other naked flames are strictly prohibited,' Mr Jones went on. 'If you see Uncle Joe using one, please remind him of the rule and provide him with a torch. And understand that this is why we're digitising the archives. I've identified the hazards, and evaluated the risks, but it would be arrogant to think I've planned for every eventuality. So, if something does happen in the future, I want to ensure some record survives.'

I was grudgingly impressed by his attitude.

Chapter Nine

Dear Toby, Mike and Izzy,

*Firstly, and most importantly, I miss you! Secondly –
and also, I suppose, fairly important – I'm alive. I'm
sorry if you've been worried about me.* ~~This strange,
mysterious, magical island I've found myself on has no
phone signal and no internet.~~ *This suits me perfectly,
hermit that I am, except that I haven't been able to contact you. Fortunately,* ~~Willum,~~ *our skipper (yes, we have
a skipper!) is going to act as postman, so please send
your reply (you'd better reply) to his address. There will
probably be quite a delay* ~~because Willum doesn't come
to the island often,~~ *but I promise to respond as soon as
I can. Also, I'm travelling to Unst soon for a daytrip, so
I'll hopefully be able to call you then.*

~~Sadly because of the confidentiality agreement I
signed, there isn't much I can write about my work,
except that I'm intrigued by, and enjoying, it. I can tell
you about my new home though. The island is beautiful – wild, rugged and so completely unlike anywhere
I've ever been. However, it is cold and wet a lot of the
time, so some things are familiar.~~

~~Although I've not seen any yet, there are apparently puffins and seals here – I wish Izzy could come here to see them. The house I'm staying in is all old stone and warm fires, and our host is lovely. Again, I probably can't write anything about her, but she makes the most amazing cakes. I'm going to be wonderfully fat when I come home!~~

~~I work with a digital archivist who's friendly and makes me laugh, and the head archivist is a sweet old man who keeps a pair of ravens as pets. I told you this was a strange and magical place! The other boss is still as pompous and pernickety as he was in the interview, but he's not here much thankfully.~~ The rest of the time we're almost like a family, which doesn't make me miss you lot any less, but does help.

But enough about me. How are you three? I want to hear everything. Is Izzy still enjoying science at school? Is she still reading about Narnia? Has mum been in touch? And are you happy to have your couch back?

I love you and miss you all, but I'm safe and happy, and won't be gone forever. So don't forget about me!

All my love, Ellie xxx

~~PS. This may seem like a really random question, but where did you send Izzy's letter to Father Christmas last year?'~~

My hand trembled as I held the letter. It was sitting on my desk in the office when I'd arrived that morning and I'd been staring at it for ten minutes. The evening before

I'd given it – sealed – to Mr Jones, along with my shopping list, for him to pass on to Willum.

Now, inspecting the thick black lines – so straight he must have used a ruler – anger boiled up inside of me. 'Where's Mr Jones?' I asked, shoving my chair back with such force that Cicero and Fluffy both leapt from their perches in consternation.

Aiden looked up from his laptop. 'What? Why?'

'Do you know where he is?'

'Er, I think I saw him somewhere in the 2000s. Is everything all right?'

'No,' I snapped, storming from the office.

Fuelled by fury, I practically ran up the spiral walkway, rehearsing what to say to him, how I'd cow him with my righteous indignation. I planned on being truly terrifying in my wrath.

Unfortunately, the journey up to the 2000s was long enough for me to remember how much I hate confrontation. With each level, I could feel my mettle wane a little more, and by the time I spotted Mr Jones ahead, my anger was almost entirely replaced by anxiety. I'd remembered not only that my natural inclination was to run *away* from disputes, not into them, but also that Mr Jones was my boss. It would be stupid to accost the person who paid me, even if he was in the wrong. Better to keep my head down and just get on with the work. That would be the smart thing to do; the safe thing.

I'd almost made my mind up to turn and head back to the office, tail tucked firmly between my legs, when Mr Jones spotted me.

'Is there something you need, Ms Lancaster?'

I was about to shake my head and walk away when an image of him casually unsealing the envelope came to me and the anger boiled up afresh.

'You opened my letter,' I accused. In my head, the words had sounded fierce, but they tiptoed gingerly out of my mouth, falling impotently onto the floor between us.

Mr Jones's expression barely changed. 'Yes, I did,' was all he said.

His indifference made me hesitate. Was I in the wrong here? My conviction was wavering, but I forced myself to press on. 'You *read* my letter.'

'Yes.'

I thought about one sentence in particular: *The other boss is still as pompous and pernickety as he was in the interview, but he's not here much thankfully*. What had possessed me to write that?

'What gives you the right . . .'

He folded his arms across his chest, surveying me as a teacher might an unruly pupil. 'The contract you signed specifically prohibited the sharing of any information. I could fire you just for putting pen to paper about your experiences here.'

'I didn't write *anything* about the work,' I protested.

'For as long as you work here, Ms Lancaster, everything about your life is confidential. Did I not make that clear to you?'

My mind stumbled as I took that in. 'Then what can I write?'

He gestured to the letter I hadn't realised was still clutched in my hand. 'The parts I didn't cross out.'

I felt angry tears spring traitorously to my eyes and had to focus all of my energy on fighting them back. Mr Jones clearly interpreted my silence as assent.

'I'm not leaving until the day after tomorrow,' he said, his tone more condescending now than clipped. 'You have time to re-write it. I'd be happy to read a second draft.'

That evening, after a day of working in furious silence, I feigned a migraine and retreated to my room. I couldn't face dinner with the man, and chose instead to stew under my covers, replaying our argument over and over again. Clementine and Aiden both knocked on my door at some point in the evening, but – being a coward – I pretended to be asleep. My redacted letter lay in a scrunched-up ball in the corner.

I couldn't say exactly what had upset me so much. The fact that he felt entitled to read my personal letter? It certainly made my blood boil, but I had signed the contract, probably giving him the legal right to do so. The fact that he had actually read it? That made me feel violated, but there wasn't anything particularly intimate about the letter. The fact that he now knew exactly what I thought of him? This made my cheeks burn with shame, but surely he already knew he was pompous and pernickety. He probably prided himself on it.

I couldn't sleep and at about one in the morning I was betrayed by my stomach. Not happy at being empty, it forced me out of my bed, into my fluffy slippers, and quietly down to the kitchen. The light had been left on and a bowl of soup stood next to the microwave. I smiled to myself: Clementine had clearly expected my late-night foraging. Bless her.

While the soup was heating, I noticed that a laptop on the table was turned on and a document was open. I shuffled a little closer and scanned the first few lines. From what I could tell, it was a report on environmental law. Not my cup of tea but I was intrigued so scanned the next few lines. And then I noticed the header of the document: Cole E. Jones.

'Does this make us even?'

I jumped in fright, the spoon I'd been holding clattering to the floor. Mr Jones stood in the doorway, looking almost like a different person in jogging bottoms and a t-shirt. One eyebrow was cocked as he looked from me to the laptop. I stepped back from it guiltily.

'I was just—'

'Reading a private document while stealing my soup?'

'I'm so sorry,' I cried, horrified. 'I didn't realise.' I moved towards the microwave but he waved a hand.

'You can have it. You must be hungry after your . . . ?'

'Stomach-ache.'

'I thought you had a migraine.'

'Yes. Migraine.' My cheeks were so hot I was surprised steam wasn't coming off them. 'All better now. But I don't want to steal your soup.'

'There's plenty more in the fridge.'

He stayed where he was and so did I, the only noise the hum of the microwave. Long seconds that felt like hours ticked by; I'd never known soup take so long to heat. I tried to think of something – anything – to say to break the strained silence.

'So . . .' I began, 'you're an environmental lawyer?'

'You sound surprised.'

'No.' That was a lie: I was very surprised. I'd pictured him in finance and banking, or as some stony-faced corporate lawyer. I'd been stereotyping, yes, but he seemed such a self-styled caricature that stereotyping felt fair game.

The soup still hadn't heated so I forced myself to carry on the conversation. 'What made you interested in environmental law?'

'It's a hangover from my tree-hugging, hippy days, I suppose.'

I gawped at him, unable to imagine the man before me – even in his casual nightclothes – as a 'tree-hugging hippy'. 'Wow, that must have been different . . .'

'That was a joke,' he said, humourlessly.

'Oh. Funny.' When would the damn soup be ready? 'What kind of environmental work do you do?'

'Small talk isn't in your job description, Ms Lancaster. Don't feel obliged.'

I was more shocked by his abruptness than offended. I struggled to think of a suitable response and in the end pretended to be amused. 'I'm English, Mr Jones. Small talk is part of my genetics.'

I would have been quite proud of my witty retort had the soup not chosen that precise moment to explode. I heard the angry eruption as it spattered all over the inside of the microwave.

'I think your soup is ready,' he said as he closed his laptop and strode from the room.

* * *

Dear Santa,

I don't really belive in you anymore because I'm 10 years old and know that your just a story. But just in case your real I want to ask for a new car for my mom. Her old car is broke and she can't get to work now so she has to get the bus and she gets home too late to make me and my sister dinner so I have to do it. You can get her any car (but my favorite color is blue so a blue one woud be nice). And if there is any money left over from that I wud like the Pokemon game. We will leave you some cookies and Rudolf a carrot because my sister (her name is Alice and she is only 7) still belives in you.

Thank you very much.

Luca

Smiling at the letter, I placed it on the pile to my left: the shortlist. This pile was considerably smaller than that on my right, which consisted mainly of requests for toys, clothes, gadgets, video games and puppies. I felt guilty placing so many children's letters into what was essentially a reject pile, but comforted myself with the fact that their authors would never know.

Aiden and Uncle Joe had been sorting through their own stacks, all of us working from the translations on the computer and – unusually for Aiden – in silence. Mr Jones, who had been brusque with me all morning (nothing new there) was coming back soon to 'check on our progress' and I was determined to deny him the pleasure of finding fault with my choices.

So when, an hour later, Mr Jones pulled me up on Luca's letter, I became instantly defensive.

'But he's not asking for himself,' I protested. 'He's asking for his mum.'

'So that he doesn't have to make dinner for his sister,' Cole countered, transferring the letter into the reject pile. 'Granted, it's less selfish than most, but it doesn't make the cut.'

I looked beseechingly across to Uncle Joe, but he wouldn't meet my eyes. I sighed.

Mr Jones continued reading through the twenty or so letters in my shortlist, cross-referencing the foreign-language ones with the translations on my computer screen. I bit my tongue as he silently placed every one of them, bar two, into the reject pile.

'I'll allow the Spanish boy who wants his friend to come out of hospital and the girl from Krakow who asks for her widower father to remarry so that he'll be happy again.'

'But what about the girl from Shanghai who wants her mother – who's been trying for another child for years – to get pregnant?'

Mr Jones sifted through the translations on my computer, found the relevant one, and quoted, 'Please let her have a baby girl so I can have a baby sister to play with. I don't want a baby brother. Boys smell.'

'Or the boy from Wales who asks for a doll-house for his sister?'

'In amongst a long list of his own toy requests. Look.' Mr Jones gestured to Uncle Joe's pile, which I could see only contained a couple of letters. Glancing over at Aiden's, I realised that his did too. I tried to conceal my bitterness harder than Aiden did his smugness; grinning at me, he patted himself on the back when Mr Jones wasn't looking.

'The shortlist needs to be short. If we could grant every single one of them, we would, but . . .'

'Grant them?' I asked. Aiden straightened as well, latching on to the word. 'Is that what you do here? Are you some kind of charity?'

Mr Jones exchanged a look with his uncle, and we all knew he'd said more than he'd meant to. 'Just be a little more discerning when you shortlist please. Now Mr Haw, let's take a look at your selection . . .'

I tried not to sulk as we went through Aiden's and Uncle Joe's apparently perfect shortlists. Nor to grind my teeth when Mr Jones set me further shortlisting practice. Determined to be ruthless, I got to work on my new stack of letters, relegating what I considered selfless requests to the reject pile until there were only three left.

'Narrow it down to one,' Mr Jones ordered.

'But you haven't read—'

'I don't have to. Discard two of them.'

I deliberated miserably through lunch and finally settled on the Sicilian girl asking *Babbo Natale* for the right donor for her hospitalised cousin. I felt heartless rejecting the other two – one asking for his mother to find a job so they could afford to pay the bills and the other asking for her parents to reconcile – and laid them softly on the other pile as if it might make the rejection gentler. My expression must have betrayed me because when I looked up, Uncle Joe cast me a sympathetic smile.

'Not nice, I know,' he said.

'But necessary,' Mr Jones added, though his tone wasn't unkind. 'When the letters start arriving in droves, you'll soon see why.'

After another hour of shortlisting the LRNCs, Uncle Joe rose stiffly and disappeared down his passageway. The three of us watched him go and then Aiden turned to Mr Jones.

'When do we get to see what's down there?'

I was glad he'd asked.

'When your job calls for it,' Mr Jones replied, sorting through the piles on Uncle Joe's desk.

Aiden pulled a face behind his back and I ducked my head to cover a smile. Then I began mustering the courage to tackle a topic I'd been meaning to bring up for a few days.

'Erm, Mr Jones?' I said. 'There was something I wanted to ask. And I didn't want to do it in front of Uncle Joe in case he thought I was criticising how things are run here.'

'And are you?' he asked without looking up from his sorting.

'Well no, but I've been thinking about record-keeping.'

'Go on.'

I glanced at Aiden and he nodded encouragingly. 'It's just that the record-keeping here seems to be . . .'

'Non-existent,' Mr Jones finished for me, finally looking up. Thankfully it didn't seem to be a question. 'I'm aware of the shortcomings of these archives and, believe me, there are many of them. An unfortunate result of generations of understaffing and the fact that the place has never been run by a professional archivist. Hence why we hired you.'

'So are you happy for me to implement some kind of system? Producing a digital index would mean that we could cross-reference the letters based on the names of the senders, look up our translations more easily, identify the ones that made the shortlist.'

Mr Jones looked at me for a moment and then nodded. 'That sounds useful.' It was the most praise he'd given me and I hated the pride I felt.

'It would mean assigning the letters catalogue numbers,' I went on happily, thinking through the logistics, 'but I wouldn't want to label them directly, so we'd need slips of paper, maybe to wrap around—'

'I'll leave the details to you,' he cut in. 'Write me a list of the supplies you'll need. I leave tomorrow so give it to me by then. Along with that letter you're re-writing.'

This punctured my momentary good mood. I hadn't looked at the letter I'd written to my brother since screwing it up and tossing it across the room. But that evening, before dinner, I forced myself to re-write it, grudgingly adhering to Mr Jones's Draconian restrictions. I worked around them by passive-aggressively starting with,

'My boss – whose character I have absolutely no opinion on whatsoever – reminded me that I signed a confidentiality agreement, and so I can't tell you anything about my work.' Knowing that Mr Jones would read that gave me an immature sense of satisfaction.

Other than Clementine, I was first into the kitchen that evening. For Mr Jones's last dinner on the island, Clementine had cooked his favourite meal – apparently to 'make sure he wants to come back' rather than to celebrate his departure.

When I saw what she was dishing up, I gave an incredulous laugh. 'Your brother's favourite meal is hot dogs?'

'Were you assuming I'm a Kobe beef kind of man?' Mr Jones asked from the doorway. As usual, he'd timed his arrival to perfection.

I tried to cover up my embarrassment with humour. 'No, I assumed you lived on a diet of orphans and kittens.' It was the kind of snappy retort I usually came up with an hour or so after it would have been funny, so gave myself a mental pat on the back. And then immediately began fretting about how the siblings – my *bosses* – would react.

I needn't have worried. Clementine roared with laughter. 'Oh snap!' She gave me a high-five of approval. 'I'm proud of you, El.'

'Orphans and kittens only at weekends.' Mr Jones was straight-faced as he began slicing hot dog buns. 'But I'm not too pompous and pernickety to enjoy hot dogs.'

My throat constricted at his words, but I resisted the urge to avert my eyes. If he hadn't wanted to know my opinion of him, he shouldn't have read my letter.

Clementine looked confused. 'I never said you were pompous and pernickety. I believe my expression was pernicious pedantry.'

'*Yours* was,' he replied, still slicing. 'Pompous and pernickety was the description given by a certain soup thief.'

'Soup thief?' Clementine looked from me to him. 'Why do I sense there's a story here that I'm not privy to?'

Aiden rescued me by suddenly waltzing through the door, declaring himself starving, closely followed by Uncle Joe. Not meeting Clementine's or Mr Jones's eyes, I followed as we all took our seats around the table.

Despite my own discomfort, most of the tension of the last few days seemed to have eased, and we fell back into casual conversation – although now there were three of us who happily stayed quiet while Clementine and Aiden chattered away.

'I'm just saying that if hot dogs are going to be your favourite meal, you at least need all the trimmings – ketchup, onions, chilli—'

Clementine shook her head. 'Cole is a purist. Mustard and nothing else. Probably because he can't actually cook anything else.'

Mr Jones made the hand gesture I'd seen him use before, and Clementine stuck her tongue out at him. Over the last few days I'd seen them both sign to each other a few times, not just profanities, and I was curious.

'You know sign language?'

Clementine glanced at her brother and he answered. 'My son is deaf.'

131

'Ah.' I wasn't sure how to respond to that. Surely not with sympathy. I knew that a lot of the deaf community didn't view their deafness as a disability, but as membership to a linguistic minority. 'That explains it then.'

'Can you sign?' Clementine asked me.

'Only the alphabet.' I made a mental note to add one last item to my list of supplies.

'Speaking of the little monster, when is Alex coming over? I haven't seen him for an age.'

'Probably Easter,' Mr Jones said, biting into his last hot dog. I'd half expected him to cut them with a knife and fork, but he was eating like a normal person. 'I'll talk to Andy about it.'

'Do! Now, who's ready for dessert? I made my brother's one true cake: marbled raspberry red velvet with peanut butter frosting.'

Afterwards, Clementine suggested a film night. 'When we were little, we'd go to the cinema once a week. And by "cinema", I mean we'd make popcorn, pick a video and turn the lights off in the living room. Who's up for it?'

I nodded while clearing away the dishes. 'That sounds great.'

'I love a film night,' Aiden agreed. 'But I have one condition. No horror.'

'I'm afraid your one condition is overruled by my one condition,' Clementine told him. 'Film selections are made collectively. And I for one love a good horror. The gorier the better.'

'So long as there's a cushion I can hide behind,' Aiden grumbled.

'Cole?'

'I have a lot of work . . .'

'I rescind the question mark,' she told him firmly. 'You're joining us whether you want to or not. That applies to you too, Uncle Joe. We'll wash the dishes tomorrow. Everyone into the living room. *Now.*'

Under Clementine's austere gaze, we filed into the lounge. I'd barely been in there since arriving at the house, partly because my bedroom was so comfortable, but also because I hadn't wanted to intrude on the family's space.

Now, the heavy drapes were closed, and a fire was already roaring in the hearth – evidence that Clementine's decision to hold a film night hadn't been a spontaneous one. I sneaked a peek at the framed photos around the place. I recognised Clementine in some of them; as a child her hair had been dark brown not bright pink, but there was no mistaking her wide grin and heart-shaped face. (Mr Jones was harder to identify because all of the children in the photographs looked happy and carefree.)

I couldn't resist old photographs – a trait of the trade, I suppose – so went to examine them more closely. One was of a family standing in front of the house; pre-extensions, it was much smaller and more symmetrical. A woman with neat curly hair and a dress straight from the 1950s shielded her eyes from the sun, while the man standing next to her was dangling two little boys above the ground by the straps of their dungarees. All four were grinning at the camera.

Uncle Joe must have seen me examining the photograph. He came up beside me and pointed to the smaller of the two boys. 'Me.'

'Really?' I grinned. 'You look like such a happy family. Was that your mother?' A nod. 'She's beautiful.'

'Beauty does run in the family,' Clementine agreed, fluttering her eyelashes. 'It's a shame for Cole that it sometimes skips a generation.'

'You're my twin,' Mr Jones reminded her dryly as he took a seat in an armchair. 'We're of the same generation.'

We all pointedly ignored him. 'And this couple?' I asked, looking to a grainy colour photograph of a bride and groom standing in the doorway of a church. I didn't know much about fashion, but the woman's long hair, full veil and elaborate, puffy-sleeved dress made me think of the 1970s.

Clementine peered over my shoulder. 'That's our very own Uncle Joe. And lovely Auntie Lorna.' Her smile was sad as she kissed her fingertip and pressed it to the bride's face. Uncle Joe reached out too and stroked his thumb down the woman's cheek. I saw then what I'd never noticed before. A plain silver band on his left hand. My throat tightened.

I noticed something else too: two gaps on the shelf where the dust suggested a pair of photographs had been removed. More pictures of Auntie Lorna, I wondered – perhaps they'd been too painful for Uncle Joe?

Clementine had moved away and was opening a cupboard with a dramatic flourish, revealing shelves of videos. 'Who needs Netflix, eh?'

'I can't believe you still watch *videos*,' Aiden said with a shake of his head as he examined them. 'Haven't you heard of Blu-ray?'

'Hey, these are vintage,' Clementine insisted.

'There is something nicely nostalgic about them,' I agreed, tracing my finger along their spines. 'The size, the weight . . . they take me back to my childhood.'

'Ah, those halcyon days of low-quality visuals and tinny audio,' Aiden replied sardonically. He pulled a few out at random and began shuffling. 'And what's a film night without waiting twenty minutes for the tape to rewind?'

Clementine threw him a grin. 'I'm glad you agree. Hey, don't be hiding *I Know What You Did Last Summer*.'

'Fine, but don't you be hiding *Star Wars*.'

'Instantly vetoed,' she said.

'Well, I instantly veto *Scream*,' he countered.

'Anyone else want to weigh in?' Clementine asked, looking around the room. 'Uncle Joe?'

When Uncle Joe smiled and shook his head, Clementine turned to me. 'Any genre preferences, El?'

'Let me guess.' Aiden's smirk was knowing rather than cruel. 'Foreign-language films.'

'Well, yes,' I admitted. 'But only because certain countries do particular genres really well. Scandinavian crime, Bollywood musicals, Japanese animation . . .'

'Plus you get to learn the language while you're reading the subtitles,' Aiden added with a wink at me. He was being sarcastic, but it was true.

'I'm curious,' Mr Jones cut in, and I instinctively drew up my defences. 'You speak various languages, and yet I remember from your interview that you haven't travelled.'

My jaw clenched and I could feel blood rushing to my cheeks. 'Is that a question?'

'No,' he replied evenly. 'Merely an observation.'

I'm sure I would have said something cuttingly witty in response had Clementine not quickly stepped in. 'Ellie's absolutely right, and I've realised my collection needs diversifying. Cole, you'll have to pick some other films up on your travels to broaden my offering. In the meantime, time's a-wasting, so let's choose something to watch tonight.'

'What's *your* genre of choice then?' Aiden asked Mr Jones, and I knew Aiden well enough now to recognise the challenge in his tone. It felt like his way of defending me, and the angry knots in my stomach unwound a little. As annoying as he could be, he was a good friend.

'Oh god, don't ask him,' Clementine groaned. 'He'll have us watching musicals.'

'Musicals?' I asked, surprised.

'Don't deny it, Cole. You made me watch *The Sound of Music* at least once a month when we were kids. And Andy told me you still . . .'

Suddenly Mr Jones was on his feet. 'I really do have too much work for this. Perhaps I'll join you for the second half of whatever you choose to watch. Thank you for dinner, Clem, I appreciate it.' And with that he was gone.

I felt a stab of anger when I saw Clementine's crest-fallen expression, but she quickly rallied. 'Well, that's one less person we've got to please. And by the way,' she added, eyeing Aiden, 'I saw you slide *Candyman* under the coffee table.'

I don't remember who won the battle that evening or what film we watched. Clearly, I didn't pay much attention to it. But I enjoyed the company, and felt far better for Mr Jones's absence.

The next day, I left my re-written letter and list of supplies on the kitchen table for Mr Jones at the crack of dawn, knowing he was leaving after breakfast, and went down to the archives before anyone had stirred.

Chapter Ten

According to my research, the population of Lerwick, the main town of the Shetlands, was under 7,000. Had I visited it straight from Manchester, I would have thought it a quaint seaport town, but after a month on an island with only three other people, it felt like New York.

Even before Willum had docked the *Valkyrie*, I'd been overwhelmed by the level of activity, and when we did find a spot to moor, I found myself surprisingly apprehensive about disembarking, already missing the peace and quiet of the island.

Aiden didn't share my sentiments: having literally leapt with joy when his phone connected to his mobile network, he bounded off the boat with the gusto of an Olympic pole-vaulter. 'See you guys at the hotel later.'

'Is it mean that I hope he's forgotten his charger?' Clementine asked.

I smiled ruefully. 'Knowing Aiden, he'd probably swim back for it.'

'Need any help here?' Clementine asked Willum, but he waved her away. He was staying with an old friend overnight and would meet us back at the *Valkyrie* the following morning. We wished him a pleasant evening and strolled into town together.

Aiden and I were there to check our account balances but also to remind ourselves that places and people still existed beyond the island. Clementine was there for work, which apparently involved picking up supplies and teaching at a local cooking school. When I'd asked Uncle Joe if he'd be coming too, he'd looked horrified, which I'd taken as a no.

We turned onto what I assumed was the high street, and I found it quite jarring to see shops, cafes and banks.

'So, the world's still here,' I said, moving to one side as a group of teenagers passed.

'I'm always a bit shell-shocked when I venture from home,' Clementine assured me. 'You'll get your civilisation-legs back in no time though.'

'Oh, I'm sure I will. Is that our hotel?' I nodded towards the large, Victorian greystone building across the road from us.

'It is indeed. We can check in at three. But now,' she said, 'if you're okay doing some solo exploring, I have to see a man about a rolling pin.'

'Erm, is that a euphemism?' I laughed, uncertain.

She looked bemused. 'No. It's serious business.'

'Don't you already have a rolling pin?'

'Not this particular rolling pin.'

'Aren't they all the same?'

She gave me a look I was familiar with from Izzy, one that made it clear how little I knew, and muttered about 'crimes against baking'.

Alone, the first thing I did was check my phone. There were dozens of messages and missed calls but none of them seemed urgent, so I did what I'd been desperate to do for a month: ring my family.

'So, she finally graces us with a call.'

I smiled. 'Toby! I'm sorry if you were worried about me.'

'You know I don't bother with worry. It's an unproductive emotion.'

In the background I could hear Mike's voice. 'He was getting ready to call the police before your letter arrived.'

'I am sorry,' I assured them both. 'Zero reception on the island and no internet.'

'Sounds barbaric.'

'It's actually quite nice,' I admitted.

'You would think that,' Toby pointed out, 'because you're stuck in the twentieth century.'

Despite the sun shining, it was cold, so I walked as I talked, holding the phone so they could see me on the camera; we chatted for nearly an hour. They were all well, my mum was still enjoying her round-the-world cruise, and Izzy had grown two centimetres and got ten out of ten on her last spelling test.

'I don't suppose you can tell us anything about *your* work?' Toby asked.

'I shouldn't. But . . .' I looked around surreptitiously, convinced that Mr Jones, master of perfect timing, would pop up any second. 'I do have a question, for Toby's ears only.'

'Go on,' Toby urged me, after Izzy had waved goodbye. 'I'm intrigued.'

'Where did you send Izzy's letter to Father Christmas?'

He laughed. 'I don't know what I was expecting, but it wasn't that. To Father Christmas, obviously.'

I rolled my eyes. 'You know what I mean.'

'The usual. Royal Mail replied.'

'You didn't send a copy somewhere else?' I pressed.

'No,' he said, clearly confused. 'Why?'

'And Izzy didn't write in silver ink, did she?'

'I wouldn't bet my life on it, but I don't think so. What's this about, Ellie? You're being very cryptic.'

'I'm sorry, I can't say.'

'Of course you can't.' He sounded cheerful, but I felt guilty. 'Any news on when you'll be coming home?'

'Not really, but I'll ask about having some time off. Maybe we could meet halfway, in Edinburgh perhaps?'

'I'll tell Mike to dig out his kilt.'

'He's not Scottish.'

'He might be.'

'His family are from Nigeria.'

'So he's *distantly* Scottish then,' Toby conceded. 'He'll still look good in a kilt.'

'I miss you guys,' I laughed.

'And we miss you too, but I'm glad you're okay. You've certainly earned your "be unboring" tick.'

Hanging up, a lump formed in my throat as a fresh wave of homesickness crashed over me. I fought back tears along with the urge to catch the next flight back to Manchester.

'Be unboring,' I reminded myself. It was time to do some exploring (and by exploring I obviously meant following the carefully planned itinerary I'd drawn up based on my travel guide's recommendations).

I divided my afternoon between exploring the Shetland Museum, meandering around the ruins of an Iron Age complex on the edge of Lerwick, and hunting for treasures in the town's only bookshop. It was one such treasure, a second-hand copy of *Shetland Folklore and Customs*, that I settled down to read in the window of an independent coffee shop. The place was busy when I first arrived, but as the afternoon drew on – the sun long ago having dipped behind the horizon – it began emptying. Eventually there was only one other person left. He was sitting across from me, at the only other window table, and it was when I glanced up to check the clock above the counter that I noticed him looking at me. The moment my eyes met his, he turned away. But there was no embarrassment in his expression; maybe he hadn't actually been watching me. He'd probably been staring into space, and I just happened to be within his eyeline. Still, I took the opportunity of his averted gaze to study him.

He was around my age. With his unkempt, shoulder-length brown hair and creased linen shirt, the word that immediately came to mind was 'bohemian'. I suspected the effect was deliberately cultivated, especially as he appeared to be sketching. He glanced up at me, then down again, continuing to draw. Was he . . . drawing *me*? Surely not. But he did keep looking across to where I was sitting, pausing, and then returning to his sketch.

Disconcerted, I decided it was time to leave. But as I went to pack my book away, he spoke.

'Don't move. I'm nearly done.' He looked up from the sketch pad and met my gaze. 'Please?'

Sketching a stranger was one thing, but asking her to stay still while you finished was surely a step too far. It was certainly a leap beyond good etiquette. Yet he seemed to have no qualms about it. And I, confined by politeness, stayed where I was. It would be rude to just leave, right? I looked across at him, uncertain and no doubt blushing, as he swept the charcoal across the page, his expression quietly intense. At least it gave me another chance to look at him.

His eyes were an intense shade of sea-green and his features delicate, with high cheekbones, narrow mouth, smooth chin and pale skin, suggesting he spent more time indoors than out. I added 'cultured' to my quick-fire assessment of him. He'd be at home, I decided, in some obscure Parisian gallery, debating the merits of a controversial art movement. While sipping on black coffee. And wearing a beret.

Ok, maybe not the beret.

My nerves increased as the minutes ticked by. How long did he expect me to stay? Was I allowed to scratch my nose? 'Are you, erm . . . nearly done?' I finally asked, trying to sound casual. As if this type of thing happened to me all the time.

He gave a distracted nod. 'Nearly,' he muttered, frowning. After a few more seconds, he dropped the charcoal to the table and pushed his fingers through his hair with a sigh, leaving a smear of black on his forehead.

Was requesting to see an artist's work a faux pas? Or would he be offended if I *didn't* ask? I'd never been the subject of a drawing before and curiosity won out. 'Can I look?'

He looked surprised but not unpleased. 'Of course,' he said, holding the sketch pad up for me to see.

If I'd been hoping – and I was – for a flattering portrait, my soul carefully captured in the caress of charcoal across paper, I was sorely disappointed. It *wasn't* a flattering portrait. In fact, it wasn't a portrait at all.

It took me a moment to register the dark, craggy shape jutting out from a swirling mass. Was that . . . an island? Was it *the* island? My breath caught and I teetered between incredulity and panic until I realised what he'd drawn. It was the front cover of my book, *Shetland Folklore and Customs*.

Was I disappointed or relieved that he hadn't been drawing me? More than anything, I was confused.

'It's stunning,' I said truthfully, 'but you do know there are some pretty nice views out there?' I gestured to the window, wondering why he'd chosen to copy a grainy photograph when he was actually *on* the Shetland Islands.

'I like to make impressions of other people's impressions,' he said. 'That photograph was one person capturing a moment. I'm reinterpreting that moment.'

The two images were admittedly very different. Although the shape of the island was the same, the photograph depicted a pleasantly green landscape above serene waters, while his sketch was all harsh lines and black shapes: a brooding island protruding from an angry sea.

'Plus, any image of an island gets my fingers itching,' he added, closing the sketch pad. 'They inspire me.'

I smiled at that. 'Me too. There's something poetic about them.'

His green eyes lit up. 'It's nice to meet a fellow admirer. I take it your love of islands brought you here?'

'How do you know I'm not a local?' I asked, amused. 'Was it the book or the accent that gave me away?' His own accent, deeply Scottish, identified *him* as a native.

He smiled. 'If you're a fan of island folklore, you should go to the Faroe Islands. There's a legend about a place called Mikladalur—'

'The selkie,' I said, delighted. 'I know this one. The selkies or sea-women were believed to come ashore every twelfth-night to shed their sealskins and dance as humans on the beach. A farmer went to watch them and fell in love with one.'

'Then stole her sealskin and forced her to marry him,' he finished for me.

'It's not a very happy story,' I remembered.

'Few are.'

'There's a statue of a selkie at Mikladalur, commemorating the story. I'd love to visit it.'

'If we left now, we could be there in roughly twelve hours.'

I laughed, but his expression was entirely earnest.

'What's stopping you?'

Maybe the fact that I've only just met you, I thought but didn't say. 'Logistics. Twelve hours, you said? I'm meeting friends for dinner soon, so don't think I'd have time to get there and back again.'

'Probably not,' he admitted. He was smiling again, but there was no humour in his voice.

'I'm not a very spontaneous person,' I explained, feeling strangely guilty. 'I'm quite boring actually.'

'A common affliction,' he nodded knowingly. 'But entirely curable.'

Be unboring.

'Would you really just jet off to the Faroe Islands on a whim?' I asked, disbelieving.

'Why not? I'm already packed.'

'I admire your spirit.'

'And I pity you yours.' It was such a blunt, cruel thing to say that I immediately thought of Mr Jones. But unlike Mr Jones, this man cringed with guilt. 'That wasn't nice of me. I'm sorry. I lack tact.'

'I guess neither of us are perfect then,' I conceded, softening.

'I'm *definitely* not.' He said it simply, without a hint of false modesty.

'Why don't you join us for dinner?' I asked suddenly. 'My friends won't mind.' I'd never been this forward before, and I could feel my traitorous cheeks reddening, but it was another tiny step towards *being unboring*.

He hesitated, and for a second I thought he'd accept. But then he gave a regretful shake of his head. 'I'd best not. But here, keep this.' He tore the drawing from his sketch pad and stood up to pass it over.

I took it, surprised. 'Thank you.'

He dropped his charcoal and sketch pad into his satchel and pulled on a slightly shabby brown raincoat. 'I enjoyed meeting you,' he said.

I stared after him, perplexed by the whole encounter and disappointed he hadn't accepted my invitation. I'd found him . . . interesting, and was sure Clementine would too. Aiden perhaps less so.

I looked down at the sketch, impressed at the sense of atmosphere he'd managed to create. I folded it into my book to keep it safe, pulled on my own coat and headed out, half hoping he'd be waiting for me, or walking back towards the coffee shop, having changed his mind about dinner. But he was nowhere to be seen.

Dismissing my disappointment, I headed to the hotel and checked into my room, which looked out onto a quiet, dusky beach and – most importantly – had a private bathroom. I'd be using the hot water with abandon.

My stomach was grumbling by this point and I wondered where the others were. I tried calling Clementine but she didn't answer, although a few minutes later a text arrived: 'Rolling pin = euphemism after all. See you tomorrow morning.'

Chuckling to myself, I sent Aiden a message asking where he was and if he wanted to eat. Half an hour – and a luxurious bubble bath – later, I headed down to the hotel bar to meet him. I smiled as I dropped into the seat opposite him, but he barely registered my arrival.

'Is everything okay?' I asked.

'What? Oh, yeah,' he shrugged, taking a swig of a beer as he scrolled through his phone. 'It's just, you know, weird being back in the real world. Apparently it's been turning just fine without us.' There was a definite edge to his tone, and I gathered he wasn't happy. I imagined it was a woman. 'Do you think it's real?'

His sudden question, so fervently delivered, took me by surprise. 'Is what real?'

'The island. The . . .' A wave of his hand, 'archives.'

I knew what he meant. I'd been wondering the same for weeks, although we'd never discussed it. It was strange it had taken us being back in the 'real' world to finally question it aloud.

'I don't know,' I admitted. 'It can't be real. And yet . . .'

'And yet,' he agreed, finally looking at me.

We stared at each other for a long moment. He was the one to look away; his phone, buzzing, commandeered his attention. When he glanced back up at me the intensity in his gaze was gone.

'At least we got paid though, right?' he asked lightly.

I let him navigate us back to an easier topic. 'Did we? I forgot to check.'

Aiden snorted. 'You do know that was the main reason Clementine brought us here, right? Speaking of Clementine, where is she?'

'She, er . . . met someone.'

He raised his eyebrows. 'Good for her.'

We sat quietly for a few minutes – a novel experience with Aiden, which was what I liked about him. I never had to think of things to say because he was always willing to fill the silence. But not this evening apparently, so I shuffled through my mental stash of small talk.

'Did you know,' I began, 'The name "Lerwick" means bay of clay in Old Norse?'

The look he gave me suggested he neither knew nor cared.

'God, I need a one-night stand,' he grumbled with a long, dramatic exhale.

I must have looked as horrified as I felt because he quickly waved his hands placatingly. 'I obviously didn't mean with you.'

Was I supposed to be relieved or offended? He gave an apologetic grimace. 'I didn't mean *obviously*. Sorry, I'm being a right dickhead. Let me buy you a drink?'

'A drink or a *drink*?' I asked cautiously.

'Just a drink,' he assured me.

Amused, I let him squirm for a moment. 'I'll have a lemonade please. And a bag of crisps, to make up for the deep wound you've inflicted on my pride.'

'Ooh, you're pushing your luck there,' he winked, pulling himself out of the armchair and draining his beer. 'Back in a sec.'

Alone, I began to wonder about the man in the coffee shop. He'd seemed interesting. And *interested*. I'd never had a one-night stand in my life, but would it be so wrong? If I was going to spend the night with a stranger, no strings attached, a handsome artist encountered on an adventure in the Shetland Islands seemed a good candidate. But I'd missed my opportunity, and seemed fated to spend the evening with Aiden, who'd be 'back in a sec'.

Except he wasn't. And neither was he back in fifteen minutes, or twenty, or thirty. Eventually I went searching for him and found him at the bar in the middle of a group of millennials, dressed for a night out. He was chatting to a leggy brunette in a sequined minidress, my lemonade and crisps sitting forgotten on the bar beside him. He certainly seemed to have cheered up. I was about to duck away but he'd already seen me. Shouting my name over the din of the group, he waved me over.

'Ellie, come meet my new friends,' he said, before rolling off a list of names. 'They're at their first stop on a bar crawl to celebrate Cara's birthday,' he added, gesturing to the brunette. 'And have invited us to join them.'

I could tell from Cara's expression that it wasn't 'us' they'd invited.

My irritation was outweighed only by my desperation to extricate myself from the situation. 'Thank you for the invite,' I said, addressing Cara, 'and happy birthday. But I should be getting to bed.'

'It's eight thirty,' Aiden helpfully pointed out. I made sure to step on his foot when grabbing my crisps, before walking away.

Back in my room, munching on my crisps and feeling sorry for myself, I did what I'd sworn not to: logged on to my social media account. Unsurprisingly, scrolling through pictures of friends, relatives and distant acquaintances all enjoying themselves did little to lift my mood. And then I saw it: the one thing that was bound to make my mood plummet still further. Gary, my banana-head of an ex, in a new relationship.

I hadn't missed him. In fact, I'd barely thought about him: a clear sign that it hadn't been true love. But seeing how happy he was in his profile picture, his arms wrapped around the waist of another woman, still knocked the breath from me. I switched off my phone, grabbed my purse and ran back down to the bar.

The group were just getting ready to leave for the second stop on their birthday bar crawl.

'Room for one more?' I asked, aiming for confident and breezy but probably sounding as awkward as I felt.

Cara looked annoyed but Aiden gave me a cheer. 'I knew there was an inner party animal deep down. Let's hit the town!'

Needless to say, I regretted it.

I can remember the second bar we went to, but not the third. I'm assured we visited three more, all of them blanks. The last thing I recall was someone saying the words, 'What, you've never had whisky? You can't live in Scotland and never try it!' And then I woke up in bed, the blinding sunlight agony in my eyes. My mouth was full of sawdust and a tiny drummer had taken up residence inside my skull. Even groaning was too much effort, so I lay still and tried to piece together the events of the night before.

It took me a few minutes to realise I wasn't in my hotel room. The wallpaper and curtains looked the same, but the furniture was arranged differently, the door where the window should be, and the wardrobe where the bathroom should be.

Mortified, I threw off the covers and jumped out of bed – the tiny drummer didn't like that. Relief that I was still dressed in the clothes I'd worn the day before was short-lived as there was a noise from the bathroom. I froze where I stood. Who was in there? Deep down, I'd hoped to run into the artist again while out with Aiden and his new friends, but I couldn't remember. Should I sneak away or stand my ground and face whoever it was I'd spent the night with?

I didn't have time to make the decision. The bathroom door opened and Aiden, wearing nothing but a towel around his waist, stepped out.

The blood fled from my face as I stood gaping at him.

'Sleeping Beauty arises,' he smiled, using another towel to dry his hair.

'Oh no, no, no,' I said, covering my face with my hands. 'This didn't happen. Please tell me this didn't happen.'

'This?' he asked. I watched between my fingers as the realisation dawned on his face, and then he burst into laughter. 'Don't worry, we didn't do anything. You couldn't find your room key so I gallantly gave up half my bed.'

I sank back onto said bed. 'Oh, thank God.'

'I'm not going to lie, El, the relief in your tone kind of stings.'

A wave of nausea tumulted over me and I lay my head down, whimpering. 'I'm sorry. I hardly ever drink.'

'You don't say.'

'On a rating scale of one to ten,' I muttered, my face pressed against a pillow, 'how much did I humiliate myself?'

'The good people of Lerwick have banned you for life.'

I peeked at Aiden, trying to gauge how serious he was being. 'Tell me truthfully.'

He gave a smug chuckle. 'You weren't that bad. Talked about your ex a little. Mentioned some handsome artist. Talked about how much you hate Mr Jones. You seriously have some issues with that guy,' he added, running a comb through his drying hair. 'But I'd be more embarrassed by the fact that you snore.'

'I don't snore.'

'You *do* snore,' he assured me, disappearing into the bathroom with some clothes. 'Enough to make me regret being chivalrous and letting you crash here. I gave up my one-night stand for you.' He re-emerged a moment later, dressed and looking fresher than he had any right to.

'I owe you one,' I mumbled gracelessly, feeling grateful, guilty and annoyed with him in equal measure.

He patted my head condescendingly and placed a key in my hand. 'I found this in your shoe, by the way.'

Clutching it, I dragged myself off the bed and trudged to the door. 'I do appreciate . . .'

'I know, I know. You can tell me how awesome I am later. Right now, you need to shower. You smell really bad.'

I gave him a withering glare, leaving the room, which he deflected with a grin and cheerful wave. 'See you downstairs for breakfast.'

An hour later, while I was half asleep in a bowl of porridge and Aiden was recounting the highlights of the night before, Clementine appeared.

'Are we witnessing the walk of shame?' Aiden teased.

'There's nothing shameful about a night of amazing sex between two consenting adults,' Clementine countered cheerfully, snatching some toast from Aiden's plate.

Aiden grabbed the slice back. 'I wouldn't know.'

'Diddums,' she mocked. 'Did someone not get lucky last night?'

'Ask Ellie.'

Wide-eyed, Clementine looked from me to Aiden. I quickly shook my head – and instantly regretted it. The tiny drummer was back. 'Don't have the energy to explain.'

'I'd ask if you had fun,' Clementine smiled sympathetically, 'but it looks like you had a little too much.' She chuckled when I gave a miserable nod. 'Fortunately, one of the best cures for a hangover is fresh air. *Unfortunately*, fresh air on a small fishing boat on choppy seas might not be.'

She was right. I spent most of the journey huddled in a corner of the wheelhouse, clutching my stomach and feeling thoroughly ashamed of myself.

Chapter Eleven

Dear Santa,

I no its the rong time of year for you but the Easter Bunny only brings candy and wat I really really want is a Playstation 4 Pro. I wrot in December asking for one but mabe my letter got lost or you forgot cos I never got one. Thats O.K. because I no how busy you are. But maybe you coud ask the Easter Bunny to bring me one.

Question: when you come to peoples houses do you use there toilets?

Thanks and goodby.

James

Smiling at the temerity of children, I secured the letter with the snake weights (courtesy of Mr Jones, who had also provided a brand new pair of wellies and, to my immense pleasure, a wide range of obscure foreign-language films – as well as digitisation equipment for Aiden) and began to input the data into the spreadsheet that was forming the digital Wish Index. Catalogue Number: 2018-369. Name: James. Address: Billings, Montana, US. I left the column labelled 'Shortlist' blank to indicate it hadn't made the cut. Then I re-rolled the scroll, wrote the catalogue number on one of the many loops of paper I'd made, secured the scroll with the loop and placed it on the trolley beside me, ready for Aiden to scan. Once scanned, Aiden would label the digital file with the catalogue number and store it in a folder designated 2018.

Our new system had been in place for a few weeks. It was simple but effective, and I slept easier knowing the letters were properly catalogued.

Uncle Joe had surprised me by asking, in his unassuming way, if I could show him how it worked. I'd expected him to flee at the sight of all the equipment, but he'd been quietly curious about it. He still hadn't touched a computer or scanner, but was happy to handwrite the catalogue numbers on the loops of paper and to run the trolley back and forth.

We were splitting our time between tackling decades of backlog and cataloguing new arrivals, of which there were a surprising number, considering it was only the end of March. Letters to the myriad versions of Father Christmas trickled steadily in from all over the world, most of them acknowledging that it was still very early *but* . . .

One was veritably local: a woman from Edinburgh wrote, asking for help with her business.

I know I shouldn't believe in you anymore, being in my forties, but I never grew out of the spirit of Christmas. And that's one of the reasons I've opened a Christmas shop in the centre of Edinburgh. Perhaps this was silly.

It was certainly silly to open in February. I haven't sold a thing. And that's why I'm writing to you, in the hope that you can send some Christmas magic my way. I need this to work.

Cammie.

It wasn't a tragic request, but it struck a chord with me.

Only one so far had made the shortlist. An eight-year-old girl from Melbourne was asking for her father to come out of hospital: *I can't wait to Xmas to right this because he might be with Baby Jesus before then so I'm righting it now. Please bring my daddy home.*

That request had upset even Aiden.

As for the backlog, we struggled to know where to start. Armed with torches, Aiden and I – accompanied by Cicero and Fluffy – had ventured into the unlit sections of the archives, but they just kept snaking down, the years going back and back and back. We'd got as far as the late 1800s when, jumping at our own shadows, we'd decided that was far enough and loaded the trolley with scrolls from 1880. There were far fewer than later decades – belief in Father Christmas clearly hadn't always been so prevalent – but still enough to keep us busy for several weeks.

Dear Father Christmas, began Josie from London, *How are you? I have been very good this year but I don't want too many presents from you because there are a lot of poor orphans and they deserve presents too. If there are enough left over then I would like a doll buggy and some oranges. But please don't come down the parlour chimney because it will be very hot. Come down the din-ing room chimney. Josie.*

Dear Santa Claus, wrote Edith from Missouri, *I am a little girl nine years old and I live in Missouri which is far away from you but I hope you can make it all the way to my house with some trifles to gladden my heart. I would like some mittens please and a sled and a doll for my little sister even though she's good only some of the time. I do hope the weather is good for your journey. Yours truly, Edith.*

Both Mr Jones and Uncle Joe had mentioned a shortlist record. When I asked Uncle Joe if I could see it, he looked suddenly anxious and told me it was lost. I wondered if there'd been an accident and didn't want to press him when he was clearly upset by it. Later that day I'd dis-creetly asked Clementine, but her response was the same.

'It's gone,' she'd said simply.

'Isn't there another copy somewhere?' The thought of records being irredeemably lost horrified me.

Clementine refused to look at me. 'No. Now, what do you fancy for dinner?'

I let it drop. While there was no way of knowing for certain which letters had been shortlisted, we could guess. While most asked for toys, clothes and food, a few made selfless requests; requests that I hoped *had* earned them a place on the list. I tried picturing a nineteenth-century archivist sitting where I was, deliberating over which letters were deserving. Would Cicero and Fluffy, known by different names then, have watched over them too?

'That would have been Hugh and Annie,' Uncle Joe told me when I'd mused aloud.

'You know who would have been the archivists here in 1880?' I'd asked, impressed.

He did some quiet calculations and then nodded. 'Great-great-great-great-great-grandfather Hugh.'

'Wow,' I breathed. 'How long has your family lived here?'

'We've always worked in the archives,' he'd said simply, before shuffling away.

The longer I was on the island, the more questions I had. But still no answers. I didn't know where the letters came from, why we were making a shortlist, and what was going to happen to it. But Uncle Joe would either pretend not to hear my questions or offer a vague non-answer, which invariably led to more questions. I tried asking Clementine, both subtly – 'Do you know when more letters will be arriving?' – and more directly – 'Where on earth do they all come from?' Neither tactic worked. Clementine would simply shake her head and say something infuriatingly cryptic like, 'I could tell you, but you won't believe me.'

I did *try* to figure it out myself. Some sense of taboo still stopped me from investigating the prohibited passageway, but when nobody was around, I'd poke around the office, digging in drawers and rummaging behind scrolls. But there was nothing. No records, no clues. Just more and more scrolls. I did some reconnaissance up in the house too, rooting through cupboards under the pretence of looking for a pen. The kitchen yielded nothing, and the only surprise in the living room was a drawer of family photographs. I'd pulled a handful out and looked through them, not expecting answers but too curious to resist.

I recognised some of the people in the images and a lot of the island backdrop. A couple were framed, and one was clearly a Christmas family photograph. There was a younger Uncle Joe, looking spry but still characteristically ragged, sitting in his usual chair, next to a Christmas tree. A slender woman with greying hair and a soft smile sat on the arm beside him. On the sofa sat a couple I didn't recognise: a rather rotund man and a dark-haired woman, both semi-obscured behind an unmistakable Clementine, possibly ten or eleven years old, doing a jumping jack in front of them. Crouched by the Christmas tree were two boys, a set of Transformers arranged between them. One could have been a pre-teen Mr Jones, but with clean-shaven cheeks and a smile, it was difficult to tell. The other boy was angled slightly away from the camera, his attention on the robots, so all I could make out was brown hair and a slim build.

The second photograph was of Mr Jones, a young woman and a toddler on a pebble beach. The woman was striking, with sharp features, paper-white skin and bright red hair, which – judging by the smattering of freckles on her nose – was natural. Her mouth was painted a bold shade of purple, and she wore a yellow mackintosh over a striped sailor top. She'd either just stepped off a yacht or out of a Gap catalogue. Mr Jones looked uncommonly casual in a loose sky-blue shirt, jeans and *sandals*. Neither was looking at the camera but at the little boy toddling between them, a sandwich in his fingers. I guessed the child was Alex, which would make the woman Andy. Mr Jones's wife. Of course she'd be beautiful. Why such a lovely picture had been hidden away I had no idea. Perhaps it had something to do with the other figure in the picture. I was assuming it was a man based on the height and build, but he was mainly obscured behind Andy. Perhaps Uncle Joe, although the only detail I could make out – a pair of heavily scuffed brown Doc Martens – didn't seem in keeping.

Meanwhile, time both in and out of the archives sped by. I'd adopted a pleasant routine of early morning strolls and long weekend walks, made all the more enjoyable now the weather was improving. It still wasn't warm or dry by any means, but I didn't always need wellies and four layers of clothes.

Evenings, too, followed a pattern: Clementine's amazing cooking (I was struggling to zip up my jeans), followed by personality questionnaires. Most evenings I'd then snuggle under my duvet with a book, but we'd designated Wednesdays and Saturdays 'cinema nights', where we took it in turns to choose a film.

I was making my way through the foreign-language films Mr Jones had sent, while being educated about classic horror by Clementine and big blockbuster movies by Aiden.

Uncle Joe joined us most evenings but always declined to choose a film himself. He seemed to enjoy the first half of whatever we chose, and then slept through the second half, gently snoring in his armchair. After the closing credits, Clementine would drape a blanket over him, and we'd tiptoe from the room.

The only grey cloud in my sky was Easter, which meant two things.

First, I would miss Izzy's Easter egg hunt, which we'd done together every year since she was old enough to appreciate chocolate. I was sure Toby and Mike would organise it in my stead, but felt glum not being there. Second, Mr Jones would be returning to the island with his son.

It would be fine – I was prepared this time. Clementine had told me when he was coming; he wouldn't catch me off guard.

Of course, I was wrong.

This time when he took me by surprise, I was lying on the floor of the living room in Harry Potter pyjamas with a wet flannel over my eyes and my legs in the air.

An hour before, I'd sludged into the kitchen with a hot water bottle clutched to my stomach and asked Clementine, busy preparing a feast, if she had any painkillers. She'd taken one look at me and clucked in sympathy.

'Aunt Flo?'

'My favourite time of month,' I'd confirmed gloomily.

'Cramps?'

'And headache.'

'I can do better than painkillers,' she assured me, turning off the stove. 'My old flatmate showed me some great yoga poses for easing period pains. Try some of them before drugs.'

Sceptical, but not wanting to offend, I followed Clementine into the living room, where she laid a cold wet flannel over my eyes to help with the headache and then manoeuvred me into various uncomfortable positions.

'And this one's the inverted leg pose. *Viparita* something-or-other.' While I lay on my back, she pulled my legs straight up and instructed me to hold them there for as long as possible. 'I'll be back soon with some herbal tea.'

'And drugs and chocolate?'

'And drugs and chocolate.' She clicked the door shut behind her and I let my legs fall. When the door opened again a few minutes later, I forced them back up into an inverted position.

'I'll take my drugs and chocolate now please. The cramps are worse.'

'I'm sorry to hear that.'

Naturally, it was Mr Jones. Yanking the flannel from my eyes, I dropped my legs and scrambled to my feet. The situation was horrifying, but to top it off, he wasn't alone. Standing beside him was a teenage boy, probably about thirteen or fourteen. Although shorter, skinnier and a little scruffier in jeans and an oversized hoodie, he was instantly recognisable as Mr Jones's son. His expression, too, was a duplicate of his father's: dead-pan.

'I, erm . . .' I began, and then shrugged in resignation. There was no point trying to salvage my pride. 'I thought it wouldn't be a proper greeting without some thorough humiliation on my part.'

Something glimmered in Mr Jones's eyes but he maintained a straight face. 'I've come to expect nothing less from you.' He signed as well as speaking aloud. 'Alex, meet Ms Lancaster. Get used to finding her in . . . unusual predicaments.'

'It's Ellie,' I signed, hoping my hand gestures were correct. 'It's nice to meet you.'

If Alex was surprised to find me signing, he didn't show it. 'And you,' he returned politely.

'And now that I can cross thorough humiliation off my to-do list, I'm going to, er . . .'

'Go in search of drugs and chocolate?' Mr Jones suggested, standing aside to make room for my exit.

'Yes. That.' And with a brief wave to Alex I ducked through the doorway and beat a hasty retreat to my room.

Clementine, being her wonderful self, came to me soon after with a fresh hot-water bottle, paracetamol and a giant bar of chocolate. 'Do you want your dinner on a tray?'

As tempting as it was, I shook my head and promised I'd be down. It would be rude to miss Alex's first evening with us. And besides, I was curious to see what kind of child Mr Jones had raised. I was expecting a sullen teenager completely estranged from his workaholic parent.

The Jones family, however, continued to surprise me.

When I entered the kitchen that evening, it was laughter that greeted me. Clementine's, Aiden's, Uncle Joe's – and Mr Jones's.

Mr Jones was laughing, actually *laughing*. And it wasn't polite or forced but loud, full-bodied and entirely genuine.

'El,' Aiden greeted me, 'you just missed Alex doing *the* best mime impression of Donald Trump.'

'I'd like to see that,' I smiled, signing the words and taking a seat.

'I thought you couldn't sign,' Clementine said. She was, as usual, busy at the stove, but half of her attention was with the rest of us.

It was Mr Jones who answered. 'Ms Lancaster requested a British Sign Language book in the last shipment.' Was that a hint of gratitude in his tone?

'I appreciate it,' Alex said, speaking as well as signing, which meant Aiden didn't need a translation.

'Well, I appreciate the excuse to learn a new language,' I enthused, ignoring Aiden's eye-roll. 'Please tell me if I sign anything wrongly. I've only been learning for a few weeks.'

Alex's eyes widened. 'Wow, you learn fast.'

'Jones Associates hires nobody but the best.' Clementine winked at me before pulling a casserole dish out of the oven. 'So, in honour of my ethically inclined nephew, for dinner tonight we'll be having: lasagne with lentil ragu and mushroom sauce; garlic bread made using dairy-free parmesan; vegan salted caramel and dark chocolate brownies, with a side of vegan coconut ice cream.' She placed the steaming lasagne into the centre of the table with a proud flourish.

'I appreciate the effort, Aunt Clem, but I'm not vegan anymore.'

Clementine's smile stayed in place, but her right eye twitched ever so slightly.

'Just joking,' Alex sniggered.

'Oh, I do love your sense of humour,' Clementine said, not sounding like she loved it *at all*. 'For that, no brownie and ice cream for you.'

'Erm . . .' came Uncle Joe's quiet voice. We all turned to him. 'What actually is a vegan?'

Once the last morsel of food was eaten, and Aiden and I had cleared away the dishes, Clementine ducked out of the room for a moment. When she returned, she was carrying a Monopoly box that looked older than the house itself.

'Family tradition,' she explained, laying it on the table. 'We play one marathon game over the course of the week, until Alex and Cole leave.'

'Or until I take over the entire board, defeating you all in the space of two hours,' Alex smiled gleefully.

'I'll remind you that happened *once*,' Mr Jones said, sorting through the paper money.

'You'll have to explain the rules.' Aiden was eyeing the board suspiciously. 'I've never played before.'

'What a sad childhood you must have had,' Clementine said, completely sincere.

'Not really,' he laughed. 'You never heard of Xbox?'

'Speaking of Xbox . . .' Alex began with a grin.

'Your dad let you bring it?' Clementine asked, incredulous.

'I invited him to write a thousand-word essay on why he should be allowed,' Mr Jones replied.

Alex's grin broadened. 'I presented a well-structured argument on how video games improve my hand-eye coordination, problem-solving skills and creative thinking.'

'It was quite convincing.' Mr Jones sounded half begrudging, half proud. 'Even if it was a load of bollocks.'

'I may need to read this essay,' Aiden said, with Mr Jones translating in sign. 'Valuable arguments for when I have a girlfriend. What games have you got?'

'Xbox talk later,' Clementine demanded, tapping the board game. 'World domination first. El, I take it you've played before?'

I grimaced. 'I know how to play but, er, maybe I shouldn't.'

'Why not?' All bar Uncle Joe asked in tandem.

'Because I can get kind of . . . competitive,' I admitted.

'We're pretty competitive too,' Alex reassured me. 'My dad's such a sore loser. You should have seen how upset he was when I beat him at Snakes and Ladders. I was seven at the time.'

Mr Jones shrugged. 'You're supposed to play to win.'

'I know, but I mean . . . *really* competitive,' I stressed. 'I've been, er, banned by my family from taking part in board games. Ever since the incident of Christmas 2012.'

Mr Jones was actually smiling at me. 'I think we can handle it.'

Two hours later, Aiden was bankrupt, and Alex and Clementine were on their last few banknotes. The board was divided between me, an unsurprisingly ruthless Mr Jones, and Uncle Joe, who'd turned out to be the dark horse of the game. He'd been quietly building his empire while the rest of us had been focused on each other.

'I think I'll put a hotel on Mayfair,' Uncle Joe said, considering his neatly arranged piles of banknotes. There was nothing combative in his tone; he seemed oblivious to the fact that he was wiping the floor with us.

'Have you reconsidered my proposal?' I asked Mr Jones on my turn. 'Regent Street in exchange for Fleet Street?'

'No thanks,' he replied blandly.

I gritted my teeth. 'You get the better end of the deal here.'

'If that were true, you wouldn't be offering it.'

'The property I'm offering you is clearly worth more . . .'

'I'm not surrendering that entire corner to you.'

'Fine,' I huffed. 'Then I'll just put two more houses on Vine and Bow Streets.' Alex passed me the houses and I rolled for my turn. I inevitably landed on one of Mr Jones's properties.

'I'm afraid that's going to cost you—'

'I know how much,' I snapped, slapping a high proportion of my dwindling notes in front of him.

'She really wasn't kidding about being competitive,' I heard Aiden whisper to Clementine.

When Mr Jones rolled the dice and landed on my most expensive property, I gave a graceless laugh. 'Oh dear, it doesn't look like you've got enough . . .'

'I'll re-mortgage Piccadilly,' he grunted.

'I'll let you off if you reconsider my proposal.'

'I've got more than enough funds to need your charity.'

Before I could retort, Clementine snatched the dice from the table and pointed to the clock. 'And on that note, shall we continue this tomorrow night?'

As usual, once I'd stepped away from the board, the aggression drained out of me. I gave them all a sheepish smile. 'Sorry if I got a little . . . carried away.'

'We like badass Ellie,' Aiden said, punching me softly on the arm.

'But,' Clementine added, 'please give me some warning if I need to hide the kitchen knives.'

The next day, Aiden and I talked Mr Jones through the new archiving system. Alex had come down as well, and Mr Jones tasked Aiden and me with putting him to work.

'Put in a few productive hours this morning,' he told Alex, 'and we'll go for a walk this afternoon.'

To my surprise, Alex didn't argue, only countered with, 'By "go for a walk" I assume you mean spend some quality father-son time playing Xbox.'

Mr Jones narrowed his eyes. 'I'll allow you to try to convince me over lunch.'

Once he'd left, I grimaced apologetically at Alex. 'I doubt this is how you wanted to spend your Easter holidays.'

He shrugged. 'It's the family business. I've been working here since I was old enough to walk. Before that, Uncle Joe apparently used to push me around on his trolley.'

'Only way to stop you from crying,' Uncle Joe said with a fond smile. I smiled too, picturing Uncle Joe a decade younger, walking the archives with a baby asleep on a bed of scrolls.

Alex was a hard worker and took to the new system quickly. For the most part I left him working alongside

Uncle Joe. The two seemed close and I didn't know how long it had been since they'd seen each other last.

'How often do you come here?' I asked Alex as he got ready to leave for lunch.

'Most school holidays.'

'My condolences,' Aiden said, with me translating. 'All I wanted to do when I was your age was hang around with my mates and maybe meet some girls.' He cocked his head to one side. 'Come to think of it, that's all I want now.'

Alex gave a dismissive gesture. 'It's not so bad. I get to see my mates at school. Sometimes it's nice seeing family.' Although he looked to Uncle Joe when he said it, I could tell he was eager to get back to the house and spend the afternoon with his dad.

That evening Clementine declared bankruptcy, Alex was forced to re-mortgage most of his properties and Mr Jones and I maintained our stalemate while Uncle Joe quietly accumulated thousands with his growing empire. I tried to rein in my combative edge, but as usual the second those dice began to roll, my ruthless alter ego came out to play.

'You should have been a businesswoman,' Mr Jones commented after a particularly brutal property negotiation.

'Stop trying to distract me,' I growled, counting my banknotes.

The next night, Alex was forced to admit defeat when he landed on one of Uncle Joe's hotels.

'I'll take an IOU,' Uncle Joe offered, looking troubled.

But Alex only laughed. 'I think I'll enjoy watching more than playing.'

'It's even better than a really vicious slasher film,' Clementine agreed, passing her nephew the bowl of popcorn. 'Only with no blood.'

'So far,' Aiden pointed out.

I'd been surprised that Aiden and Clementine, both out of the game, had stuck around, but they seemed rapt. I knew they'd taken bets on who would win, and that Clementine was in my corner while Aiden was backing Mr Jones.

In the end, they both lost.

On the fourth and last night of Mr Jones's and Alex's visit, a particularly ill-fated dice roll saw me land on Uncle Joe's most expensive property.

'No!' I cried, immediately scrambling to sell my hotels and houses. But it wasn't enough. I'd lost. It took all of my willpower not to throw the board across the room and storm out. Instead, I rose calmly from the table and told them I'd be back in a few minutes. By the time I returned to the kitchen, I was able to laugh at myself again.

Aiden shook his head as I sat back down. 'That was disappointing.'

'Very disappointing,' Clementine agreed. 'We were all ready to witness the incident of Easter 2018.'

'You might still,' Alex noted, nodding to his father. Mr Jones was hanging on by a few meagre properties and, to my joy, was out of the game the next round. But he didn't seem to mind crowning Uncle Joe the champion. He just seemed pleased to have defeated me. Charming.

'Oh, have I won?' Uncle Joe asked, genuinely surprised.

It was still early in the evening, so Aiden and Alex went to play on the Xbox, while the rest of us stayed in the kitchen.

'How has Alex been in the archives this week?' Mr Jones asked, and it took me a moment to realise he was talking to me.

'He's been great,' I enthused, glad that I didn't have to lie. 'He's such a hard worker. And it's been lovely having him around.'

'He is a pretty sweet kid,' Clementine agreed. 'And you know I don't say that lightly.'

'Do you not like children?' I asked, surprised.

'I understand that we need them to continue our species,' she granted, 'and they're useful to have around when you're old and falling apart, because who else is going to look after you? But pregnancy? Childbirth? I honestly don't know how you did it, Ellie.'

'I don't have children,' I reminded her.

'Well, you did—'

Mr Jones growled Clementine's name in warning and she clamped her hand over her mouth.

Realisation slowly dawned on me. 'You know about Izzy?' I asked, confused. So few people knew. Not because I was ashamed of it, but because I saw no reason to broadcast it. How could they have found out? Had they talked to a close member of my family? Or had they been digging through my confidential medical records? They were the only two ways I could think of, and I wouldn't put either past Mr Jones. Unless . . .

'I'm sorry,' Clementine was saying, looking miserable. 'I forgot that it wasn't, you know, common knowledge.'

'It isn't,' I replied. 'I don't mind you knowing about it, but how *do* you know?'

Clementine looked to her brother and he sighed, clearly annoyed. 'Come with me and I'll show you.'

He led me down into the archives, which were as still and silent as usual. We didn't speak as we walked, but I was too preoccupied to worry about it being awkward.

Mr Jones stopped at *2011* and scanned the top shelf. He pulled out a scroll and opened it to check, nodding. 'We used it as one of your references.'

He passed it to me and I immediately recognised my handwriting. Trying to ignore Mr Jones's eyes on me, I read.

Dear Father Christmas,

I know it's still a while until Christmas and I'm too old to be writing to you, let alone believe in you, but this is an 'explore every avenue' situation. I hope it doesn't offend you that I've also prayed to several different deities for this. I don't mind who hears me, I just hope someone does. You see, my brother and his husband are desperate for a baby, and I want so much to help them because they'll be fantastic dads. I've offered to be a surrogate, but the first round of IVF didn't work and we can only afford one more. So please, please, please can you throw a

*little magic my way and let it work this time? I'll be
eternally grateful. Wishing you a (very early) Merry
Christmas.*

Love from Ellie

When I looked up from the letter I so vividly remembered writing, Mr Jones averted his gaze. 'It made the
shortlist,' he said quietly.

I had no words. This letter was meant to explain how
Clementine and Mr Jones knew I'd given birth to Izzy,
but it only amplified the mystery. How had it found its
way here? I certainly hadn't posted it; I'd followed the
old custom of placing it in the hearth. At that point I'd
moved back in with Mum after university and our house
didn't have an open fire, so I'd stuffed it behind the electric one. I hadn't told anybody about it, and it had been
left behind when my mum had sold the house.

'How . . .?'

Mr Jones gave me a level look. 'I'm a lawyer and even
I don't ask how anymore.'

I read my letter again. 'Okay,' I finally said, re-rolling
it and passing it back to him. 'I won't ask either.'

Chapter Twelve

I contemplated the bauble for long moments. It was shiny, bright and gaudy; a red-nosed reindeer crafted in sequins. Perfect for Christmas, and Izzy would love it. It was also on the expensive side, but that wasn't why I hesitated. It wasn't just a bauble. It represented something more. To buy it would be a tiny act of defiance and I hadn't yet decided if the rebellion was worth it.

It had started forty-eight hours ago, on the morning of my birthday. I'd been conflicted for weeks about whether to mention the date. As much as I hated being the centre of attention, I'd always loved my May birthday. It was the one day a year I had a free pass to do precisely what I wanted – which usually involved spending the majority of the day in bed with books and pastries, before going out for a low-key meal with friends. Toby, Mike and Izzy would usually make a big fuss of me on the closest Saturday, taking me to the zoo or cinema. I'd pretend I didn't need the fuss but obviously secretly enjoyed it.

But I felt too embarrassed mentioning it to my island family. There was no way to casually drop it into the conversation without implying I expected the spotlight on me.

Of course, with Clementine around, I needn't have worried that it would pass by unacknowledged. In fact, I should have worried about the opposite.

I came into the kitchen on my birthday morning to find it entirely overtaken by banners and balloons. Clementine, Aiden and Uncle Joe were lying in wait for me, wearing paper hats and proffering a colossal candle-topped cinnamon roll. Conducted by Clementine, they launched into 'Happy Birthday to You' while I covered my burning face.

The second the candles were out, Clementine waved an envelope under my nose and insisted I open it. Inside was a printout for a hotel reservation in Edinburgh, dated for that weekend.

'Group road trip!' Clementine beamed. 'I mean that metaphorically of course, as it's mainly boats and planes.'

'You shouldn't have,' I beamed, overwhelmed. 'Thank you.'

'We really should,' Aiden assured me. 'I need some time back in civilisation and this was the perfect excuse. So thank *you*.'

'Are we all going?' I asked.

'Uncle Joe's holding down the fort here,' Clementine said, smiling at her uncle. 'But the rest of us are coming. Cole and Alex are based in Edinburgh, so we'll see them too.'

Surprisingly, the thought didn't fill me with dread. My only disappointment was that Toby, Mike and Izzy wouldn't be there.

I shouldn't have underestimated Clementine.

Checking into the hotel the next day, I heard a familiar voice behind me.

'Auntie Ellie!'

Spinning in amazement, I saw my three favourite people rushing into the hotel lobby. By the time I'd registered that they were really there, they'd swept me into a suffocating group hug.

'I've missed you all so much,' I gasped, trying to catch my breath.

Izzy had her arms wrapped tightly around my waist. 'I missed you too.'

'We all did,' Mike said.

Toby lifted his head. 'Are you Clementine?' Clementine, who was standing at the reception desk, nodded. Toby pulled her into the family scrum; she submitted happily. 'You're an angel for organising this.'

Once we'd checked in, Clementine ducked away to meet Mr Jones and Alex. Aiden, who lived in Edinburgh, was staying with his old flatmates and spending the weekend with his own friends and relatives. This left me with Toby, Mike and Izzy. I could easily have spent the entire time in the hotel room, just basking in my family's company. But we were in Scotland's capital city for the first time and my brother knew me all too well.

'Let's see it,' he ordered.

I didn't bother denying it. Happily, I handed over the checklist I'd written when expecting to be exploring Edinburgh alone.

'Item number one,' he read aloud, 'visit Edinburgh Castle. Okay, let's go!'

I'd thought Lerwick was busy after a couple of months on the island. Edinburgh was over fifty times the size and I'd now been in isolation for five months. This time though, I was too busy enjoying my family to let it overwhelm me.

We managed to fit a week's worth of sightseeing into that one day. Toby, in full tourist mode, insisted we cliché every experience: we sipped Irn Bru while watching the bagpipe player on Princes Street, munched on shortbread as we climbed up the Scott Monument and walked the Royal Mile. We went into every single whisky and kilt shop we passed. And that evening we watched the sun set over the city as we sat amid the columns of the National Monument on Calton Hill, feasting on fish and chips. We three adults were shattered, but Izzy had found her second wind.

'Hide and seek?' she suggested hopefully.

'I've got a better idea,' Toby said. 'It's called the sitting game.'

'How do you play?' my niece asked.

'We all sit for a very long time and the person who's best at sitting wins.'

Izzy chewed on her lip, unconvinced. Laughing, I pulled myself to my feet. 'I'll play hide and seek. Do you want to count first or hide?'

'You put us to shame,' Mike scolded, but Toby waved him down.

'Ellie loves being the favourite auntie. Let her earn the accolade.'

'It's true,' I admitted. 'The only reason I put up with the two of you is to see Izzy.'

'Ouch,' Toby said without looking up from his chips. 'You break my heart. Now go entertain my daughter.'

Five minutes later, I crouched behind one of the columns as Izzy counted loudly a few feet away.

'You often find Ms Lancaster in unusual predicaments.' For the first time, my heart didn't drop at the sound of his voice. I looked over my shoulder to see Mr Jones, Clementine and Alex standing below the monument, all three looking up at me in amusement. I put my finger to my lips before signing, 'Very important game of hide and seek.'

'She's here!' Clementine instantly shouted.

I threw the traitor a glare as Izzy whipped round the column. 'Found you!'

'Small world,' Clementine said, as we all headed to the front of the monument, where Toby and Mike were winning at the sitting game. I made the introductions, hesitating at Mr Jones. Even after all this time, I didn't feel comfortable referring to him as Cole, especially as he'd never given me permission to. But that was how he introduced himself when I gestured to him and lamely said nothing.

I turned to Izzy. 'And this is – well, actually, why don't you sign your name? I'll do it with you.' I'd taught her the alphabet a few months before going to the island and we'd practised that afternoon. Shyly she came forward and together we spelled out her name. Alex nodded approvingly.

'So, what do you make of Edinburgh?' Clementine asked, flopping down next to Mike.

'Windy,' Izzy replied. 'And there's a lot of up.'

We all laughed at her assessment. 'It is, and there is,' Mike agreed. 'But it's a beautiful city.'

'It really is,' I smiled. 'Thank you so much for arranging this, Clementine.'

We sat in silence for a moment, then Mike, suddenly formal, turned to Mr Jones. 'So, Cole, what do you do?'

Toby wiggled his eyebrows. 'If you're allowed to talk about it, that is.' I gave him a sharp kick.

Mr Jones glanced at me briefly before answering. 'Primarily, I'm an environmental lawyer.'

That piqued Izzy's interest. 'You save the whales?'

'He's not that kind of environmental lawyer,' I said gently.

'Actually, he is.' Alex's manner was matter-of-fact.

I turned to Mr Jones, both abashed and intrigued. 'You are?'

He gave me a level look and then shifted his focus to Izzy. 'I try to stop people hurting whales.'

Izzy gave a delighted smile. 'So, you save them.'

'I *try* to.' He paused. 'I've been in Japan for the last few weeks, *trying*.'

I couldn't help myself. 'Oh Japan, wow. What's it like?'

'Not particularly respectful towards the Convention on Trade in Endangered Species.'

I frowned. 'There's more to the country than that.'

He cocked an eyebrow. 'Have you been?'

'No,' I admitted grudgingly. 'But I know you shouldn't judge a place based wholly on the illegal actions of a small minority.'

'Just as you shouldn't judge a place based wholly on the pictures in a travel guidebook.'

I felt my cheeks burning as my anger intermingled with embarrassment. I forced myself to hold Mr Jones's cool gaze, and the moment became uncomfortably long as everyone else averted their own eyes.

In the end it was Alex who broke the charged silence.

'Do you want to climb up Arthur's Seat with me and my dad tomorrow?' he suddenly asked, looking directly at me.

With Toby, Mike and Izzy heading back to Manchester first thing, I was tempted. 'Thank you very much for the invite,' I said, genuinely touched. 'But I don't want to intrude on father-son time.'

Alex waved the same dismissive hand I'd seen Clementine use a hundred times before. 'We've had plenty of father-son time. Come.'

I looked to Mr Jones, trying to gauge if I'd be an unwanted third wheel. His expression was guarded but he gave a shrug. 'You can't come to Edinburgh and not climb Arthur's Seat.' I noticed that he hadn't specifically said I was welcome. But it would seem rude to decline Alex's invitation, so I nodded.

'That would be lovely. Are you coming too, Clementine?'

'Get up early on my holiday to hike up a muddy volcano? Tempting. Very tempting. But I'm afraid I have a date with room service and then the jacuzzi.'

Later that evening, with Izzy asleep in the room next door, Toby, Mike and I snuggled into hotel bathrobes and raided the mini-bar. I still wasn't drinking after the

Lerwick incident, so nursed a can of pop while the men cracked open tiny bottles of whisky.

'So you and Cole, huh?' Toby asked, flopping onto the bed.

I frowned at him.

'Don't play all innocent with me, missy.'

'Me and Mr Jones?' I laughed, baffled. 'I thought you knew me better than that. He really isn't my type.'

'Handsome. Serious. Professional. Good dad. Saving the world one whale at a time. He's anyone's type. Hell, if I wasn't married . . .' He looked over to Mike, who was grimacing at the mini-bar price list. 'No offence, Darling. Love you.'

'Love you too,' Mike replied absently, sliding the price list out of sight.

The next morning when I said goodbye to my family on the steps of the hotel, we hugged four times before I reluctantly pointed out that they were going to miss their train.

'Look after them,' I whispered to Izzy during our final embrace.

She squeezed me tightly. 'I always do.'

'And you look after yourself,' Mike said, blowing me a kiss.

'Enjoy your romantic volcano walk with the hunky whale champion.' Toby's wink didn't have quite the same effect with watery eyes.

'There's nothing romantic about it,' I cried, exasperated. 'We're going with his son.'

But it turned out we weren't.

Mr Jones was the only one waiting for me in the car park at the foot of Arthur's Seat. He saw me and, looking displeased, held up his phone.

'Alex just messaged. He's coming down with a cold.'

'Oh. That's a shame.' I stayed where I stood, unsure if we'd go ahead. Mr Jones certainly didn't seem happy to be there, and I would have preferred to walk alone rather than having to make polite conversation. But after replying to Alex, Mr Jones gestured towards the footpath.

'Shall we get started then?'

I nodded and fell into step beside him.

It was a warm and sunny Sunday, so the trails were busy. A steady stream of walkers passed us on their way down. Fortuitously, this meant that Mr Jones and I had to walk in single file, minimising the need for talk – which was just as well, because after five minutes, I was embarrassingly out of breath. I really needed to get more exercise. Mr Jones, of course, showed no signs of tiredness as he strode up the steady incline in front of me.

We reached the peak along with six others, whose accents and voluble awe marked them as American tourists. The summit was marked by a stone monument, obscured behind another crowd of tourists taking selfies. Mr Jones bypassed them and found a quiet spot a few metres away. He sat on a rock close to the edge, leaving enough room for me – but I stayed standing, enjoying the views.

'I won't bite,' Mr Jones eventually said.

Sheepishly I sat beside him and let a moment pass before saying, 'I hope Alex is okay.'

He surprised me by barking a laugh. 'Oh, I'm sure he's absolutely fine.'

'But he said . . .'

'I know what he said. I also know how he thinks. Invite you to come with us and then drop out at the last minute.' He gave me a sideways glance and, seeing my confusion, sighed. 'For an intelligent person, Ms Lancaster, you can be quite obtuse at times. He's trying to set us up.'

My confusion doubled. 'But your wife . . .'

'My *ex*-wife. Alex's mother and I have been separated for three years, divorced for two.'

The revelation shocked me. 'Oh. I'm sorry.'

I wasn't sorry. I felt something very different to sorry: an emotion I'd have to shelve for now and examine later.

'Why would you be sorry?' he asked. 'Andy and I made each other happy for a time. That ended. We can still be friends.'

'That's a very healthy attitude,' I commended. 'I wish I shared it.' I thought of the petty vengeances I'd exacted on Gary and was relieved Mr Jones didn't ask me to elaborate.

'I just wish Alex could stop worrying about me being alone,' he continued, looking out towards the city. 'Trying to set me up with random women because he thinks I'm unhappy.'

When Aiden had shown a blatant lack of attraction to me in Lerwick, I'd been more relieved than offended. But Mr Jones's casual dismissal – 'random women' – stung and I was thrown. Not by his indifference, but my reaction to it. Again, I told myself, *shelve now, examine later.*

'Have you spoken to Alex about it?' I asked gently. For now, I'd just be pleased that he was showing his human side. I sensed it wouldn't last long, so would make the most of it.

'Of course. But he thinks he knows best.'

'It's a good thing that you've raised such a confident and considerate boy,' I pointed out.

He smiled at that. 'I can't take all the credit. Andy's always been a great mum.'

As curious as I was about their marriage and why it had ended, I kept my mouth shut. We sat in what I felt was a companionable silence for a few minutes, before Mr Jones broke it. 'This is where Andy and I decided to get married.'

It was such an intimate thing for him to volunteer that I was convinced I'd heard wrong. But he went on. 'I suppose that's why Alex sent us up here. He thinks it's romantic.'

'It is beautiful,' I said, keeping my tone neutral. 'Did you get down on one knee?'

He laughed. 'Andy would have declared me a misogynist if I'd tried. Besides, our engagement was more of a mutual arrangement. We hadn't graduated, she was pregnant and her family were as old-fashioned as she was progressive.'

'Romantic,' I said wryly, and then instantly worried he'd take offence. But he simply nodded.

'I've never been particularly good at romantic gestures.'

You don't say, was on the tip of my tongue but I swallowed it down. There was, I felt, only so much sass I could get away with. 'I've never been particularly good at receiving them,' I said instead. 'My ex-boyfriend Gary sent me flowers at work for my birthday and I was so embarrassed that I threw them away before any of my colleagues saw.'

'What's so embarrassing about flowers?'

'The flowers were lovely. But the whole public display . . .' I shuddered to get my point across.

He looked at me, amused. 'I'll make a note that if I ever have need to buy you flowers, I should sneak them to you surreptitiously.'

'That would be appreciated,' I laughed.

He must have clocked the unexpected direction our conversation had taken at the same time I did. Suddenly his manner changed. He straightened and looked away just as the blood flooded my cheeks.

'We should head back down,' he declared, standing. 'I'm sure there are things you want to do on your last day here.'

'Yes,' I agreed, glad of the change in topic. I rose and together we headed towards the path. 'There's a Christmas shop I want to visit. It's called Santa's Workshop: Terrestrial Branch. A letter arrived in the archives about it. The owner's really struggling and I thought it would be nice . . .'

Mr Jones stopped so abruptly that I almost walked into him. He turned, his expression grim. 'You read about it in a letter?'

'Yes, it was one of the early ones.'

He was shaking his head. 'You can't go.'

'Why?'

'It's not your job to act on the letters. You catalogue and you shortlist. The rest is up to somebody else.'

I wanted to ask who, but something held me back. 'I wouldn't be *acting* on the letter. I'm only going to buy a bauble. That won't fulfil the owner's wish and save her business.'

'We don't interfere.' His tone was firm, his expression steely. 'If something appears in a letter then it's off-limits.'

I wanted to remind him that while I wasn't on the clock, my shopping habits were none of his concern. But I knew it would be futile. He wasn't going to bend on this, and it seemed silly to fight over something as trivial as a bauble.

Still, it didn't stop me from heading straight to the Christmas shop once we'd coolly parted ways at the foot of Arthur's Seat.

I wasn't surprised business was poor. It was hidden away down a small side street, and the fact it was a warm May day, making the merry Christmas jingles seem incongruous, probably didn't help either. I wasn't surprised to find the shop empty, bar the blonde, middle-aged woman – who I assumed was Cammie – sitting behind the counter. She jumped, startled by my entrance.

'Can I help you?' she asked.

I felt like an intruder. Her letter hadn't been particularly intimate, but I knew, from Mr Jones reading mine, how violating it could feel. It was too late now though. I forced a breezy smile. 'I'm just browsing, thanks.'

'Oh, of course, of course. Take as long as you need. Let me know if there's anything I can help with.'

I perused the bauble section, not yet having decided if I would buy anything. Mr Jones had been so adamant about me not interfering that I was second-guessing myself. But was it really interfering if I bought just one little thing?

More importantly – would Mr Jones ever find out?

In the end it wasn't the bright red-nosed reindeer bauble that persuaded me. It was Cammie's words in her letter – *that's why I'm writing to you, in the hope that you can send some Christmas magic my way. I need this to work* – and knowing that her request wouldn't be shortlisted. One single bauble wouldn't save her business. But it would give her a little bit of happiness.

'I'll take this, please,' I said, holding up the reindeer. Cammie's answering smile was worth the small rebellion.

Chapter Thirteen

The sight of Uncle Joe outside in the fresh air was incongruous: I'd never seen him in natural light, and he looked ten years younger for the sunshine on his face and the wind in his wiry grey hair.

It had been a week since Edinburgh, and we'd brought the nice weather back to the island with us. The warmth had tempted me further afield that Saturday and I'd been following the coast north when, to my surprise, I'd stumbled upon Uncle Joe. He was sitting on a cliff-top bench overlooking the sea.

He seemed lost in thought and, not wanting to disturb, I turned to walk in the opposite direction. But he wasn't alone. Perched either side of him on the bench were Fluffy and Cicero, jarringly out of place in daylight but characteristically vigilant. Within seconds, they'd alerted Uncle Joe to my presence with heralding caws. Noticing me, he looked startled, but by that point we'd been working together for nearly half a year and, with a tentative smile, he patted the space on the bench beside him. Even Fluffy obligingly hopped along the backrest to make room for me.

We sat in comfortable silence for long moments, listening to the crash of the waves below. I realised two things sitting there: firstly, we were probably at the northernmost tip of the island; and secondly, there were wildflowers everywhere. With my limited botanical knowledge, daisies and buttercups were the only two species I could identify, but there were many others, from cushions of delicate pink flowers to odd, feathery tufts of white.

It was Uncle Joe who finally broke the silence. 'My Lorna loved this spot.' He was gazing out across a flawless blue sky, his smile tinged with sadness. 'Nothing north of here but heaven,' she'd say.'

'It's beautiful,' I agreed. 'Is this her bench?'

He ran his fingers over the glossy white wood of the seat and nodded. 'A gift to her. Made it for our tenth wedding anniversary.'

'You made this?'

He chuckled. 'Wasn't always an archivist.'

'And the flowers?' I asked, gesturing to the swaying carpet of colour stretching between us and the cliff edge.

'Planted the seeds for her. She loved wildflowers.' It was so rare for him to volunteer information unprompted that I held my breath, not wanting to spook him. 'Hated to see them cut. Said they belonged with the earth below and sky above.' He was quiet for a minute, then he gave a wry smile. 'Shame it took her two years to admit as much to me. Two years of me courting her with neat bouquets. Hated to hurt my feelings, she said. Just like her. Always putting other people first.'

'I wish I could have met her,' I said quietly.

'You would've liked her. And she'd have liked you.'

Had anyone else said this, I would have brushed it aside as a polite thing to say. But coming from Uncle Joe, it wrapped me in a warmth that had nothing to do with the sunshine.

We lapsed back into silence. After ten minutes, I squeezed his hand before standing up, giving him a smile, and continuing along the coast as it curved south-west.

The path gradually descended as I walked on, and the rocky coastline gave way to a long pebble beach where the waves met land more gently. I regretted not bringing a book; it would have been a lovely spot to sit and while away the afternoon.

It was then that I saw yet another resident of the island: Mr Jones. Or, more accurately, the back of Mr Jones as he walked away from me, a good distance up the beach. I assumed it was him because of the dark hair, height and the simple fact that there was nobody else it could be. A black shape was hovering close to his head and another was perched on his shoulder. The ravens had clearly forsaken Uncle Joe – temporarily at least.

I was surprised to see him. Clementine hadn't mentioned his visit. And it was strange to find him here, at the point of the island probably furthest from the dock. He seemed to be walking quickly, with purpose, rather than a leisurely stroll.

I didn't even consider not following him. I wasn't being clandestine: I'd announce my presence once I caught up with him. My pace was slightly slower than his, but if he turned and saw me, I'd wave – there wasn't anything to hide behind anyway.

After about a mile, he veered away from the sea towards the cliffs. And then suddenly he disappeared. Frowning, I scanned the beach ahead, but saw no sign of either man or birds. I broke into a jog, too curious to let it go.

It was only when I was much closer that I saw the cave in the rock face. It wasn't large, but sufficient for Mr Jones to have squeezed into. I hesitated at its threshold. Had he noticed me following and slipped inside to hide? Or was this his intended destination?

I couldn't see how deep it went, so I pulled out my phone and wasted three minutes trying to figure out how to turn the torch on before discovering it was actually a passageway, just wide and tall enough to admit one person. The surprisingly smooth ground ran level for a few feet and then began declining. Knowing full well it was a stupid thing to do – I'd watched enough horror films by now, courtesy of Clementine – I shone the light in front of me and began the descent. I stopped every few steps but there were no sounds bar the muted waves behind me and my hammering heart.

I'm not scared, I told myself.

You bloody well should be, myself retorted.

I was *willingly* walking down a narrow subterranean passageway with nothing but my phone for light. Nobody knew I was there. I had no idea where it led. Any number of things could go wrong, from cave-ins and sudden drops to cannibalistic mole-people. If I were watching myself in a film, I'd be shaking my head in despair and saying she deserves to be eaten.

But the island held so many secrets; so many mysteries I'd accepted as unsolvable. I wanted to unravel just one. And if Mr Jones had come here, it must lead somewhere.

And it did.

Ahead of me was a bright archway – bright enough that as I drew closer, I could turn off the torch. I approached cautiously in case Mr Jones was just beyond the exit, and peered rather than stepped out of the passageway. I don't know what I was expecting but it certainly wasn't what I encountered.

The vast cavern stretched a good few hundred feet up, forming a craggy dome that opened to the blue sky above. In front of me was a wide circular space, just unsymmetrical enough to be natural. The floor itself was smooth, with an almost polished finish – what I could see of it anyway. Because the ground was covered in paper. *A lot* of paper. White sheets blanketed nearly every inch, laid out like feathers on a bird's wing. Even more bizarrely, several gardening rakes, rusty with age, were propped against the cavern's rocky walls.

Scanning the area, I saw no sign of Mr Jones. A slightly raised path, clear of paper, ran around the edge of the cavern to a similar looking passageway on the opposite side. He must have gone that way. Reassured that I was alone, I knelt to study the papers closest to me, but they were blank. I didn't touch them: I had no idea what I'd walked into and didn't want to break a taboo – *or unleash a curse*, I thought, not entirely in jest.

I was baffled. Anywhere else in the world, I'd assume it was some obscure art installation. But here, in an underground cavern on an island in the North Sea with a population of four (six including the ravens)?

I reached the other passageway. Having already risked the cannibalistic mole-people, it seemed silly to turn back now so I ploughed on – and walked straight into what I recognised as Uncle Joe's trolley. There were no scrolls on it and no sign, of course, of Uncle Joe. I shifted it to one side and sidled past, wondering if Mr Jones, wherever he was, would hear.

The path branched off, giving me three options, but I only hesitated for a moment. The middle passage was illuminated by old-style electric lighting. The other two stretched into darkness. Even for me, it was an easy decision. I followed the lit passage upwards for about five minutes, passing other darkened tunnels, and seeing and hearing nothing to indicate that Mr Jones was nearby.

And then, suddenly, I stepped into the office. Bizarrely, given that I'd spent most days there for the past five months, I didn't recognise it at first. But there was my desk and my laptop and the jumper I'd left hanging over the back of my chair on Friday. I'd just never entered the room from this angle before and everything felt backwards. I realised I'd come from the prohibited passageway only Uncle Joe was allowed down.

* * *

Walking into the kitchen that evening, I expected to find Mr Jones at the table. But it was the usual trio and nobody else.

'Is your brother not joining us?' I asked Clementine as Aiden and I set the table.

She looked confused. 'My brother? I don't think even my cooking is worth the trek from Edinburgh.'

'But isn't he here?'

'Not that I'm aware of. In fact, I'm fairly sure he's in Japan for that case he's working on.' Clementine placed a steaming vat of stew in the centre of the table and gave me a suggestive wink. 'Thinking about Cole a little too much, are we?'

I was too confused to be embarrassed. Granted, I'd not seen his face, but who else could it have been?

'I thought I saw someone,' I explained, filling up the water jug. 'Down on the beach. He went into a cave.' I glanced at Uncle Joe, wondering if he'd guess where I was referring to. I desperately wanted to ask about the paper, but didn't want to admit I'd unwittingly found myself in the out-of-bounds passageway, so kept it vague. 'It led into a tunnel.'

Uncle Joe's expression gave nothing away. He seemed more focused on his food than me, and I wasn't sure he was even listening.

'The island's riddled with tunnels,' Clementine said. 'But I don't know who you saw. Are you sure it wasn't a seal?'

I was beginning to doubt myself now. Maybe my mind *had* been playing tricks on me. Tearing off a chunk of bread and dipping it into the stew, I shrugged.

Thankfully, Aiden began talking about the algorithms for the *Psychology of Cake* cookbook. I let the conversation distract me, and by the time Clementine served up miniature sticky toffee tarts with a side of personality quiz, I'd convinced myself that I hadn't seen anyone on the beach.

But that evening, instead of letting Aiden and me wash the dishes, Clementine announced she and Uncle Joe would do it. I hung around outside the closed door just long enough to hear Clementine ask, 'You don't think it was . . .?'

And Uncle Joe, surprisingly firm, respond, 'No.'

Not who? Yet another mystery to add to the pile. As for the question of the paper-filled cavern . . . I had to trust that its answer would come in its own time.

* * *

'I've seen him too.'

The following morning, Uncle Joe and I had been working in the office for about an hour, with Aiden up in the house on his laptop, when Uncle Joe suddenly broke the silence.

I didn't need to ask what he was talking about, although I was surprised he'd brought it up. I didn't think he'd been paying attention the previous evening.

I looked up from the German letter I was translating.

He was studying the items on his desk, touching each one lightly – a sign, I now recognised, that he was nervous. 'No,' he said, his fingers brushing his neat row of pencils. 'It wasn't Cole.'

'Who was it?'

Uncle Joe said nothing for a moment as he contemplated a pencil sharpener. 'I saw him first when I was nine years old,' he began quietly. 'December. Heavy snow. I'd gone out for more firewood. Saw him in the distance, Bill and Ben circling around him. Thought it was my father at first but then saw my father in the window of the house.' He began straightening the papers in front of him. 'Seen him a few more times over the years. Saw him when I was twenty, right here in this room. Looking through the scrolls. Disappeared when I turned the lights on.'

I felt foolish asking, but it needed to be asked. 'Like . . . a ghost?'

Uncle Joe looked even more uncomfortable. 'Don't know about ghosts. But he did disappear. Told my granny about it and she nodded like she knew him. Said she'd seen him too when she was a wee lassie. Called him Pete.'

'But who – what – is he?'

He shook his head. 'Don't know. Maybe an ancestor. The first one of our family to work here.' He gestured to the scroll-filled room around us. 'First one of us who was here to help.'

'To help?' My tone was heavy with the burning need for confirmation. 'To help who? With what?'

When Uncle Joe finally looked up from his desk, his expression said enough. It told me that I already knew.

Chapter Fourteen

Father Christmas was in the kitchen, tucking into a buttered crumpet.

He was exactly as you'd expect: white beard, rotund belly, jolly smile. True, he wasn't wearing a fur-trimmed Santa suit and hat, but his dressing gown was bright red. And there was a definite twinkle in his eye when I walked into the kitchen and stopped abruptly.

I may have been half asleep – it *was* early on a Saturday morning – but I was certain it wasn't a dream.

'Phew, I thought you were my wife,' he said, brushing crumbs from his beard. 'If she happens to ask, I was eating an apple.'

His accent was Scottish. This surprised me. I'd never thought of Father Christmas having an accent.

I watched him throw a surreptitious glance to the doorway behind me and sneak another crumpet under the grill. What should I say? That it was an honour to meet him? Should I thank him for his service? Or should I aim for poise, and casually introduce myself as if I didn't know who he was?

He seemed oblivious to my dilemma. Once the crumpet was toasting, he wiped his hand on his dressing gown and held it out to me with a broad smile. 'You must be short form of Roosevelt, Dashwood and Powell. Such a pleasure to meet you.'

Still too shocked to be perplexed by what he'd said, I lifted my hand to his; he didn't shake it, but bowed low and kissed it instead.

'Might I interest milady in some bread debris for a domesticated animal?' He gestured to the crumpets.

'I . . . er, no. Thank you.'

Maybe I was dreaming. Maybe all these months on the island had taken their toll on my sanity. Or maybe, just maybe . . .

While he bent down to check on his crumpet, I backed out of the room – and ran straight into Clementine.

'Had breakfast already?' she asked.

'I don't know how to say this,' I muttered, dazed. 'But . . . I think Father Christmas is in the kitchen.'

Clementine raised an eyebrow. 'Father Christmas?' And then, a grin breaking across her face, she whizzed past me with a high-pitched 'Dad!' and flung herself at him.

With a roar of delight, he wrapped her in a bear hug that pulled her a good foot off the floor.

Did that mean that Clementine and Mr Jones were the children of . . . ? I couldn't finish the thought. It was too ludicrous.

And yet . . . it made a peculiar kind of sense.

Clementine – fortunately – put me to rights before I shared my theory.

'Ellie, I can assure you that Father Christmas is not in the kitchen,' she called out to me, a laugh tickling her voice. 'Not even Saint Nick could eat *six* crumpets before the rest of us come down for breakfast. Only my dad has that superhuman ability. But that's the *only* superhuman ability my *entirely human* dad possesses.'

Oh.

It was, considering everything, an honest mistake to make.

'What's this about Father Christmas?' her father asked as I traipsed back into the room, abashed. But Clementine gave me a wink and talked over him.

'Ellie, Clyde. Clyde, Ellie.'

'I've already had the honour of meeting the lovely Lady Neither Roosevelt nor Rigby,' the man – Clyde – said with a flamboyant bow, before turning to rummage through the fridge.

Clementine shook her head at me in apparent despair. 'He's a cryptic crossword compiler who refuses to retire. You'll get used to him talking in riddles, but you'll only understand half of what he says.'

So, I wasn't entirely losing my mind then. I gave an embarrassed smile and came further into the room. 'Sorry I didn't say much before. I was just – surprised to see you.'

'No need to apologise, my dear,' he assured me, emerging from the fridge triumphantly holding up a jar of jam. 'Is this blackberry? Of course you were surprised. We didn't tell anyone we were coming.'

'Where's Mum? And does she know you're raiding the kitchen?'

'Getting the others sorted.' He took a spoonful of jam. 'And no.'

I wondered who these 'others' were and whether Mr Jones was among them. It would make a refreshing change if I could be prepared before meeting him again – not stuck in a swamp, or lying on the floor with my legs in the air, or hiding from my niece behind a gothic pillar.

The kitchen door opened again and a woman, probably in her late fifties, entered. She had dark hair, slightly touched by silver and elegantly coiffed, the same brown eyes as Mr Jones and the same wide, thin lips as Clementine. I knew before she introduced herself that she was their mother.

'You must be Ellie. It's nice to meet you. I'm Alison,' she said, shaking my hand briskly. Her accent was English, probably southern.

Alex was just behind her, followed by Mr Jones. When his dark eyes met mine he gave the briefest of nods, but there was some warmth in his tone when he said, 'Ms Lancaster.'

I smiled shyly and moved back to let him pass, just as Aiden joined us.

The kitchen was big, but felt crowded, so I wasn't surprised when Uncle Joe appeared for a few seconds, took in the scene, and hastily retreated. Clementine and Clyde exchanged knowing smiles.

'So,' Clementine asked, 'much as I love seeing you all, is there a reason for your visit?'

Her mother smiled, 'It's the summer solstice this week. What better reason?'

Clementine gave a gleeful shriek. 'We've not thrown the summer solstice party for years.'

'We thought it was time to remedy that,' Alison said simply.

'Is it traditional to celebrate the summer solstice here then?' I asked, intrigued.

'We focus so much on midwinter on the island, we like to redress the balance. Plus, this marks the start of the busy season,' Alison explained.

Once breakfast had been eaten and the dishes washed, I turned to Clementine expectantly. 'What should I be doing for the solstice?'

She waved a hand. 'Just enjoy it! It's officially a three-day holiday, so no work. And on the third evening, we'll have a party!'

As much as I loved the archives, a break sounded wonderful. Feeling like a teenager whose school has unexpectedly closed for the day, I giddily grabbed a handful of books and snacks, and headed outside to replenish my dwindling vitamin D supplies.

I'd recently discovered an ideal reading spot just east of the pier. A grassy valley that dipped down to the coastline; it was high enough to provide a perfect view of the sea but protected enough on both sides to be sheltered from the wind. I'd just perched myself at the foot of my usual birch and begun reading the first page of a book about a woman walking the Camino de Santiago, a pilgrimage route to the shrine of Saint James in Galicia, Spain, when a shadow fell across me.

I looked up to see Mr Jones, dressed in hiking boots and a fleece, and carrying a briefcase.

'I'm afraid this particular tree is reserved,' he said.

A few months ago, I probably would have apologised and vacated the spot. But I knew him better now and was more confident distinguishing between his sober and droll tones.

'I didn't see a sign,' I retorted.

He raised an eyebrow. 'I didn't think there'd be much competition for a valley I've had exclusive use of all my life.'

'A forgivable oversight,' I assured him. He allowed himself a smile. 'So, I'm not the only one who thinks this is the best spot on the island?'

'Not the only nor the first. I'd come here as a boy to get away from my annoying twin sister.'

'I can imagine that,' I laughed, then nodded to the briefcase. 'Would you bring legal documents to read then too?'

He glanced down as if he'd forgotten he was carrying it. 'Back then it was adventure books.'

'The best kind,' I grinned, holding up my reading material.

He read the title. 'Any good?'

'Ask me again in fifty pages.'

'I will.' He stayed where he was for what felt like a long moment, and I realised with surprise that he was waiting for an invitation. I was also surprised I didn't mind issuing one.

'You know, I think this valley just might be big enough for the two of us.'

He smiled then, in a way that made his chocolate brown eyes seem lighter. 'I'm willing to test that theory if you are.' His tone turned serious. 'But I understand if you'd prefer the solitude.'

'Not at all,' I said, a little too quickly.

He sat a polite distance away from me, amidst the long grass and wildflowers. He looked comfortable there, even allowing his usually poker-straight back to relax a little. Only the briefcase seemed out of place.

I'd been reading in a silence punctuated only by the sound of the wind and the turning of pages for about an hour, when Mr Jones's voice drifted over to me.

'Read your fifty pages yet?'

I smiled without looking up. 'Forty-two.'

He sniffed in a way that communicated disapproval of my reading pace but said nothing. My smile widened. Eight pages later, I looked over to him. He was busy highlighting a passage in a document but seemed to sense I'd stopped reading.

'And your assessment?' he asked.

'Enjoyable so far. The writer has a real talent for description. I feel like I've been there.'

'Haven't you?'

'I've never been to Spain, although I'd love to do the pilgrimage one day.'

'Why not today?' His tone was light but there was a definite challenge in the question. Suddenly I was reminded of the artist I'd met in Lerwick, who'd, seemingly seriously, invited me to travel to the Faroe Islands with him. I wondered if he'd gone himself in the end.

'A minor detail of two thousand miles between here and there,' I replied to Mr Jones, refusing to rise to the bait. 'Have *you* walked it?'

'I was there a few years ago when the local authorities were assessing the environmental impact of the pilgrimage.'

Of course. 'What was it like?'

'I didn't see much of it. I was working.'

I didn't want to be drawn into another argument, so stopped myself from asking how he could visit such beautiful places without *seeing* them. I knew he'd retaliate by pointing out my hypocrisy. How could I read about such beautiful places but never visit them?

'Maybe you'd like to borrow my book?' I offered instead.

I could tell he was about to instinctively reject my offer, but he reconsidered. 'It's been a long time since I read something other than treatises and reports.'

I set the book down between us. 'It's there if you want to take a break from work. I won't read any more of it today.'

'Why not?'

'I ration my English reading,' I admitted, picking up a Mandarin book on the history of Beijing's Forbidden City.

'Of course you do. And I'm the one who should take a break from work?'

Giving an accepting shrug, I settled down to read. After a few minutes I heard movement and, out of the corner of my eye, saw Mr Jones reaching for the book. Like somebody trying not to startle a deer, I stayed very still. After a few minutes more, I glanced up to see him leaning against the trunk of another tree, engrossed in the Camino de Santiago. Feeling smug, I returned to Beijing.

The day flowed on in a peaceful haze of sunshine and literature. At one point, Mr Jones peeled a tangerine and, without saying anything, passed me half. An hour later, I returned the favour – but it was only when Mr Jones closed the book and handed it back to me that we finally spoke.

'You finished it?' I asked, surprised. How long had we been reading? The sun was still high, but it was midsummer, and it wouldn't be setting until late.

'The author uses ten words where one would do,' he concluded, 'but maybe that's how she makes you feel as if you're there. I enjoyed it.' He looked to the papers that had sat untouched by his briefcase all afternoon, and I could tell he was weighing up whether or not it had been a worthwhile distraction.

'I'm glad you enjoyed it,' I said, packing away my belongings. 'We should head back before they send out a search party for us.'

'Indeed, Ms Lancaster.'

'Do you think maybe it's time you called me Ellie?'

The corners of his lips twitched. 'Maybe. But only if you call me Cole.'

'It's a deal. Cole.' His name felt foreign on my tongue, but I was glad we were finally past the formality of Mr and Ms. We'd known each other over six months, after all.

* * *

The next day, we found ourselves back in the valley, sharing the odd word and snack, but otherwise reading in silence. I'd brought one of my favourite books with me – an anthology of Māori myths re-worked into modern stories by Māori writers – in the hope that Cole would turn up. I placed it between us with a pointed, 'If you're interested in whales . . .'

Cole had also come prepared. He swapped my book for *The Hitchhiker's Guide to the Galaxy*. 'One of my favourites as a kid.'

'I'm not really into sci-fi,' I admitted, picking it up doubtfully.

'But you are into travel writing,' he pointed out. 'Think of it as a . . . cosmic travel guide.'

And that's exactly what it was. I loved every page of it, laughing out loud at some sections, and justifying it as a foreign-language book because of the myriad made-up terms it contained. Cole seemed equally engrossed in the book I'd brought, not once opening his briefcase.

The next day followed the same pattern, only this time Cole was waiting outside the house for me after breakfast and we walked to the valley together.

'What have you brought me today?' he asked, as we settled down beneath our respective trees. I noticed he hadn't even bothered to bring his briefcase.

Grinning, I pulled out the funniest book in my collection: a comedic take on Homer's *The Odyssey* from the perspective of a rubber duck. Toby and Mike had bought it as a going-away present when I'd come to work for Jones Associates. Their handwritten inscription told me to have a 'quacking adventure'.

To my surprise and delight, the book Cole offered in exchange was entitled *Pioneering Penwomen: A history of female travel writers*.

'I saw it in a charity shop a few weeks ago and thought of you,' was all he said, handing it over.

I held it delicately, like the precious treasure it was.

That afternoon as we walked back up to the house, I noticed movement in the distance. Clementine, Clyde and Alex were en route from the pier to one of the beaches, lugging two barrels between them.

'Ah,' Cole said. 'That means Willum's here, with refreshments and other items Clementine requested. He and his wife will stay and join the party.'

'Should I be worried?' I asked, only half joking.

He paused. 'My mother vetoed most of Clementine's suggestions.'

'That doesn't entirely reassure me.'

'It's just one of my sister's parties.'

I cast him a dark look. 'That reassures me even less.'

When I went to my room, I found a garland of wildflowers lying outside the door, perched on top of a folded white garment. Beside them was a handwritten note: *Wear these or suffer my wrath*. There was no doubting who'd written it. Across the corridor a similar bundle awaited Aiden.

With trepidation I unfurled the garment. It was a simple linen dress, white, knee-length and sleeveless. More revealing than my usual outfits, I slipped it on – partly because I didn't want to cross Clementine; partly because

I felt I should enter into the spirit of the occasion, but also because my wardrobe was otherwise limited to smart-casual, or oversized woolly jumpers. Positioning the garland on my head, I braved the mirror.

My gaze instantly homed in on the flaws. The tan lines on my shoulders from my weekend ramblings. My pasty legs. My straw-coloured hair, halfway down my back, in desperate need of a trim. My waist, perceptibly thicker after six months of Clementine's cooking.

Shrugging on a bulky cardigan, I peeped sheepishly round the kitchen door before entering. To my relief, it seemed Clementine had dictated everyone else's ensembles as well, although I noted with envy that the older women's – Alison and Mary, Willum's wife, who had introduced herself to me earlier, pulling me into a hug – dresses were ankle-length. The men wore loose linen shirts and trousers. Clyde had daisies in his beard; Alex wore a garland around his neck. Even Mr Jones – Cole, I reminded myself – had followed the dress code, albeit minus the flowers, and I was taken aback by how relaxed he looked – although his hair and beard were cut too neatly for him to seem entirely bohemian.

He looked at me from the other side of the kitchen table, his expression unreadable. I touched the garland self-consciously and felt myself blush.

'Oh, you look lovely,' Mary gushed.

'The Uffizi would place your portrait between a Seignac and a Botticelli,' Clyde declared.

'I don't think the cardigan is regulation,' Cole said simply.

I hadn't expected a more enthusiastic reaction from him. But expectation and hope were two different things.

Alex rolled his eyes. 'Believe it or not, that's my dad's way of saying you look hot.'

I avoided making eye contact with Cole as I said, 'I highly doubt that. But thank you, Alex. You look very festive.'

'I wear this on the condition that *nobody* takes *any* photos.' Alex punctuated each word with a strict glare at each person in the room.

'Too late!' There was the click of a phone camera as Aiden jumped into the room. I was pleased to see he was fully kitted out, too, with the flowers hanging around his neck.

He flopped down onto a chair. 'Where's Clementine?' He didn't ask about Uncle Joe, the only other person absent. We all knew he'd be holed up in the archives until the house emptied again.

'I'm here!' Clementine trilled. She looked at me. 'And don't think I haven't noticed the contraband cardigan, missy.'

I pretended I'd not heard as we formed a procession down to the beach, where a bonfire was set up. It wasn't yet lit, thankfully – it was still warm out, and I was too self-conscious to remove my cardigan.

'Be on your guard,' Aiden muttered darkly to me. 'This is where they burn the outsiders.'

Alex chuckled as he passed. 'Like lambs to the slaughter . . .'

Along with the bonfire was a barbecue, picnic blankets, various musical instruments and an inordinate number of barrels.

'Simmer Dim,' Mary told me, proffering a glass of golden-coloured ale. 'It means summer twilight. Brewed at Valhalla, the UK's most northerly brewery. My cousin works there,' she added with a wink, 'so I get a discount.'

Accepting the glass with a smile, I folded myself down onto one of the blankets. Alison and Alex began playing a card game, which Aiden joined. Clyde and Cole stood by the barbecue, deep in conversation. Willum and Clementine sat together, providing background music with a couple of guitars while people called out requests. Mary, who'd been passing out drinks, came to join me.

'Room on the blanket for one more?'

'Of course.' I shifted to make more space for her.

'Enjoying the party so far?'

'It's definitely a novel experience.' Worrying that could be taken as a negative, I added, 'I'm loving it.'

Mary kicked off her sandals and buried her toes in the sand. 'Me too! I don't normally have permission to come to the island. You should consider yourself lucky, being here every day.'

'I am lucky,' I agreed, intrigued by what she'd said. 'But do you really need permission to come here? Willum travels over a lot; couldn't you come with him?'

'Willum rarely steps off the *Valkyrie* when he's here,' she pointed out. 'My husband's family have known the Joneses for generations. They trust him, but they're still very . . .' She looked over at Cole and Clyde, considering her words, '. . . protective of their island. And rightly so. It's a magical place.'

I gathered she meant 'magical' in a metaphorical sense. But there was an intense curiosity in her eyes as she turned to survey the land stretching out behind us.

'It certainly is,' I nodded, a little wary. I felt we were skirting a taboo subject, one I'd dropped some time ago.

'Do you know what Osk means?' Mary asked, taking a sip of her ale.

It was the name Willum and Clementine had given the island. *We call it Osk.* I shook my head.

'It's Old Norse for "wish". Sweet, wouldn't you say?'

I was considering this new nugget of knowledge, when Clyde's voice boomed over to us from the barbecue. 'Who's ready for food?'

The evening segued pleasantly into night. At some point Clyde disappeared and returned with Uncle Joe in tow. He looked uneasy but accepted a glass of ale from Clyde, and I gestured for him to sit beside me.

'I'm glad you came,' I said, and it was true. Even though he rarely spoke, I'd felt his absence. His smile said he'd rather be elsewhere, but after a few sips of ale he seemed to relax. Eventually Willum joined us, and soon the two men fell into a quiet conversation of few words and long pauses.

Not long after, Mary began to play the fiddle and Clementine tried to coax people into dancing. Aiden gallantly offered his arm and the pair began a do-si-do, soon joined by Clyde and Alison. I glanced discreetly at Cole, who was sitting with Alex the next blanket over, wondering if he might ask. Perhaps my gaze wasn't very subtle because Mary, sitting beside me, called over to him.

'You cannot refuse to dance, I am sure, when so much beauty is before you.' I recognised the line from *Pride and Prejudice* and was mortified when Mary paused in her fiddling to point the bow at me.

Cole looked across at us. What was that in his expression? Not quite distaste, but there was certainly no enthusiasm.

'Go on Dad, ask her to dance,' Alex prompted, smirking.

His obvious reluctance stung, especially considering how much I'd enjoyed his company over the last few days. I'd *thought* he'd enjoyed mine. I blame the ale for my response. 'He doesn't have to dance with me. I'm just some random woman after all.'

I regretted it instantly and tried to take the edge off with an awkward laugh, but the bitterness was impossible to conceal. I hadn't realised Cole's words had stayed with me but clearly they'd cut deep.

I certainly didn't expect Cole to have remembered his throwaway comment, so his reaction surprised me. He gave me a very direct look and said, 'You're not some random woman, Ellie. I was wrong to have said that. I apologise.' He spoke frankly, with no hint of embarrassment, even with Mary and Alex there. The man was unflappable.

Of course, *I* was blushing furiously. I cleared my throat and looked away. 'Thank you.'

There was an uncomfortable silence, which Mary and Alex broke simultaneously – Mary resuming the fiddle while Alex leapt to his feet, offering himself as a dance partner. Grateful, I grasped his hand and let him pull me to where Clyde was demonstrating the moves to a traditional ceilidh dance he called 'The Dashing White Sergeant'.

'Thank you,' I mouthed to Alex as Clyde ushered us into position.

He shrugged. 'Don't take anything my dad says personally. He has an incurable condition.'

'Oh?'

'It's called being an asshole.' He grinned. 'Fortunately, it's not hereditary.'

I snorted and then tried focusing on Clyde's instructions, all too aware that Cole would be watching us. 'I'm sorry in advance for how bad my dancing is.'

'Well, I can't even hear the music, so I'll be copying you.'

'Then I guess we'll both be terrible.'

I was proved correct, but had a lot of fun in the process. Clyde and Alison were good, but the rest of us forgot the formations the second Mary started playing. We consistently went the wrong way, stood on each other's feet, elbowed each other and ended in a tangled, laughing mass on the floor. Then we did it all again, at least ten more times, working our way through Mary and Clyde's repertoire.

The night was a blur of dancing and laughing, interspersed with more food and drink. The sun had set and the North Sea was tranquil beneath a lilac sky by the time the bonfire's flames started to peter out.

'It's time to leap the bonfire,' Clementine announced, gesturing for us to gather.

I turned to Mary. 'Does that involve what I think it involves?'

She hitched up the skirt of her dress in answer. 'It's for luck.'

'I don't know how lucky I'll feel with a burnt backside,' I muttered, but didn't consider abstaining. Even Aiden was rolling up his trouser legs, although he looked a little anxious.

The flames were low now though, the bonfire nearly out. Clementine went first, whooping as she leapt. I held my breath but she made it look easy. Others followed – Willum and Mary hand-in-hand, Alex with a roar. Cole, characteristically composed, looked like he was completing a minor business transaction. And then they were all shouting my name, urging me on.

I gripped my dress tightly, glad for the first time that it was so short. Then I ran across the sand and leapt, letting out an involuntary shriek of laughter as I cleared the flames and landed with a stumble. A firm hand gripped my arm, steadying me before quickly pulling away. Still laughing, I looked up to see Cole and instantly sobered. It may have been the fire reflected in his eyes, but I'd never seen him look so intense.

'Thanks,' I muttered, a little flustered. 'It wasn't the graceful landing I'd hoped for.'

The look he gave me was incredulous. 'You really have *no* idea, do you?'

He stared at me for what felt like a very long moment, and suddenly the space between us felt immense. My arm was hot where he'd clasped it briefly. Too briefly. Why hadn't his fingers lingered just a little longer? The fleeting touch implied indifference, and yet . . . There was something in his expression, in the way he gazed down at me, direct but hesitant at the same time, that told me he wanted to bridge the distance as much as I did.

Whether it was the magic of the evening, the crackle of the bonfire, the beauty of the beach or too much ale, I don't know, but I found the courage to take a step closer. Close enough that with one more step we would be touching. I raised my face to his, an invitation, a challenge, for him to make that final move. And then . . .

'Bollocks!'

Aiden's voice pierced the moment, unceremoniously shattering it. I jumped guiltily back like a thief caught red-handed and spun just in time to see Aiden running into the sea, the bottom of his trousers on fire.

Chapter Fifteen

The cloud wasn't like the others. They were wispy things, but this was dark, dense and moving far faster than – and in the opposite direction to – the gentle breeze. Speeding towards the island, it looked like a cloud on a mission. I blinked, rubbed my eyes, checked again, but it was still there.

I was on my way back to the house after my morning walk and headed straight for the kitchen. Everyone bar the usual inhabitants had already left, but Clementine, Aiden and Uncle Joe were there, munching on their breakfasts.

'You see that, right?' I pointed out of the window.

The three of them followed my finger and Clementine gave a squeal halfway between excited and anxious. 'The first flurry!' I'd noticed her looking out of the window frequently over the last few weeks, as if hoping for something. I hadn't asked, knowing Clementine had no problems sharing when she wanted to. Perhaps this was what she'd been waiting for?

'Snow in August?' After the changeable weather of the summer so far, I shouldn't have been sceptical.

'Not that kind of flurry. The *wishfall*.' Clementine turned to Uncle Joe, her expression uncharacteristically fretful. 'Is the printer full?'

A few weeks before, Uncle Joe had appeared in the office with a large stack of plain paper, saying enigmatically, 'Printer needs filling.' A bemused Aiden had pointed out, once Uncle Joe had disappeared along the forbidden passageway, that we didn't have a printer.

Uncle Joe nodded and set down the piece of toast he'd been eating. 'Best head to the post room.'

'Let's all go,' Clementine said. 'I love the first wishfall. And Ellie and Aiden should see it too. Come on, we don't want to miss it.'

Led by an impatient Clementine, we hurried to our office, Uncle Joe retrieving his trolley en route. Aiden cocked an eyebrow at me as we entered the usually prohibited passage. I still hadn't told anyone about accidentally stumbling across the cavern via a 'back door', but didn't have to fake my look of curiosity: I was still eager for an explanation, and intrigued by the peculiar cloud.

Clementine ushered us into the cavern, which was as I remembered: a vast conical space, its floor blanketed in paper. It opened up to a sky much darker than it should have been. Was it the cloud? It seemed to fill the space above us.

'What the . . .' Aiden began, scanning the paper-filled cavern, but Clementine interrupted him.

'Hush,' she hissed, staring intensely up. She was clearly nervous, and I noticed Uncle Joe was looking a little apprehensive too. 'Any second now,' Clementine whispered. 'Grab a rake everyone.'

Nonplussed, I reached for one of the rusty rakes I'd noticed last time. Clementine and Uncle Joe held theirs at the ready, still watching the cloud above in anxious anticipation.

Aiden, gingerly holding his rake, met my eyes. 'Have they gone mad?' he mouthed.

I'd witnessed a lot of strange things since coming to the island, often accepting them without pushing for explanations. But this time I was thinking the same as Aiden.

'Clementine,' I began, but she dismissed me with a distracted 'shh', her gaze still on the cloud.

And then it started snowing.

The cloud dispelled its load softly, delicately, at odds with its foreboding hue. Snowflakes drifted down through the skylight, fluttering rather than falling. At first, I was too busy watching their descent to notice what happened when they reached the ground. But then I saw that some of the pieces of paper had begun to curl. The snow was landing on the paper – of course, there was nowhere else for it to go – but bizarrely the flakes seemed to settle in the very centre of each piece of paper, one per sheet. Perfectly aligned.

If that seems incredible, what happened next had me doubting my own sanity.

The snow didn't simply melt into the paper. Instead, it seemed to spill out in silver tendrils across the surface. The snaking lines shifted slowly, forming what looked to be words. Words, then sentences. I examined one close to my feet and made out the words '*Cher Père Noël*'. Before I could read more, the paper began to furl. Like a flower at day's end, it curled gently into itself.

It had become one of the scrolls I was so used to seeing in the archives.

'They fell right,' Clementine whispered, the relief in her voice unmistakable. She was speaking more to herself than to the rest of us, but then she turned to Uncle Joe with a grin. 'They fell right!'

Uncle Joe's return smile was a little shaky. 'That they did.'

Without warning, Clementine pulled Aiden and me into a group hug. 'You're clearly doing something right, guys.'

'What do you mean?' I gasped as she squeezed the wind out of me.

'Never mind,' she said, letting go and gesturing back to the snow. 'It's too beautiful not to watch.'

Aiden was shaking his head, looking bewildered. 'What *is* it?'

'The wishfall.'

'And that is . . . ?'

Clementine gave a wry smile. 'The start of the busy season. Now come on,' she ordered, hoisting her rake, 'let's get to work.'

'Work' was the wrong word for the fun we had gathering in the rolled-up scrolls. The incongruous rakes were less incongruous when I realised their purpose: retrieving the scrolls without having to step onto the paper-strewn floor. We collected armfuls at a time and deposited them on the trolley before going back for more. The task quickly turned competitive, and we jostled over scrolls, laughingly knocking each other's rakes out of the way. Even Uncle Joe joined in, smiling as he and Clementine tallied their 'catches'.

'Fifteen, sixteen, seventeen,' he said, expertly raking three in at once.

'Cheat!' Clementine declared.

'Hey, that was mine!' I cried when Aiden hustled a scroll from beneath my rake.

Aiden smirked as he fished it from the floor. '*Was* being the operative word.'

There were, it transpired, several layers of paper, but just as I feared we might run out, the snow began to ease. The last few flakes fell and as the others raked them in, I watched the skylight. The cloud had disappeared now, leaving wisps of white against a blue sky.

'And that, ladies and gentlemen,' Clementine puffed, leaning on her rake, 'was the first wishfall.'

From that moment on, the work was non-stop. Hundreds of letters had arrived that morning and just when we'd finished translating, cataloguing and short-listing them, another black cloud appeared on the horizon. That time only Aiden and I watched the flurry, still mesmerised by the whole process as another few hundred letters were snowflaked into existence.

'I just don't understand,' Aiden admitted, crouching down to examine the transformation from snowflake to letter. 'Is it some kind of invisible ink?'

I'd considered this theory myself but it didn't explain the sudden appearance of a dark cloud, in an otherwise clear sky, or snowflakes that landed in the centre of each piece of paper with perfect precision.

Aiden seemed to be thinking the same as he peered up at the opening above us. 'Some kind of snow machine?' he mumbled, taking several photos of the falling flakes with his phone and zooming in on them, as if looking for some clue.

I found myself less eager to explain the phenomenon. The magic of the island – and I no longer meant that metaphorically – allowed mysteries to remain mysteries. And I had more than enough work archiving wishes to keep my mind occupied. The letters were literally pouring in, and it was still only August.

* * *

August slid towards September, the letters coming thick and fast and the 'printer' needing frequent re-stocking. Translating had become my full-time job, and the others had taken over the archival work. Even Clementine helped out, but we were constantly running behind.

'How on earth did Uncle Joe cope alone all these years?' I asked Clementine as we raked in the latest flurry. The backlog was giving me sleepless nights on top of twelve-hour days.

'He wasn't alone,' she replied, and her expression became suddenly guarded.

'Your aunt Lorna?' I asked, remembering the photo of Uncle Joe on his wedding day. When she nodded, I went to ask another question, but she cut over me.

'My parents too. They'll be here soon and then it'll be all hands on deck,' she said, depositing the last armful of scrolls onto the trolley.

I wanted to ask if Cole would be coming to help but knew the sly smile it would earn me. Even without asking, Clementine threw me a knowing look.

'Sadly, my brother's tied up with work until December. But don't worry, you'll see him before then in Edinburgh.'

She was talking about the trip we had planned for November. Her publishers had teamed up with an Edinburgh bookshop to host a charity 'Evening with Clementine', where guests would sample some of the most popular cakes from *Calorifica* and get a sneak preview of *The Psychology of Cake*. I was assured it would be a festive, glitzy affair, and, despite myself, was looking forward to it. The prospect of seeing Cole again had nothing to do with it – or that's what I told myself.

I didn't know how I felt about sharing the island with Clyde and Alison. It was a relief there'd be more hands in the archives, but I was possessive of my new home and family. Even though Clyde and Alison had far greater claims to both, I was a little worried about their imminent arrival, hoping they wouldn't upset the equilibrium. I'd not spent much time with them at midsummer, but it'd been enough for me to decide that Clyde, with his habit of speaking in riddles, was tiring and Alison intimidating. Their first evening back on the island confirmed this.

'I'm off to the H-I-J-K-L-M-N-O wardrobe,' Clyde declared halfway through dinner, excusing himself from the table briefly. I couldn't decide if he enjoyed being cryptic or was genuinely unaware of it.

But at least he was cheerful, which was more than could be said for Alison. Her lips seemed set in a constant pout of disapproval and, although she rarely said anything negative, her critical gaze spoke volumes. It was normally aimed at Clyde, particularly when he added salt to his food or reached for a second portion. Clementine fell victim to it too, when she casually dropped the f-word in a sentence and when she ate a biscuit she'd dropped on the floor, invoking 'the five-second rule'. Alison was perfectly cordial to me, but I got the impression she was weighing me up, and kept wondering when she'd declare me wanting.

'So, you have an MA in archiving?' she asked me, that first evening.

'In Information and Library Studies,' I replied, feeling like I was being interviewed again.

'A practical humanities qualification,' she said, with a hint of approval. She glanced at her husband. 'Unlike English Literature.'

Clyde winked at me. 'Forgive the immunologist her cynicism. She may not perceive the poetry in the petri dish but it penetrates the soul nonetheless, and evinces the simple fact that whether we look to the pages of a book, the strokes of a painting or the patterns of genetic code, we are all seeking the truths of the world.'

I blinked once, twice, then turned to Alison. 'You're an immunologist?' I asked, latching on to the only part of his speech I'd understood.

'Yes,' she said, dabbing her mouth with a napkin. I waited for more, but none came. Cole was making more and more sense to me. 'So, they've been falling right?' she asked suddenly, turning to Clementine.

Clementine grinned. 'Every single one of them.'

'The wishfalls?' I asked, remembering what Clementine had said about the first one having fallen 'right'. 'Do they normally fall . . . wrong?'

Clementine exchanged a cautious look with her parents before saying, 'Sometimes. But there's no point talking about that because it's all fixed now. I told you bringing in Ellie and Aiden would do the trick,' she added to Alison and Clyde with a triumphant grin.

After that first evening – forcing smiles for Clyde's benefit and second-guessing myself under Alison's scrutiny – I decided two extra pairs of hands in the archives weren't worth the cost. The office, once a quiet, comfortable place to work, was suddenly crowded and noisy, and I felt on edge whenever I was there.

But if my time on the island had taught me anything, it's that first impressions can be misleading. I'd been apprehensive about Clementine and Cole when I'd first met them, about Aiden and Uncle Joe and even about the archives. But now I couldn't imagine life without them. And so I resolved to put aside my misgivings and give my new colleagues a chance.

It helped when I realised nobody else instantly understood Clyde's riddles. I felt less stupid and started to enjoy trying to solve them. I also began to appreciate his boisterous energy and enthusiasm.

Alison, on the other hand, worked quietly, meticulously and tirelessly, her fingers like lightning on the keyboard as she ploughed through piles of letters. At first, I'd been expecting her to take charge, but on her first day in the archives, she'd turned to me and said, 'Tell me what to do.'

It wasn't only Alison's work ethic that made me slowly warm to her. The more time I spent in her company, the more I realised that her disdain was in fact affectionate disparagement, and her disapproval, exasperated amusement. And my time with Cole had taught me that blunt doesn't necessarily mean hostile. When she gave me a one-word answer, it wasn't (necessarily) because she was rude or didn't want to converse. She simply didn't feel the need to elaborate. (It took me a lot less time to realise this with Alison than it had with Cole.)

With two extra bodies in the archives, Clementine could return to her own work, and the evening taste-tests and personality quizzes resumed. Like Uncle Joe, Alison and Clyde were exempt (much to Clyde's chagrin) as Clementine already knew their favourite cakes, but apparently she was also close to identifying mine and Aiden's, which meant *The Psychology of Cake* was nearing completion.

One evening, instead of the usual samples, Clementine placed dishes concealed beneath silver cloches in front of us.

'I've compiled all of my data,' she announced, 'and believe that I've worked out each of your one true cakes. If I'm right, then I'm ready to send off *The Psychology of Cake* to my agent. So be honest.'

With a flourish she lifted the cloches, revealing a slice of cake on each – although, as usual with Clementine, 'cake' was too simple a word. They were works of art. The one in front of Aiden was beautiful in its simplicity: dark brown with spirals of pistachios and gold-sprayed coffee beans and the strong, bitter scent of espresso. Mine was more rustic; triple-layered carrot cake, oozing with frosting and generously sprinkled with coconut shavings. Four pairs of eyes watched in anticipation as Aiden and I picked up our forks and took our first bites.

It was pure bliss.

'Well?' Clementine demanded, impatient.

I shook my head in awe as I savoured my fourth mouthful. 'Clementine, this is amazing.' Fifth mouthful. 'Genuinely the best cake I've *ever tasted*.' Sixth. 'No hyperbole.' Seventh. 'Is that cinnamon in the frosting?'

Clementine grinned. 'Of course. Ellie Lancaster's one true cake wouldn't be complete without cinnamon frosting. Aiden?'

He laid his fork down, sat back and let the tension build as he considered his response. 'Three words,' he finally said, picking up his fork again. 'Better than sex.'

Everyone cheered.

'How did you know that carrot cake's my absolute favourite? And with coconut and cinnamon? I would never have thought of that combination, but it works *so* well,' I said, once I'd scraped the plate clean – not having even *considered* offering to share it.

Clementine tapped the side of her nose. 'That's for me to know and for you to find out – for an RRP of £19.99.'

* * *

Clementine's work may have been nearly finished, but the rest of us were getting busier. Each day seemed to bring another wishfall. Even with help from Alison and Clyde, and then Alex, who was staying for a couple of weeks during the school holidays, the letters were piling up, and I missed more than a couple of meals and film nights trying to catch up. I was determined that every single letter would be properly translated, recorded and archived. Every one of them would have its chance at the shortlist.

One night, hours after the others had left, as I sat hunched over a letter from Seoul, a sandwich suddenly appeared in front of me. I looked up, expecting to see Clementine, but it was Alison, shaking her head in despair.

'You'll burn yourself out if you carry on like this.'

'I know,' I admitted, gratefully taking the sandwich. 'But it—'

'No buts,' she said sharply. 'Do you think this place will fall apart without you?'

I blushed. 'Not fall *apart*, but some of the letters might fall through the cracks if I slack off.'

'Wrong,' Alison sniffed. 'This island and these archives have been here for a long time. A very, very long time.

They survived without you. And *that* is why Clyde and I are taking over while you take a break.'

I knew she was right. Although the piles of scrolls were weighing on me, I realised I'd benefit from one evening off, and probably work better for it.

'Okay,' I sighed, reluctantly pushing away from the desk. 'But I'll be back first thing tomorrow morning.'

'Wrong again. You'll be on your way to the mainland first thing tomorrow morning.'

'I – what?'

Just then Clementine came skipping in, flourishing my backpack – which she'd clearly carried all the way down through the archives just for effect. 'Get packing, girly. It's mini-break time.'

Resistance was futile. No matter how or what I argued, nobody would listen. The Joneses even pulled rank, reminding me they were my employers and I was con-tractually obliged to do as they say. I didn't think going away with Clementine was actually in my job descrip-tion, but remembering how dense the contract had been, I couldn't be sure. So I obediently packed my bag, left an entirely redundant list of instructions for the archives, and let Clementine tow me down to the pier in the early hours of the following morning.

It turned out that Clementine had been invited as a guest speaker at the Ludlow Food Festival. I'd heard of the event, held every September in the castle grounds of a Shropshire market town. I'd never been, but I'd read about it, and knew it was a major date on the culinary calendar.

'Are you sure you want me to come?' I asked as we stood on the pier watching the *Valkyrie* cut through the waves towards us. 'Me, the confectionery philistine?'

'I like to think that eight months of living with me has taught you something,' Clementine sniggered. 'Now you at least know the difference between sponge and pound cake, between frosting and icing, between a scraper and an icing knife.' I said nothing, letting her assume she was right. 'Besides, you don't need to know how to cook to enjoy a food festival. You just need to know how to eat.'

'Well, I am expert at that,' I admitted.

This would be my first time back in England since January. I knew from their letters that Toby, Mike and Izzy were away – rendezvousing with my mum somewhere in the Canary Islands – but I was disappointed to hear Cole wouldn't be there. Though I wouldn't admit how disappointed, not even to myself.

'He has no interest in listening to his sister talk about cakes,' Clementine assured me, giving me a sideways look. 'Why do you ask?'

'No reason.'

It seemed I'd have to settle for a relaxing weekend away from the archives. And I was determined to not spend a moment thinking about those letters piling up without me, or dreading the mountain of translating, transcribing and cataloguing that would greet me on my return. Not a single moment. Nuh-uh.

Of course, I spent *many* moments on the long journey – boat, bus, boat, plane, plane, train – to the West Midlands doing precisely that. But by the time we reached Ludlow, my worry was all spent. It helped that Ludlow was a beautiful riverside town of timber-framed buildings, historic churches and picturesque bridges, and that we were staying in a quaint guest house with a view of the castle and courtyard, filled with festival tents. It helped that the sun was shining, the breeze warm. And it helped there was absolutely nothing I could do about the work I was missing.

Clementine had dinner with her agent to discuss her talk, scheduled for the following morning, and the progress of *The Psychology of Cake*. She invited me but I declined and instead explored the castle grounds and then, when I'd exhausted every corner of every sandstone chapel, every vaulted chamber, every roofless tower, the cornucopia of food stalls. I filled up on free samples but still spent a small fortune, unable to resist the breads, cheeses, pies, jams and chutneys. Laden with enough to feed a small army, I weaved my way through the crowds, more boisterous around the beer tents, out of the gatehouse, and down a quiet street. I was heading for the river – the Teme, according to my guidebook – beneath the castle promontory. I followed a narrow path until I found a quiet spot, where I kicked off my sandals and, dangling my feet into the cool water, ate more than I should while reading the next book in my new favourite series, pilfered from the Joneses' collection: *So Long, and Thanks for All the Fish*.

The next morning, Clementine laughed when I told her I'd be attending her talk.

'Don't be ridiculous,' she cried. 'You get your fill of my talking and baking at home. Go listen to somebody else.'

But I was curious to see her perform to an audience. She would, I guessed, exude confidence and humour – and I wasn't wrong. From the moment she appeared on stage dancing to the 1950s song 'If I Knew You Were Comin' I'd've Baked a Cake', everyone in the audience was laughing. And she kept them laughing for the next hour, with terrible cake puns and hilarious anecdotes of kitchen failures – 'So it turns out your family won't appreciate you trying out sprout-based frosting on Christmas cake – who knew?' – as she spoke of the inspiration behind her baking.

The crowd applauded when she announced she'd be sticking around to sign copies of *Calorifica*. I was amazed at her confidence in front of an audience a hundred strong. I was even more in awe that it never once tipped over into arrogance, even though a long queue quickly formed, most people already clutching a copy of her book. I considered queuing up myself, for the amusement it would give Clementine, but decided she was far too busy. So I began to back out of the tent – and it was then that I heard the voice behind me.

'It's nice to see you again.'

I spun, hoping – but no. It wasn't Cole. Long brown hair, intense green eyes, creased baggy shirt with the sleeves rolled up. I knew him but couldn't think where from, and then it struck me.

'You're the artist from the coffee shop in Lerwick.'

He nodded. 'You remember me.'

'*You* remember *me?*' I asked, letting the surprise show in my voice.

'Of course.'

Flustered, I couldn't think of a reply, but he suggested we talk somewhere less crowded. Once outside, we headed to a cluster of tables, quiet until the beer tents opened.

I slid onto the bench opposite him, buying myself a moment by sipping a juice I'd been carting around all morning, and then finally asked, 'So, what are you doing here?'

'I like food as much as the next starving artist. Unhappy to see me?'

'No, not at all. Just surprised. You're a long way from Lerwick.'

'I don't live in Lerwick.'

'Oh?' I was hoping he'd divulge where he did live, but he changed the subject.

'That was an interesting event. I never realised you could milk an hour's talk and twenty-six puns out of cake-baking.'

'You counted?' I asked, amused.

'It deserved to be quantified. Quite the feat.'

'I'll tell Clementine you approve.' I regretted the words as soon as I said them, convinced he'd think I was bragging about knowing her, but he barely reacted.

'Is she a friend?'

'The best I could ask for,' I answered earnestly. 'As bubbly and funny as she seems. And she *really* likes to feed people.'

'Yes. She does.'

I'd been about to take another sip but stopped, surprised. 'You know her?'

He cocked his head to one side. 'Once upon a time.'

'Wow, small world.' Later, I'd cringe at my naiveté. 'I'm sure she'd love to see—' I began, but again he changed the subject. He seemed to be good at that.

'How much do you know about Ludlow Castle?'

'Only what I've read in my travel guide,' I admitted.

He stood up. 'I want to show you something.'

My interest piqued, I let him lead me through the stalls, growing increasingly busy as the morning wore on, to a tower on the northern edge of the old bailey. It was half in ruins and, to my relief, he didn't suggest we climb it.

'In the twelfth century, a woman named Marion de la Bruyere lived here. At the time, Ludlow Castle was being held against enemies, but Marion was in love with one of those enemies, a knight named Arnold de Lys. She'd hang a rope down from this tower, Pendover Tower,' he pointed up, 'for him to climb.'

'Why do I sense this story doesn't have a happy ending?' I asked grimly.

'Because love stories rarely do. One night de Lys deliberately left the rope hanging behind him and a hundred soldiers followed. Ludlow Castle was taken by the enemy and Marion realised she'd been betrayed.'

'I hope she got her revenge.'

'She snatched his sword and cut his throat.'

A different vengeance for a different time, I thought, remembering the lightbulbs I'd stolen from Gary and the social media passwords I'd changed. 'A little extreme but it gets the point across. Did she at least get a happy ending?'

'She threw herself from the tower.'

'Oh. I guess not then.'

'Her ghost apparently still haunts the tower.' He looked up and I followed his gaze. 'It's said that if you visit this particular spot at dusk, you'll see her.'

'Sad, but I do love a good ghost story.' I turned back to him with a smile. 'How do you know so much folklore?'

'I like to dig into alternative histories. There's always more to a place than meets the eye.' At this point, his eyes met mine. 'But you already know that, don't you?' His tone, almost accusatory, took me aback.

I tensed, glancing nervously around. This part of the castle was still busy, but nobody was within earshot. 'What do you mean?'

He kept his eyes locked on mine. 'Has Clementine ever mentioned the name Niall?'

It didn't ring a bell. 'No. Should she?'

He laughed then, but it was half bitter and half sad. 'No, I suppose not.' He broke eye contact and ran his fingers, speckled with paint, through his hair. 'Perhaps you should ask her.'

Crossing my arms over my chest, suddenly cold in the shadow of the tower, I nodded. 'Okay. I will.'

'Thank you.' And, with that, he turned and strode away.

Some instinct stopped me from running straight to Clementine to ask about him. I wanted to broach the subject carefully, to not give too much away before I could gauge her reaction. I'd spent eight months accepting vague explanations about the island and the archives, but in this case I was determined to get a real answer.

We were meeting for an early dinner later that day, so I waited until we were sitting in the beer garden of one of Ludlow's many pubs before tentatively raising the subject.

'Clementine?'

'Mm?' she asked distractedly, busy perusing the extensive list of beers on tap.

'There's something I need to ask you.'

She picked up on the serious tone and abruptly focused her attention on me. 'Ask me anything. I'll answer if I can.'

I fidgeted nervously with the menu. 'Does the name . . . Niall mean anything to you?'

I could see instantly that it did. She straightened, abruptly tense.

'Where did you hear that name?' she whispered.

The truth was on the tip of my tongue. The artist in the coffee shop, who'd drawn me a picture of an island; the man who said he'd known her, *once upon a time*. I'd had a few hours to think about it, and the only theory I'd come up with was that he was a former lover. She'd never mentioned any serious relationships, but that didn't mean she'd never had one. But before I could voice any of this, Clementine's expression shifted from shock into sadness, and she asked another question.

'Does Uncle Joe talk about him?'

This was unexpected. 'Uncle Joe?' I asked, confused.

'Or Alex, maybe?' Clementine wondered aloud. 'I know for a fact Cole won't have mentioned him.'

'Clementine,' I sighed, tired of the puzzle. 'Who *is* Niall?'

The sorrow on her face intensified. 'My cousin. Uncle Joe's son. He . . . left the family. He's not welcome on the island anymore.'

Chapter Sixteen

I wasn't heading towards the base of Pendover Tower at dusk expecting to spot Marion de la Bruyere. I was hoping to see Niall again. I had no idea where he was staying and no way of contacting him, so when I remembered him mentioning the ghost, I had nothing to lose. My instincts were right. He was already there – waiting for me rather than her, I hoped. He was leaning against the wall of the tower, sketching. One pencil was in his hand, another tucked behind his ear.

He didn't notice my approach, so I deliberately scuffed my foot on a stone to announce myself. There was still plenty of noise coming from the food stalls – particularly in the vicinity of the beer tents – but this corner of the castle was quiet. He heard me and looked up. Even after only two encounters, I could easily read his smile. He was pleased to see me, but not surprised. He'd trusted that I'd come. The guileless honesty in his face was refreshing after so long on the island. Books, I decided, were better open.

But as he studied my face, the smile faded. 'What did she tell you?'

I had to remind myself that his apparent sincerity didn't mean I could trust him. I kept my distance, my arms crossed over my chest. 'Not much.'

'She must have told you something for you to be looking at me like that.'

'I'm not looking like—'

'You're trying to decide if I'm a dolphin or a shark. It's OK. I'm not offended. I'd just like to know what Clementine said about me.'

'That you're her cousin. You grew up on the island with her and Cole. When they left for university, you stayed. To train under Uncle – your father. To be the next archivist.'

He flipped his sketchbook closed and straightened. 'So far, so true.'

'But that you're no longer . . .'

'I'm exiled,' he said with a nod. 'Did she tell you why?'

Clementine had been closed-mouthed, the way she always was when I asked about the island. Clearly shaken by my question, she'd given a very brief and cryptic answer before pretending to get a text from her agent saying she was needed elsewhere. After months of living on the island without anyone even mentioning his name, I knew I needed to turn to Niall himself for any explanation.

'She said that some of it's Uncle Joe's story to tell, some of it's Cole's. But, ultimately, you didn't . . . respect the wishes of the island?'

A bitter twist turned his lips. 'What a sad way of wording it.'

I wasn't naive enough to believe him over Clementine, but family dynamics could be complicated. He deserved a chance to tell his side of the story. 'How would you word it then?'

238

He gave me a very direct look, his eyes piercing. 'Did you know, hundreds of years ago, in parts of Europe, it was believed that Saint Nicholas had a helper? The Dutch called him *Zwarte Piet*. Some think he was a human companion or servant; others that he was a spirit or a kobold. Whoever he was, he was supposed to assist Saint Nicholas. His main job was determining who was worthy of a gift and making a list for the saint, who was apparently too busy to do it himself.'

I did know that. I'd come across the information in my surreptitious island research. It was a well-circulated piece of Christmas folklore; a piece I'd tucked away in my mental archive when I'd resolved not to ask any more questions about the island. Was now the time to pull it out and dust it off? Perhaps.

Niall's smile was comradely. 'Of course, you already knew that. You probably already know that a lot of historians theorise that Father Christmas is linked to the Norse god Odin. According to many European traditions, Odin – or Woden – was a bearded old man who travelled across the winter sky on an eight-legged horse, doling out gifts to the good and punishments to the bad. Probably the original Father Christmas. He had helpers too. They'd listen down the chimneys of mortals so they could tell Odin who was worthy and who wasn't. Do you know what form those helpers took?'

I shook my head, clearly not having delved this far into the research rabbit hole. His smile turned triumphant. 'Ravens. Two black ravens.'

I felt my mouth form an involuntary 'O'. 'Is that . . . really true?'

'Look up the names "Huginn and Muninn" if you don't believe me. There are lots of stories about them.'

'So what you're saying . . .' I began, matching this new information with the theories I'd already formed. He nodded, urging me on, but I pulled myself back. I needed to be direct, even if it felt rude. 'You're not answering my question. Why aren't you on the island anymore?'

When he spoke, it was with an earnestness I couldn't doubt. 'I realised that if we're the helpers now, we should do more. We don't have to rely on the island for everything. There are some wishes we can fulfil ourselves. *Should* fulfil ourselves, even. Wishes that involve getting out there in the world. The others . . .' He ran his fingers through his hair, clearly frustrated, 'well, let's just say they didn't like my ideas.'

I thought of the Christmas bauble I'd bought in Edinburgh. My own little rebellion; my conviction that not all wishes need miracles. And of Cole's own conviction, so crisply dictated as we'd sat on Arthur's Seat: *We don't interfere.* I could certainly imagine Cole taking offence at Niall's idea to 'get out there in the world'.

Some of what I was thinking must have shown on my face because Niall smiled again. This time it was a smile of relief. 'You agree with me, don't you?'

Saying 'yes' aloud would have been a betrayal of Cole and Clementine, of Uncle Joe and the archives. But I couldn't stop myself from thinking it. I *did* agree with him. Whatever the island's mystery was, whatever its power, I believed we could do more than just catalogue wishes. We had the power to grant some ourselves, even if only in tiny, mundane ways.

Niall read my silence correctly, his expression quietly victorious. 'You know exactly what I mean. You feel it too. But let me guess – the others won't hear any of it.'

Again, I wasn't prepared to vocalise my agreement. To turn it into something tangible. I didn't know Niall at all, while Clementine was my best friend, Uncle Joe was like family and Cole was . . . whatever Cole was. My loyalties lay with them. Even if . . .

'No,' I said, more sharply than I'd intended. 'I'm sorry. Thank you for sharing, but I can't talk about this. I could ask Clementine—'

'There's no point,' he said, the disappointment on his face painful to see. 'They've made their minds up and there's no shifting them.'

'But they're your family. Surely they want you back.' It was true that nobody had mentioned Niall. But with hindsight, there *were* signs of his absence. The sorrow and regret in Uncle Joe's eyes when he thought nobody was looking. The times Clementine had been on the cusp of saying a name before choking it back. The framed family photographs hidden in a drawer: a boy playing with his Christmas toys, turned away from the camera, and a Doc-Marten-shod man obscured behind Andy on a beach.

'You clearly have a more forgiving family than I do,' he said with a hopeless shrug.

'But I'm sure I—'

He cut across me with an air of finality. 'Thanks, but there's nothing you can do. There's no happy reunion on the cards. The prodigal son won't be returning.' His words were dismal but he was smiling again. 'I'm just glad to have met you. To know the archives will be well looked after in your hands. I want them to stay that way, so can I offer some advice?' I nodded tentatively. 'Don't tell the others about me. If they knew we'd been talking, they wouldn't trust you. Cole especially.'

I could believe that. But I couldn't commit either way, so instead I asked, 'What will you do?'

He laughed. 'What I've been doing all this time. Travelling. Living. Drawing. And on that note . . .' He lifted his sketchpad, jotted something down, tore out a sheet of paper and held it out to me. I studied it before taking it. The pencil sketch lacked colour and detail but even upside down, I recognised the distinct slopes and sharp edges that shaped the island. My island. Scrawled beneath it was a phone number.

'In case you're ever out in the world and want to talk,' he explained.

I hesitated. Was accepting his number a betrayal? I felt guilty taking it, but I'd already disappointed him – hurt him, even – by biting my tongue when I could have told him he wasn't alone. Accepting this small token of friendship was the least I could do.

'Thank you,' I said, gently taking the sheet of paper.

He gave a nod and a sad smile, painfully reminiscent of Uncle Joe's, and turned to walk away. I watched him go, holding the island in my hand and knowing nothing would be simple again.

*　*　*

Clementine didn't stop talking for the whole journey back to Edinburgh. She chatted about the people she'd met at the festival, the food she'd sampled, the baking tips she'd learned, the weather, the comfort of our seats on the train, the quantity of sheep we were passing, the weather again. But not once did she mention Niall. It was as if the conversation we'd skimmed the day before had never happened. And yet now I knew he existed, the omission was impossible to ignore. And I knew Clementine well enough by then to recognise the avoidance tactic. Niall wasn't part of her conversation, but he was everywhere else.

At some point during my sleepless night, I'd decided if Niall's name was mentioned, I'd come clean. I'd tell Clementine about meeting him. I'd show her the sketch and his phone number. I'd try to convince her to call him, to take that first step towards reconciliation. But her steadfast determination to avoid the topic censored my mouth too. I had too many thoughts and feelings to sort through. So I kept Niall's sketch tucked away in an inner pocket of my backpack and nodded as Clementine remarked on a particularly large cow in the field we were passing.

In fact, I was paying very little attention to our surroundings. I barely even noticed the familiar red-brick houses and industrial buildings of my home city as we changed trains in Manchester Piccadilly. I hardly registered the silhouette of Arthur's Seat or the craggy cliff leading up to Edinburgh Castle as we transferred to the airport train at Waverley. And I didn't notice the man sit next to me on the plane that would take us to the Shetland Islands until the surprised voice of Clementine – in the window seat on my other side – pierced through my reverie.

'What are *you* doing here?'

I thought for the briefest of moments – not long enough to consider how I'd react – that I'd turn to see Niall. But instead of unkempt long hair and sincere green eyes, I found myself facing a familiar neat beard and level gaze.

You'd think by then I'd have become accustomed to meeting Cole in unexpected places. But I still found myself flummoxed and flustered, glad that he was looking beyond me to his sister.

'I finished some business early and decided a trip home was overdue,' he explained casually, clicking his seatbelt in place. 'I had your flight details and thought I'd travel up with you.'

'Oh, you thought that, did you?' Clementine asked coyly. 'How very . . . brotherly of you.'

'I wanted to see Alex, and we can travel back to Edinburgh together in a week.'

'Uh-huh. Alex. Right.' With a knowing glance at me, she pulled out a magazine from her bag and disappeared behind it. 'See you guys in Sumburgh.'

I felt trapped. Sandwiched between the siblings with a ninety-minute flight ahead, there was no way to avoid Cole. But how could I talk to him without him realising I was hiding something? He may have been aloof, but he was also astute. He was a lawyer after all. He knew how to read people. And my secret would be written all over my face.

'It's nice to see you,' I said hastily, keeping my gaze on the back of the seat in front of me. 'But I didn't sleep well last night. I was planning on napping. I'll, erm, be better company later.' I closed my eyes without waiting for a response.

But closing my eyes only heightened my other senses. I couldn't ignore the brush of his shirtsleeve against my elbow on our shared armrest or the brief graze of his knee against mine. I couldn't ignore the sounds of him drinking from a water bottle or turning the pages of whatever he was reading (I resisted the urge to peak). Couldn't ignore the smell of his aftershave, subtly woody. I took it all in, my mind juggling conflicting emotions. Happiness that he was there, right next to me. Guilt at the secret I was keeping. And anger. Anger at what Niall had told me, at the rules of the island, at my own cowardice.

I managed to fake sleep for what felt an interminably long journey. And once we arrived at Sumburgh Airport, I feigned post-nap grogginess, trailing behind Cole and Clementine as we headed for the car park. It was only when Cole opened the boot of a shiny grey car and gestured for me to unload my backpack into it that I realised we weren't at a bus stop.

'It's a rental,' Cole explained, registering my confusion.

'Cole doesn't do public transport unless he has to,' Clementine smirked, tossing her own luggage in. 'Not that I'm complaining.'

'I enjoy the drive.' He gave me a surprisingly sheepish smile. 'It's the one time I have a valid excuse for not working.'

My return smile clearly wasn't convincing enough, because he quickly dropped his. Avoiding eye contact I reached for the handle of a rear passenger door, but Clementine beat me to it.

'I'm declaring dominion over the backseat,' she announced, throwing herself in before I could even blink. 'It's *my* turn to nap. You keep my brother company on the drive.'

I couldn't very well say no. And I couldn't fake more sleep without raising suspicion, so I settled resolutely into the front seat. Clementine was already snoring by the time Cole had pulled out of the car park and onto the A-road that would take us to our first ferry terminal. I said nothing because I didn't want to risk saying the wrong thing, and Cole said nothing because silence was his default setting.

Clementine woke up just as we disembarked from the ferry at Belmont. It was only a ten-minute drive then to Unst, where I was hoping Willum would be waiting to take us the last leg of the journey. Back home, where I could sort out my feelings. But, although the *Valkyrie* sat bobbing in the harbour, neither Willum nor Mary were home.

'The bus was due much later,' Cole explained. 'I tried phoning them to say we'd be coming earlier by car but got no answer.'

'Well, in that case,' Clementine heaved a dramatic sigh, 'I guess I'll be resuming my nap. Wake me up when Willum's ready to set sail and not a nanosecond before.'

She left us standing in the late afternoon sun.

'A stroll to stretch our legs?' Cole suggested. Before I could fabricate an excuse, he added, 'There's something I need to ask you.'

The knots in my stomach tightened into tangled snarls, but I tried to look nonchalant as I followed him along the edge of the harbour. The sky was particularly blue, the sunlight gilding the ocean particularly brilliant, but I couldn't appreciate the scenery. I was too aware of Cole walking beside me, clearly mulling over how to ask his question. A question, I assumed, that would be about Niall.

So it took me by surprise when he stopped, turned to look at me, and said with concern, 'Are you unhappy on the island?'

'I – what? No. Why?'

He held my gaze, his brown eyes searching. 'You seem . . . unenthusiastic about returning.'

I almost laughed at the absurdity of the suggestion. 'No. I can't wait to get back.'

A flicker of relief crossed his face, but he wasn't convinced. 'I know how isolating it can feel. You're not the first person to wish it was more connected. Trust me,' he added wryly, 'Clem and I grew up there. I lost count of the letters we sent in bottles or the times we smuggled phones back onto the island with us, but they'd never connect. Once, when we were coming home from university, we even spent a small fortune on a brick-sized satphone. It was meant to be one of the best, able to connect from anywhere on Earth.' I cocked an eyebrow at him, and he shrugged philosophically. 'Let's just say we demanded a refund.'

'The island doesn't like or allow it,' I mumbled, remembering what Clementine had first said when Aiden asked about phone signal, all those months ago. I'd thought it was odd wording back then. Now I knew it was entirely appropriate.

Cole nodded. 'I know you must miss your family. Clementine told me they were away, that you didn't have a chance to see them on this trip. I'm sorry about that.'

I pretended to watch two seagulls battle over half a sandwich. Cole's worry for me, so unexpected, multiplied my guilt tenfold. *Tell him*, I ordered myself. *Tell him about Niall.* But everything had been going so well before I'd discovered who Niall was. My work, my home on the island, had felt so right. Would bringing Niall up ruin that? The Jones family clearly avoided the topic for a reason. Would it be fairer on everyone to just do as Niall had advised and keep our meeting a secret? *Not even a secret*, a different, more cowardly inner voice reasoned. *Just not important enough to mention.*

It was a long moment before I spoke, and the words that came out of my mouth weren't lies. 'I do miss my family. A lot. It's hard, not being able to even call or email them. To have to wait for Willum to come to the island just to send them a letter. To need an excuse to come to Unst, just so I can connect to Mary's Wi-Fi. But,' I added, emphasising the truth of my words by returning his gaze, 'I'm *not* unhappy on the island. I love it there. It's . . . home.'

While he didn't smile, the uneasy set to his jaw loosened. He nodded. 'That's good to hear. Because—'

'Och no, don't tell us we got the wrong time,' a familiar female voice cried out behind us. We turned to see Willum and Mary climbing out of a tiny, ancient-looking three-wheeled car. 'Willum, get our girl ready while I put the kettle on. We're just back from the shops. I've got ice lollies.'

'Our girl'– *Valkyrie* – was soon pulling out of the harbour. Cole and Willum took the wheelhouse while Clementine and I stood on deck, waving goodbye to Mary and eating our rapidly melting ice lollies. I'd planned on spending the entire journey in the sunshine, but once land had disappeared behind us, Cole asked me to join them at the wheel.

I glanced at Clementine, who shrugged, and went inside. Willum gave me a nod of greeting, looking strangely amused, but said nothing. So I turned to Cole, whose eyes were on the line where the turquoise of the sea greeted the azure of the sky. 'I want to try something.'

'Okay . . .' I said warily.

'Where's the island?'

'Pardon?'

'Humour me. Point to the island.'

I looked to the horizon but not a single shape interrupted the vast blue. No island, no mist. Nothing but the North Sea.

'I can't see the island,' I said, looking confusedly from Cole to Willum. 'Should I be able to see it?'

'No,' Cole replied. 'But can you tell me which direction it's in?'

I moved to point forwards: it made sense that we'd be travelling directly towards it. But something tugged at me, some less logical instinct that made me want to turn to the left. The uncanny sense that our destination grazed the edge of my vision.

'I don't know why but . . . that way?' I pointed left across the placid sea.

Cole looked to Willum who gave a barely discernible nod, a wry twist to his lips. Cole's expression didn't change in response, although he turned to study me for a moment. Then he focused again on Willum, nodded and stepped out of the wheelhouse.

Baffled, I looked to Willum for explanation. 'Do you know what that was about?'

In response, he backed away from the wheel. 'Lesson one: left takes you left, right takes you right. Lesson two: don't bother with a compass. They don't work out here. And lesson three: don't hit any rocks. The rest of it, we'll get to.' When I did nothing but stand there gawping at him, he pointed with his thumb towards Cole, who was standing with Clementine on deck. He was saying something to his sister that made her look up in surprise, but I couldn't hear what. Judging from the way she spun to look towards the wheelhouse, I guessed they were discussing me.

'Just been given a new commission,' Willum went on gruffly. 'Teach you how to get our girl out there and back again in one piece.'

Stunned, I continued gaping like an idiot. 'But . . . why?'

'Because like it or not, I'm not going to be around forever. Can't ferry anyone when I'm six feet under. But I'm thinking I've got plenty of time to get you worthy of the old girl.' He reached over to tap the wheel affectionately, then nodded for me to take hold.

'But why me? I can't even drive a car.'

His tone suggested the answer was obvious. 'You know where the island is.'

'So I was right?' I looked out towards that specific stretch of skyline that was implausibly beckoning me.

Willum nodded.

'But still—'

'The lad's offering you something here, something I didn't expect him to offer anyone,' Willum cut in, uncharacteristically firm. He didn't have to name Cole for me to understand. 'It'll mean more freedom for you. Eventually. I'd recommend not looking this gift horse in the mouth. I'd also recommend taking the wheel soon,' he added. 'Otherwise we'll be crossing into Norwegian territory. And I don't have a permit.'

Hesitantly I reached for the wheel. It felt as if I was being given something precious, something sacred. The wheel was more than metal and plastic in my hands. As Willum had said, it was the promise of freedom. Of one day being able to come and go as I pleased, not subject to someone else's schedule. I tentatively turned the wheel a fraction to the left, glancing over my shoulder at Willum. He pulled a face, clearly unimpressed, so I turned further until I felt a tug and the *Valkyrie* felt right in the water.

Chapter Seventeen

*. . . if we're the helpers now, we should do more. We don't
have to rely on the island for everything. There are some
wishes we can fulfil ourselves. Should fulfil ourselves, even.
Wishes that involve getting out there in the world . . .*

Niall's words, imprinted on my memory, had been
haunting me all week. But now, they fortified me.

Sitting with the whole family, bar Uncle Joe, at the
kitchen table, I fidgeted with the bag on my lap. I'd
planned on getting the ordeal over and done with at the
start of the meal. Best to have it out of the way. But
the food was disappearing, and I still hadn't opened my
mouth. I picked at my plate listlessly, not noticing what
it was, and avoided Cole's gaze the entire time – as I'd
done practically all week.

As cutlery clattered, I decided it was now or never. No
matter how much I was dreading it, it needed to be done.
Cole and Alex were heading back to the mainland the
following morning, and I wanted everyone here.

With Clyde and Clementine at the table, there was
no point waiting for a lull in the conversation. I made
myself cut in, breathlessly blurting out the words, 'I need
to show you all something.'

To my surprise, everyone instantly stopped talking, and I felt my cheeks redden as all eyes turned curiously to me. Taking a deep breath, I unclasped my bag and pulled out the three letters. Rolled up, they were instantly recognisable as belonging to the archives, and Cole frowned in clear disapproval.

'They shouldn't have been removed—'

'Just read them,' I begged, handing one to Clementine on my left, another to Alex on my right and the other to Alison across from me. 'Please.'

Clearly perplexed but willing to humour me, they read in silence. The letters were short, read in mere seconds, and I gestured for them to pass them around. Cole took one, I wasn't sure which, and studied it with a frown, as if he'd already decided he wouldn't like the contents. And sure enough, before he'd even finished, he was shaking his head.

'No.'

I made myself meet his gaze. 'But you don't even know—'

'We *don't* act on them.'

'Act on what?' Aiden asked. He reached for a letter, quickly scanned it, then looked quizzically to me. 'I don't understand.'

Cole ignored him, focused on me. 'We don't act on them,' he repeated.

Alex signed for his father's attention. 'Why not?'

'Because that's our rule.'

'A rule needs a reason,' Alex retorted. I'd always liked him, but in that moment he was my favourite person on the planet.

253

'There's a very good reason,' Cole replied. His tone was even, his temper kept in check no doubt by years of arguing legal cases. 'Keeping our secret is imperative—'

'Why?' It was Aiden who interrupted this time. 'I don't get why keeping everything a secret is so important.'

'You're not a member of this family . . .'

'So my opinion's invalid?'

'That's not what he meant,' Clyde protested at the same time as Clementine shouted, 'Guys, stop! Let's at least listen to what Ellie has to say.'

All eyes turned back to me. I took a deep breath. 'These are selfless, time-sensitive requests that are in our power to grant.'

'They don't *need* granting,' Cole replied. 'Nobody's life is on the line.'

'No, but these three letters stand for three unhappy kids. Kids we can easily make happy, without revealing anything about the island.' Tormented by Niall's words and my own certainty that they were true, I'd spent every spare, private moment over the last week trawling through the Wish Index. I'd been trying to find letters that met four criteria: selfless, time-sensitive, possible to grant and to do so covertly. I'd identified three.

One was from Jack, a boy in Cincinnati whose little brother had a birthday soon. Jack was convinced their mother, in 'jail in Marysville', would forget to send a card. *Please remind her Santa.* Another was from Alina who lived just outside Volgograd, whose best friend was being bullied. *She has stopped coming to school now and when her parents make her, she cries all the way there,* the translation read. *Last time I thought they were going to break her arm. I promised I wouldn't tell the teachers though, so can you please make them stop hurting her?* And the third came from a boy named Abeo who had just moved into a flat with his mother in Hackney, London: *We had to leeve all our ferniter so my mum has nuffing to sit on when shes werking and her backs herts and she cries. I know its erly but can you send her a chair please for Xmas? Shes been good all year.*

'These are easy enough to help with,' I insisted, my focus on Cole.

'Do you think we have endless time and resources?'

'Enough to buy a couple of second-hand chairs in Hackney.'

'And how can we help the girl being bullied?'

'Send a message to the school about the situation, stressing how serious it is. With internet access we could see which primary schools are close to Alina's address and send them emails. And with the internet we could also look into how many prisons there are in Marysville, Ohio. There can't be that many. We could send Jack's mum a little boy's birthday card to the prison – if she has the same surname as Jack then it should reach her. It'll remind her about her son's birthday, and she could sign the card and send it herself.'

'You've given this a lot of thought,' Alison said, speaking for the first time.

'It deserves a lot of thought,' I countered.

'And what makes you think these cases are worthy?' Cole asked.

'They're just kids. How can they not be "worthy"?'

'We get millions of letters from children,' Alison pointed out, not unkindly. 'We can't possibly respond to them all.'

'That's not what she's suggesting,' Alex argued. 'Just the ones that we can answer. Just because Mum—'

'This has nothing to do with your mother,' Cole signed, his gestures sharp. *What does this mean?* I wondered, my curiosity matching my frustration.

Alex clenched his jaw, looking as stubborn as his father. I didn't recognise the sign he gave but could guess based on the combination of horned animal and excrement.

I expected Cole to scold him, but he just sighed. If I'd been hoping he'd say more about his ex-wife, shedding some light on this new development, I was disappointed. 'It's not our job to answer the letters,' he said, looking from Alex to me. 'It never has been.'

'Not our job?' I repeated, my frustration once more eclipsing my curiosity. I couldn't believe what I was hearing. 'It doesn't matter if it's our job or not. Surely it's our duty as *human beings*.'

Cole clearly didn't agree – I hadn't really expected him to. But Cole wasn't the only one there. I scanned the other faces, desperate to see some solidarity or, if not that, a little credence. I was disappointed. Clyde's and Aiden's expressions were apologetic, as if they knew my fight was futile and weren't willing to bet on a losing horse. Alison's was speculative but non-committal. Alex was clearly frustrated but pessimistic. I turned to Clementine.

I'd been counting on her as my staunchest ally in this – as both my closest friend and a fond rule-breaker. But she'd been uncharacteristically quiet through the whole exchange. Looking at her now, I didn't immediately recognise the emotions on her face because I'd never seen them there before. Awkwardness, regret, pity. She was even averting her eyes.

'Clementine?' I asked hesitantly, unsure that I wanted her to answer.

Her mouth twisted in apology. 'I'm sorry El. This is just . . . how we've always done things.'

I'd been prepared to battle Cole. I'd even been prepared to battle Alison and Clyde. But not Clementine. Angry tears sprang to my eyes as I scraped the chair back and shot to my feet.

'"This is how we've always done things" is *never* a valid argument,' I retorted, my voice steadier than I'd expected it to be. 'We can do more. And if we're here to help, which I believe we are, then we *should* do more.' They were Niall's words, adapted, but I meant every one of them.

Cole's expression turned from angry to icy. Everyone else in the room bar Aiden seemed to straighten, and I sensed recognition. They'd heard these words before, or some variation of them.

I could see Cole's jaw clench as he gathered the letters and rose. 'May I remind you, Ms Lancaster, that you are our employee and are paid to do a job? Your job is to translate and archive, not to interfere in family matters. Is that clear?'

I was already standing so it was easy to retreat. 'Consider my position well and truly clarified,' I said thickly, before fleeing from the room.

* * *

When somebody knocked on my bedroom door that evening, I was expecting Aiden or Clementine, not Cole.

'Can we talk?' he asked through the closed door.

I glanced at myself in the mirror – Harry Potter pyjamas and messy, post-shower hair. With a sigh, I opened the door a tiny crack. He seemed both annoyed and amused.

'I'm not here to kill you. As tempting as the prospect is.'

Grudgingly, I opened the door a little further.

'May I come in?' he asked, clearly exasperated.

It would feel strange to have him in my bedroom – not necessarily unwelcome, but more intimate than I was prepared for. But insisting he stay out in the hallway would seem both petulant and prudish so, stepping aside, I let him in. Closing the door behind him, the room suddenly felt a lot smaller. And had there always only been one chair? Cole gestured to it questioningly and I nodded, sitting awkwardly on the bed.

'I'll be gone in the morning and didn't want to leave things as they were,' he began, not looking uncomfortable in the slightest. 'I apologise for how I spoke to you. It was . . . distasteful of me to pull rank like that. Especially as nobody here sees you as just an employee.'

'But I'm not family,' I finished for him.

'No,' he answered simply. 'And I won't apologise for maintaining the way my family has always done things. What you're asking us to do is noble. It's kind. But my family's job is to protect the island at all costs.'

'Why does it need protecting?' I asked. 'What does it need protecting *from?*' *And what does any of this have to do with Alex's mother – your ex-wife?* I was desperate to ask but too cowardly to.

'From damage,' he said, refusing to elaborate. 'Don't blame Clementine for siding with me. She knows how important this is, but that won't stop her from feeling guilty. If you need somebody to be angry with, be angry with me. Don't let this ruin your friendship with her.'

'I'm not angry.' It was a lie. I was *very* angry, but his concern for his sister momentarily softened it. 'And of course I won't let it ruin my friendship with Clementine.'

He nodded, something like gratitude in his eyes. But I wouldn't let him distract me. 'I just think our job can be more than protecting the island,' I ploughed on. 'We can help it by doing some of the work ourselves. By answering the wishes that we're able to. We won't be betraying the island by doing that. We won't be giving up its secret. I want to protect the island as much as you do. I *do*,' I insisted when he raised a sceptical eyebrow. 'I may not have grown up here and my family may not have lived here for generations, but I can see how special it is. I want to keep its secret.'

I think he was surprised by my earnestness; the scepticism certainly left his face. But it won me no ground.

'Good. Then you'll understand why we can't answer any of the letters. They're not written for us.'

'Maybe some of them *are*.' But even as I forged on, I knew it was hopeless. His mind was set in marble.

He seemed to sense my surrender. 'I'm sorry to have disappointed you,' he said, sounding sincere. 'I don't disagree with your sentiment. I just have to think of the bigger picture.'

There was no point demanding further explanation. He'd said what he was going to say on the matter.

Hugging myself, I nodded. 'Okay.'

'Okay?' He seemed surprised. Relieved.

'There's no point fighting you on this. It's your island. I understand I'm here as an employee.' I'd meant to sound resigned, but the words came out bitter and surly.

'No,' he said sharply, leaning forward in the chair. 'This is *your* island too. You may not understand it yet, but the island does want you here.' It was such an uncharacteristically whimsical thing for him to say that I was certain I'd misheard. I didn't mishear his next words though. '*I* want you here.'

'Do you?' I asked. But then I realised he was just referring to my job. He wanted me there because of my work in the archives. My implementation of the new system. My efficiency with the translations. At least it was an endorsement of sorts . . .

'Isn't it obvious?' His face, so close to mine, was intense.

'Nothing here is obvious,' I admitted, flustered and frustrated. 'Everything is the exact opposite of obvious. Obscure. If that's the right antonym. Incomprehensible.

Ungraspable.' I was rambling because I was nervous. And I was nervous because of the space between us. Space that felt far too little and far too much at the same time. I was angry with him. I didn't understand him. I hated that he'd dismissed my proposal so absolutely. But none of that stopped me from wanting to bridge those last few centimetres of charged air between us and . . .

Before I could even finish the thought, Cole was on his feet and at the door.

'I'm glad we talked,' he said, stepping out into the hallway. 'Goodnight. Ellie.'

And he was gone.

* * *

I like to think I would have come to the decision on my own. That I'd been bold enough, determined enough, to not need a push. But truth be told I did need the push. And it came in the form of three letters.

For months now, I'd been aware of a presence. Although 'aware' isn't the right word. It was more that I'd been sensing something *other*. Shadows glimpsed from the corner of my eye that didn't belong to anyone. Footsteps that never materialised. A vague feeling of being watched on late nights working alone in the archives. It wasn't frightening or even discomforting; there was no threat there. If anything, it felt companionable. Those moments emerging from long stretches of deep focus, finding myself in an empty office, everyone else long in bed, were less lonely. It was probably just

Cicero and Fluffy keeping discreet vigil nearby, I'd reasoned. Or my fatigued mind playing tricks on me.

But then late one night – or very early one morning – I found myself in the cavernous post room mid-wishfall. Snowflakes drifted onto the expectant sheets, and walking amongst them was a figure. He was partly obscured by the falling wishes but was clearly a 'he'. I strained my eyes and saw Cole. But then he shifted and was suddenly Niall, with those intense sea-green eyes. Kneeling, he was moving from letter to letter. I watched, transfixed, as he read each of them in the seconds before they furled into scrolls. His actions were deliberate, focused. He was looking for something. After seconds, minutes, or hours, he seemed to find it. He picked one scroll up, but then continued searching as more wishes fell. Some indeterminate time later, he selected another, and then one more. With the three scrolls in his hands, he straightened, turned and looked directly at me. It wasn't Niall and it wasn't Cole. I didn't know this man.

And yet I did.

He nodded to me, solemn, and held out the scrolls. There was a sense of significant meaning in the gesture. I knew with absolute certainty that what the letters contained was important, vitally so. That I needed to read them. But also, that in accepting them, I'd be accepting the responsibility that came with them.

I didn't hesitate. I reached out my hands to take them.

But just as my fingers curled around the crisp parchment, my eyes opened and I was at my desk in the empty office, my head pillowed in my arms. A letter from

Chengdu lay weighted open to one side, half translated on a laptop that hadn't yet entered sleep mode. I must have nodded off. It was only a dream.

But no.

Did you know, hundreds of years ago, in parts of Europe, it was believed that Saint Nicholas had a helper? ... Some think he was a human companion or servant; others that he was a spirit ... Niall's words were playing in my mind as I walked down to the post room. I knew what I'd find there. Not a man. Not a servant or a spirit. But three letters, curled up on the otherwise virgin sheets of paper.

Three wishes, waiting for me.

Chapter Eighteen

'If you so much as glance at that cardigan, I'll rip off each of the buttons, sharpen them into teeny, tiny shanks and stab your eyes out with them.'

'Has anyone ever told you you've got a really dark sense of humour?' I asked, averting my gaze from said cardigan. I *had* just been about to reach for it.

Clementine cocked an eyebrow. 'Who said I was joking?'

We were in Edingurgh for the 'Evening with Clementine'. Four days of civilisation stretched ahead of me. It was November so the city had put away its pumpkins and plastic skeletons for another year, and the tinsel was out in force. There was a Christmas tree in every shop window and festive markets had already popped up in Princes Street Gardens. Lights twinkled, sleet fell and a sea of woolly-hatted heads ducked in and out of shops as the season's spending began.

Clementine and I made up two of those heads, because she had deemed it necessary to go dress shopping. She'd asked me the week before what I planned on wearing for the launch. When I'd gingerly shown her my nicest outfit – which had admittedly included a cardigan – she declared me a 'hopeless self-stereotyping bookworm who dresses like a nana' and announced her plans to 'sexy' me up.

'And it's my big event so you have to wear whatever I choose,' she informed me in a tone (her usual) that brooked no argument. I'd gone along with it, partly because it *was* her big event and, truth be told, partly because Mr Jones – Cole – was going to be there.

I was regretting it now, though, as Clementine piled slinky, sequined dresses into my arms, and me into the changing rooms. None of the outfits suited me; they were all too revealing, too gaudy or too tight (I blame Clementine's baking) in all the wrong places, and I refused to show Clementine any of them. She sat outside sulking while I shimmied back into my jeans and jumper.

'It's fine,' she rallied as I apologetically passed the dozen dresses to the shop assistant. 'Edinburgh has no shortage of clothes shops.'

My heart sank. 'The event's *tonight*, Clementine. Surely you have more important things to do than—'

But she'd already grabbed my arm and hustled me into the shop next door. 'The speech is written and *my* outfit's sorted. Getting my best friend properly decked out is number three on the priority list.'

Hearing her describe me as her best friend meant my protest died on my lips. I let her shove another dozen dresses into my arms.

It took three more shops, but I finally found a dress we could agree on. Simple dusty pink silk, 1940s style, that kept my shoulders covered but pinched in at the waist and was low enough in the chest to meet Clementine's approval.

'I have just the cardigan to match,' I said as the cashier folded it into a bag for me. At Clementine's growl, I gave her a placating pat on the arm. 'Joking.'

'You better bloody had be. But we do need to find you some matching underwear.'

'Now *you're* joking. Nobody's going to see my underwear.'

'Oh no?' She gave that infuriating smile but didn't push it. We'd spent longer shopping than planned and had an early dinner reservation, giving us time to head back to the hotel afterwards to get ready for the big event. We'd agreed to meet the others (bar Uncle Joe, who was gratefully holding down the fort) at the restaurant – Clementine's favourite.

I should have been relieved to escape underwear shopping, but I was unsure about dinner. As much as I wanted to see Cole again, I also *didn't* want to see him again. Not after two months of absence. Two months of playing back those moments we'd shared in my bedroom, furious with him but wanting his arms around me. Wanting his lips on mine. Wondering if he felt the same. I'd had two months of safe fantasies, where I'd opted to ignore the fact he'd chosen to leave when he could have stayed.

Two months where I'd also ignored the job I had to do.

* * *

I should have known better than to expect a fancy restaurant. It was Clementine's choice so of course it was
a quirky family-run place – Mexican, judging from the
name and decor. It was busy, especially considering it
was still only late afternoon, and the hostess led us to the
only vacant table. To my relief, Clementine and I were
the first to arrive.

Jittery, I read the menu three times, re-arranged my
cutlery five, and looked up every time the door opened.
Clementine chuckled as she sipped on her tequila sunrise.

'Anxious about seeing a certain someone?'

Before I could respond, we were suddenly swept up
in a flurry of greetings as Alison, Clyde, Alex and Aiden
assembled around the table. I kept my eyes on them
rather than looking for Cole, but perhaps my *not looking* was obvious because Alex signed, 'My dad's stuck in
a meeting. He'll be at the event though.'

I tried not to let my warring relief and disappointment show, aiming for a nonchalant shrug. Alex's smile
was a lot like his aunt's.

Once everyone's drinks had arrived, Clyde clinked his
knife against his glass and cleared his throat. 'I'll keep
this brief.' He ignored Alison's delicate snort. 'We con-
gregate here in this delightful establishment to honour
my wonderfully talented daughter, whose successes rival
the greatest thinkers and artists of the past . . .'

'Dad, it's just a cookbook,' Clementine laughed.

'As Michelangelo protested, "It's just a bit of ceiling
paint".'

Clementine grinned. 'A fair comparison. Continue.'

The toast lasted about five minutes and would have gone on longer had Alison not-so-subtly pointed out that the nacho cheese was congealing. We raised our glasses to Clementine and tucked in.

Three hours later, it was Clementine's turn to give a speech – to the crowd who'd turned out for her charity evening. She looked stunning with kingfisher-blue hair, recently coloured, and a 1950s-style dress, the fabric polka-dotted with cherries.

'I won't bore you with a long list of "thank yous" because nobody cares – and you can always read the acknowledgements when you buy my upcoming book. Notice how I said "when" and not "if",' she added, with a laugh.

'But there are two people I *do* need to thank. Ellie and Aiden. Where are you?' She looked out into the crowd from her podium. I shrank back at the same time as Aiden, standing next to me, held his arms over his head and waved. 'Oh yes. Hi guys.' She waved back. 'Stop hiding Ellie. So anyway, these two have been my guinea pigs over the last ten months, taste-testing and answering questionnaire after questionnaire. Aiden was a huge help with the algorithms – I won't share the details with you because I don't understand them myself – and both of them deserve a huge thanks along with another ten months' worth of free cake.' She winked at me from across the sea of chuckling heads. 'So, no more talking from me. I'll see you all back here for the launch next year. In the meantime, please bugger off and enjoy the evening. And eat some cake!'

I clapped along with the rest of the crowd, my smile genuine. For once in my life, this was my type of party.

Not only was the venue a bookshop, but the catering consisted entirely of confectionery – one of Clementine's stipulations – and the decorations seamlessly wove rustic Christmas with a quirky baking theme. The bunting was made from miniature aprons, the baubles on the Christmas trees were tiny cakes, the cushions on the stools were shaped like giant mince pies and the vases were filled with holly-entwined whisks and spatulas.

I was also feeling surprisingly good about myself. Aiden had wolf-whistled when he'd seen me, which I took as a compliment. I'd made an effort with my hair, curling it in a slight 1940s style, in keeping with my dress, and had applied a little blusher and dusty pink lipstick. I'd even resisted wearing a cardigan.

I hadn't seen Cole yet, but was ready to. I subtly scanned the crowd, making my way over to the table laden with cakes. I'd just reached the end of the queue and was scanning the myriad delectables when Clementine appeared beside me. 'Why bother pretending to deliberate? We both know you're going to choose the carrot cake.'

'Maybe I'm in a chocolate mood,' I laughed, gesturing to the Black Forest brownie.

With a snort she plonked a brownie and a generous slice of carrot cake onto a plate. 'Life's too short to choose only one.'

'It's your evening. Who am I to argue?'

An elderly couple, reaching for their own cakes, interrupted us to congratulate Clementine. They talked for a few minutes, enthusing over her recipes and asking advice on specific baking problems they'd encountered.

Just then a petite woman with bobbed white-blonde hair and bright red lips scooted over.

'You're meant to be mingling,' she hissed to Clementine.

'I am,' Clementine replied innocently.

The woman narrowed her eyes. 'You've got books to promote.'

'Isn't that your job? I bake cakes; you promote books.'

'Everyone's here to talk to you, not me.'

'Everyone's here for the free cake, actually,' Clementine muttered, but she threw me an apologetic smile. 'Sorry, it looks like I've got an evening of shameless schmoozing ahead of me. This is Viv, my editor, by the way.'

'I guessed,' I laughed, holding out my hand. Viv shook it but was busy surveying the crowd.

'Oh excellent, the reviewer from the *Herald*'s here. Hop to it Clementine, and let the shameless schmoozing commence.'

The pair moved away, and suddenly I was on my own in the middle of the room holding two slices of cake. Glancing around, everyone I knew was busy talking to someone else. I could try to stealthily slip into one of their conversations, or better yet, I could pretend to be confident and join a group of strangers.

Or I could do what I'd normally do when finding myself alone in an awkward social situation: retreat to the toilets.

The toilets were on the lower ground level, so I made my way downstairs – and that's when I saw Cole.

For just a moment, it felt like a cheesy romcom. There I was, in a new dress, descending a flight of stairs as Cole, wearing a dark blue shirt and black jeans, glanced up and saw me. But that was where the daydream ended.

Granted, I didn't fall down the stairs, but I was too occupied with trying not to fall down them that I didn't have a chance to note his expression. Was he smiling or serious? I had no idea. He didn't hold his hand out for me as I reached the bottom. There was no wry comment when I faced him, and his expression was as inscrutable as ever.

But then he opened his mouth and said, 'You look . . .' And in that moment no other two words could have made me happier.

He trailed off, his sentence incomplete. As if lost for words. Cole was never lost for words. He could have meant to say anything. *You look . . . tired. You look . . . cold. You look . . . hungry* – I was still carrying two slices of cake after all. But there was an intensity to his tone that made me believe it was something more significant. Maybe I was reading too much into it, but the moment felt heavy with unspoken things. I wanted so desperately for him to reach out and tenderly tuck a stray hair behind my ear or graze my cheek with a fingertip. One touch, any touch, just to tell me that he felt something for me. And then he was moving forward and . . .

'If you're wanting the loo, they're out of paper.'

The woman had come up behind Cole, making me jump and entirely, albeit unwittingly, ruining the moment. I forced a polite smile at her as she brushed

271

past and began climbing the stairs. Cole and I locked gazes and, at the same moment, both burst out laughing.

It was like a dam had opened. Once we started, we couldn't stop. Here was that rare full-bodied laugh I'd hear from Cole when Alex was around. One that lightened his eyes and loosened his limbs. When it finally subsided, Cole straightened and put his hands into his pockets and gave a surprisingly rueful smile.

'I've congratulated Clementine, applauded her speech and promised to buy ten copies of her book when it's published. My brotherly duty is fulfilled. Do you want to go for a walk?'

The question took me aback. 'With you?'

He rolled his eyes. 'Yes, with me.'

'I . . .'

I had a job to do. But I had time. Just enough to permit myself one selfish walk.

'Yes,' I said. 'I'd love to.'

'Do you want to finish those first?' he asked, eyeing the cakes.

I set them down on a nearby stand. 'After the last few months, even I'm getting a little sick of cakes. But you must *never* tell Clementine that,' I added.

'I'll take your secret to the grave,' he promised solemnly. 'Shall I wait here while you . . . ?' He raised his eyebrows. I blinked at him, confused, and he gestured behind us.

'Oh, I don't actually need the toilet,' I admitted. 'I was just going there to hide.'

'Of course you were.' He didn't bother to ask what from. 'Let's go then.'

I felt like a teenager skipping school as we grabbed our coats and snuck out of the shop. Only Clementine noticed us leave. She was standing at the centre of a group of people but saw us through a gap between two heads. She gave a cheery wave and an even bigger grin as we slipped through the door.

It was dark and cold outside, drizzling slightly, but Princes Street was still busy. Shops were open late to accommodate the pre-Christmas spending, and the festive illuminations kept the night from feeling dreary. I pulled my bobble hat over my ears, burrowed into my scarf and turned to Cole.

'Where to?'

He glanced around, clearly lacking inspiration. 'The Christmas markets?'

I'd never been to Edinburgh's Christmas markets before, but they were pretty similar to the Manchester ones. Wooden huts flanking streets that felt too narrow as hundreds of people congregated, most of them feeling claustrophobic and frustrated, wondering why they went every year, and knowing they'd be going again the year after. The smell of mulled wine, roasted hog and plum strudel. The clamour of chatter and Christmas songs. The stalls selling fresh wreaths, and candles, and wooden toys, and felt hats people bought but never wore.

In my experience, the markets worked best (and they'd been an annual ritual for me in Manchester) if you ignored anything non-perishable and instead snacked your way around. I admitted this to Cole and he seemed amused.

'What would you start with?'

'Hot chocolate and marshmallows,' I replied instantly. 'Tasty but also practical: holding it keeps your hands warm.'

He was quiet for a moment as we wove our way through the thickening crowd and then suddenly, I'd lost him. I stood on tiptoes, straining to see over the ocean of woolly hats, but he was gone. And then, just as suddenly, he was beside me again, passing me a hot chocolate. With marshmallows.

I grinned, taking the proffered cup. 'Thanks.'

'I'm just glad I'm not wearing a white shirt this time.' I frowned in confusion and then, remembering the first hot chocolate I'd drunk with him, gave a ruffled laugh.

'I made a really good first impression, right?'

'There's no better way to start a job interview than to spray your prospective employer with a hot beverage.'

'I thought so too.'

Just then someone jostled me from behind. Cole snatched the cup out of my hands before it could – inevitably – spill all over him. Shaking his head, he passed it back to me.

I gave an impish smile as we wound our way through a group of teenagers taking selfies in front of a giant nutcracker.

'I'm surprised you wanted to come,' I admitted.

He shrugged. 'It was a good excuse.'

'For what?'

The look he gave me mingled exasperation with something less familiar. Something I couldn't read. I met his gaze, willing – challenging – him to put that expression into words.

I shouldn't have been surprised when he rose to my challenge with characteristic frankness.

'To spend the evening with you.'

We couldn't stop; we were surrounded on all sides by stalls and people. I was disappointed and relieved in equal measure that I wouldn't have to figure out what to do or say next. But I did resist the urge to bury my face in my scarf, instead letting him see the smile his words had kindled.

I waited until we were nearing the edge of the market, the crowds thinning, before I moved to walk right beside him.

'You know,' I began, sounding far more confident than I felt, 'if you wanted to hold my hand, I wouldn't entirely hate it.'

He didn't look at me, but I could sense his smile. 'No?'

'No.'

And then his fingers were lacing mine. I couldn't tell you if his hand was soft or hard, hot or cold. Just that it felt *right*. I'd held hands with ex-boyfriends before, but it had always felt forced. With Cole it felt strangely normal, as if it were something we'd always done. And, chaste and charged at the same time, it was a chance to touch. Not enough but enough for now.

It would have to be enough, I reminded myself. But I pushed the thought away. I could allow myself this one thing.

We moved slowly away from the market and found ourselves on the quieter cobbled streets of Edinburgh's

Old Town. We walked with no direction in mind. We walked and we talked.

I asked him about work. Not just to be polite, but because I was genuinely interested. And because I loved how animated he became as he talked about the different cases he was working on. His passion was contagious, and I felt my anger bubble as he described some of the injustices his company were working to overcome, and my pride swell as he – candidly, without arrogance – recounted his recent victories.

And he asked me about my life in Manchester, what my hobbies and ambitions had been, and about all the places I wanted to visit. This time there was no judgement in his tone when he told me I should start acting on my bucket list.

'And you should start enjoying the places you visit,' I gently chided.

'Well, when I travel to Japan next for work, you'll have to come with me and educate me on the ways of a tourist.'

He said the words casually, as if it were so simple, as if there was nothing momentous in his proposal. I smiled but said nothing, feeling a coldness that had nothing to do with the icy night air.

Suddenly I noticed a clock on the side of a building. It was nearly midnight.

'Is that the right time?' How had the evening disappeared so quickly?

Cole pulled his hand out of mine to check his watch and nodded. 'Do you turn into a pumpkin at the strike of twelve?'

I acknowledged his joke with a weak smile, looking around, trying to get my bearings. Where was the hotel from here? 'I should really be getting back,' I said, panic mounting.

Cole looked confused but didn't press me. 'We're not far from your hotel. I'll take you.'

We walked the rest of the way in silence. My hand was cold and empty without his, but he didn't reach for me again and I didn't want to complicate matters by reaching for him. I set a brisk pace and as soon as we reached my hotel, turned to him to say goodnight.

'Thank you for a lovely evening,' I said, desperately wishing it wasn't over. Wanting so much to ask him to stay. Knowing absolutely that I couldn't.

He seemed to sense my reluctant dismissal but didn't comment on it. There was the briefest of hesitations before he nodded, suddenly formal again, and stepped back.

'Goodnight, Ellie.'

'Goodnight, Cole.'

I didn't have time to watch him stride away, no matter how much I wanted to. The second he turned, I ran up the steps into the hotel lobby.

The concierge greeted me with a tip of his hat. 'Ms Lancaster,' he smiled, reaching behind the counter to pass me the rucksack I'd left in his care earlier. 'Perfect timing. Your taxi to the airport is just a minute away.'

Chapter Nineteen

I'd had a taxi ride, a flight and another taxi ride to decide on the right thing to say. But now the time had come, the only thing I could think was *please don't be too late, please don't be too late, please don't be too late.* I don't know who I was praying to. All I knew was that it was a bitterly cold night and if I was too late, I'd never forgive myself.

I hadn't brought the letter with me. Taking it from the island felt wrong, so I'd copied it out instead. The copy sat in my bag, but I didn't need it. I could picture the original, word for word.

Penned in an untidy scrawl, as if the writer had no smooth surface to lean the paper on, it read:

Dear Santy,

I stopped believing in you years ago and I'll be throwing this letter in the bin anyway, so I don't know why I'm writing it. Maybe I'm trying to turn back time to when I was a kid and everything was simpler. Nothing's simple now. I didn't want to leave home. I don't want to be here. But I can't go back. Not just because I don't have the money to get home but because I'm a

278

coward. What if Mam and Dad don't want me back?
I know they love me but can they forgive me? I don't
know how much longer I can last. Nights are so cold
now and

I just want to go home.
Ethan

All the letters that arrived in the archives contained
addresses. Although written in the same handwriting
as the related request, they were so uniform in their
placement and specificity I'd begun to suspect they were
later additions. But by whom? And how? I had no idea.
Like most things on the island, it was a mystery, one I'd
chosen to accept rather than question.

The address this letter bore was *The red sleeping bag,*
Parnell Street, Dublin, Ireland.

Since reading Ethan's note, I'd not stopped picturing
him. I had no idea what he really looked like, of course,
but I imagined him a lot like Alex: a lanky teenager with
dark hair and eyes that hadn't seen anywhere near enough
of the world to be alone in it. Huddled in a sleeping bag,
cold and hungry. Hands shaking as he scratched out the
letter he never planned on sending on a scrap bit of paper.

I'd been thinking of Cammie and her Christmas shop
too, empty and on the brink of shutting down back in
May. Her grateful smile when I'd bought the bauble had
meant I'd felt no guilt in disobeying Cole's rules. Besides,
no harm had been done by my tiny insurrection. The
island's secrets remained safe. And here was the chance to
do something much more important than buy a bauble –

something that could mean the difference between life and death. How could I not take it?

That said, this task was far more difficult than buying a bauble. For one, I hadn't anticipated how long Parnell Street was. It was early on Saturday morning, and the stretch of shops, cafes and hotels was still sleeping, as were the figures hunched in doorways, faceless cocoons of nylon and newspaper. I hated myself for passing them as I searched for Ethan, telling myself that helping only one may not be enough, but it was a start.

Ethan's letter had said 'the red sleeping bag' and so that's what I looked for. Most were so dirty and worn they'd forgotten their original colours, but none seemed like they might have once been red. I was nearing the end of the street when I started to really worry. The best-case scenario was that he'd found the courage – and funds – to go home. The worst-case scenario . . . didn't bear thinking about.

The *likeliest* scenario was that he'd moved to a different part of the city. I had no way of knowing when that letter had been sent. But some instinct told me Ethan had written it recently, and *was* still here. Why else had it been 'given' to me, back on the island?

I was nearing the end of Parnell Street when I noticed a doorway in a side alley. The morning was grey enough for the tiny triangle of colour poking out to be conspicuous. I moved nearer and saw that there was indeed a sleeping bag tucked into the meagre shelter, although red was a generous description. Soiled and torn, it looked more brown, but *maybe* it had once been red. And, judging from its shape, it was occupied.

I crept closer, my heart hammering. Was it him? Whoever lay there was angled into the doorway. I tried to get a better view, but the hood of the sleeping bag was fastened tightly around their head. Perhaps if I . . .

Just then my foot connected with an empty can. The noise it made was quiet, but clear enough. The sleeping bag suddenly lurched upright and I found myself face-to-face with its occupant. Again, to call him a teenager would be generous. Perhaps if the world had treated him more kindly, he would be a teenager. But his face was so gaunt and ashen that he looked like an old man, and what little hair I could see beneath his frayed woollen hat was grey with grease and dirt. Only his blue eyes, wide and bright with fear, suggested an age close to the boy who'd written that letter. I couldn't guarantee this was Ethan, but he was there and he needed help.

He seemed panicked, instantly alert. 'I'm leaving, I'm leaving,' he said, unzipping his sleeping bag and shuffling out of it. His voice, distinctly Irish, was young. And he looked smaller out of the nylon padding, even though he was wearing several layers of clothes.

I held up my hands, apologetic. 'No, I'm not here to – I don't . . .' I trailed off lamely. This was where I was supposed to say something – *anything* – about how he should go home and how I was there to help him. I'd given the speech enough times in my head. But there in that cold, dirty alleyway, all words failed me. And suddenly I was gripped by fear. Fear that he wouldn't want my help. Fear that, even if he did, he'd want to know how I'd come to be there. His life was more important than any secret, but I was determined to protect the archives if I could.

'I'm sorry,' I finally said. 'I didn't mean to wake you.'

But he was rolling up the sleeping bag with practised movements and fingers that trembled in the early morning chill. He'd clearly had to pack up hastily many times before. And then, without a backwards glance, he scurried out of the alley. I stood there for one long, deflated moment, and then hesitantly followed him onto Parnell Street.

He didn't seem to have a destination in mind. Keeping close to the buildings, he moved slowly along the street, pausing in a few doorways before settling on the shuttered entry to a Chinese takeaway. Scanning his surroundings nervously, he curled into the alcove, his back to the road. I stood a few buildings down from him, unsure of what to do next.

The idea that finally struck me was simple but fitting. He'd written a letter asking for help. I'd write one back.

I'd brought only hand luggage with me to Dublin, leaving my suitcase at the hotel in Edinburgh. But I was certain there'd be paper and a pen somewhere in the depths of my backpack. And, sure enough, after a few minutes of rummaging, I found it. Leaning the scrap of paper against the back of my *Ireland* travel guide, I kept it short.

'Please use this money to go home. Your family love and miss you – of course they'll forgive you.' I considered how to sign off and decided on a simple, 'Merry Christmas.'

Not even my bag could produce an envelope, but I had an old shopping list that I folded into a sleeve.

I wrote 'A Gift' on the front so that he'd open it, then slid the letter inside and reached for my purse. Not knowing where 'home' was for Ethan, I had no idea how much he'd need to get there. But for the first time in my life, I had money to spare – thanks to a generous wage and no living expenses. The cash I slipped inside would be more than enough to get Ethan anywhere within Ireland.

I'd been keeping one eye on his shrouded form and he hadn't moved since lying down. Fairly confident he was asleep, I edged closer. A glance up and down the street to make sure nobody was watching, and then, as stealthily as I could, I placed the makeshift envelope in a crease of his sleeping bag, surprised – and relieved – he didn't stir.

I toyed with the option of leaving only briefly. A flight to Edinburgh departed in a few hours; if I headed straight to the airport, I could be back at my hotel before the day's end. Cole and the others might not even realise I'd gone. I wouldn't have to suffer their disappointment and reproaches; wouldn't have to defend my defiance. I could have my metaphorical cake and eat it too. It was tempting. Very tempting.

But I couldn't leave without knowing this was Ethan's last night on the streets. After all, I had no idea why he was in Dublin in the first place. Had he been running to or from something? Any number of things could drive a teenage boy from his family. I couldn't assume it was a simple matter of money.

Across the road from where Ethan lay was a coffee shop, just opening for the morning. I was their first customer.

Wrapping my fingers around a hot drink to tempt some feeling back into them, I perched on a stool in the window and watched the red sleeping bag. It didn't move for a very long time. Minutes trickled slowly by, enough that my drink grew cold and, even though the barista didn't seem to care, I felt the need to order another to justify staying. I was halfway through that one when my phone rang, making me jump. Anxiety and guilt swept over me when I saw Clementine's name displayed on the screen. *She doesn't know where you are*, I reminded myself, but that only intensified the guilt. I switched the phone to silent and slipped it back into my pocket.

As I sat staring at a dormant sleeping bag, the street around us slowly waking, I found myself growing impatient. I shifted restlessly, tapping my fingers against the edge of the table. It didn't help that I couldn't get comfortable. Considering my stool's sole purpose was to accommodate a sitting person, you'd think it wouldn't be quite so tiny and quite so hard.

I pulled my phone out to check the time and saw another missed call from Clementine and a message that read, 'Don't tell me you've raided the hotel buffet breakfast without me.'

I was considering whether or not to respond when a movement caught my eye. Across the road, Ethan had shifted to a sitting position. I strained my eyes trying to make out if he'd found the envelope, but I couldn't see his hands and his face was still obscured by the hood of his sleeping bag. He was still for what felt like a very long time and then suddenly I caught a flash of white –

perhaps my note – and he looked up and down the street. Even at a distance I could read the shock and confusion on his face. There was also a hint of suspicion and fear as he tucked something – the money? – into his myriad layers and hurriedly rolled his sleeping bag up.

He was moving so quickly now that I had to rush out of the coffee shop to keep him in sight. Obviously, I'd never tailed anyone before and it wasn't like it looked in films, especially now the street was growing busy. I wove in and out of people, half jogging to keep up as Ethan dashed to one end of Parnell Street. He definitely had a destination in mind but, completely unfamiliar with Dublin, I couldn't guess where.

Ten minutes later, and he'd moved away from the now busy thoroughfare of Parnell Street and seemed to be heading into a quieter part of the city centre. Hotels and chain eateries gave way to offices, closed for the weekend. It was harder to blend in when there was no crowd, so I took my phone out (briefly registering I had two more missed calls) and pretended to be texting whenever Ethan glanced back, hoping he wouldn't recognise me from earlier that morning.

With another look over his shoulder, he suddenly turned into an alleyway. I couldn't follow him without making it obvious. Instead, I made to walk past, trying to catch a glimpse of where he was heading. He'd stopped, just a few feet away. I froze, assuming I'd been discovered and was about to be confronted, but his back was to me. He was stock-still, and I couldn't tell why. There didn't seem to be anything of interest down there, just a few bins, some graffiti on the walls and a parked car. Then I noticed movement within the car. The windows were tinted, but I could just about make out two faces.

I hurriedly stepped back, positioning myself at the corner of the alley at an angle that kept me out of the car's line of sight but able to see Ethan. He was still just standing there. His hand was in his pocket and I wondered if that was where he'd stashed the money. As naive as I was, I could guess at his dilemma.

I held my breath as he pulled something out of his pocket. But it wasn't the money. It was a scrap of paper, bearing a few scrawled lines of writing. My note. He gazed down at it for a long moment, then up at the car again. Even from the outside I could tell the moment was tense, heavy with a decision to be made. With careful movements, Ethan folded the note and returned it to his pocket.

And then, so quickly it took a moment for me to register, he broke into a run. Not towards the car but away from it, back the way he'd come. He brushed past me, barely noticing my presence. He was running so fast that, before I could collect myself, he'd turned another corner and was gone. I took off at a run too, but he was nowhere to be seen. Slowing, I looked up and down the other side streets. There was no sign of him.

I roamed the area for about twenty minutes, knowing it was pointless: he was long gone by now, wherever he was heading. I had no doubt he'd reached a personal crossroads, and all I could do was trust he'd made the right decision.

What now? There was another flight to Edinburgh that afternoon. Trying not to feel defeated, I followed

the map on my phone to the central bus station. A timetable on the wall told me I had a fifteen-minute wait
before the next airport-bound bus. It was midday on a
Saturday and the depot was heaving, but I managed to
find a free spot on a bench. Then, with resignation, I
pulled out my phone. It was time to face the music.

There were three more missed calls, two from Clementine and one from Aiden, and another message from
Clementine asking where I was. I toyed with the option
of phoning Aiden and asking him to cover for me. There
was no reason the others would doubt him if he said I'd
spent the day sightseeing in Edinburgh by myself or even
that I'd caught an impromptu flight to Manchester to
visit Mike, Toby and Izzy.

There was no need for Clementine and Cole to ever
find out what I'd done. I was sure Aiden would keep my
little insurgence a secret. I could go back to the island –
back to the life I'd grown to love – without consequence.
The thought of not returning, of never stepping foot in
the archives or Clementine's kitchen again, was almost
unfathomable. That place was my home. Those people
were my family. Would I really risk losing it all for the sake
of a stranger? A stranger I probably hadn't even helped.

'Excuse me, miss.' The voice, young with an Irish lilt,
pulled me from my worries. I looked up and there he
was. Ethan.

The sleeping bag was nowhere to be seen but there
was no hiding his nights on Dublin's streets. He hugged
himself beneath the frayed layers of clothes, and his eyes
were somewhere between haunted and panicked. But

there was a stubborn set to his mouth I was sure hadn't been there before. And he was looking directly at me.

So he had noticed me then. Wondering how I was going to explain the note, I stood up hesitantly. He took a step back.

'I'm really sorry for troubling you,' he went on. 'But I was wondering if I could . . .' Nervously he glanced at the phone in my hand.

'You want to use my phone?' I asked, nonplussed.

He nodded, apologetic. 'I really need to phone my mam.' At the word 'mam' his voice broke and he suddenly looked a lot younger. Pretending not to notice the tears in his eyes, I passed him the phone.

He looked surprised I'd given it so freely. But now he had it in his hand, he didn't seem to know what to do with it. I thought for a horrible moment that he couldn't remember his mother's number. But then, with a shaky sigh, he hit a sequence of buttons and held the mobile to his ear.

Please pick up, please pick up, please pick up, I begged.

And she did, almost immediately.

'Mam?' Ethan whispered, turning away from me.

I could hear a woman's voice on the other end but not what she was saying. 'I'm sorry,' Ethan murmured after a moment. 'I'm okay. But I want to come home.'

She said something that made his shoulders convulse. He covered his face with his free hand and heaved a sob. A middle-aged woman passing by gave him a concerned look. I tried to reassure her with a smile but, not knowing what Ethan's mother was saying, couldn't muster one.

Between sobs he managed to choke out the words 'Dublin' and 'bus station'. She said something that made him shake his head. 'No, don't come. I've enough to get to Limerick. Can you come get me from there?' Whatever she said next made his whole body sag – with relief or defeat, I couldn't tell. But then he whispered, 'Thank you Mammy. I . . . love you too,' and I was so happy I wanted to hug him.

Ethan turned to me then, almost as if he could sense my joy. I tried to moderate my smile. 'No, this isn't my phone. I borrowed it,' he continued, meeting my eyes. 'The bus gets into Limerick at half seven, so . . . I'll see you then?' Whatever she said in response made him smile and, in that second, I caught a glimpse of the teenage boy he'd once been. He hung up and passed me back my phone, suddenly awkward.

'Thanks, that was decent of you.'

'You're welcome.' I hesitated, wanting just one more confirmation. 'Is everything okay?'

He rubbed his arms self-consciously but managed a small smile. 'Yeah. It is now. Thanks again.' Ducking his head in farewell, he moved away, disappearing amidst the crowds.

I watched him go, my heart swelling. And then I looked down at the phone in my hand, torn. Wanting to share this victory with the people who would most understand it, my thumb hesitated over the 'C's. I didn't know how the Jones siblings would react to my rule-breaking. More accurately, I didn't *want* to know. But they were still the people I instinctively wanted to call first, to celebrate with.

But Ethan's wasn't the only letter I had copied in my bag. In the dream that wasn't a dream, there were two others. Ethan's was the first, but it was the second I was thinking about now.

Six simple words, plus the address of a flat in Edinburgh: *Let me come home. From Niall.*

Thinking logically, I knew that hundreds if not thousands of Nialls must have written Christmas letters. Rationally, I couldn't guarantee this was the Niall I'd met, but logic had no place in my life right then. I *knew* who had written that letter. And I also knew I'd been directed to it for a reason.

I bypassed the 'C's on my phone, scrolled down to the 'N's, and pressed 'call'. By the fifth ring I'd begun to worry, but then he answered.

'Hello?'

'It's Ellie. I need to meet you,' I said firmly. 'You were right.'

Chapter Twenty

I hadn't expected Niall to be at Edinburgh Airport; we'd agreed to meet near the university. But I stepped groggily into the arrivals lounge and there he was.

We'd only crossed paths twice, the last time three months ago, but he looked exactly as I remembered. Long brown hair, slightly unkempt, with those intense green eyes. He seemed happy to see me, his expression as readable and ingenuous as I recalled. I'd worried our meeting would be awkward, but he left no room for tension.

'You did a good deed today,' he said, launching straight in with a reassuring smile. 'You know that, right?'

I nodded. I'd expected the triumph felt in the wake of Ethan's call home to have slipped into doubt on the flight back to Scotland. But it hadn't. I was certain – in a completely uncharacteristic way – I'd done the right thing. That was why instead of calling Aiden, or Clementine, or Cole, I'd called Niall. When he'd given me his phone number three months before, back in Ludlow, I'd never expected to use it. But after Dublin, I didn't want to face disappointment and admonishments, to have to defend myself. I wanted someone to celebrate with, someone who, like me, believed we could – and should – do more to help. Perhaps together we could start to convince the others.

'I'm proud of you,' he said, earnest.

'Thanks. You'll be the only one,' I added dryly.

'Not necessarily. There's someone I want you to meet. Will you come with me?'

I hesitated, suddenly uncertain. Niall may have been Uncle Joe's son, but how much did I know about him? It was one thing to meet him in a public place, but another to follow him to who knew where? Clearly sensing my doubt, he gave an understanding smile.

'Don't worry, she's one of us. Trust me?'

'What do you mean, one of us?'

'She's on our side, you'll see.'

Deciding to trust him for now, I gestured for him to lead the way.

'You won't regret it,' he promised, looking quietly triumphant as he turned and began weaving through the crowd.

As I followed him towards the airport bus terminal, I was thinking again about his letter: *Let me come home. From Niall.*

I wasn't sure how much I could help. But whoever or whatever had given me the scroll clearly expected me to try, and – I hoped – believed I might succeed.

I wasn't sure what we'd talk about on the bus journey into the city, but Niall made conversation easy. The second we were sitting he turned to me, his eyes bright, and said, 'Tell me about this boy in Dublin. Do you think he went home?'

So I told him about Ethan, about the way he'd seemed so old and wrung out, but also so young and vulnerable. Niall listened intently, compassion in his eyes, and I realised he must know how Ethan felt. *Let me come home . . .*

Before I knew it, Edinburgh appeared, with its tall sandstone buildings and looming castle. We changed buses at Waverley train station, apparently heading for an area on the south side of the city called Morningside. By the time we stepped off the bus it was dark, but I could tell it was a leafy residential suburb consisting mainly of independent shops and cafes, and Victorian tenements. It was outside one of the latter that Niall stopped. Looking both excited and nervous, he pressed a buzzer and waited. After a moment, a woman's voice came through the intercom.

'Hello?'

'It's Niall.'

This was greeted by silence, and I noticed the briefest shiver of worry in Niall's expression. But then the woman's voice came again.

'Okay. Come up,' she said, sounding tired. His smile returning, Niall pushed open the door and headed for the stone staircase.

I hesitated, apprehensive about who was waiting for us. But I could see plenty of lights on in the surrounding flats. Lots of people to hear me scream and call the police, if it came to that. I followed slowly.

The building had clearly been gentrified. It had a homely, distinctly middle-class feel to it. The stairs were swept clean, the walls warmly painted and most of the apartment doors we passed were fronted with welcome mats and flanked by house plants or the occasional Christmas decoration.

On the third floor, a blue door was already open. Standing in the threshold was a woman in her thirties. Curly red hair pinned up, wide lips, a scattering of freckles on otherwise flawless skin. She was artfully casual in bare feet, capri trousers and an oversized white jumper that hung off one shoulder. The instant she opened the door I recognised her.

She didn't see me at first. Her gaze was focused on Niall – and she didn't look happy.

'You can't just show up,' she said, her accent English. 'You're lucky Alex is away for the week on a school trip. What do you want, Niall?'

A framed photo hidden in a drawer. A family on a beach. Cole, looking younger and happier. A toddler. A figure, half obscured behind a woman with red hair, wide lips and freckles.

A little older, a little narrower, more guarded, this woman was unmistakably Andy. Alex's mother. Cole's ex-wife.

I didn't have a moment to contemplate the implications of this before Niall stepped to one side and gestured to me. 'I brought Ellie.'

Surprise flitted across her face as she eyed me speculatively. It was ridiculous given the circumstances, but I was painfully aware of my scrunched airplane clothes and hair that hadn't seen a comb in over twenty-four hours. 'The new archivist?' she asked.

'She answered a letter today, Miranda.'

Miranda – Andy – raised a neat eyebrow and stepped aside. 'Come in then.' She padded down a hallway, its walls covered in the kind of modern art I'd never understand, to a stylish, open-plan lounge and kitchen. It still had some original Victorian features – the fireplace, the high ceiling, timber window frames – but the colour scheme, slate grey and mustard, was distinctly modern.

'Can I get you anything?' she asked, peering into a stainless-steel fridge. 'I've got sparkling water, red wine, iced coffee. Alex's stash of pop that he thinks I don't know about. And some left-over phad thai.' She lifted the lid, sniffed its contents and snapped the lid back down. 'Scratch that. No phad thai.'

She appeared to be making the offer to me rather than to Niall. I just shook my head. I'd yet to say anything. What *could* I say?

She folded herself onto the vast charcoal couch and nodded for us to sit too. Niall took a seat on the opposite end of the couch, while I tentatively perched on an armchair – which, I realised belatedly, turned out to be the kind that swivels. I began spinning, got halfway around, and decided it would be easiest to continue. Facing them again, I stamped my feet down to anchor myself in place.

'This is a, er, fun chair,' I mumbled.

Andy smiled but there was little warmth in it. 'So, you're the new archivist.'

It wasn't a question, which meant I didn't have to reply. I was already in breach of my contract with Jones Associates, of course, but talking to this woman – essentially a stranger, albeit one who'd been married to Cole – about the island felt a step too far. Niall was different because he'd always been the one volunteering information. I'd talked about Ethan, yes, but not how I'd found his letter. I'd talked about Clementine but never about the house or the archives.

'I'm Ellie,' I said neutrally.

'It's nice to meet you, Ellie. I've been curious about you.'

'I'm sorry but I don't know who you are . . . ?'

'She's our resident scientist,' Niall added, which earned him a brief glower from Andy. 'Will you show her your research?'

'Later maybe,' she said with a breeziness I didn't entirely trust. 'I want to hear more about Ellie's experiences.'

What had I walked into here? 'I'm sorry, I can't share those with you.' I tried for a breezy tone too, but wasn't convincing.

She gave a knowing chuckle. 'Let me guess, Cole made you sign a confidentiality agreement. He does love those. He even worked one into our prenup.' She studied me in silence for a moment and then, placing her drink on the glass coffee table, leant forward. 'Why did you bring her here?' She was talking to Niall but still looking at me.

'I told you. She answered a letter. She agrees with us about the island.'

'What precisely is it you agree with?' she asked. Her body language was casual, her tone conversational, but there was no mistaking the sharpness of her scrutiny. I felt like a frog on a table being dissected.

I looked to Niall, uncertainly, and he gave a reassuring smile. 'Don't worry. Miranda's one of us. She knows about the island. Hell, she knows more than anyone about the island. You can talk to her.'

'What do you want me to say?' I asked cautiously. 'If she already knows everything, what can I possibly add?'

'Tell her that you agree with us, that we're all on the same page. And then we can start working together.'

'It's a bit early for that,' Andy said at the same time as I asked, 'What do you mean, start working together?'

Niall's voice was intense. 'On the letters. What you've been doing already, only we work as a team. Just get us back to the island and I can carry on with my work, Miranda can carry on with hers, and we can help the way we're supposed to.'

I felt the first subtle tendrils of unease as Niall spoke, his expression almost feverish. 'You want my help to go back to the island?' I asked, looking from Niall to Andy.

Andy didn't respond but Niall laughed. 'Of course we do.'

'Well, I'm sure if you talked to Cole and Clementine—'

'I already told you,' Niall cut in, impatient. 'They wouldn't listen to us then; they won't listen now. We had too many questions and too many ideas. We're exiled. Only you can get us back.'

'How?'

Niall rose. 'Come with me and I'll show you. Miranda?'

I sensed a weariness from Andy as she stood too and nodded. 'Okay. I'll drive.'

Having come this far, I couldn't refuse to go with them, no matter how uneasy I felt sliding into the front passenger seat of Andy's Mini. With Niall squeezed into the back – I sensed, distractedly grateful, to make me feel safer upfront – we drove. I took a moment to brave looking at my phone. More missed calls and messages, this time from Toby as well – clearly Clementine had been in touch with him. I hated letting them worry and wondered how long it would be before they called the police. I sent a hasty, vaguely reassuring message to them all, hoping it would convince them I was still alive and hadn't been kidnapped: I'd call them as soon as I could, I said, but there was something I needed to do first.

I didn't know enough about Edinburgh's layout to judge whether we were travelling north or south, out of the city or towards the centre. But in the orange glow of the street lights, I could see tenements and parks were giving way to high-rise flats and betting shops. More people were on the streets here, spilling out of or into pubs.

How is it still only Saturday? I wondered, amazed by how much had happened in such little time. Only yesterday, I'd been dress shopping with Clementine; only last night, I'd held hands with Cole as we walked the streets of Edinburgh. Now I was being driven by Cole's ex-wife to god knows where.

God knows where turned out to be the home of Cole's exiled cousin – a tiny apartment above a chippy. The street sign matched the address on Niall's letter, and the door sported chipped paint and three locks.

Niall went in first, flipping a switch that did absolutely nothing.

'When did you last pay your electricity bill?' Andy sighed.

'Not recently enough, it seems,' Niall replied with an admirable lack of concern. 'I'll dig out some candles.'

As he disappeared inside, Andy turned to me and said quietly, 'He was getting better.' There was no mistaking the admonishment in her tone. Taken aback, I opened my mouth to ask what she meant, but she'd already turned to follow Niall into the flat, using her phone as a torch.

I lingered indecisively on the threshold. Was it stupid of me to follow? The sensible thing for me to do would be to leave, call Cole or Clementine, and tell them everything. But in front of me was an open door and possible answers. And there *had* to be a reason I'd been given Niall's letter . . .

I stepped inside. By the time I reached the room at the end of the hallway, Niall had lit several candles, and I froze in shock.

There was barely any furniture, just one desk and countless easels. And on every easel was a painting, each in a different style, ranging from bold, bright cubes of colour to dark lines slashing harshly across the canvas. But there was no mistaking what they all depicted.

The island.

I was relieved Niall wasn't looking at me – he was rummaging in the desk – and didn't see my reaction. Andy's attention, however, *was* on me. She didn't look surprised by the paintings, just eyed them briefly, her mouth set in a thin, grim line, before turning to gauge my response. I tried to hide how unnerved I was but knew it was obvious. She gave a subtle nod, as if confirming something, though I didn't know what.

There was a sudden clatter and we both jumped. Niall had cleared the desk by sweeping everything to the floor.

'Take a look at this,' he said as he set a couple of candles down and slapped a large sheet between them.

I looked to Andy, unsure, but with a resigned shrug she moved closer. I followed to see it was a nautical chart. There was one mass of land, depicted in pale brown, at the bottom, and I could make out a couple of words I recognised: 'UNST' and 'Baltasound'. But otherwise, the chart was a vast blue littered with lines, crosses and numbers I didn't understand.

I touched an x with my fingertip. 'What are these?'

'All the places the island isn't,' Niall replied.

I glanced at Andy again. And again, she seemed more sad than surprised.

'I've looked everywhere. Willum won't take me – he's too loyal to my dad. But I've tried others. Other fishermen, other boats. They take my money, but they can't find the island. Going west, we got as far as the Faroe Islands; east, we got to Bergen. North we just kept going until we had to turn back. Nothing but sea.' He shook his head, seeming at a loss. 'No hint of home, no matter how hard I search. But,' he peered up at me, suddenly excited, 'we've got you now. You can help.'

Before I could say anything, Niall rifled through one of the desk drawers and pulled out reams of handwritten documents. The writing on them was scrawled, difficult to read and I didn't have a chance to make out any of the words as Niall tossed them onto the desk before passing me a large, leather-bound book.

'What's this?' I asked, taking it gingerly.

'The shortlists.'

I gave a gasp of surprise. But it made sense. Hadn't Uncle Joe and Clementine told me a written record of shortlists had been 'lost'? Now I knew what they meant.

'How do you have this?' I asked gently, trying to keep my tone free of judgement.

'I brought it with me when I left the island, and then . . . couldn't get back. I needed it, you see. To do the work. Open it and look.'

I did as he asked. It was a thick book, heavy with words, and clearly old. Judging by its binding and paper quality, I estimated it to be an early twentieth-century notebook. Opening the first page, I saw hand-drawn lines marking out columns, with names to the left, addresses in the centre and transcriptions of letters on the right. The script, slanted cursive with its elongated 's's that looked more like 'f's, dated it earlier, to the nineteenth century. And then I saw the numbers written at the top of the page, confirming my estimate: *1864*.

I'd only managed to skim the first entry – a boy called Howard, from an illegible town ending with 'Creek' in Georgia, was asking for his big brother to return from the war – when Niall took the book from me. Flicking two-thirds through, he passed it back.

'This is my work.'

301

The handwriting here was just as difficult to read, but modern. Blue biro and a ruler had been used to mark the columns, and the number at the top of the page dated it two years previously. Names, addresses and transcribed letters filled the page, but to my alarm, most of them had been obscured behind decisive lines of black marker.

'Why are they crossed out?' I asked, unable to keep the disquiet from my tone.

'Because they weren't worthy,' Niall said, as if it was obvious. 'Don't worry, I did my research. Here,' He passed me a sheet of paper at random from the pile on the desk.

I looked down and saw a name and address scrawled at the top: *Mattia from Treviso*. Beneath that was a hand-written list of times and events: *8.20 left the apartment for work. 8.30 bought coffee. 8.55 reached work.* And so on, until *23.05 turned apartment light off, presumably to bed.* It was an itinerary, presumably Mattia's. Two events were highlighted. One in green read: *13.45 passed the wallet test.* The other, in red: *18.30 failed the homeless man test.* Beneath it all, in bold, unforgiving letters: *UNWORTHY.*

Niall misread the alarm on my face for confusion. He passed me a handful of papers. 'Read more and you'll understand what I've been doing.'

Fighting a wave of nausea, I scanned names, places and highlighted events. Some were simple observations, while others were clearly orchestrated. Cristina from Miercurea Ciuc had 'passed the dropped wallet test' but 'failed the charity donations test'. *UNWORTHY.* Martha from Tampico had 'failed to help a bullied classmate when the opportunity arose'. *UNWORTHY*. Egil from Støren had 'passed the lost phone test' but 'failed the old woman test'. *UNWORTHY*. Looking back at the notebook, I could just about make out these names and addresses beneath the black lines.

My stomach turned at the wrongness of it. Not the removal of the record book from the island – after all, I was hiding three copied letters in my own bag. But all those black lines. All those crossed out names. Looking down at the other sheets of paper on the desk, I saw they followed the same pattern as Mattia's record. I couldn't make out the details of Julya from Maladzyechna or Bailey from Wānaka, but they'd clearly been deemed undeserving too.

Unable to face Niall, I turned to Andy instead. For the first time, she refused to meet my gaze.

'You see how important this work is,' Niall was saying, brushing the records off the chart so we could see all those places the island wasn't. 'Help me get back home and we can carry on with this together.'

Revulsion swept over me like an icy wave. *This* was what he'd meant by doing more, going out into the world. Not helping people, but testing them.

I opened my mouth, not sure what words were going to come out but hoping they could adequately express my horror. Andy, though, gave an almost imperceptible shake of her head and I clamped my mouth shut, opening it again only after I'd considered my words carefully.

'What makes you think I can get you back to the island?'

His smile was so sincere and eager I nearly forgot the repulsion I'd been feeling only seconds ago. 'You're the archivist now.' He repeated his words from earlier. 'So the island will show itself to you.'

As senseless as it seemed, I knew he was right. With a boat and somebody driving us, I could navigate. I could follow that invisible line tethering me to the island. I could get Niall home. But I also knew, without a shadow of a doubt, that I shouldn't. His letter may have pled to come home, but this wasn't right.

'I'm so sorry, Niall,' I whispered. 'But no.' I was about to add 'I can't', but that would have been a lie.

The room fell into silence. Niall and Andy stared at me. Andy looked surprised; Niall shocked and then, abruptly, relieved.

'You're worried you won't be able to find the island,' he said, his tone gently understanding. 'But trust me, it'll let you.'

'No,' I said again, before I could back down. 'I won't take you without talking to the others. I don't have the right.' His expression of relief turned to one of grief, and I hastened to reassure him. 'But I *will* help. I'll get Clementine and Cole to meet you. You can talk this through, fix things without having to sneak back onto—'

But Niall grabbed a nearby easel and hurled it across the room. 'You're not listening!' he screamed, his face contorted in rage. I jumped back in fright. Andy, who'd barely flinched, stepped towards Niall and placed her hand on his shoulder.

I expected him to lash out but when he turned to her, I saw it wasn't rage in his face at all but despair. 'She isn't listening,' he said, his voice anguished. 'She won't help me get home. Back to . . .' He closed his eyes as the tears came. I stood frozen to the spot, seemingly forgotten. After a long moment, he opened his eyes again and ran his fingers through his ragged hair. 'If she won't take me, I'll go myself.'

Pulling out of Andy's grip, he moved back to the chart, tracing a space between crosses. 'There are still places I haven't looked. That area north of the oil fields. Or further into the Norwegian Sea. Maybe even east beyond the Faroe Islands. I don't need a skipper, just a boat. Plenty of supplies and I can just keep going.'

'Niall . . .' Andy began.

'Don't try to talk me out of this, Miranda. I *need* to get back.'

Pursing her lips together, Andy was silent for a moment. Then she nodded. 'I won't try to talk you out of this. But let me talk to Ellie. You've given her a lot to think about.' She took the notebook from my hands and closed it with a decisive snap. 'Why don't you go out and get us some drinks? Give me some time to talk with her alone, woman to woman.'

It spoke of how much he trusted Andy that, after only a few seconds of hesitation, he nodded. 'If you think it'll help.'

The second the front door closed, Andy slammed the notebook onto the desk.

'What have you done?' she hissed, her eyes blazing. Gone was the coolly aloof woman from a moment ago.

I stepped back defensively. 'What do you mean?'

'He was getting better. He was learning to forget a little, live a little. And then you come along—'

'I didn't exactly "come along",' I protested. 'We met by chance.'

'By chance?' she scoffed. 'How gullible are you? You met in Lerwick, right? Niall knew Clementine was going to be there doing a book signing. He follows all her events online. He was waiting in the harbour for Willum's boat. He saw you and the other new archivist, and decided to follow you. There was nothing random about your meeting. He'd planned it. The same with Ludlow.'

Cold fingers of unease crept up my spine.

'How do you know this?' I whispered, ashamed by how stupid I'd been.

'Because he tells me *everything*.' Her words weren't smug or possessive. She wasn't boasting. She was drained and jaded. 'He called me thirty times from Lerwick, updating me constantly. He phoned me straight after meeting you in the coffee shop, convinced you'd help. I tried to warn him but . . .' She shrugged, her mouth a bitter twist. 'The spark was reignited. That was his metaphor, not mine. All that time trying to heal him, trying to help him forget and move on, wasted. He was back to where he started, desperate to be on that goddamn island, continuing his *work*.' She said the final word as if it tasted foul on her tongue.

306

I looked down at the chart and paper records scattered across the desk and felt sick. 'I didn't know. I thought he just . . . wanted to get home and help people.'

'That's what he thinks too. But as you can see,' she tapped Mattias's record with a short but neatly manicured fingernail. 'His idea of helping people doesn't align with the rest of the family's.'

'Does it . . . align with yours?' I asked uneasily. I was remembering how Alex had mentioned his mother when arguing with Cole about answering the letters. *This has nothing to do with your mother,* Cole had said, convincing nobody.

Andy moved away from the desk to retrieve the picture Niall had hurled across the room. With precise movements, she righted the easel and remounted the canvas. I was no expert, but its abstract style of sharp, choppy lines, forming a collage of the island from twenty different angles, made me think of Picasso.

'Once upon a time it did,' Andy replied, studying the painting. 'But not now.' She turned back to me then, met my eyes. 'I've made mistakes. I'm human. But I've been trying to make up for them, for Alex's sake. And for Niall's. I feel . . . responsible for him, in a way. Protective. He looks like a man but really, he's just a child. Just a child wanting to go home.'

I thought of Ethan then, and wanted to cry,

'Back to his dad. He's *furious* with Joe but misses him fiercely, even if he'll never admit it to himself. They used to fight a lot, back on the island, even when Niall was a kid, apparently. And he'd run off and hide somewhere, in a cave or up a tree, but Joe would always find him so they could make amends. Niall used to say the island told Joe where he was hiding, but really, I think that's just parenthood. Have you got children?'

She glanced at me, and although my mind instantly went to Izzy, I shook my head.

'I wouldn't believe it if I wasn't a mother,' she continued. 'But there is a tether between parent and child. A kind of radar. And I think . . .' Her fingers traced the vivid red of the painting's island. 'I think he's still just waiting for his dad to find him and take him home. But without Joe . . .' Striding back towards the desk, she gestured to the cross-littered chart. 'Do you know how many times he's nearly died trying to find the island? Those waters are dangerous and Willum's the only one who can navigate them safely. Niall's wrecked one boat already. Nearly drowned falling off another during a storm. And now he's determined to go alone.'

'Then we need to stop him,' I said.

Andy gave a sad smile, her eyes still on the painting. 'You can't stop Niall. That's what I used to . . . admire about him. When he's made up his mind, he's like a tsunami. Indomitable. But so very destructive.'

'Then what are we going to do?' I asked, feeling helpless. 'Should I take him? If it would be less dangerous—'

'No,' she interrupted sharply. 'He can't go back there. You were right to refuse. I may not fully believe in all of . . . this,' she said, gesturing to the paintings, 'but I know he's even more destructive *on* that blasted island. And, as much as I want to protect him, I also want to protect *it*.'

Before I could begin on the thousand questions I had, the front door opened and Niall strode in, a cone of chips in one hand and two cans of pop stacked in the other. He looked from Andy to me, hopeful, expectant. He clearly had a lot of faith in Andy's powers of persuasion.

Andy negated the need for me to think of something to say. 'She isn't coming, Niall. But I'll come with you.'

My mind turned to those letters; the three given to me by the island. The first from Ethan, sleeping rough in Dublin. The second from Niall, pleading to come home.

The third was finally beginning to make sense.
To whom it may concern, it had begun.

Apologies for the formality but I don't know who I should be addressing. The island? Some magical being I don't believe in? Or the family I lost? Either way, I'm sorry. I'm so sorry for betraying your trust. I see mystery and I need to find answers, that's who I am, but everything I did was wrong. I see that now. Perhaps it is too late. But if we are all allowed one wish then this is mine: to make amends and to be forgiven. And, if I'm permitted a second wish, to earn back what I so carelessly and selfishly lost.

Yours faithfully,
Andy

309

Chapter Twenty-One

Clementine was uncharacteristically silent as we drove out of Uyeasound. Nobody in the small coastal village, overlooking a strait on the south side of Unst, had seen anyone matching Niall and Andy's descriptions, let alone sold or loaned a boat to them. Another harbour, another dead end. But Unst was small; there were only so many piers and marinas they could have launched from, and, having spent the last five hours travelling down the coast from Baltasound in Mary's borrowed old banger, we'd been to most of them on the eastern side. We'd knocked on every door, ventured into every pub, approached every anchored boat. Nothing.

We'd called both Andy and Niall's phones repeatedly, but both had been switched off. We'd contacted the Shetland coastguard but, with no idea of where they'd sailed from, they could do little to help. At Willum's suggestion, we'd phoned the Shetland Fishermen's Association based in Lerwick, who'd put a call out to their members but heard nothing back. So for now all we could do was search the harbours and hope that somebody somewhere had seen the pair set off.

Cole and Alex were combing the west-side harbours of Unst; Aiden, Alison and Clyde were scouring the coastlines of Yell, immediately south to us, while Willum and Mary were sailing from pier to pier on the smaller northern islands. Frequent phone check-ins confirmed they were having no success either.

'I think that's the last one until we're back at Belmont,' I said grimly, studying the map we'd bought back on the mainland.

'Call Cole,' Clementine said, her attention wholly on the road. It was well maintained, but narrow, and the sleet whipping sideways made driving difficult. On top of that, it was growing dark, and we didn't have the luxury of street lights.

I didn't want to speak to Cole. He'd barely said two words to me since I'd phoned from Niall's flat, panicking. Niall and Andy had already left – I'd not been able to convince them to wait – and I'd told Cole everything. Meeting Niall in Lerwick and again in Ludlow. The few titbits of information I'd gleaned from him and from Clementine. The letter from Ethan, leading me to Dublin. The letter from Niall, leading me back to Edinburgh. I didn't mention Andy's letter, but did confess I'd met his ex-wife. Cole listened in silence and once I'd finished, told me he was coming to get me.

His knuckles were white on the steering wheel when he pulled up outside Niall's flat at nearly midnight. I'd been too scared to notice the cold, but my feet and hands were numb when I climbed into the passenger seat, and my tears of guilt and worry had nearly frozen to my cheeks.

'I'm so sorry,' I choked out.

Cole wouldn't look at me. 'We can talk about this after. There are more pressing issues. I've called Clementine and Willum, and the coastguard. We've not sent word to Uncle Joe yet though. We don't want to worry him.'

He may not have been willing to talk or meet my gaze, but he still buckled my seat belt for me when my fingers were too chilled to do the job. I also noticed he turned the heating up when he thought I wasn't looking. But he remained stonily silent. And while Clementine and the others peppered me with urgent questions on the flight to Shetland, he kept himself apart, his face unreadable.

Bracing myself now, I phoned him. There was no preamble.

'Anything?'

'Nothing. Sorry. We're headed to Belmont next.'

'We're already there. No sign of them.' There was a moment's silence and then, in a resigned tone, 'There's nothing more we can do today. This storm's set in for the night. Head back to Baltasound. We'll meet you there and sleep at Willum and Mary's. They're staying with Mary's cousin on Fetlar tonight.'

'Have you heard anything from Aiden and—'

'Checked into a guesthouse on Yell for the night. See you soon.' There was a beep and he was gone.

I relayed what he'd said to Clementine, who gave a grim nod. After her questions on the plane, we hadn't spoken much either. It would only take us ten minutes to reach Baltasound, Unst being so small. Ten minutes of us being alone together; I had to use them.

'I'm so sorry, Clementine,' I blurted out.

'What for, exactly?' she asked, her eyes still on the road. It wasn't the question of somebody who thought me blameless. It was the question of somebody who wanted an itemised list of my many misdeeds.

I swallowed down what little pride I had left and began. 'I'm sorry for Dublin. I'm not sorry for going there and helping that boy – it was the right thing to do, I'm certain of it – but I shouldn't have snuck off. I should have told you. And I'm sorry for not answering my phone while I was there and making you worry.'

Clementine said nothing. My verdict would come only once the list was complete.

'And I'm sorry for not telling you about Niall,' I went on. 'As soon as I knew who he was, I should have told you. He asked me not to, but I shouldn't have listened. It was stupid of me. And I'm sorry for not telling you about Niall's letter, and for calling him instead of you when I came back from Dublin. And for going to meet Andy. And for being the one that sparked off his . . . obsession again. Without me, none of this would have happened.'

'One hundred per cent correct,' Clementine nodded. There was silence for a moment, punctuated only by the squeak of the wipers. And then she sighed. 'One hundred per cent forgiven.'

'What?' I asked, startled. 'Really?'

'Don't misunderstand, I was mad. *Really* mad. And I'm *really* worried about Niall and Andy. But I know you acted with good intentions, and perhaps if we'd been more honest with you, you would have trusted us.'

The relief I felt was immense. Much remained to be concerned about – not least, as Clementine had noted, the safety of Niall and Andy – but discovering my friend-ship was still intact felt like someone taking a huge, weighty backpack off my shoulders. I had a lot of other suitcases to deal with yet, but my load was much lighter for her forgiveness.

'Thank you,' I said, knowing those two words could never convey my depth of gratitude, but hoping she could sense it anyway. 'I doubt everyone else will feel the same.'

She gave me a sideways glance. 'Don't worry about my brother. I'll deal with him.'

We arrived at Baltasound to a harbour so dark we could see neither boats nor water. It seemed odd letting our-selves into Mary and Willum's bungalow without them, but Mary had insisted we sleep and eat there, so we set about making a big plate of sandwiches in time for Cole and Alex's arrival.

The glaring glow of a headlight across the kitchen wall announced their approach. The howling wind cov-ered the sound of the engine, but a few moments later we heard the front door open and footsteps leading into the lounge. Bearing the plate of sandwiches, Clemen-tine stepped out of the kitchen, gesturing with a flick of her kingfisher-blue head for me to follow. I dithered, wondering if I should make myself scarce. But there was nowhere to hide except the bathroom, and I couldn't very well stay in there all evening. So, I braced myself for a chilly – or heated – reunion with Cole, and followed Clementine into the lounge.

Cole was kneeling in front of the traditional wood-burner and I could tell he was tense. The nod he gave me as I stepped into the room was neither cold nor angry. It was cursory, distracted, and I realised nothing he was feeling was about *me*. Clementine may have been too generous to hold a grudge, but Cole was consumed by other emotions, chief amongst them fear. It was the same fear that haunted Alex as he stood by the window look-ing out onto the violent night.

I hadn't expected Cole to tell Alex about the situation. Camping with his school in the Pentland Hills, south of the city, he could have remained blissfully ignorant while the adults sorted everything out. But honesty was clearly Cole's default parenting policy. He'd texted his son, explaining the circumstances and giving him the option of staying put or joining us. Though I didn't know what Alex had said in response, I knew that Cole had picked him up. They'd not left each other's sides since.

Clementine offered Alex a sandwich, but he shook his head.

Cole moved away from the log burner, already health-ily crackling, and touched Alex's shoulder. 'You should have something,' he signed.

'Not hungry,' Alex replied.

'Then sleep,' Cole insisted. 'You'll be no use to any of us if you can't keep your eyes open tomorrow. Mary said to use their bed, so use it. The rest of us will sleep in here.'

Alex looked exhausted. Wan and leaden, he leant into Cole's arms and let his father lead him from the room. Sharing concerned looks, Clementine and I perched either end of the sofa and picked listlessly at a sandwich each.

When Cole came back into the room ten minutes later, there was one expression discernible on his otherwise unreadable face. Anger.

'Why would she do this?' he demanded, pacing over to the window to assume Alex's vigil. 'Why risk her safety for *him*? Why put *his* needs before her own son?'

Clementine held out her hands in a helpless gesture. 'Maybe she doesn't realise how dangerous it is.'

She definitely realises, I thought, but didn't say aloud. 'Maybe she let her worry for Niall cloud her judgement?' I offered tentatively. 'He was . . . very determined. She didn't think we'd be able to stop him.'

'Then she should have just let him go,' Cole said, his voice quiet and measured but no less livid. 'He's already ruined so much.'

'How?' I asked. It wasn't the right time to demand answers, but it never would be.

Cole didn't acknowledge my question. He was still staring out of the window, and either hadn't heard or wasn't willing to reply. But Clementine, casting me a reassuring look, barked her brother's name.

'No more secrets,' she ordered, her mouth a stubborn line. 'Ellie kept all this from us because we were keeping so much from her. Let's break this stupid circle of secrecy once and for all.'

I would have bet my life's savings that Cole would refuse. That he'd declare me undeserving of answers, or say we could discuss it another time, or simply ignore Clementine altogether. But he turned from the window, met my eyes, and with a resigned sigh, lowered himself into the armchair by the window. 'What do you want to know?'

Taken aback by this sudden invitation, I sat mute for a long, embarrassing moment. The myriad questions I'd been compiling for nearly a year suddenly fled my mind, and even as I managed to reel them back in, I didn't know which to ask first. Was there a finite number of questions Cole would be willing to answer? Feeling like the beneficiary of a genie's three wishes, I had to choose my words carefully.

'Why did you exile Niall from the island?'

The slight raising of an eyebrow indicated that Cole was surprised. A glance at Clementine confirmed she was too.

'I didn't,' Cole replied. 'The island did.'

Not too long ago, his response would have seemed absurd. Now it was perfectly believable. Accepting the island's agency without question, I pressed on. 'Why? How? What did he do?'

The siblings exchanged a long look, and it was Clementine who eventually spoke. 'There's no simple answer to that. If you want to understand then we'll need to start at the beginning, back when we were just kids.'

'If you're willing to tell me, I want to hear,' I said.

Clementine sighed. 'The three of us grew up together on the island. We were practically siblings. There was barely any age gap between the three of us; we played the same games, read the same books, watched the same videos. As really young children, I was probably closer to Niall than to Cole. But when we hit our teens, things began to change. *He* began to change.' She was clutching a cushion, fidgeting with the tassels. 'We used to fantasise about getting off the island. You know, the way every kid thinks every patch of grass is greener than their own. Don't get me wrong, we loved the island, and our parents made sure we had plenty of time on the mainland. To make friends, to visit places, to get used to life on the outside. But we wanted some independence. So, unsurprisingly, the moment me and Cole turned eighteen, off we skipped to university. But Niall . . .'

'Decided he belonged on the island,' Cole interjected. 'Uncle Joe had been training him as archivist, and that's where he felt he belonged.'

'He wasn't pressured to stay,' Clementine added. 'He was encouraged to go off-island and "find himself". He just didn't want to.'

'Why not?'

The pair exchanged another look. 'How much do you know about Auntie Lorna?' Clementine asked.

'Uncle Joe's wife? Not much.' Uncle Joe rarely spoke about her, though I knew he thought of her often. 'I've seen her bench and garden.'

Clementine grinned fondly. 'Lorna loved that spot. Well, she loved the whole island. She always said it was home from the moment she first stepped foot on it. She never wanted to leave, not even for short trips back to

Scotland. Which was why it was . . . so hard . . .' Her smile faded, and she looked to Cole.

'Which was why it was so hard when she became ill,' Cole continued for her. His voice was detached, his expression remote, but I could see he was as pained as his sister. 'And her treatment meant leaving the island. She refused at first, but Uncle Joe begged.'

'Niall begged too,' Clementine said. 'He loved his mum so much. He was just a kid at the time—'

'He was twenty-one,' Cole cut in sharply.

'Technically, but he'd barely left the island. He didn't know anyone beyond his family. We were his only friends, and we were both gone. His parents were his entire world.'

Cole gave a slight nod, as if acknowledging Clementine's words. 'Lorna didn't want to leave the island but, in the end, she acquiesced and went to hospital in Lerwick. We all thought she'd get better and be home soon – but she never came back.'

'We scattered her ashes on the island,' Clementine continued after a moment of silence. 'At her spot. It seemed to give Uncle Joe some peace, allowed him to begin healing. But Niall . . . I don't think he ever healed. He'd asked her to leave the island for the treatment, argued when she'd wanted to stay. The guilt . . .'

'It wasn't just guilt,' Cole said stiffly. 'It was anger too.'

'Who was he angry with?' I asked. 'Himself?'

'Partly.' Clementine replied at the same time Cole said, 'The island. He blamed the island.'

I frowned. 'But why—'

'We'd always written letters to the island,' Clementine said. 'As kids. In secret. We wanted things just like everyone else. The usual stuff: toys, books, clothes. I remember one Christmas I asked for a Mr Frosty Snow Cone Maker; Cole wanted a set of fantasy books – you always were a geek, weren't you? – and Niall a typewriter. We'd write our letters and sneak them into the post room.'

'Did you ever get what you'd asked for?'

Clementine snorted. 'Yes. But only because our parents read our requests. But then Auntie Lorna got sick.'

'And Niall began writing more and more letters.' Cole's tone was grim. 'Every day, he wrote, asking for Lorna to recover, to come home.'

Clementine gave a helpless shrug. 'He and Uncle Joe were in Lerwick with her when she died. When they came back to the island, Niall went straight down to the archives and, well . . .'

'He turned the place upside down,' Cole said, his eyes steely. 'He tore up letters, broke furniture, smashed bulbs and then started a fire.'

'That could have been an accident,' Clementine interjected.

Cole's sigh indicated they'd had this argument many times before. 'The damage he caused was immense, but we were all grieving, in our own ways. Niall's way was anger. We thought, with time, he'd let it go. But he didn't. He couldn't understand why his letter hadn't been answered. In his mind, it was a selfless request, and who was worthier of a miracle than Lorna, who'd dedicated so much of her life to the island? So why had she died

320

while others lived? Why had his wish not been granted when others had? He became obsessed with finding the answers to these questions.'

'Did he find them?' I asked. I thought of the short-lists Niall had shown me, the names scored out. The files detailing failed tests of Niall's own devising. Tests of worthiness.

Cole levelled his gaze at me. 'No. His search was fruitless. But it was also long, consuming and harmful – not just to Niall.'

'Who else did it harm?' My voice was smaller than I wanted it to be.

Cole's expression turned even harder. 'My wife.'

I shouldn't have been surprised by those two words, but they still threw me off balance. It was obvious there was a connection between Andy and Niall, not just because they'd stayed in touch off-island, but in how they interacted. They were close, or had been. Andy worried for him, and he trusted her, that much was obvi-ous. But the way Cole said those two words, as if grind-ing something bitter through his teeth, made me think there was more.

I didn't expect Cole to elaborate, but he went on.

'Andy was never supposed to stay on the island. We were going to carry on living in Edinburgh, raise Alex there. She'd find a job. She had a Master's in Environ-mental Chemistry and she wanted to put it to good use, not just work in the island's archives.' Later, running through his words in my mind, I'd be hurt by this throw-away comment that so casually belittled my work. But right then I was too engrossed to register it. 'Except, after giving birth, she became despondent, withdrawn.'

'Post-natal depression?' I asked gently.

Cole nodded. 'She didn't get on with her family, so I thought the best thing would be to stay with mine for a while. She liked my parents and Clem, and they would support us. So we moved to the island, just temporarily. But one month turned to two, which turned to three, then to four. I needed to be in Edinburgh for work, but Andy didn't want to leave. I came back as often as I could but,' he sighed, rubbing his eyes tiredly, 'it wasn't enough.'

'It wasn't your fault,' Clementine insisted.

'It was my decision to leave my wife and son on the island rather than stay with them. That was my fault and there's no denying it, Clem.'

'Well, then it's *my* fault for not realising what was happening with Niall,' Clementine countered. 'I was there. I should have known something was wrong.'

'It wasn't your responsibility,' Cole assured her.

I was desperate to ask what had happened but sensed I'd gain more answers by staying silent.

'Lorna had been gone for two years by then,' Clementine explained. 'Both Uncle Joe and Niall had let themselves be swallowed up by the archives. We barely saw them. All they did was work, work, work. But while Uncle Joe seemed to find some comfort in it, Niall just grew more and more . . .' Looking miserable, she grasped for the right word. 'Intense. Obsessed. And then Andy was there, and she was sad and beautiful and intrigued by the island, and I think Niall saw her as a kind of,

I don't know, kindred spirit. She seemed to be the only one who could make him smile, and we all thought she was good for him. But . . . Andy started taking Alex down to the archives nearly every day. She'd push him down there in the pram and not come back for hours. I assumed she was helping Niall with the archiving because she was bored and maybe a little lonely.' Clementine's eyes flicked guiltily towards Cole. 'But it was more than that.'

She didn't seem to want to elaborate, looking to her brother hesitantly. Cole took up the story.

'Eventually Andy and Alex came back to Edinburgh with me. Andy started her doctorate and seemed to be better, happier. But she still wanted to go back to the island whenever we had the chance. A weekend here, a week there. At first, I was pleased. Pleased she liked my home and my family, pleased Alex would grow up on the island as well as the city. But when it started to interfere with Andy's work, I grew suspicious. I'd never been possessive or jealous, but I knew something was wrong. So, I asked her.' He leant over to tend to the log burner. 'She came clean straight away. As if she'd been desperate for me to ask.'

I held my breath, my heart drumming in my ears.

'They were studying the island,' Cole continued, his face impassive. 'Running experiments. Andy had been sneaking letters back to her labs in Edinburgh to analyse the writing. And she'd collected some of the wishfall mid-descent and conducted trace element analysis on it, comparing it with samples of snow from elsewhere.'

He said this matter-of-factly, but his words felt like a fist to my stomach. The *wrongness* of it. I'd felt guilty taking transcripts of letters from the island. The thought of somebody taking *original* scrolls away and running experiments on them was inexplicably but inherently appalling. And catching the wishfall, letting it melt into water rather than words – the idea was abhorrent. Wishes stoppered in test tubes, diluted, sampled, run through machines, stored in sanitised laboratories . . . It was unthinkable.

'The tests all came back inconclusive. But that only intrigued her more. And she wanted me to join her *research project*.' Cole gave a shake of his head. 'Those are the words she used. That's what the island was to her. A science problem that needed solving.' He shrugged. 'I tried to convince her to leave the island alone, to respect its mysteries. But she was stubborn. As am I.' Once more, he levelled his gaze at me. 'Our divorce petition cited irreconcilable differences.'

Swallowing, I nodded. 'And Niall?'

Clementine took up the thread. 'He carried on as if nothing had happened. For years he worked quietly in the archives while the rest of us came and went. We thought, without Andy, he was okay.' She gave a bitter laugh. 'When he went on his first trip to the mainland, I genuinely thought it was a good thing. That he was finally recovered, curious enough about the world to go and live in it, meet new people. But he wasn't travelling to meet people. He was testing them.'

'I saw,' I whispered, looking from brother to sister. 'He showed me the shortlist, with names scratched out. Tests of morality, I guess you'd call them. It was . . . disturbing.'

Clementine looked away, clearly upset. Cole was inscrutable. 'Yes,' he said. 'Disturbing. And destructive. To Niall, but also to the island.'

'How?'

'Things started going wrong,' Clementine explained. 'Almost like Niall was corrupting things somehow. As if he'd become toxic. The archives had always preserved the letters no matter what. But rain fell into the post-room for the first time, washing away the writing. And the wishfalls started to become . . .' She spent a moment searching for the right word. 'Imprecise. They didn't fall where they were supposed to. They landed elsewhere on the island and, without paper, were lost to us. Sometimes we'd watch them falling into the sea.'

I closed my eyes. Now I knew why Clementine and Uncle Joe had been so relieved when that first wishfall had landed where it should. *They fell right*, Clementine had said.

'We didn't know why it was happening. Didn't connect it to Niall,' Clementine went on. 'But he was the only one who didn't seem concerned. If anything, he seemed glad, in a twisted way. As if breaking the island was somehow fixing him. He carried on going back and forth between home and the mainland, and things on the island went from bad to worse. And then suddenly, one day, he couldn't come home. Willum tried to bring him back, but the sea was too rough. And when they tried again, they couldn't find the island.'

As if suddenly cold, Clementine reached for a crocheted blanket draped on the sofa arm and wrapped it around her shoulders. 'Willum's been sailing to the island nearly all his life, never had any trouble. Always known which direction to travel. But suddenly the island wasn't where it was supposed to be. No matter how much he searched, it eluded him. Mary told me later he was worried it was something he'd done, but by that time Uncle Joe had found Niall's records. The tests of morality, as you put it. Who was worthy and who wasn't. And we realised he'd taken the shortlists with him. We knew then it was Niall who wasn't welcome back.'

I now understood what Cole had meant earlier. 'The island exiled him,' I breathed.

'Uncle Joe was devastated,' Clementine said, shaking her head at the memory. 'Not angry with his son, but heartbroken. It was as if Niall had died. He kind of . . . went into mourning. He'd always been quiet, closed off. But he just sort of stopped living, refusing to step foot off the island.'

'He exiled himself *to* the island,' I said, comprehension dawning.

Clementine nodded grimly. 'I guess so.'

I curled my knees to my chest and hugged myself. Despite the roaring fire, I'd also grown cold.

Suddenly noticing the time, Cole said, 'We should try to sleep.'

Nodding, Clementine pulled herself up and headed for the door, tiredly mumbling, 'Bathroom.'

Cole and I were alone. He turned off the main light, letting the room sink into the dim glow of a single lamp, and I was suddenly nervous.

'Do you want the sofa?' I asked.

'I'll take the chair. You and Clem have the sofa,' he replied, lowering himself into the armchair by the window.

I steeled myself. There was a lot that needed to be said between us and, though now wasn't the right time for that, I had to get two things off my chest.

'Thank you. For telling me.'

He met my eyes across the darkened room. 'Clem was right. It was time you knew.'

'And,' I added, returning his gaze. 'I'm sorry. I hate that you're angry with me.'

He watched me for a long moment, his expression unreadable. Then he turned to look out of the window. The night was too dark to reveal anything, but we could hear the furious wind and the ceaseless hammering of rain against the roof. I tried not to picture Niall and Andy out there in a boat.

'I'm not angry with you, Ellie,' he said softly. 'I just want Alex's mum back safely.'

I didn't expect to sleep. But I was exhausted and, with Cole stationed in the armchair and Clementine curled up on the sofa next to me, I drifted into a dream.

Andy stood in the post room, wishfall drifting around her as scrolls furled at her feet. Then she lifted her head and spoke. 'I think he's still waiting for his dad to find him and take him home.' But she wasn't speaking to me. Suddenly I was aware of another presence and turned. There, in the archway, was a figure. The man who was one moment Cole, the next moment Niall, and then just himself. The man who'd given me the three wishes all those dreams ago. Andy was looking at him, but his gaze was fixed on me. He nodded.

I jerked awake, expecting it to be the middle of the night still. But the sky through the window was a sullen grey and from the silence – punctuated only by a ticking clock and Clementine's snores – it seemed that the storm had ebbed. I looked across at Cole, who was in the arm-chair but awake. I didn't know whether I'd disturbed him with my sudden movement, or if he'd simply not slept, but he looked tired. More tired than I'd ever seen him.

'Can you ask Willum to come back here?' I asked without preamble, pulling my dishevelled hair from my face. 'I need to get to the island. I need to see Uncle Joe.'

Chapter Twenty-Two

Uncle Joe didn't know, of course, that Niall was missing, so I was confident I'd find him in the archives, busy adding to the Wish Index. We should have been back yesterday, but he'd have put our delay down to the storm, and would, I guessed, greet me in his usual unassuming manner – and I'd tell him as gently as I could about Niall. And then I'd tell him my theory. The theory I hadn't been able to explain to Cole or Clementine, which was why they'd continued their search, while I sped to the island with Willum, rehearsing my speech.

Except my rehearsal hadn't accounted for Uncle Joe waiting at the end of the pier as we approached. Perhaps he'd come to watch for our arrival, given we were a day late? But as we drew closer, I noticed his expression. It wasn't one of relief but fear. There was no way he could know about Niall and the events on the mainland. And yet, as the *Valkyrie* pulled up alongside the pier, he stepped aboard before Willum had a chance to cut the engine.

'Quickly now,' he said grimly.

Willum and I exchanged a look but didn't ask for explanation. Within seconds we were back at sea, speeding south.

'You know about Niall?' I asked. Uncle Joe nodded. 'How? And how did you know we were coming?'

He gave a slight shrug, his eyes on the southern horizon. 'Same way you knew to come for me, I reckon.'

I knew how momentous this was for him, leaving the island. And yet he didn't give it a backwards glance. 'Can you find him?'

'Always could before.' His words sounded confident, but his eyes told a different story. It wasn't doubt he could find his son, I knew. It was doubt he'd find him in time. Instinctively I reached for his hand, and he didn't pull away.

Once we'd cut through the mist to the grey day the other side, Willum asked for direction. Uncle Joe peered across the steely waves, looking for something that none of us could see. After a moment he gestured to one side, and Willum bid the *Valkyrie* follow. She flew obediently and steadily, even at high speed, towards the sharp edge of sea and sky and, eventually, a dark ribbon of land. Unst.

'To Baltasound?' Willum called from the wheelhouse, shouting to be heard over the wind.

Uncle Joe studied the horizon for a second and then shook his head, pointing left. I had little sense of direction but guessed he was leading us south-west, and scanned the craggy shoreline, hoping not to see the debris of a boat smashed against rocks. But Uncle Joe continued to stare ahead. Andy had described it as a kind of radar and I wondered if it was anything like the pull that guided me to the island. Insubstantial, invisible and yet very much *there*. Impossible to explain, and impossible to ignore.

A familiar shape appeared. A small mass of land crested by a squat, white tower. Muckle Flugga. At first I saw no signs of life other than seagulls, but then I noticed movement. Precariously steep stone steps descended from the lighthouse to a tiny wave-battered pier. Standing on the pier were two figures. Both were wearing raincoats, the hoods tightened in place against the bitter wind, and I knew it was Niall and Andy. Beside them, leaning grace-lessly on its side, was their boat. From this distance, it looked no bigger than a rowing boat; as we drew closer, I realised with horror it *was* a rowing boat, far better suited to a leisurely lake meander than the harsh North Sea. No wonder we'd had no luck identifying a chartered boat or borrowed fishing vessel. The thought that they'd take a rowing boat out to sea had never crossed our minds. *What had they been thinking?*

Willum slowed the *Valkyrie*'s approach, and I could understand why. Navigating the sharp rocks that jutted out from the surf either side of the pier was going to take concentration and a steady hand. But I had no doubt he'd see us safely to land.

I could tell from Niall and Andy's body language that they hadn't noticed us. If I was reading Andy's desper-ate hand gestures correctly, they seemed to be arguing. And then abruptly Niall turned to look out to where we slinked gingerly through the water. Andy followed his gaze and shouted to us, waving her arms wide. But Niall grabbed the rowing boat and dragged it along the pier, heaving it into the water just as Willum carefully pulled the *Valkyrie* up alongside Andy.

'You have to stop him,' she cried, her tone and expression frantic. 'He won't listen to me.'

Moving with more speed than I'd have thought possible, Uncle Joe leapt from deck to pier. Without even glancing at Andy, he ran to Niall who jumped into the rowing boat. It rocked violently under his weight, but he kept his balance long enough to sit, and then, grasping an oar with one hand, made to push himself away from the pier with his other. But then he froze.

I still don't know what Uncle Joe said to him. What words could have drawn him back from the brink. He didn't look at his father, who seemed small and frail once more as he stood at the edge of the pier, but he was clearly listening.

'He'd tried everything,' Andy said, sounding dazed now rather than panicked. 'But he hadn't tried this. So reckless, so dangerous. He thought that if he needed it, if it was a matter of life or death, the island would show itself to him. Rather than let him die.'

I turned from Niall, still sitting rigid as his father spoke in words too quiet to reach us, and looked at Andy. Beneath her hood, her lips were chapped and tinged blue by the cold, and she had a nasty graze across her cheek. She was shivering. I moved to take off my coat, but Willum was suddenly beside me, passing over a rough, grey blanket. I stepped off the *Valkyrie* and wrapped the blanket around Andy's shaking shoulders, while Willum poured something hot out of his flask.

'I didn't really think he'd go through with it.' She sounded close to tears. 'I told him it was suicide. He'd never make it, not in that thing. But he was so determined. I couldn't let him go alone. But then the storm . . . And Alex,' she choked. 'I kept thinking about Alex. About everything I was risking, everything I was leaving behind. I begged him to take us to the lighthouse. We just about made it before the storm came. But once the storm passed, he was going, whether I went with him or not.' She looked to me, her gaze focusing. Hardening. 'He'd rather die than give up.'

I turned back to Niall. Uncle Joe was crouched now, reaching down to him in the boat. Saying something only Niall could hear. I held my breath, expecting Niall to push off from the pier at any second. But then suddenly he dropped his head into his hands, and began sobbing. His boat would have been tugged away by the current if Uncle Joe hadn't been gripping its side. Andy and I rushed over to help, but Niall didn't seem to notice us. Uncle Joe gave me a brief, grateful smile, and took his son's hands.

'Come now, my boy,' he urged, quiet and gentle. 'I'm here. You're home now.'

* * *

Nobody spoke as we approached Baltasound just in time to see the last strip of wintry sun slip from the day. At the first sign of a signal, I'd phoned Cole to tell him the news, so I wasn't surprised to see him, Alex and Clementine at the harbour.

Niall and Uncle Joe had been silent all the way from Muckle Flugga, huddled together on the floor of the deck,

333

beneath one of Willum's blankets. Niall hadn't looked at me once, too wrapped up in the fury of emotions that had brought him so close to the edge. Anger and sorrow were still clearly written on his face, but in the slump of his body against his father's small but surprisingly solid frame, I read surrender. And, I hoped, the first whisper of comfort.

Throughout the journey, Andy had stood in the wheel-house with Willum, her hands clamped around a cup of coffee, her gaze fixed on the horizon, and I saw in it the same determination that I'd seen in Uncle Joe's – both of them seeking out their sons.

Nearly a full year I'd had. A full year of the family, the island, the magic. I'd stolen some selfish moments with Cole. Warm summer days reading beneath trees and a cold winter's evening in Edinburgh I'd always cherish. But it had been a borrowed year and now everything was back the way it should be, and I could take comfort in knowing that I'd played a part in that. I'd helped Ethan find his way home, and, in an indirect way, I'd helped Niall too. Two letters answered.

But the island had given me three letters, and it was the third I was thinking about.

Perhaps it is too late, Andy had written, *but if we are all allowed one wish then this is mine: to make amends and to be forgiven. And, if I'm permitted a second wish, to earn back what I so carelessly and selfishly lost.*

At the time, I hadn't *known* it was Cole's ex-wife. But I'd suspected. After all, how many other Andys knew about the island? Likewise, I'd been in the dark about her involvement with Niall and the archives, so didn't understand what she sought to make amends for. But now I knew – and although forgiveness wasn't mine to give, I knew I could help grant her second wish.

By walking away.

And so I did.

Nobody witnessed me slip off the *Valkyrie*. And nobody noticed that I didn't follow them to Willum and Mary's house, slinking off down the road instead, the torch on my phone lighting the way. I wouldn't let myself be bitter about it. Niall and Andy deserved forgiveness, and Cole and Andy's marriage deserved a second chance. They clearly still loved each other. Andy had wished to earn back what she'd lost, and Cole's worry for her over the last two days suggested far deeper feelings than he'd admit – probably even to himself. But their only obstacle had been Andy's scientific curiosity, which she now seemed resolved to relinquish.

To think I might be an obstacle would be self-important delusion. I wasn't even stepping back – I'd never really been in the way. Cole and I had done nothing more than hold hands. It may have meant something to me, but for him? I was a minor distraction; the harmless side character relevant to the story only insofar as she helped the main protagonists find their way to each other again.

Taking myself discreetly out of the picture now rather than later was best for everyone. There'd be no guilt on Cole's part for reconciling with Andy, no awkwardness on the island with me hanging around as the superfluous third wheel. Andy's wish would be granted, Cole's happiness assured and the island's mandate for me fulfilled. *And* I wouldn't have to torment myself by witnessing it all.

As much as I believed these words, as convinced as I was that I was making the right decision, walking away was still the most difficult thing I'd ever done. Knowing I'd never see the archives again, no longer be part of the island's family, left me with a hollowness I didn't think could ever be filled. But sacrifices weren't meant to be painless.

Huddled inside the shelter with only Bobby the puffin for company and fifteen minutes until the next bus, I agonised over what message to send Cole and Clementine. I was, of course, taking the coward's way out and saying goodbye via text. But what could I write that would convince them this was the best thing for everyone?

I didn't have time to settle on an answer. When headlights illuminated the dark road, I assumed it was the bus arriving early. But as it drew closer I realised it was a car. Cole's rental car, to be precise, with Cole behind the wheel and Clementine in the front passenger seat. They pulled up alongside the shelter and Clementine opened her door.

'Where are you going?' she demanded.

My heart sank. So much for the coward's way out.

Cole stood on the other side of the vehicle, his eyes searching my face. Unable to meet his gaze, I focused on Clementine.

'I need to go home,' I said, my voice cracking.

'Why?' she asked, striding forward. 'Has something happened to Izzy? Toby?'

My eyes were stinging with tears. 'No. I need to go home *for me*.'

There was a confused silence that I felt the need to fill. 'I knew when I left the island last that I'd be going to Dublin to help Ethan. I knew there was a strong possibility I wouldn't return after disobeying your rules. So I made sure all my stuff was packed away neatly. Would you mind sending it to me? Obviously knock the costs off my pay. And there's no rush at all. Please wait until after Christmas when things are quieter.' I bit my lip, bracing myself against a fresh wave of guilt. 'I'm so sorry that I'm leaving at such a busy time, and without giving notice . . .'

'We don't care about *that*,' Clementine snapped. 'We care about *you*. Why on earth are you leaving? You're happy on the island, working in the archives. You can't deny it.'

'I am,' I nodded. 'I mean, I was. It was one of the best years of my life.'

'So stick around for a second and a third.' Clementine opened the rear passenger door and gestured for me to climb in.

I shook my head, trying not to look as miserable as I felt. I *had* to seem confident and unwavering. 'I need to go home.'

'But *why?*' Clementine looked bewildered. I still wasn't risking eye contact with Cole, all too aware of my weak resolve. The right – or wrong – look from him would have me folding.

This needed to be convincing, so I strayed as close to the truth as I dared. 'Seeing you reunited made me want my own family.'

'That's fine,' Clementine shrugged. 'Totally under-standable. Go see them – then come back to the island.'

I shook my head, firmer this time. 'I've done what you employed me for. You don't need me now.' Before she could protest, I slogged on. 'And if I came back, I wouldn't be happy.' The thought of not returning to the island was painful, but not as painful as the thought of seeing Cole and Andy together there.

Clementine frowned, looking more hurt than con-fused now. 'But you're *family*.'

'Clementine.' Cole's tone was clipped, stern. I forced myself to look at him and saw only that impenetrable mask. 'She's an adult, entitled to make her own decisions.'

Clementine turned to her brother, aghast. 'Don't tell me you're OK with this.'

His jaw seemed to clench ever so slightly, but I detected no other signs of displeasure. He looked exactly as he had the day of my interview in the coffee shop – albeit more tired and less formally dressed. He'd clearly reached the same conclusion I had. That it would be eas-ier for everyone involved if I slipped unobtrusively away.

'I'll stay in touch,' I assured Clementine. 'And if you're ever in Manchester . . .'

Her face was an open book of warring emotions. To my relief, incredulity and anger lost ground to concern, and she grabbed my gloved hands in her bright red mit-tens. 'I don't know why you're leaving us but if it's what you need, then . . . OK. I'll miss you like crazy but I trust you.' She pulled me into a fierce bear hug. 'You're my best friend wherever you live, geography be damned.'

'Ditto,' I said, prolonging the hug to give myself a chance to force back my tears.

'Are you sure you have to go right now though?' she asked as we separated. 'Stay with us tonight; travel to Manchester tomorrow.'

And spend the night under the same roof as Cole and Andy? Perhaps it was selfish of me, but I'd save myself that pain at least. 'Simpler this way,' I said thickly, not trusting myself to say more.

Clementine scowled again but seemed to think better of arguing. 'Fine, but we're driving you to the ferry terminal.'

'Honestly, I don't—'

But Cole cut me off. 'We're driving you to the ferry terminal.'

His tone was so final I couldn't argue. But suddenly headlights appeared, and the bus bound for Belmont Ferry Terminal approached. If not providence, then it was at least a lucky escape. Pulling up behind Cole's rental, the bus driver opened the door and called out, 'Anyone joining us?'

I hesitated only for a second before murmuring 'Thank you for everything' – probably too quietly for them to hear – and sprinting towards the bus. I didn't look back. I focused on the driver as I paid my fare. Focused on the floor as I walked up the aisle. And then sat on the far side so I wouldn't have to see their faces one last time.

And so they wouldn't see my tears.

Chapter Twenty-Three

The angel's smile was cruelly mocking.

Last Christmas, I could have sworn it was lovingly benevolent. But a lot could change in a year.

It was the early hours of the morning when I finally broke. I threw the covers back from the sofa-bed, marched across the living room and yanked her down from the top of the tree. In my hands, the derision in her expression was even harder to ignore so I stuffed her, wings first, into a nearby cupboard, and slammed the door.

Later that morning, Toby and Mike noticed her absence but, glancing at me, neither commented. Children have less tact.

'Where's the fairy?' Izzy asked, peering over her bowl of cereal at the crownless Christmas tree.

'Retired from service,' I sniffed.

'Why?' she demanded.

I dragged my spoon morosely through my porridge. 'I didn't like the way she was looking at me.'

It had been three weeks. Three weeks since I'd left Cole and the others in Baltasound. Aiden had called as I'd travelled back down to Manchester, but I didn't answer. I waited until I was cocooned in Toby's sofa-bed to send

WINTER'S WISHFALL

him a message, and another to Clementine, thanking them for a wonderful year and wishing them a merry Christmas. They'd both tried to call me, but I didn't pick up, and then everything went quiet.

'Their loss,' Toby had assured me, shouldering my backpack as he'd greeted me at the train station.

'And our gain,' Mike added.

Izzy, clutching my hand as we walked through the busy station, leant into me. 'I'm so glad you're home.'

I'd sunk my fingers into her curly hair and felt a little bit warmer. 'So am I, sweetie.' The look my brother flashed me told me I'd need to lie more convincingly.

At their house, the sofa-bed had welcomed me as if I'd never been away. But I *had* been away and even though nothing had really changed in my absence, *everything* had changed. I'd thought being back in the world, solid and familiar, would render the island a distant, surreal dream. But it was the opposite. It was this world that felt immaterial, while the island stayed sharp and vivid in my mind.

I could remember every detail. The salty wind that blustered all year round. The vibrant purple of heather. The warm, sweet smell of Clementine's kitchen. The squeaking wheels of Uncle Joe's scroll-laden trolley. The cold shower that indicated Aiden had beaten me to the bathroom. The feel of the rake in my hands as I harvested wishes. Cole's laughter, so coveted for being so hard-won. If I closed my eyes, I could easily be back there, all five senses brimming with memories – while out in the 'real world', everything was tepid and colourless. November had tipped into December and the city was awash with Christmas lights and tinsel, but to me, it was monochrome. Christmas music was grating. I was indifferent to the festive television adverts that usually made me cry. Snow was just dirty street slush waiting to happen. Chocolates didn't taste right, not even the green triangles. It was all a bitter reminder of where I wasn't. I'd expected to feel fulfilled. Hoped my conviction that I was doing the right thing would translate into happiness, or at least contentment. But it hadn't.

I wouldn't let myself mope though. I'd done enough of that the Christmas before. I was back home with people I loved. I had Toby to make me laugh and Mike to lend a sympathetic ear. I had a year of Izzy's life to catch up on, and some work ahead of me if I wanted my title as 'favourite auntie' restored, Mike's sister having staged a coup in my absence. I was back where I needed to be, with my family, and it was time to get my life in order.

Obviously the first step was compiling a to-do list. Item one on the list: 'Write a list.' The second: 'Get a job.' The third: 'Stop sponging off your brother and get your own place.' In the original draft, the fourth item was 'be happy', but before getting it laminated, I'd revised this to make it more achievable: 'Be content.'

'You got it laminated?' Mike asked, baffled.

'This is Ellie you're talking to,' Toby pointed out. 'If it's not worth laminating, it's not worth doing.'

I nodded. 'Truer words have never been spoken.'

My brother-in-law was still bemused. 'But how will you cross the items off?'

I picked up my permanent marker and blacked out the first item with a victorious smile.

The second was going to be harder. For one, vacancies were scarce, especially in the library and archives sector. Councils were ruthlessly slashing jobs to save money, and positions in private archives rarely cropped up. I also had the added problem of how to update my CV; for the last ten months I'd been in full-time employment, but what details could I include in an application? Even citing 'Jones Associates' might be seen as a breach of confidentiality, and I certainly couldn't put Cole or Clementine's names down as references. Besides, how would I describe my duties? Raking up letters to Father Christmas and populating the Wish Index in between eating a lot of cake?

In the end I kept it vague: 'Modernising records in a growing private archive, details subject to confidentiality agreement.'

Fortunately, Toby was, of course, a recruitment guru, and he worked his magic quickly. Within a week, I had three interviews lined up. One was for the role of temporary bookseller for the Christmas period, another for a customer services officer in a museum archive, the third a part-time school library assistant. None of them particularly appealed but I couldn't afford to be fussy. So, I dusted off my white shirt, smart trousers and polite interview smile.

I tried my best to seem engaged, but the interviews felt stiflingly mundane. Not a single mention of favourite hot chocolate flavours, Christmas films or socks.

'How do you organise and prioritise your work?'

'What is the key to success when communicating with the public?'

'Share an experience when you applied new technology in your job.'

My answers were equally bland. I said what they expected me to say and avoided drawing on recent examples. When they asked about my last position, I tried to change the subject. Perhaps it was this caginess that failed me, or maybe the interviewers sensed my lack of enthusiasm. Either way, I didn't get the jobs.

'You don't seem that bothered,' Toby observed when I told him.

We were sitting in the living room while Mike and Izzy worked on her Christmas play costume. This year, she was one of the penguins who helped build Father Christmas a runway for his sleigh after his original one melted.

'There aren't any penguins in the North Pole,' I'd whispered to Toby when Izzy had first announced her role, two weeks earlier.

'*That's* the issue you're seeing here?' he'd asked, incredulous. 'Not the fact that the Christmas play has been hijacked and turned into a commentary on climate change?'

'It's good that kids are learning about current issues,' Mike had argued, before adding, 'but I'm not sure about the zoological aspects. I mean, how is a flock of flightless birds, with not a single opposable thumb between them, supposed to build a runway?'

'Can reindeer really fly?' Izzy asked, pointedly. We blinked at each other, stumped. 'And it's not a flock. It's a *waddle* of penguins. Miss Beecham told us.'

Mike smiled proudly at his daughter. 'Touché, little genius.'

Two weeks later, while Mike was pinning a white crest to Izzy's black onesie, Toby glowered at me. 'I'm not going to keep getting you interviews if you don't even want a job.'

I was indignant. 'It's not my fault.'

'Whose fault is it then? You're more than qualified so it's got nothing to do with lack of experience. Employers aren't stupid, Ellie. They know you don't want the job.'

'But I do want the job.' It was only when I said it aloud and tasted the lie on my lips, that I realised how untrue it was. 'Okay,' I admitted grudgingly, 'maybe it is my fault. I'll try harder next time. Promise.'

'Good,' Toby sniffed, passing me his phone. 'Because I've got another interview lined up for you on Tuesday.' I looked at the screen and recognised the University of Manchester's logo.

I scanned the email. The university wanted an archivist to work in their library's special collections, collaborating with a team of scholars on a project exploring the history of travel literature.

'This is—' I began.

'The perfect job for you, yes,' Toby finished. 'You're welcome.'

The interview was in five days, but because the library was currently undergoing a refurbishment, it would be held in a less formal setting. In a coffee shop on – I gasped.

'It's the same place.'

'Same place as what?' Toby asked, taking his phone back.

'The coffee shop. It's the same venue as . . . before.' Toby and Mike knew what I meant. 'How many coffee shops are there in Manchester? That's a pretty big coincidence.'

'Maybe it's a sign,' Mike suggested as he moved on to Izzy's penguin tail.

'A sign of what?' I asked dubiously, at the same time as Toby reminded his husband, 'You don't believe in signs.'

Mike gave a shrug. 'If you want to see a sign then you see a sign. And it means whatever you want it to mean.'

Mike's words stayed with me over the next five days. Did I want to see a sign in this coincidence? And what did I want it to mean? I honestly didn't know.

On the morning of the interview, everything went as planned. No breakfast spillages on my outfit. Mike had a late shift at work and offered to drive me, so no need to cycle or even brave the bus. I reached the city centre with half an hour to spare and decided to get to the coffee shop early. It hadn't rained at all in the last few days (a record for Manchester) so there were no puddles to accidentally step in. I was uncharacteristically dry, tidy and composed.

It was only as I approached the coffee shop that a thought occurred to me. Maybe the venue wasn't a coincidence at all. Perhaps the whole interview was a ruse; a ploy architected by Cole or Clementine, in league with Toby.

Clandestine was definitely their style. Never mind that they hadn't tried to contact me in weeks. Had they just been waiting for the right time? And was now the right time?

Both dread and hope churned my stomach as I surveyed the scattering of tables and armchairs, looking for Cole's familiar face or a flash of Clementine's kingfisher-blue hair. But there was no sign of them. I didn't know if I was relieved or disappointed. There was, however, a neat, slender middle-aged woman wearing a blue blazer and a polite smile.

'Eleanor Lancaster?' she enquired.

I stepped closer, nodding. 'I'm a bit early, sorry.'

She gave a soft laugh. 'Never apologise for being early. It's lovely to meet you.' Rising from her seat, she held out her hand. 'I'm Nicola Blythe. Can I get you a drink?'

The interview went well; Toby would have been proud. Nicola's gentle manner put me at ease instantly. She asked interesting questions and it felt more like a chat between two enthusiastic archivists than an interrogation. When she eventually began wrapping up, I was astounded to realise we'd been talking for nearly two hours. And, as arrogant as it sounds, I wasn't surprised when, just before taking her leave, she whispered conspiratorially, 'Obviously I can't *officially* confirm now, but *unofficially* you'll hear from me very soon.'

It had been the perfect interview for the perfect job. So why, when I stepped out of the coffee shop a few minutes later, did I not feel like celebrating? If anything, I wanted to chase after Nicola and tell her I was sorry, but – contrary to every logical argument – it wasn't the job for me.

If I'd been looking for signs, the second was the Christmas elf.

He was standing just outside the entrance to the Arndale shopping centre, his bright green elf hat and twirly-toed slippers at odds with the vape he was puffing on. I didn't recognise him as I passed, but he called out my name.

My mouth fell open in surprise. 'Gary?'

My ex-boyfriend gave an abashed smile. 'Call me Buddy the Christmas Elf.'

Aside from the ridiculous outfit, he looked exactly the same. Lanky, clean-shaven, with a hint of blond hair sticking out from under his elf hat. He was studying me too, probably noting my slight weight gain and the fact my hair hadn't been cut in nearly a year.

'It's been ages,' he said unnecessarily. 'How've you been? You look smart,' he added before I could answer, gesturing to my outfit.

'I've just come from a job interview.'

'Oh.' He took a puff of his vape. 'Have you been on the job hunt since last year?'

'I had another job in between,' I replied, wondering how I could politely extricate myself from the conversation.

'You're probably wondering what happened to my job,' he said, touching the bell on the top of his hat self-consciously.

'Did you leave the Hanky Chief?' I asked, genuinely curious.

'The company went into liquidation. I didn't even get a decent payout.' He shrugged indifferently. 'I'll find something better.'

I couldn't resist glancing down at his twirly green boo-
ties and he shifted on his feet, satisfyingly embarrassed.

If the first sign was the coffee shop, and the second
the Christmas elf, then the third – and by far the most
significant – was waiting for me outside Toby's house.

Uncle Joe was jarringly out of place in the real world.
He seemed to know it too, because he looked uneasy,
lost almost, standing there beneath a porch festooned
with Christmas fairy lights.

I froze at the end of the front path, stunned at the
sight of him. He froze when he saw me too, but his
expression was one of relief. After a moment's hesitation he nodded to me in greeting. Perplexed, I moved
towards him.

'Uncle Joe?'

He gave one of his unassuming smiles. 'I'm happy to
see you.'

'I'm happy to see you too,' I replied earnestly. 'But
why are you – no, wait. You must be freezing. Let's get
inside.' Without waiting for him to respond, I fumbled
in my pocket for the key and pushed the door open. The
driveway had been empty, and the house was quiet; Toby
was still at work, Izzy at school and Mike must have left
for his late shift already. I was glad of the privacy as I
ushered Uncle Joe towards the lounge, where I gestured
for him to sit.

'Can I get you anything to drink? Tea, coffee?'

Shaking his head, he perched warily on the edge of
the couch.

'Anything to eat?' I pressed, strangely nervous in his presence.

Again, he shook his head. 'Thank you, though,' he mumbled, pulling off his gloves.

'Can I take your coat?'

'Can't be here long,' he replied, keeping it on.

I sat in the armchair opposite him, grasping for something to say. I couldn't very well ask what he was doing here, so instead opted for the banal, 'Did you come by train?'

He nodded.

'Was it busy? I imagine it would be, this time of year. Everyone coming into the city to do their Christmas shopping. I hope you got a seat.'

Another nod.

'Well,' I said, flustered, 'I, er . . .'

'You're not where you're supposed to be.' He didn't look at me as he spoke, but gazed shyly around the room and fidgeted with his gloves. His tone was firm though. 'The island was right when you were there. First time in a long time. It needs you.'

It was beyond flattering to hear those words, but I was at a loss for how to respond. 'I'm sorry,' I eventually mumbled.

He nodded sadly. 'Me too.'

Opting for the safe, cowardly route, I changed the subject. 'How have you been?'

I didn't know if he'd acquiesce to my blatant redirection, but the ghost of a smile touched his lips. 'With my son again.'

I beamed, so glad to see the happiness this clearly gave him. And pleased to hear Niall wasn't alone. 'How is he?'

'Doing a little better.' Uncle Joe forced himself to look me in the eye. 'He . . . sends his apologies. For involving you. I'm sorry too.'

My instinct was to brush the apology aside, but in truth Niall had hurt me. I'd thought he was a friend, an ally, but he'd kept so much back. Still, he hadn't done it out of spite. He'd been hurt himself, damaged, and seen me as a potential route to fixing things. I gave Uncle Joe a gentle smile. 'I don't blame him. I'm glad he's doing better.' I hesitated and then abruptly made my decision. 'I saw him again. The man on the island. Your granny called him Pete?'

Uncle Joe nodded slowly.

'He . . . showed me some letters. Some wishes I thought it was my job to grant. One of those was from Niall.' I wanted to explain why I'd left. I wanted him to know I'd been doing what I believed was right, had been following the wishes of the island. But I wouldn't tell him what those letters said. It didn't feel right to voice their wishes, which weren't mine to share. The letters were archived anyway – once I'd copied them out, I'd indexed and catalogued them as with all the rest. If he wanted to read them he could.

He didn't seem surprised by my disclosure. 'Thank you,' was all he said. I didn't know if he was thanking me for sharing the information or for trying to act on Niall's letter, but either way I was grateful at his simple acceptance of my story.

351

We sat in less awkward silence for a moment. 'Are you staying in Baltasound or did you go back home?' I eventually asked.

I couldn't mistake the trace of longing in his eyes. 'Neither. In Edinburgh while we figure things out.'

'That must be hard for you,' I said softly. 'Being off the island.'

He bobbed his head slightly. 'Been quite an adjustment. World's changed a lot since I was last in it. Faster, louder. Or maybe it's me who's changed.'

'It's probably a bit of both. The world feels faster and louder to me too, and I've not been out of it for that long. But you'll go back to the island, right?' I was desperate to hear him say yes. The island needed Uncle Joe far more than me.

It was a relief to see him nod. 'Eventually. Maybe he can come back with me too. I reckon the island will forgive him. Still a long way to go, but he's getting the help he needs. I'm there, and Andy looks after us both, so—'

'Andy?' I interrupted, confused.

'Offered to let us stay with her but we didn't want to be too much trouble. We're at Niall's flat, but she pops by to bring us—'

'Why isn't she on the island?'

He frowned, looking as puzzled as I felt. 'Why would she be?'

'Isn't Cole on the island?'

'Yes, he's there. With Alex. They're always there over Christmas.'

'But Andy . . . isn't?'

His bewilderment didn't lessen. 'No. She's in Edinburgh.'

I floundered. 'Oh. OK. I just assumed she'd be there with them. You know, with her and Cole . . .' I didn't want to have to say it aloud, but Uncle Joe clearly wasn't following. 'With them being back together.'

'Back together?' Uncle Joe raised a bushy, grey eyebrow. 'My nephew? And Andy?'

'They were married,' I pointed out – unnecessarily, I thought.

'Married, yes. But happy? Not for a long while.' For the first time, he met my gaze. 'Cole has forgiven her. They're reconciled. Friends. Parents. A family, with Alex. But not *together*.'

'Oh,' was all I could think to say. I sat stunned. I'd been so certain they'd found their way back to each other, the mistakes of the past firmly behind them. If Andy had redeemed herself, and Cole had forgiven her, then what else stood in their way?

Uncle Joe finally seemed to understand, and answered my silent question. 'They're meant for others. It's not been said aloud, but the way she is with Niall . . .'

'Niall and Andy?' I asked, shocked. I'd known they were close, but hadn't considered a romantic attachment.

Uncle Joe only shrugged. 'Who can say? Maybe in time. And my nephew . . .'

His words trailed off, but I grasped hold of them like a lifeline. 'What about Cole?'

'My dear girl,' he said, his tone kind. 'Do you really not know?'

I looked down at my shoes. The smart black ones I'd worn for the interview I'd already forgotten about. I wouldn't ask coyly, *know what?* Because I *did* know. And I was ashamed it had taken Uncle Joe travelling all these miles to tell me.

He seemed to sense the direction of my thoughts. With a little cough, he stood up and began pulling on his gloves. 'Hope to see you again.'

'You're leaving so soon?' I asked, standing too.

'Train to catch. Didn't want to leave him alone long but needed to see you.'

'I – thank you,' was all I could think of to say, following him dazedly to the front door. 'Can I at least order you a taxi to the station?'

His eyes creased with a smile as he pulled out an ancient-looking mobile phone, with a little stumpy aerial. 'Can call one myself.' Proudly, he turned the phone over to show me a few numbers handwritten on a piece of paper taped to its rear, one of which was labelled *Manchester taxi.*

I choked back a laugh. 'You're practically a millennial.'

Chuckling, he began walking down the garden path. But as he reached the street, he turned to look at me. 'Hard to reach the island this time of year. Don't leave your decision too late or it'll be made for you.'

Panic set in as I watched him retreat, hunched over his phone as he dialled. But I knew then that I'd made my decision.

It seemed everyone else knew too.

When I phoned Toby a few minutes later, he answered with, 'Does this mean we can put the angel back on the Christmas tree?'

'How did you know?' I asked.

I could practically hear the eye-roll.

'Am I doing the right thing?'

'The "right thing" is a myth. It doesn't exist. There are just a bunch of things and you get to pick one.'

I snickered down the phone. 'Thank you for those words of wisdom.' A pause. 'Will Izzy be very angry with me?'

'Why would she be?'

'Because I won't be home for Christmas.'

'She loves you and wants you to be happy, just as I do. Plus,' he added, a smile in his voice, 'it sounds like you *are* going to be home for Christmas.'

It was my turn to roll my eyes. 'I'll be in touch as soon as I can.' And, my stomach flipping with a concoction of giddy excitement, impatience and rattling nerves, I hung up. Then I flung some bits and pieces into a rucksack and began the long, long journey home.

Chapter Twenty-Four

Bobby the puffin was wearing a red-and-white Santa hat. He stood vigil outside his bus shelter, which was bedecked for the season with tinsel, a miniature plastic Christmas tree atop the set of drawers and a sprig of mistletoe in the open doorway. I patted Bobby on the head as I passed, feeling a swell of affection for him.

In the last twenty-four hours, I'd experienced sleepy airport terminals, foggy bus windows and a bitterly cold ferry crossing. It was still bitterly cold, and the sun was dipping low, gilding the fields and stone walls of Baltasound. To my right, the North Sea rippled amber.

I didn't have Willum and Mary's phone number and had been worrying about how they'd react to me turning up on their doorstep unannounced. Or – worse – what if they were out? Away? It was a huge relief when Mary opened the door at my knock, blinked once in bewilderment and then enveloped me in a fierce hug.

'By the angels, what are you doing here?' she demanded, mid-hug.

Before I could answer, she pulled me into the divinely warm house and ushered me down the hallway to the lounge, where Willum occupied the fireside armchair

– and was, to my consternation, reading a well-known teen vampire novel.

If he was surprised by my sudden appearance, the fisherman didn't show it. He glanced up, nodded a greeting and, with a simple, 'Might be a window tomorrow morning if the weather holds,' resumed reading.

I'd been convinced they'd tell me I was too late, that the island was unreachable now. Hearing Willum offer this morsel of hope, I sagged with relief. Mary was quickly beside me, forcing me onto the sofa.

'You look like you've had a long journey, hen,' Mary clucked sympathetically, seeming to conjure a steaming cup of tea from thin air. I took it gratefully, hoping it would nurse some feelings back into my fingers.

'Can you really take me tomorrow?' I asked Willum, afraid to allow myself too much hope.

Setting a hand-painted plate of mince pies on the coffee table between us, Mary lowered herself into another armchair and answered for her husband. 'Only if this clear weather holds. It'd be too dangerous otherwise.'

'What's the forecast?'

Behind his book, Willum snorted. Mary's smile was indulgent. 'Usually wrong. Best just to check the sky tomorrow morning.'

'I'll pay you of course.'

'Hundred quid,' Willum said, but Mary reached over to slap his arm.

'Pay him no mind and definitely pay him no money. The Joneses give him a very generous annual wage for ferrying to Osk.'

'Are you sure?'

'Surer than sure,' Mary insisted. Behind his book, Willum grinned.

Fighting back a yawn, I was too tired to argue further. 'Thank you so much. Is there a . . . hotel anywhere?' After the enormous favour they'd already promised, I didn't want them to think I expected an invitation. Nevertheless, I was immensely relieved when Mary chided me for the question.

'A hotel? What a thing to say! Shame on you. You'll not be going back out there in the dark. As you know, we can't offer a bed as such, but the couch pulls out and the grandkids say it's comfier than any bed. Willum, go get the spare duvet and some sheets.'

With a long-suffering sigh, Willum set down his book and shuffled out. I didn't see him return. I didn't even know I'd closed my eyes until I opened them again and found myself still in the armchair but cocooned in a blanket, with sunlight streaming through a gap in the curtains.

Sunlight.

The pastel sky was punctuated only by seagulls; there wasn't a cloud in sight. With a triumphant smile I made my way to the kitchen.

'Good morning,' Mary beamed. 'The hot water's on and I've put clean towels in the bathroom. You go enjoy a shower while Willum gets her ready.'

I didn't need to ask who 'she' was.

* * *

When freshly showered, I made my way to the *Valkyrie*. I found both Mary and Willum in the wheelhouse, munching on bacon sandwiches – which I politely declined when Mary offered me one, my stomach churning with excitement and nerves. But I was glad of the flask of tea she'd brought, the morning being as cold as it was bright.

'Let's away with us then,' Mary announced, throwing her crusts to the gulls.

I was surprised she was joining us; she never had before.

'It's too nice a day to be cooped up inside,' she explained.

With my declined sandwich clutched in his mouth, Willum steered the *Valkyrie* away from the pier and out to sea. As Baltasound disappeared behind us, Mary headed onto deck armed with a sketch pad and pencils of various shades of blue tucked behind her ears. I followed, standing at the prow as if it would help me see the island sooner. I tried to enjoy the voyage: the views of Unst's craggy coastline, the growing hint of warmth from the sun, the briny wind filling my nostrils. But now I'd made it to the final stage of my journey, the worry of whether I'd reach the island in time had been replaced by a new fear. What would happen when I got there? Had I been forgiven for my trip to Dublin? Forgiven for my unwitting collusion with Niall? Would they even want me back after I walked away?

Even with most of her attention devoted to sketching, Mary seemed to sense my thoughts.

'There's no use fretting,' she said beside me. 'I don't know why you didn't head back with the others. And I don't know why you've left it so late to come now. But I do know you're nearly home and that's the important thing.'

I smiled at Mary, surprisingly heartened by her words. She was right: there was no use fretting. It wouldn't accomplish anything. They'd either want me back or they wouldn't, and there was nothing I could do about it in the meantime.

But 'meantime' seemed to last forever. Had this part of the journey always dragged so? I felt we'd been travelling for hours, though neither Willum or Mary seemed to realise that either time had slowed, or the North Sea expanded. Just when I was about to ask how much further, I noticed a smudge of grey in the otherwise unbroken blue sky ahead: the wall of mist that seemed to perpetually shield the island from the rest of Scotland. We were nearly there.

'I never get used to it,' Mary admitted ten minutes later, as Willum sailed us into the dense fog. She put down her sketch pad and peered out into the silver haze.

I felt, as always, as if I were passing from one world into another.

The sensation was strengthened by the change in weather. We'd left blue skies behind and now, as we cut through the mist onto the other side, we were greeted by steely clouds. They seemed to converge over the dark mass of land that sat directly ahead of us.

I was excited about seeing the island again, its colours and shapes so familiar to me now, and gave the weather very little mind. But Willum seemed troubled.

'Don't like the look of those clouds,' he muttered.

'We've come this far,' Mary exclaimed, then cursed as the wind – significantly stronger this side of the fog – dislodged one of the pencils from behind her ear and bore it down into the waves. 'Well, it can be an offering to the sea deities.'

Suddenly I realised how ominous the clouds looked. The sea was a lot choppier here as well. 'Will you be able to get there safely?'

Willum studied the island's coastline for a long moment and then nodded. 'But we'll want to be gone again as soon as we've dropped you. No visit this time, Mary.'

Mary looked disappointed but nodded. 'I've never seen a storm look so . . . *concentrated*.'

The clouds seemed to grow even darker as we approached the island, and I was glad of my waterproof anorak.

'Are you sure you'll be okay getting up to the house, hen?' Mary asked when Willum pulled the *Valkyrie* up to the pier. She had to shout over the howl of the wind.

'I'll be fine,' I promised, my feet itching to be on the island. 'Thank you so much, both of you. You don't know how grateful I am.'

Mary's eyes twinkled when she smiled. 'Oh hen, I think we do.' She pulled me into a bear hug and then gestured to the pier. 'Away with you. Get up to the house before the storm breaks. We'll see you in the new year.'

Relief washed over me as I stepped off the boat and onto land. It had been a long journey, in more ways than one, but I'd finally made it back. And nothing, I thought, breaking into a run, could get in my way now.

I was mistaken.

The first snowflake fell just as I turned to wave good-bye to Mary and Willum. Although 'snowflake' and 'fell' were the wrong words – it was a sharp, icy dart that whipped across my vision. And then another and then another, until all I could see was a torrent of silver amid the foreboding blackness. It may have been morning still, but it felt like night. I hunched down against the vicious wind and pushed forward, but as the flurry grew heavier, the path was quickly obscured beneath a layer of snow. At least I knew the house was at the top of the slope, so as long as I kept going up, I would be there soon.

Except I wasn't. I knew from my many pre-breakfast walks that the journey from pier to house shouldn't take this long. Where was the house? And how had it become *so cold?* The wind cut through my thermal insulated clothes with mocking ease and whipped at my face, drawing tears from my eyes. After a few moments I realised I was no longer walking uphill. I took a few steps to the right then to the left, but there was no slope. I looked around, desperate for some familiar landmark. A tree, a rock, anything I might recognise. But there was only snow and darkness.

'Is anybody out there?' I cried. 'Cole? Clementine? It's Ellie!' But no matter how loudly I shouted, my words were lost to the roaring wind.

By then, the tears freezing onto my cheeks were provoked as much by frustration as the wind. And the more

I walked, and the faster the snow fell, the more that frustration slid into worry.

Growing up in England, the weather was something to complain about, not fear. At its most malicious, it could flood a river or render a road impassable with snow or ice. It rarely posed a danger to life. And so, when Mary had asked if I'd be okay making my way up to the house, I hadn't thought twice about my answer. That now seemed reckless.

Words from Ethan's letter drifted into my mind. *I don't know how much longer I can last. Nights are so cold now* . . . I'd always been privileged, with a roof over my head. I'd never faced cold like this. Never had to wonder if I was going to survive it.

Even 'survive' was a word I'd used so blithely. Would I survive my first day of work? Would I survive seeing my ex-boyfriend again? Would I survive until lunch on an empty stomach? I'd never had to contemplate the word's truest meaning. But I did now.

How long had I been walking? Minutes? Hours? Days? Time was meaningless and there was still no sign of the house. It wasn't where it was supposed to be and I was going to die. It was surprising how calmly I accepted this idea.

I tried. I tried really hard, walking and walking and searching and stumbling and walking. Retracing my steps. Shouting into the wind. More walking, more searching, more stumbling, but it was no use.

The world was nothing more than a blur of black, white and the greys in between.

I couldn't feel my fingers and toes anymore, not at all. I could barely feel any part of me. A distant voice told me that was a bad sign. I also knew it wasn't good that the shivering had stopped, but I couldn't bring myself to care.

A shape emerged from the billowing grey and I recognised it as a tree. I trudged up to it on leaden legs and collapsed against its trunk, the snow enveloping me. It was as good a place to die as any.

I dropped my chin to my chest and closed my eyes. So tired.

Chapter Twenty-Five

At first, I thought the cracking signalled the breaking of ice.

A thought formed, more exasperated than scared. *It's not enough for me to die from hypothermia. I have to die drowning in a frozen lake.*

Then I remembered there weren't any lakes on the island. And I realised I wasn't cold anymore; I could feel my limbs, even my fingers and toes, and they were *warm*. Forcing my eyes open, I saw what was making the cracking sounds. A fire. A wonderful, glorious, life-saving fire. Not even the first human to discover that sticks and flint, if struck just so, could produce fire was as awed as I by the sight of those orange flames.

I could also see that the wind and snow had stopped – not just eased but ceased entirely.

And I could see the man sitting on the other side of the fire, watching me.

I knew instantly it was the man I'd followed on the beach all those months before, the man who'd visited my dream to show me those three letters and tell me, indirectly, how to reach Niall.

He looked like Cole. But it definitely wasn't him. This man was older, his dark hair and beard silvered slightly as well as fuller and rougher. His nose was slightly longer, his face leaner, his eyes more akin to Niall's sea-green.

I wasn't afraid, and it had nothing to do with courage. I wasn't even surprised. I accepted his presence with an easy familiarity. He wasn't smiling, but there was a softness to his expression as our eyes met across the flames.

'You're going to tell me I need to wake up and keep moving, aren't you?' I said.

He nodded.

'I don't think I can,' I admitted. My mind might know I needed to stand, but my body was reluctant.

The man nodded again, his meaning clear. *You can. You must.*

'A little longer,' I pleaded, basking in the warmth.

He gave me a direct look, so reminiscent of Cole. *No. Now.*

And so I did. And as I did, both fire and man disappeared, and the storm raged on once more. I couldn't move my legs; I couldn't even feel them. I tried to call out for help, but a pathetic whimper was the only sound that came.

Looking up, I could just about make out a shadow standing over me. Perhaps it was the man, but I couldn't see clearly enough. It was more likely just the tree.

It would be so easy to close my eyes again. That warm, cosy fire was waiting for me behind my eyelids, I was certain. There was no use trying to stand. Even if I made it to my feet, walking was beyond me – and pointless anyway. I'd never find the house.

No. Now.

I don't know if the voice was mine or his. But it compelled me to try. Grunting with the effort, I managed to nudge one leg with the other, then tried to stand. The icy blasts buffeted me persistently, forcing me back, but somehow on my second attempt I managed an upright position.

What now?

My eyes sought the shadow again and I realised it had moved. *Was* moving. Away from me, but slowly. Whether it was the clarity of the dream I'd just had, or the knowledge there was no better option, I decided to follow it. Miraculously, one foot obeyed my command to slide forward. Then, after a terrifyingly long moment, the other foot shifted too. I was moving. It was painfully slow, but it was progress. And the dark shape that cut through the snow seemed to be waiting for me.

I'd like to say love kept me going. That images of Izzy and Toby and Clementine and Cole were flashing through my mind, urging me on; that the thought of never seeing them again was so abhorrent it galvanised me. In truth, I was too numb to think of anything or anyone. I was moving because somehow I could – and I would keep moving until I couldn't anymore. At least then I could know I'd died trying my hardest. Not that I'd know anything by that point.

One step. Two steps. Three, four, five. I could have been walking for minutes or an eternity. I kept my eyes glued to the dark shape in front of me, not caring that it was probably an hallucination. Whatever it was, it drew me forward.

This time when the wind and snow stopped, I knew it was real. My body felt too heavy, the numbness too aggressive, for it to be a dream. Had it got darker? Black seemed to surround me on all sides but I was too far gone to wonder why.

A brief tingling sensation on my arm halted me, and more words – his or mine? – echoed in my mind.

Rest now.

I didn't need telling twice. I was gone before I hit the floor.

A long, long darkness.

Then dreams. Indistinct, more noises and colours than images. A frantic cawing.

More darkness.

Then a voice, garbled, as if underwater. Only two words. *She's here . . .*

Just enough sensation in my face to wonder if something was touching it.

Then the feeling of being enveloped. Lifted.

More darkness.

A tingling. Subtle but growing. Feeling eking into my shoulders, my legs, my arms. My hands. My feet.

And then every inch of my body, a million daggers. A million scorching flames.

Let it stop. Please just let it stop.

Blessed darkness.

No dreams.

A vague sense of time passing was the first clue I was alive. The second was the raw pain lying in wait for me every time I tried to surface. The first few times, that pain was all I could feel. Red and intense and merciless. But then the red was a little less red, and my other senses began to stir. Lights, shapes. Voices again. Indistinct still, but soft and soothing. Fingers on my forehead. A vague awareness, based on the lampshade above, that I was back in my old room on the island. Something smooth and warm on my lips; the instinct to swallow as liquid passed over my tongue.

The pain became less intense. I was conscious enough to know that I had eyes and should open them. And myself enough to worry that whoever was looking after me must surely be losing their patience by now. It was this more than anything else that meant this time when I dragged myself to the surface, I stayed there.

Somebody was dabbing something cool on my right hand. The contact hurt and soothed in equal measure. I forced my eyes open to look at whoever was tending me. Of all the people on the island, Willum was the last person I expected to see sitting beside my bed, focused on applying a gel labelled *Aloe Vera* to my hand. The same expression of calm concentration on his face as when he piloted the *Valkyrie*. Glancing down at my hand, I flinched. Large, ugly red blisters covered my fingers. Turning my head, I saw the same on my other hand.

The movement alerted Willum to the fact I was conscious. Meeting my eyes, he gave the warmest smile I'd ever seen from him.

'Awake.'

'Awake,' I croaked.

'Gave people a scare,' he chided.

I grimaced. 'Sorry.'

'No permanent damage done.' He resumed his task, rubbing gel into the back of my thumb. 'Mostly frostnip. Some superficial frostbite. Toes, fingers, nose. You're lucky. Only first degree. Just need to keep on top of the pain and blisters.'

Just then there was a knock on the door, and it opened slightly. 'I thought I heard voices . . .'

There'd been no time to prepare for my reunion with Cole. But in that moment I didn't care I was wearing pyjamas and my hands and probably nose were covered in blisters and my hair was probably a state. I was just so glad to see his face, even if he did look a little different. His eyes seemed darker, his beard less kempt. And he did *not* look happy to see me.

Willum pulled back from me. 'Go easy on her lad,' he warned, handing Cole the gel. 'Left hand and face still need doing.' And with that, he slipped from the room, closing the door behind him.

Cole's blazing eyes bore into me, his mouth set in a furious line.

'I'm sorry for leaving so suddenly . . .'

'I'm not angry about that,' he snapped, striding forward. In a charged silence, he moved the chair to the other side of my bed and continued where Willum had left off. Despite his anger, his fingers were gentle, hesitant even. 'Does it hurt?'

'What *are* you angry about?' I demanded, ignoring his question.

'Do you know how stupid it was to come back to the island? To take such a reckless risk?' His voice was a growl, but his touch tender. 'Do you know how close you came to—'

'I didn't know,' I interrupted. 'I didn't know how dangerous it was going to be. I just thought . . .'

'If Willum and Mary hadn't been forced back by the storm and told us you were here,' he went on, refusing to meet my eyes. 'If the ravens hadn't somehow found you in the miles of tunnels . . .' He shook his head as if to banish the thought.

'So, you do care then?' I shot at him, showing perhaps less maturity than I should have.

His expression turned incredulous. '*Of course* I care.'

I'd been so convinced his worry for Andy and relief at her safety meant he still loved her. And that she, given the letter she'd written to the island, still loved him. I'd been so certain that the right thing for me to do was to step back and let them be a family again.

But love is not a clean-cut category. It's not an absolute. Cole and Andy could care for each other without wanting to be together. Uncle Joe had assured me they were just friends. They were family in that they were Alex's parents, but that was all. I could believe that now. It was the other part of the equation I needed some confirmation on.

'Did you think about me?' I hoped 'when I wasn't here' was implied.

The look he gave me was one of blatant exasperation. 'Do you really need to ask?'

'Apparently,' I muttered. My hands salved, he'd already reached over to begin smoothing the gel across my nose. I was too invested in the conversation to feel awkward, but he leant back to look me directly in the eyes.

'Every day. Most minutes of every day, if you must know.' His tone was level, unabashed.

As clichéd as it was, I gulped. 'Do you mean that?'

With a frustrated sigh, he resumed smoothing the gel over my nose. 'You know how I feel.'

'I really don't,' I assured him.

'I've made my feelings for you quite clear—'

'As clear as stone.'

'*You* are the one who left without any warning.'

'Oh, I'm sorry I didn't honour my two weeks' notice,' I snapped, sitting straighter in bed. It was difficult to project imperious indignance half submerged by pillows.

'That's not what I meant. But while we're on the subject, you *were* in breach of your contract.'

My anger surged. But before I could form a suitably cutting rebuttal, I noticed the wry twist of his lips, the glint of humour in his eyes, and the outrage abruptly dissolved. Instead, I laughed.

'I didn't comply with my contract,' I nodded in mock solemnity. 'Does this mean I don't have a job to come back to?'

He set the gel to one side but didn't move. 'That depends.'

'On what?'

'On whether you want your job back.'

'That depends,' I countered, unable to keep a straight face.

'On what?'

'On whether I get a pay rise.'

I'd expected a teasing response but instead his eyes, fully serious now, roamed my face. 'Do you really want to be here?'

I held up my blistered fingers. 'Isn't the proof in the frostbite?'

Annoyance flitted across his face. 'That's not something to joke about.'

'And my determination to come back isn't something to doubt. Of course I want to. You may not believe it, but this is my home now.'

This time when he stroked my cheek, it wasn't to administer the salve. His words, though simple, meant the world to me. 'So it is.'

It was with a sense of inevitability that Clementine chose that precise moment to come crashing through the door. But I was so happy to see her that it was a welcome intrusion. She looked from me to Cole, grinning broadly.

'Am I interrupting?'

'Yes,' Cole replied, slowly withdrawing his fingers from my cheek.

'Don't care,' Clementine declared as she rushed over to the bed, grimacing as she looked at my hands. 'Oh Ellie, you silly, wonderful human being. I'm so glad you didn't die.'

'I'm pretty pleased about it myself,' I assured her wryly.

I hadn't yet decided whether to tell them about the mysterious man who'd delivered Niall and Andy's wishes to me via a dream. The same man who had apparently led me through a blizzard to the shelter of one of the island's many subterranean passageways. I doubted they'd believe me. But if I was going to stay, I didn't want any more secrets. *And if you don't do it now, you never will*, I told myself firmly.

'There's something I need to tell you both.'

'Ooh, a juicy secret?' Rubbing her hands together with glee, Clementine parked herself on the edge of my bed. 'Let me guess: You're an undercover journalist here to unearth the secrets of the archives and go public with them, your eye on a Pulitzer? Or a spy from our competitors in the South Pole, sent for a little corporate espionage? No, wait. It's worse, isn't it? You're an archival *auditor*.'

Cole gave his sister a withering look, but I couldn't help laughing. 'Not that,' I promised her. 'But it is about the archives. About why I left in the first place and why I . . . didn't come back with you.' I averted my eyes at that point, preferring to examine my blistered hands than witness Cole's expression. 'I was trying to help answer some letters. I think the island wanted me to. Or at least somebody who works on the island. A man. Uncle Joe knows who I mean. Someone the family's seen before.' I looked up just as the pair exchanged a glance. Cole was about to speak, but I cut him off. 'Before you say anything, I wasn't hallucinating. Granted, I was dreaming, but the dreams meant something. They're significant. Somebody or something was trying to send me a message, to prompt me to do something, and I couldn't ignore it. I couldn't ignore the letters. The one from Ethan in Dublin was heart-breaking, and the other two—'

'Ellie,' Cole interrupted.

I spoke over him, not wanting to stop for fear I'd never start again. 'I won't tell you what the letters said, but—'

'Ellie,' Clementine repeated, her tone exasperated. 'We know!'

'You know?' I asked, looking from one to the other.

'We saw the letters,' she explained. 'When you didn't come back with us, we looked through the most recently archived letters. We saw the one from Niall, the one from Andy. We figured that's why you'd gone AWOL.'

I turned to Cole. So, he'd read Andy's letter, and knew I had too. He met my gaze directly and held it but didn't say anything. It was Clementine who continued.

'We wanted to come back for you.' Her eyes flicked meaningfully to Cole. 'But knew Willum wouldn't be returning to the island until the new year. Well, we *thought* he wouldn't be. So, we had to wait. We, erm . . . weren't happy about it.' Again, she gave her brother a sideways glance. 'But I knew you'd be back,' she added, her smile smug. 'Never doubted it for a second.'

'That makes one of us,' I admitted. 'I didn't think I'd ever see the island or any of you again.'

'Ha!' she scoffed. 'The island was never going to let you go. Once it's decided it likes somebody, it just keeps reeling them back in.' She lowered her tone, mock sinister. 'There's no escaping now.'

It was with consternation that I discovered I'd been asleep for a full day. Willum ordered me, in his usual curt manner, to stay in bed for at least two more. He also wouldn't allow any further visits, stating that I needed rest.

Clementine pouted but, like me, didn't dare resist. 'I know not to argue with Nurse Willum.' Giving me an apologetic wave and silently mouthing that she'd try to sneak in later, she ducked out of the door.

Willum turned to Cole. 'You too,' he growled. 'I hear there's plenty of work to be getting on with downstairs.'

I knew he was referring to the archives. Christmas was just round the corner and I could only imagine how busy they were, especially with Uncle Joe's absence. I felt a stab of guilt.

'I chose the worst time to become bed-bound, didn't I?'

'Get yourself better and then you can join us,' Cole promised.

'She'll get better faster with sleep,' Willum insisted.

Cole looked reluctant to leave but I knew the pressure of the archives would be weighing on him – and, as Clementine had said, you don't argue with Nurse Willum.

Over the next two days, Willum returned intermittently to check on my blisters, cleaning them and applying salve. He seemed pleased with how quickly I was healing, and confident there wouldn't be any lasting damage. Satisfied that the pain was manageable and

I was getting enough rest, some of the others were permitted short visits, to bring me meals and break up the tedium.

When Aiden visited, he spent the first five minutes sulking. Refusing to look at me, he dumped the tray of food at the foot of my bed, collapsed into the chair with his arms crossed, and began muttering under his breath. Most of what he said was inaudible, but I picked up 'so much for friendship' and 'buggering off without telling me'.

'I didn't want to get you mixed up in everything,' I protested.

He harrumphed. 'Life's so dull here I would've appreciated getting mixed up in it.'

Sensing his anger was only superficial, I gave a smile. 'How about I promise that next time I make a huge mess of something, I'll drag you into it? I could even put all the blame on you, if you'd like.'

With a sideways glance at me, he gave a grudging shrug. 'I suppose that's a fair enough offer. You're off the hook. But I mean it – at the first whiff of excitement or trouble, I want to be there in the thick of it.'

'I never knew you were so loyal.'

'Not loyal. The verb you're looking for is *bored*.'

I liked him enough in that moment not to correct his grammar.

Despite the boredom he complained about, Aiden seemed happier than he had all year. I sensed he'd finally begun to adapt to life on the island – or life on the island had begun to adapt to him. He'd invested in a Blu-ray player, set it up in the lounge and convinced Clementine to work through all the Marvel films with him. Clyde (in another word: Alison) had commissioned him to help get Clyde into shape, and so the pair had begun a regime of running through the archives together every morning on their way to work. 'And by "run" I mean walk quickly,' he added, 'but it's a start.' And the algorithmic system he'd set up for Clementine's *Psychology of Cake* was proving so successful that he'd decided to develop it the following year, after the Christmas rush.

'There are literally dozens of potential applications for it, all big money-earners,' he assured me.

'So you're planning on leaving then?' I asked, hoping I sounded more supportive than disappointed.

'Not necessarily,' he shrugged, reaching for the tray and setting it on my lap. 'I can develop my ideas here. It's not so bad on the island. And maybe, I don't know, I could be more of a seasonal worker. We'll see.'

Alex too had come to visit, wielding a pack of playing cards and some Jaffa Cakes. Without preamble, he announced he was going to teach me poker and, in exchange for saving his mother's life, he'd let me win the first three hands. We played for Jaffa Cakes.

Despite their efforts to keep my cabin fever at bay, I was anxious to be out of bed and help with the pre-Christmas rush, knowing how swamped they must be in Uncle Joe's absence. Although whenever I asked, they all assured me everything was under control, the slightly dazed look in their eyes, not to mention the bags beneath, told a different story.

And so, hours before the sluggish winter sun began to pinken the horizon on the day of my liberation, I was out of bed and getting myself ready.

I'd avoided glancing in the mirror on my earlier expeditions to the toilet, but this time I braved it. My face wasn't as bad as I'd feared. My cheeks were red and chapped, and the blisters on my nose had begun to peel, as they had on my fingers. I washed gingerly, declining Clementine's offer of help but grateful for it all the same. Aiden grumbling through the door of our shared bathroom that I should 'get a move on' made me smile. He seemed as eager as I was for things to return to normal. Well, as normal as they could be on an island that shouldn't exist, where letters fell in flurries and turned to wishes to be indexed and archived.

Although most of the dexterity had returned to my hands, it took me a long time to dress. I had to pull up the trousers and worm my arms through the sleeves of the jumper carefully, trying not to catch the raw skin. Walking took even longer with the pain in my toes, and I was glad of Uncle Joe's cane, borrowed via Willum, even if it was embarrassing entering the kitchen with it.

The place was in chaos and, at first, my entrance went unnoticed. Other than Uncle Joe, the whole family were there – plus Willum and Mary, who were trapped on the island until the weather turned in the new year. Alex was monitoring the toaster, one slice already in his mouth, while Aiden slathered jam on another. Clyde, squeezed into incongruous running shorts and t-shirt, was rummaging in the fridge. Willum and Mary were standing to one side shovelling down bowls of porridge and Clementine was stacking sandwiches into precarious piles, cling-filming them onto plates before they toppled. Only Alison was seated, calmly sprinkling seeds onto her granola, while Cole was pouring a cup of coffee and turning to the door.

'Five minutes until we need to be down there,' he announced, before catching sight of me and halting. His face, sharp with tension, seemed to soften.

I gave the gathering a timid smile. 'Room for one more?'

Everyone cheered, and just like that, I was where I should be.

'Hurrah!' Clyde toasted me with a glass of smoothie. 'The Empress of the Archives returns!'

I may have returned, but the journey to the archives was painfully slow (why had nobody thought to install a lift yet?) – probably all the more so for my eagerness to be there. This time, as I stepped onto the platform overlooking the vast cavern of scrolls, the awe I felt was accompanied by the warm fuzziness of homecoming. I hobbled to the railing and looked down, breathing in the familiar scents of paper, salt and earth. Aiden and Clyde had already run ahead – I could hear Clyde's deep breathing and Aiden's words of encouragement as they disappeared below – Clementine, Alex and Willum following at a less laboured, but still efficient, pace.

'Can you make it?' Cole asked, moving to stand beside me.

'Of course. Maybe even before Christmas,' I said, only half joking.

Mary appeared on my other side, offering her arm. 'You head down, love. I'll look after her.'

I nodded to Cole, knowing he'd be more use in the archives than straggling with me. Besides, I wanted the chance to speak with Mary. I hadn't seen her since stepping off the *Valkyrie* three days ago and there was something I needed to say.

I waited until the others were out of sight. 'I'm so sorry you can't go home for Christmas,' I said, feeling wretched. The guilt had plagued my bedrest far more than the boredom. 'It's completely my fault.'

'Are you kidding?' Mary snorted. 'This has been a dream come true. I always knew there was something special about this island, but to find out about the letters. I mean, wow.'

It was only then I realised the significance of Mary and Willum accompanying us to the archives. So, the Joneses had shared their secret. I was glad of that; Willum and Mary deserved to know, and I was certain could be trusted. But I wished the circumstances were different.

'What about your family?' I asked glumly.

She waved a dismissive hand. 'The grandkids are holidaying in Bali with their parents. Besides, even if they weren't, do you think I'd rather be peeling potatoes and burning a turkey than enjoying this magical place?'

She had a valid point. 'I owe you and Willum a lot for getting me here,' I said. 'In more ways than one.'

Mary squeezed my arm. 'Well, we owe *you* for getting *us* here. Willum's been ferrying the family for decades, and

I've known the Joneses since Cole and Clementine were wee tykes. We've never been invited into the archives. Until now. So, let's call it even.'

Mary and I eventually reached the office. I'd prepared myself for a backlog, maybe a few trolleys' worth of scrolls. I hadn't anticipated *mountains* of them. Every surface was littered with letters, including the floor and desks. To my alarm, they lay amidst half-full coffee cups, crumb-covered plates, empty biscuit wrappers and browning banana peels: the debris left by eight people working long shifts. And wading through it all were the Joneses.

'Got one here for the shortlist,' Clementine called, holding up a scroll. She was sitting in the corner with Alex, both surrounded by letters. 'Where's that pile again?'

'Somewhere on this desk I think,' Clyde replied. 'Or maybe on one of the others . . .'

'Here,' Cole said, gesturing absently to the shelf behind him. He seemed to be working his way through the contents of one of the trolleys.

Everywhere I looked were scenes of horror. Scrolls held open with various makeshift paperweights: cups, glasses, an incongruous slipper. Letters stained by coffee rings and soup splashes. Scrolls peeking out from under furniture, obviously forgotten. There wasn't a snake weight in sight.

Even Uncle Joe, who'd never seemed particularly concerned by proper archival protocol, would have been dismayed.

Just then I noticed a bottle of ketchup on one of the desks. It was lying opened on its side, its *bright red* contents dangerously close to oozing onto the *clean white* scroll below. With a cry of panic, I rushed forward, forgetting how sore my feet were and inevitably falling over them. Mary caught me before I hit the floor, but not before everyone had turned to look at me, their expressions ranging from concerned to amused. Alison followed my line of sight and noticed the ketchup bottle. With excruciating calmness, she crossed to it and, just in the nick of time, flipped the lid back on.

Clyde threw his wife a sheepish smile. 'Oops.'

'Oops,' I repeated in a whisper, incredulous. I sensed that all eyes were still on me, though my own were busy jumping from one appalling mess to another. Had the Joneses been *trying* to cause chaos in my absence?

'I don't . . . what *happened* here?'

Alison and the others turned from me to survey the room. I was expecting abashed realisation to dawn, but everyone continued to look bemused.

'We've been working,' Clementine said. 'I told you it gets busy this time of year.'

'Busy, yes. But this . . .' I turned to the shelf next to me where a Pepsi can weighed down one of the scrolls. Removing the can I cringed at the brown circle it left, and tried dabbing it away.

'I think she's upset it's a little messy,' Alex posited.

'A little messy?' I cried. 'This is *anarchy!*'

Aiden snorted. 'Anarchy? I don't think—'

But I cut across him. 'What system are you following here? How do you know which scrolls have been read and which haven't? Who's entering the details into the database? I don't see a single computer turned on. Nobody seems to be cataloguing the letters at all. And don't get me started on the number of archive *violations* I'm witnessing here.'

I could see everyone's confusion slowly shift to amusement, which just incited me all the more. I cast my most disapproving scowl across the room. 'Don't you dare smile.'

But they weren't just smiling. They were laughing. Every single one of them.

'Archive violations?' Clementine guffawed.

'This is serious,' I insisted. 'How can you get anything done in this . . . this . . . there isn't a word strong enough to fully communicate the wilful mayhem I'm witnessing here.'

That just made them laugh all the harder. Even Willum and Alison. I folded my arms across my chest and waited for the hilarity to subside.

'It is a little haphazard,' Cole finally admitted.

'But it's how we always work,' Clementine added.

'And we get by every year,' Alison finished.

'Well,' I sniffed, making a show of rolling up my sleeves (remembering belatedly how cold it was but too proud to reverse the action). 'That was before you hired a professional. And we don't do *haphazard* in my archives. I'll draw up a proper rota but for now, Cole and Clementine, you're on clean-up duty. I don't want to see a single cup, plate, crisp packet or apple core within ten feet of a scroll. Willum, Mary and Clyde, we need three clearly marked piles of scrolls: one for those in the shortlist, one for those that didn't make the cut and one for those that haven't been read yet. Once that's done and the trolleys are clear, you're on harvesting duty. Alison and I will read and translate the letters while Alex and Aiden transcribe into the database and label them. When this room's spotless, Cole and Clementine can help with the cataloguing. We'll rotate jobs every three hours, with breaks in between – and snacks consumed a safe distance away. And these,' I added, picking up a snake weight from beneath a jumble of scrolls, 'have a purpose. Please use them.'

There was a moment's silence during which I could practically hear the surprised blinking. It was just long enough for me to wonder whether I'd overstretched my authority. But then, all at once, there was a chorus of 'Yes, boss' that sounded entirely sincere.

It was both the longest and shortest week of my life. There wasn't enough time to work through the hordes of letters that blizzarded onto the island daily – there was barely even enough time to rake them up and transport them to the office. And yet the days seemed to expand, like a container stretching to accommodate whatever filled it. It wasn't that time dragged; more like it indulged us. We seemed able to achieve three hours' worth of work in one, which was exactly the rate we needed to keep pace with the incoming flurries.

When I noticed, I joked that the clocks were on our side.

The Joneses looked at me with mild exasperation. 'How else would we get through it all?' Alison asked.

Like every other uncanny feature of the island, I was expected to accept it and move on. So I did.

I missed Uncle Joe though. Every time I stepped into the office, I expected to see him sitting at his desk, half obscured behind a pile of scrolls, or to hear the squeak of his trolley wheels.

The others would momentarily forget too. More than once I'd seen Clementine tally up the sandwiches for our packed lunches, counting Uncle Joe's amongst them, and Clyde would frequently look up from his work and glance around the office, as if looking for his brother.

But then we'd remember. And although it felt wrong without him, the wishfall continued to fall as it should, and the ravens continued to watch over us. It was as if the island knew – as did we – that Uncle Joe was where he needed to be. And that he wouldn't be gone forever. We kept him there with us by talking about him, sharing funny stories and wondering aloud what he was doing at that very moment. At first everybody tiptoed around the subject of Niall. But once his name had been spoken a few times – furtively, in quiet, tentative tones – it began to lose its air of anathema. Reminiscences about family life on the island could now include him. 'Do you recall that time, when Cole, Clementine and Niall were kids . . .' Clyde would say, and nobody would flinch. 'I remember when Niall used to . . .' Clementine would offer, and there would be no sharp intakes of breath. Even Cole tolerated this unspoken lifting of the taboo. He didn't talk about

Niall, but he stopped stiffening whenever the name was mentioned.

He'd forgiven Andy. Perhaps he could forgive Niall too.

One morning, four short days until Christmas, I checked the rota and noticed that my name had been crossed off 'Reading and Translation Duty' and scribbled into the box for 'Harvesting Duty'. Next to Cole's name.

'Oh, what a surprise,' Clementine said as she peered over my shoulder, in a tone confirming it was anything but.

Cole gave his sister an exasperated look, but when he met my eyes he smiled. 'Shall we?'

There were a few knowing nudges as we passed through the office, which I tried my best to ignore. Things were already awkward without everyone else's expectations. This would be our first time alone together since I was bed-bound; life had been so hectic over the last week that we hadn't had a second to ourselves. And the weight of our many almost-moments lay heavy in the silence as we pushed a trolley each down to what the Joneses called the 'post room'.

Despite being harvested the evening before, the floor was once again blanketed in letters. There must have been a heavy flurry overnight. Trying not to calculate how much cataloguing it would require, I reached for a rake. It would be nice, even for just a short time, to give my mind a rest and let my body do some work.

'I think you're going to win this race,' I admitted, adjusting my grip. Although the blisters were nearly fully healed now, my fingers were still swollen and ungainly.

'I'll give you a head start,' Cole assured me. 'I wouldn't want my victory marred by having an unfair advantage.'

I smiled and began gathering the letters in. I liked that he hadn't asked if I was up for the work. Other than his outburst when I'd first regained consciousness, he hadn't said a word about my wounds. There had been no gallant proffering of his arm for support, though everybody else had offered, even Aiden. And there had been no scolding me for working longer hours than Willum advised, nor for skipping meals and occasionally sleeping at my desk overnight. A few months ago, I would have been convinced his lack of chivalry indicated a lack of care. But I knew him better now. It simply meant he trusted me to know my own capabilities. Still, I saw his eyes shift discreetly over my fingers as I flexed them, a flash of concern quickly covered up.

We harvested silently for a while, beside each other but not touching. When he did finally talk, it was to ask a question.

'What brought you back?'

I didn't look at him and took my time before giving an answer. 'Mainly Uncle Joe. But even without him, I think I would have made the right decision in the end.'

'Why?' His tone was casual, but the question charged.

I braved an honest answer. 'Because I feel I belong here. And because I missed you.'

Glancing at him out of the corner of my eye, I saw that his expression was unreadable. 'Good.'

We reached down to pull in a pile of scrolls at the same time. There was no accident in the way his hand brushed mine. I stilled, watching as his fingers gently moved over my knuckles, then into my palm, and slowly up my wrist. Like the last time our hands had clasped, there was both tenderness and electricity in the contact. A promise.

And when we both looked up at the same time, I knew there'd be no more waiting.

It didn't matter who moved first. All that mattered was that his lips were suddenly on mine. It was a fierce kiss, both soft and urgent. One of his hands was in my hair, the other on my waist, pulling me closer. My arms wrapped themselves around his neck, drawing him down to me. He tasted of the island. Salt water air, clay and earth, open flames. His lips caressing, tasting me in turn. We breathlessly broke for air but like magnets our mouths found each other again. He pushed me gently against the rock wall behind us, his body pressing against mine as his kiss travelled from my lips to my cheek, my jaw, my neck.

I'd had kisses before, most of them with Gary. Some had been just okay; others had been nice. None had made everything else in the world fall away, filling me with a pressing need to kiss again, and again.

Suddenly there were too many layers of fabric between us. My hands sought the hem of his shirt, and slipped beneath it to find the bare skin of his back, warm against my cold fingers as I pulled him harder towards me. Wanting to feel his hands on me too, I broke away just long enough to shrug my jumper over my head. The shirt beneath took longer. There was a question in Cole's eyes as his fingers moved over the buttons, and in answer, I yanked at the last few, expecting them to break, but the damn things were too strong. We both laughed as he undid them and then his lips were on my shoulder.

Later, we lay tangled in a blanket of clothes on the rock floor. He stretched out behind me, his beard tickling the crook of my neck and his arm around me, keeping the cold at bay. I had no idea of the time but knew it was long past the end of our shift. Nobody had come to find us though. Or if they had, we hadn't noticed. And didn't care. I felt his lips brush my shoulder blade as another flurry of wishes began falling from the sky.

Chapter Twenty-Six

The shortlist was more of a longlist. A very, very long-list: one thousand letters that needed narrowing down to one hundred.

'So few?' I'd asked at the start, daunted.

Clementine's expression was apologetic, but her tone firm. 'It never takes more than that. Sometimes it's less.'

I didn't ask what 'it' was. The time for those kinds of questions was long past.

For the first time since my return to the island, there was tension. Everybody seemed to have a different idea of which letters should make the *final* shortlist. At first, I had kept quiet, not knowing how much I should contribute to what was essentially the family business. But they insisted I had as much right to a say as the rest of them, which was as warming as it was daunting.

Ethan's face crossed my mind whenever we placed another scroll into the 'no' pile and guilt weighed heavily on the rare instances I voted against a request. And nothing could stop the indignant anger from bubbling up each time a letter I'd chosen to champion was cut, and the others clearly felt the same.

391

'We fall out over this every year,' Cole assured me. 'We always make it through to the other side.'

'Usually unscathed,' Clyde added.

Knowing this didn't make the job any easier though.

By sunset on Christmas Eve, we had our final shortlist.

I still didn't know what would become of these letters; how the wishes they contained would be granted. But I didn't doubt that they would be.

* * *

'What's this about?'

Cole's expression gave nothing away, but Clementine looked like a child trying – and failing – to hide an exciting secret. It was Christmas morning, and we were – currently – the only three up.

'Wait a sec, I want to do it right,' she said, gesturing to the table. 'Have a seat.'

I perched on a chair apprehensively as Clementine directed Cole to sit opposite me and then positioned herself beside him. Christmas crackers and snowflake-patterned napkins – when Clementine had found time to decorate the house, I wasn't sure, but decorate she had; there were lights and tinsel and reindeer ornaments everywhere, not to mention a huge tree that dominated the kitchen – were pushed aside to make room for a clipboard that seemed to materialise from nowhere.

'What is this?' I asked again.

'Job interview,' she replied, clicking briskly down on a pen. 'Favourite Christmas film?'

Assuming this was some reinstatement ritual – and knowing that, where Cole and Clementine were concerned, it would be entirely serious – I saw no option but to humour them. 'All of them.'

'That's not what you said last time,' Clementine remarked, making a few notes behind her clipboard. 'Can you be a bit more specific?'

'I've realised there's no such thing as a bad Christmas film,' I insisted. 'And choosing one is like . . . erm . . . picking your favourite star in the heavens.' I was overselling it. Clementine was nodding earnestly, but Cole rolled his eyes.

Clementine gestured to my slippers. 'What socks are you wearing under those?'

'Three pairs,' I replied. 'Including the Christmas ones you kindly lent me.'

She nodded her approval and made another note. 'Good choice.'

'And what will you be having for your Christmas breakfast this morning?'

'A mountain of pastries prepared by my good friend – and excellent baker – Clementine Jones.'

'Another good choice. Well, *Mr Jones*,' she said, turning to Cole. 'I think I've got everything I need. Do you have her reference?'

Also seemingly from nowhere, Cole pulled out a plastic wallet containing a page from a newspaper. 'Right here.' As he handed it to me, I saw the words *Limerick Post* printed at the top of the page, and the headline 'Home for Christmas'. Below it were two grainy photographs: a beaming middle-aged woman with her arm around the shoulders of a teenage boy; and a hand-written note.

Ethan's face was transformed by a smile and the beneficial effects of a few hot meals. I probably wouldn't have recognised him from the picture without reading its caption: *Mystery do-gooder reunites runaway teen with mother in time for Christmas*. Beside this was a photo of the note I'd hastily scribbled for him.

The piece was short, not touching on Ethan's reasons for running away and giving only vague details of his time on the streets, but it contained a quote from him. *'I'd basically given up. But then one morning I woke up and there was the note and enough money to get me home . . .'*

His mother was quoted as well. *'Whoever you are, wherever you are, thank you, with all my heart. And merry Christmas to you too.'*

My cheeks were wet with tears by the time I'd finished reading. I looked up at Cole and Clementine, prepared for their admonishments – but they were both smiling. There was no reproach in either of their expressions. If anything, they looked proud.

'You were right. We were wrong,' Cole said simply, taking the newspaper from my hand and looking at the photo of Ethan and his mother. 'Because of you, this boy's safe. And the world's still none the wiser about us.'

'It turns out not all wishes need magic. Or maybe it's just a different kind of magic,' Clementine suggested. 'We were so used to doing things one way we couldn't see an alternative. Thank you for showing us.'

Warmth spread through me at their words, and I gave a tentative smile. 'How did you find the story?'

'I was keeping an eye out,' Cole replied. 'Ever since your . . . excursion to Dublin.'

'And you're not mad?' I was still a little perturbed by their smiles.

'We're not mad,' Clementine clarified.

'So, does this mean . . .?'

'That we'll try it your way,' Cole nodded. 'And see where it takes us.'

'In fact, we've already started.' Clementine gestured to the foot of the tree. I followed her gaze to find a bevy of baubles still wrapped in tissue paper, spilling from a large box. Printed across the box were the words *Delivery from Santa's Workshop: Terrestrial Branch.* I recognised the name instantly.

'The Christmas shop in Edinburgh.'

Cole shrugged as if the gesture was insignificant. 'We needed new decorations.'

'So,' Clementine went on, grinning now. 'Following a successful interview and a positive reference, we'd like to offer you a promotion. As well as your current duties, how would you like to be the overseer of our second shortlist? Job title, courtesy of Dad: Minister of the Mundane Miracles.'

'Of course,' Cole added, 'we should let you know that it will involve foreign travel.'

Did they really mean it? Had my actions actually convinced them to go against generations of tradition? If so, that would be a lot of responsibility on my shoulders.

But also, so much precious opportunity. Stunned into silence, all I could manage was a dazed nod.

Clementine clapped her hands together. 'Excellent. Now we can give you your Christmas present.'

A rectangular parcel wrapped in red-and-gold paper suddenly appeared on the table. Cole passed it across to me. It was heavier than it looked. Curiously, and a little cautiously, I unwrapped it – and immediately burst out laughing. It was a contract for the role of 'Minister of Mundane Miracles'.

'Do you need to take it home to read it first?' Cole asked dryly.

'Thank you, yes,' I replied, remembering the last contract he'd had me sign. 'My previous employer wasn't half as considerate.'

'Sounds like a real asshole,' Cole observed, poker-faced.

I gave a wry smile. 'He turned out all right in the end.'

Clementine rolled her eyes. 'As much as I love the flirting, could we move things along please? We've got other presents to open, snowmen to build, charades to play and ridiculous amounts of chocolate to consume – and time's a wastin'.'

Chuckling, I reached for the pen in Clementine's hand, opened the contract and signed.